Praise for *Ninth House*

"In this mesmerizing novel, Leigh Bardugo introduces us to Alex, a high-school dropout who gets a free ride to Yale because of a unique talent. Bardugo's New Haven is plausible and frightening, and I was one rapt reader." —Charlaine Harris, bestselling author of the True Blood series

"With an aura of both enchantment and authenticity, Bardugo's compulsively readable novel leaves a portal ajar for equally dazzling sequels." —*Kirkus Reviews* (starred review)

"Atmospheric . . . Part mystery, part story of a young woman finding purpose in a dark world." —*Booklist* (starred review)

"Genuinely terrific . . . The world-building is rock solid, the plot is propulsive, and readers will be clamoring for a sequel as soon as they read the last page." —*Library Journal* (starred review)

"Excellent . . . Bardugo gives [her protagonist] a thoroughly engaging mix of rough edge, courage, and cynicism." —*Publishers Weekly* (starred review)

"Instantly gripping . . . Creepy and thrilling . . . The world of this book is so consistent and enveloping that pages seem to rush by." —*BookPage* (starred review)

"Simultaneously elegant and grotesque, eerie and earthbound . . . Wry, uncanny, original, and, above all, an engrossing, unnerving thriller." —*The Washington Post*

NINTH HOUSE

Also by Leigh Bardugo

The Shadow and Bone Trilogy

Shadow and Bone

Siege and Storm

Ruin and Rising

The Six of Crows Duology

Six of Crows

Crooked Kingdom

The Language of Thorns

King of Scars

NINTH HOUSE

Leigh Bardugo

FLATIRON
BOOKS
NEW YORK

NINTH HOUSE. Copyright © 2019 by Leigh Bardugo. Map and endpaper art copyright © 2019 by Leigh Bardugo. All rights reserved. Printed in the United States of America. For information, address Flatiron Books, 120 Broadway, New York, NY 10271.

www.flatironbooks.com

Designed by Donna Sinisgalli Noetzel

Map by Rhys Davies and WB

Endpaper illustration by Travis DeMello

The Library of Congress has cataloged the hardcover edition as follows:

Names: Bardugo, Leigh, author.
Title: Ninth house / Leigh Bardugo.
Description: First U.S. edition. | New York : Flatiron Books, 2019.
Identifiers: LCCN 2019019855| ISBN 9781250313072 (hardcover) | ISBN 9781250258397 (international, sold outside the U.S., subject to rights availability) | ISBN 9781250313089 (ebook)
Subjects: | GSAFD: Occult fiction.
Classification: LCC PS3602.A775325 N56 2019 | DDC 813/.6—dc23
LC record available at https://lccn.loc.gov/2019019855

ISBN 978-1-250-75136-2 (trade paperback)

Our books may be purchased in bulk for promotional, educational, or business use. Please contact your local bookseller or the Macmillan Corporate and Premium Sales Department at 1-800-221-7945, extension 5442, or by email at MacmillanSpecialMarkets@macmillan.com.

First Flatiron Books Paperback Edition: 2020

10 9 8 7 6 5

To Hedwig, Nima, Em, and Les—
for the many rescues.

Ay una moza y una moza   que nonse espanta de la muerte
porque tiene padre y madre   y sus doge hermanos cazados.
Caza de tre tabacades   y un cortijo enladriado.
En medio de aquel cortijo   havia un mansanale
que da mansanas de amores   en vierno y en verano.
Adientro de aquel cortijo   siete grutas hay fraguada.
En cada gruta y gruta   ay echado cadenado. . . .
El huerco que fue ligero   se entró por el cadenado.

—La Moza y El Huerco

There is a girl, a girl who does not fear death
Because she has her father and her mother and her twelve
    hunter brothers,
A home of three floors and a barnyard farmhouse,
In the middle of the farm, an apple tree that gives love apples
    in the winter and summer.
In the farm there are seven grottos,
Each and every grotto secured. . . .
Death was light and slipped in through the lock.

—Death and the Girl, Sephardic ballad

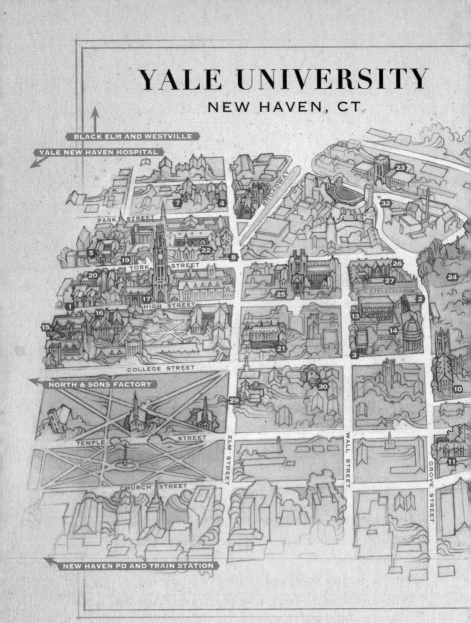

YALE UNIVERSITY

NEW HAVEN, CT

BLACK ELM AND WESTVILLE

YALE NEW HAVEN HOSPITAL

BROADWAY

PARK STREET

YORK STREET

HIGH STREET

COLLEGE STREET

NORTH & SONS FACTORY

TEMPLE STREET

CHURCH STREET

ELM STREET

WALL STREET

GROVE STREET

NEW HAVEN PD AND TRAIN STATION

1 SKULL & BONES
2 BOOK & SNAKE
3 SCROLL & KEY
4 MANUSCRIPT
5 WOLF'S HEAD
6 BERZELIUS
7 ST. ELMO
8 THE HUTCH
9 IL BASTONE

10 SHEFFIELD-STERLING-STRATHCONA
   HALL
11 ROSENFELD HALL
12 FORESTRY SCHOOL
13 BEINECKE RARE BOOK &
   MANUSCRIPT LIBRARY
14 COMMONS
15 VANDERBILT HALL
16 LINSLY-CHITTENDEN HALL

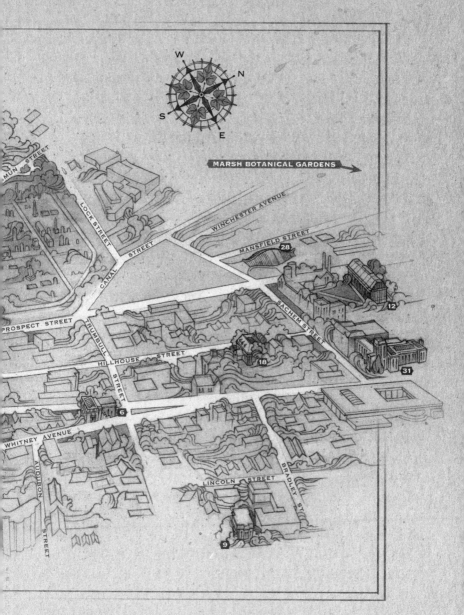

MARSH BOTANICAL GARDENS

NINTH HOUSE

Prologue

Early Spring

By the time Alex managed to get the blood out of her good wool coat, it was too warm to wear it. Spring had come on grudgingly; pale blue mornings failed to deepen, turning instead to moist, sullen afternoons, and stubborn frost lined the road in high, dirty meringues. But sometime around mid-March, the slices of lawn between the stone paths of Old Campus began to sweat themselves free of snow, emerging wet, black, and tufty with matted grass, and Alex found herself notched into the window seat in the rooms hidden on the top floor of 268 York, reading *Suggested Requirements for Lethe Candidates*.

She heard the clock on the mantel tick, the chiming of the bell as customers came and went in the clothing store below. The secret rooms above the shop were affectionately known as the Hutch by Lethe members, and the commercial space beneath them had been, at varying times, a shoe store, a wilderness outfitter, and a twenty-four-hour Wawa mini-mart with its own Taco Bell counter. The Lethe diaries from those years were filled with complaints about the stink of refried beans and grilled onions seeping up through the floor—until 1995, when someone had enchanted the Hutch and the back staircase that led to the alley so that they smelled always of fabric softener and clove.

Alex had discovered the pamphlet of Lethe House guidelines sometime in the blurred weeks after the incident at the mansion on Orange. She had checked her email only once since then on the Hutch's old desktop, seen the long string of messages from Dean Sandow, and logged off. She'd let the battery run down on her phone, ignored her classes, watched the branches sprout leaves at the knuckles like a woman trying on rings. She ate all the food in the pantries and freezer—the fancy cheeses and packs of smoked salmon first, then the cans of beans and syrup-soaked peaches in boxes marked EMERGENCY RATIONS. When they were gone, she ordered takeout aggressively, charging it all to Darlington's still-active account. The trip down and up the stairs was tiring enough that she had to rest before she tore into her lunch or dinner, and sometimes she didn't bother to eat at all, just fell asleep in the window seat or on the floor beside the plastic bags and foil-wrapped containers. No one came to check on her. There was no one left.

The pamphlet was cheaply printed, bound with staples, a black-and-white picture of Harkness Tower on the cover, *We Are the Shepherds* printed beneath it. She doubted the Lethe House founders had Johnny Cash in mind when they'd chosen their motto, but every time she saw those words she thought of Christmastime, of lying on the old mattress in Len's squat in Van Nuys, room spinning, a half-eaten can of cranberry sauce on the floor beside her, and Johnny Cash singing, *"We are the shepherds, we walked 'cross the mountains. We left our flocks when the new star appeared."* She thought of Len rolling over, sliding his hand under her shirt, murmuring into her ear, "Those are some shitty shepherds."

The guidelines for Lethe House candidates were located near the back of the pamphlet and had last been updated in 1962.

> *High academic achievement with an emphasis on*
> *   history and chemistry.*
> *Facility with languages and a working knowledge of*
> *   Latin and Greek.*
> *Good physical health and hygiene. Evidence of a*
> *   regular fitness regimen encouraged.*

Exhibits signs of a steady character with a mind
toward discretion.
An interest in the arcane is discouraged, as this is a
frequent indicator of an "outsider" disposition.
Should demonstrate no squeamishness toward the
realities of the human body.
MORS VINCIT OMNIA.

Alex—whose knowledge of Latin was less than working—looked it up: Death conquers all. But in the margin, someone had scrawled *irrumat* over *vincit,* nearly obliterating the original with blue ballpoint pen.

Beneath the Lethe requirements, an addendum read: *Standards for candidates have been relaxed in two circumstances: Lowell Scott (B.A., English, 1909) and Sinclair Bell Braverman (no degree, 1950), with mixed results.*

Another note had been scratched into the margin here, this one clearly in Darlington's jagged, EKG-like scrawl: *Alex Stern.* She thought of the blood soaking the carpet of the old Anderson mansion black. She thought of the dean—the startled white of his femur jutting from his thigh, the stink of wild dogs filling the air.

Alex set aside the aluminum container of cold falafel from Mamoun's, wiped her hands on her Lethe House sweats. She limped to the bathroom, popped open the bottle of zolpidem, and tucked one beneath her tongue. She cupped her hand beneath the faucet, watched the water pour over her fingers, listened to the grim sucking sound from the mouth of the drain. *Standards for candidates have been relaxed in two circumstances.*

For the first time in weeks, she looked at the girl in the water-speckled mirror, watched as that bruised girl lifted her tank top, the cotton stained yellow with pus. The wound in Alex's side was a deep divot, crusted black. The bite had left a visible curve that she knew would heal badly, if it healed at all. Her map had been changed. Her coastline altered. *Mors irrumat omnia.* Death fucks us all.

Alex touched her fingers gently to the hot red skin surrounding the teeth marks. The wound was getting infected. She felt some kind of concern, her mind nudging her toward self-preservation, but the idea of picking up the phone, getting a ride to the under-grad health center—the sequence of actions each new action would incite—was overwhelming, and the warm, dull throb of her body setting fire to itself had become almost companionable. Maybe she'd get a fever, start hallucinating.

She eyed the thrust of her ribs, the blue veins like downed power lines beneath her fading bruises. Her lips were feathered with chapped skin. She thought of her name inked into the margins of the pamphlet—the third circumstance.

"Results were decidedly mixed," she said, startled by the husky rattle of her voice. She laughed and the drain seemed to chuckle with her. Maybe she already had a fever.

In the fluorescent glare of the bathroom lights, she gripped the edges of the bite in her side and dug her fingers into it, pinching the flesh around her stitches until the pain dropped over her like a mantle, the blackout coming on in a welcome rush.

That was in the spring. But the trouble had begun on a night in the full dark of winter, when Tara Hutchins died and Alex still thought she might get away with everything.

Skull and Bones, oldest of the landed societies, first of the eight Houses of the Veil, founded in 1832. The Bonesmen can boast more presidents, publishers, captains of industry, and cabinet members than any other society (for a full list of its alumni, please see Appendix C), and perhaps "boast" is the right word. The Bonesmen are aware of their influence and expect the deference of Lethe delegates. They would do well to remember their own motto: *Rich or poor, all are equal in death.* Conduct yourself with the discretion and diplomacy warranted by your office and association with Lethe, but remember always that our duty is not to prop up the vanity of Yale's best and brightest but to stand between the living and the dead.

—*from* The Life of Lethe: Procedures and
Protocols of the Ninth House

The Bonesmen fancy themselves titans among pissants, and ain't that a bite. But who am I to quibble when the drinks are stiff and the girls are pretty?

—Lethe Days Diary of George Petit
(Saybrook College '56)

1

Winter

Alex hurried across the wide, alien plane of Beinecke Plaza, boots thudding over flat squares of clean concrete. The giant cube of the rare-books collection seemed to float above its lower story. During the day its panels glowed amber, a burnished golden hive, less a library than a temple. At night it just looked like a tomb. This part of campus didn't quite fit with the rest of Yale—no gray stone or Gothic arches, no rebellious little outcroppings of red-brick buildings, which Darlington had explained were not actually Colonial but only meant to look that way. He'd explained the reasons for the way Beinecke had been built, the way it was supposed to mirror and slot into this corner of the campus architecture, but it still felt like a seventies sci-fi movie to her, like the students should all be wearing unitards or too-short tunics, drinking something called the Extract, eating food in pellets. Even the big metal sculpture that she now knew was by Alexander Calder reminded her of a giant lava lamp in negative.

"It's Calder," she murmured beneath her breath. That was the way people here talked about art. Nothing was *by* anyone. The sculpture is Calder. The painting is Rothko. The house is Neutra.

And Alex was late. She had begun the night with good intentions, determined to get ahead of her Modern British Novel essay and leave with plenty of time to make it to the prognostication. But she'd fallen asleep in one of the Sterling Library reading rooms, a copy of *Nostromo* gripped loosely in her hand, feet propped on a heating duct. At half past ten, she'd woken with a start, drool trickling across her cheek. Her startled "Shit!" had gone off like a shotgun blast in the quiet of the library, and she'd buried her face in her scarf as she slung her bag over her shoulder and made her escape.

Now she cut through Commons, beneath the rotunda where the names of the war dead were carved deep into the marble, and stone figures stood vigil—Peace, Devotion, Memory, and finally Courage, who wore a helmet and shield and little else and had always looked to Alex more like a stripper than a mourner. She charged down the steps and across the intersection of College and Grove.

The campus had a way of changing faces from hour to hour and block to block so that Alex always felt as if she were meeting it for the first time. Tonight it was a sleepwalker, breathing deep and even. The people she passed on her way to SSS seemed locked in a dream, soft-eyed, faces turned to one another, steam rising off the cups of coffee in their gloved hands. She had the eerie sense that they were dreaming her, a girl in a dark coat who would disappear when they woke.

Sheffield-Sterling-Strathcona Hall was drowsing too, the classrooms closed up tight, hallways cast in energy-saving half-light. Alex took the stairs to the second floor and heard noise echoing from one of the lecture halls. The Yale Social screened movies there every Thursday night. Mercy had tacked the schedule to the door of their dorm room, but Alex hadn't bothered to study it. Her Thursdays were full.

Tripp Helmuth slouched against the wall beside the doors to the lecture hall. He acknowledged Alex with a heavy-lidded nod. Even in the dim light, she could see his eyes were bloodshot. No doubt he'd smoked before he showed up tonight. Maybe that was why the elder Bonesmen had stuck him on guard duty. Or maybe he'd volunteered.

"You're late," he said. "They started."

Alex ignored him, glanced once over her shoulder to make sure the hallway was clear. She didn't owe Tripp Helmuth an excuse, and it would look weak to offer one. She pressed her thumb into a barely visible notch in the paneling. The wall was supposed to swing open smoothly, but it always stuck. She gave it a hard nudge with her shoulder and stumbled as it jolted open.

"Easy, killer," said Tripp.

Alex shut the door behind her and edged down the narrow passage in the dark.

Unfortunately, Tripp was right. The prognostication had already begun. Alex entered the old operating theater as quietly as she could.

The room was a windowless chamber, sandwiched between the lecture hall and a classroom that grad students used for discussion sections. It was a forgotten remnant of the old medical school, which had held its classes here in SSS before it moved to its own buildings. The managers of the trust that funded Skull and Bones had sealed up the room's entrance and disguised it with new paneling sometime around 1932. All facts Alex had gleaned from *Lethe: A Legacy* when she probably should have been reading *Nostromo*.

No one spared Alex a glance. All eyes were on the Haruspex, his lean face hidden behind a surgical mask, pale blue robes spattered with blood. His latex-gloved hands moved methodically through the bowels of the—patient? Subject? Sacrifice? Alex wasn't sure which term applied to the man on the table. Not "sacrifice." *He's supposed to live.* Ensuring that was part of her job. She'd see him safely through this ordeal and back to the hospital ward he'd been taken from. *But what about a year from now?* she wondered. *Five years from now?*

Alex glanced at the man on the table: Michael Reyes. She'd read his file two weeks ago, when he was selected for the ritual. The flaps of his stomach were pinned back with steel clips and his abdomen looked like it was blooming, a plump pink orchid, plush and red at its center. *Tell me that doesn't leave a mark.* But she had her own future to worry about. Reyes would manage.

Alex averted her eyes, tried to breathe through her nose as her stomach roiled and coppery saliva flooded her mouth. She'd seen plenty of bad injuries but always on the dead. There was something much worse about a living wound, a human body tethered to life by nothing but the steady metallic beep of a monitor. She had candied ginger in her pocket for nausea—one of Darlington's tips—but she couldn't quite bring herself to take it out and unwrap it.

Instead, she focused her gaze on some middle distance as the Haruspex called out a series of numbers and letters—stock symbols and share prices for companies traded publicly on the New York Stock Exchange. Later in the night he'd move on to the NASDAQ, Euronext, and the Asian markets. Alex didn't bother trying to decipher them. The orders to buy, sell, or hold were given in impenetrable Dutch, the language of commerce, the first stock exchange, old New York, and the official language of the Bonesmen. When Skull and Bones was founded, too many students knew Greek and Latin. Their dealings had required something more obscure.

"Dutch is harder to pronounce," Darlington had told her. "Besides, it gives the Bonesmen an excuse to visit Amsterdam." Of course, Darlington knew Latin, Greek, and Dutch. He also spoke French, Mandarin, and passable Portuguese. Alex had just started Spanish II. Between the classes she'd taken in grade school and her grandmother's mishmash of Ladino sayings, she'd thought it would be an easy grade. She hadn't counted on things like the subjunctive. But she could just about ask if Gloria might like to go to the discotheque tomorrow night.

A burst of muffled gunfire rattled through the wall from the screening next door. The Haruspex looked up from the slick pink mess of Michael Reyes's small intestine, his irritation apparent.

Scarface, Alex realized as the music swelled and a chorus of rowdy voices thundered in unison, *"You wanna fuck with me? Okay. You wanna play rough?"* The audience chanting along like it was *Rocky Horror*. She must have seen *Scarface* a hundred times. It was one of Len's favorites. He was predictable that way, loved everything *hard*—as if he'd mailed away for a How to Be Gangster kit. When they'd met Hellie near the Venice boardwalk, her golden hair like a parted curtain for the theater of her big blue eyes, Alex had thought instantly of Michelle Pfeiffer in her satin shift. All she'd been missing was the smooth sheaf of bangs. But Alex didn't want to think about Hellie tonight, not with the stink of blood in the air. Len and Hellie were her old life. They didn't belong at Yale. Then again, neither did Alex.

Despite the memories, Alex was grateful for any noise that would cover the wet sounds of the Haruspex pawing through Michael Reyes's gut. What did he see there? Darlington had said the prognostications were no different than someone reading the future in the cards of a tarot deck or a handful of animal bones. But it sure looked different. And sounded more specific. *You're missing someone. You will find happiness in the new year.* Those were the kinds of things fortune-tellers said—vague, comforting.

Alex eyed the Bonesmen, robed and hooded, crowded around the body on the table, the undergrad Scribe taking down the predictions that would be passed on to hedge-fund managers and private investors all over the world to keep the Bonesmen and their alumni financially secure. Former presidents, diplomats, at least one director of the CIA—all of them Bonesmen. Alex thought of Tony Montana, soaking in his hot tub, speechifying: *You know what capitalism is?* Alex glanced at Michael Reyes's prone body. *Tony, you have no idea.*

She caught a flicker of movement from the benches that overlooked the operating arena. The theater had two local Grays who always sat in the same places, just a few rows apart: a female mental patient who'd had her ovaries and uterus removed in a hysterectomy in 1926, for which she would have been paid six dollars if she'd survived the procedure; and a male, a medical student. He'd frozen to death in an opium den thousands of miles away, sometime around 1880, but kept returning here to sit in his old seat and look down on whatever passed for life below. Prognostications only happened in the theater four times a year, at the start of each fiscal quarter, but that seemed to be enough to suit him.

Darlington liked to say that dealing with ghosts was like riding the subway: *Do not make eye contact. Do not smile. Do not engage. Otherwise, you never know what might follow you home.* Easier said than done when the only other thing to look at in the room was a man playing with another man's innards like they were mah-jongg tiles.

She remembered Darlington's shock when he'd realized she could not only see ghosts without the help of any potion or spell but see them in color. He'd been weirdly furious. She'd enjoyed that.

"What kinds of color?" he'd asked, sliding his feet off the coffee table, his heavy black boots thunking on the slatted floor of the parlor at Il Bastone.

"Just color. Like an old Polaroid. Why? What do you see?"

"They look gray," he'd snapped. "That's why they're called Grays."

She'd shrugged, knowing her nonchalance would make Darlington even angrier. "It isn't a big deal."

"Not to you," he'd muttered, and stomped away. He'd spent the rest of the day in the training room, working up a cranky sweat.

She'd felt smug at the time, glad not everything came so easily to him. But now, moving in a circle around the perimeter of the theater, checking the little chalk markings made at every compass point, she just felt jittery and unprepared. That was the way she'd felt since she'd taken her first step on campus. No, before that. From the time Dean Sandow had sat down beside her hospital bed, tapped the handcuffs on her wrist with his nicotine-stained fingers, and said, "We are offering you an opportunity." But that was the old Alex. The Alex of Hellie and Len. Yale Alex had never worn handcuffs, never gotten into a fight, never fucked a stranger in a bathroom to make up her boyfriend's vig. Yale Alex struggled but didn't complain. She was a good girl trying to keep up.

And failing. She should have been here early to observe the making of the signs and ensure the circle was secure. Grays as old as the ones hovering on the tiered benches above didn't tend to make trouble even when drawn by blood, but prognostications were big magic and her job was to verify that the Bonesmen followed proper procedures, stayed cautious. She was playacting, though. She'd spent the previous night cramming, trying to memorize the correct signs and proportions of chalk, charcoal, and bone. She'd made *flash cards,* for fuck's sake, and forced herself to shuffle through them in between bouts of Joseph Conrad.

Alex thought the markings looked okay, but she knew her signs of protection about as well as her modern British novels. When she'd attended the fall-quarter prognostication with Darlington, had she really paid attention? No. She'd been too busy sucking on ginger candy, reeling from the strangeness of it all, and praying she wouldn't humiliate herself by puking. She'd thought she had plenty of time to learn with Darlington looking over her shoulder. But they'd both been wrong about that.

"*Voorhoofd!*" the Haruspex called, and one of the Bonesmen darted forward. Melinda? Miranda? Alex couldn't remember the redhead's name, only that she was in an all-female a cappella group called Whim 'n Rhythm. The girl patted the Haruspex's forehead with a white cloth and melted back into the group.

Alex tried not to look at the man on the table, but her eyes darted to his face anyway. *Michael Reyes, age forty-eight, diagnosed paranoid schizophrenic.* Would Reyes remember any of it when he woke? When he tried to tell someone would they just call him crazy? Alex knew exactly what that was like. *It could be me on that table.*

"The Bonesmen like them as nuts as possible," Darlington had told her. "They think it makes for better predictions." When she'd asked him why, he'd just said, "The crazier the *victima*, the closer to God."

"Is that true?"

"*It is only through mystery and madness that the soul is revealed*," he'd quoted. Then he'd shrugged. "Their bank balances say yes."

"And we're okay with this?" Alex had asked Darlington. "With people getting cut open so Chauncey can redecorate his summer home?"

"Never met a Chauncey," he'd said. "Still hoping." Then he'd paused, standing in the armory, his face grave. "Nothing is going to stop this. Too many powerful people rely on what the societies can do. Before Lethe existed, no one was keeping watch. So you can make futile bleating noises in protest and lose your scholarship, or you can stay here, do your job, and do the most good you can."

Even then, she'd wondered if that was only part of the story, if Darlington's desire to know *everything* bound him to Lethe just as surely as any sense of duty. But she'd stayed quiet then and she intended to stay quiet now.

Michael Reyes had been found in one of the public beds at Yale New Haven. To the outside world he looked like any other patient: a vagrant, the type who passed through psych wards and emergency rooms and jails, on his meds, then off. He had a brother in New Jersey who was listed as his next of kin and who had signed off on what was supposed to be a routine medical procedure for the treatment of a scarred bowel.

Reyes was cared for solely by a nurse named Jean Gatdula, who'd worked three night shifts in a row. She didn't blink or cause a fuss when, through what appeared to be a scheduling error, she was slated for two more evenings in the ward. That week her colleagues may or may not have noticed that she always came to work with a huge handbag. In it was stowed a little cooler that she used to carry Michael Reyes's meals: a dove's heart for clarity, geranium root, and a dish of bitter herbs. Gatdula had no idea what the food did or what fate awaited Michael Reyes any more than she knew what became of any of the "special" patients she tended to. She didn't even know whom she worked for, only that once every month she received a much-needed check to offset the gambling debts her husband racked up at the Foxwoods blackjack tables.

Alex wasn't sure if it was her imagination or if she really could smell the ground parsley speckling Reyes's insides, but her own stomach gave another warning flutter. She was desperate for fresh air, sweating beneath her layers. The operating theater was kept ice cold, fed by vents separate from the rest of the building, but the huge portable halogens used to light the proceedings still radiated heat.

A low moan sounded. Alex's gaze shot to Michael Reyes, a terrible image flashing through her mind: Reyes waking to find himself strapped to a table, surrounded by hooded figures, his insides on the outside. But his eyes were closed, his chest rising and falling in steady rhythm. The moan continued, louder now. Maybe someone else was feeling sick? But none of the Bonesmen looked distressed. Their faces glowed like studious moons in the dim theater, eyes trained on the proceedings.

Still the moan climbed, a low wind building, churning through the room and bouncing off its dark-wood walls. *No direct eye contact,* Alex warned herself. *Just look to see if the Grays—*She choked back a startled grunt.

The Grays were no longer in their seats.

They leaned over the railing that surrounded the operating theater, fingers gripping the wood, necks craned, their bodies stretching toward the very edge of the chalk circle like animals straining to drink from the lip of a watering hole.

Don't look. It was Darlington's voice, his warning. *Don't look too closely.* It was too easy for a Gray to form a bond, to attach itself to you. And it was more dangerous because she already knew these Grays' histories. They had been around so long that generations of

Lethe delegates had documented their pasts. But their names had been redacted from all documents.

"If you don't know a name," Darlington had explained, "you can't think it, and then you won't be tempted to say it." A name was a kind of intimacy.

Don't look. But Darlington wasn't here.

The female Gray was naked, her small breasts puckered from the cold as they must have been in death. She lifted a hand to the open wound of her belly, touched the flesh there fondly, like a woman coyly indicating that she was expecting. They hadn't sewn her up. The boy—and he was a boy, skinny and tender-featured—wore a sloppy bottle-green jacket and stained trousers. Grays always appeared as they had in the moment of death. But there was something obscene about them side by side, one naked, the other clothed.

Every muscle in the Grays' bodies strained, their eyes wide and staring, their lips yawning open. The black holes of their mouths were caverns, and from them that bleak keening rose, not really a moan at all but something flat and inhuman. Alex thought of the wasps' nest she'd found in the garage beneath her mother's Studio City apartment one summer, the mindless buzz of insects in a dark place.

The Haruspex kept reciting in Dutch. Another Bonesman held a glass of water to the Scribe's lips as he continued his transcriptions. The smell of blood and herbs and shit hung dense in the air.

The Grays arced forward inch by inch, trembling, lips distended, their mouths too wide now, as if their jaws had unhinged. The whole room seemed to vibrate.

But only Alex could see them.

That was why Lethe had brought her here, why Dean Sandow had grudgingly made his golden offer to a girl in handcuffs. Still, Alex looked around, hoping for someone else to understand, for anyone to offer their help.

She took a step back, heart rabbiting in her chest. Grays were docile, vague, especially Grays this old. At least Alex thought they were. Was this one of the lessons Darlington hadn't gotten to yet?

She racked her brain for the few incantations Darlington had taught her last semester, spells of protection. She could use death words in a pinch. Would they work on Grays in this state? She should have put salt in her pockets, caramels to distract them, anything. *Basic stuff,* Darlington said in her head. *Easy to master.*

The wood beneath the Grays' fingers began to bend and creak. Now the redheaded a cappella girl looked up, wondering where the creaking had come from.

The wood was going to splinter. The signs must have been made incorrectly; the circle of protection would not hold. Alex looked right and left at the useless Bonesmen in their ridiculous robes. If Darlington were here, he would stay and fight, make sure the Grays were contained and Reyes was kept safe.

The halogens dimmed, surged.

"Fuck you, Darlington," Alex muttered beneath her breath, already turning on her heel to run.

Boom.

The room shook. Alex stumbled. The Haruspex and the rest of the Bonesmen looked at her, scowling.

Boom.

The sound of something knocking from the next world. Something big. Something that should not be let through.

"Is our Dante drunk?" muttered the Haruspex.

Boom.

Alex opened her mouth to scream, to tell them to run before whatever was holding that thing back gave way.

The moaning dropped away suddenly, completely, as if stoppered in a bottle. The monitor beeped. The lights hummed.

The Grays were back in their seats, ignoring each other, ignoring her.

Beneath her coat, Alex's blouse clung wetly to her, soaked through with sweat. She could smell her own sour fear thick on her skin. The halogens still shone hot and white. The theater pulsed heat like an organ suffused with blood. The Bonesmen were staring. Next door, the credits rolled.

Alex could see the spot where the Grays had gripped the railing, white slivers of wood splayed like corn silk.

"Sorry," Alex said. She bent at the knees and vomited onto the stone floor.

When they finally stitched up Michael Reyes, it was nearly 3 a.m. The Haruspex and most of the other Bonesmen had left hours before to shower off the ritual and prepare for a party that would last well past dawn.

The Haruspex might head directly back to New York in the creamy leather seat of a black town car, or he might stay for the festivities and take his pick of willing undergrad girls or boys or both. She'd been told "attending to" the Haruspex was considered an honor, and Alex supposed if you were high enough and drunk enough, it might feel like that was the case, but it sure sounded like being pimped out to the man who paid the bills.

The redhead—Miranda, it turned out, "like in *The Tempest*"—had helped Alex clean up the vomit. She'd been genuinely nice about it and Alex had almost felt bad for not remembering her name.

Reyes had been transported out of the building on a gurney, cloaked in obfuscation veils that made him look like a bunch of AV equipment piled beneath protective plastic sheeting. It was the most risky part of the whole night's endeavor as far as the safety of the society went. Skull and Bones didn't really excel at anything other than prognostication, and of course the members of Manuscript weren't interested in sharing their glamours with another society. The magic binding Reyes's veils wobbled with every bump, the gurney coming into and out of focus, the blips and bleeps from the medical equipment and the ventilator still audible. If anyone stopped to take a close look at what was being wheeled down the hallway, the Bonesmen would have some real trouble—though Alex doubted it would be anything they couldn't buy their way out of.

She would check in on Reyes once he was back on the ward and then again in a week to make sure he was healing without complications. There had been casualties following prognostications before, though only one since Lethe had been founded in 1898 to monitor the societies. A group of Bonesmen had accidentally killed a vagrant during a hastily planned emergency reading after the stock-market crash of 1929. Prognostications had been banned for the next four years, and Bones had been threatened with the loss of its massive red stone tomb on High Street. "That's why we exist," Darlington had said as Alex turned the pages listing the names of each *victima* and prognostication date in the Lethe records. "We are the shepherds, Stern."

But he'd cringed when Alex pointed to an inscription in one of the margins of *Lethe: A Legacy*. "*NMDH?*"

"No more dead hobos," he'd said on a sigh.

So much for the noble mission of Lethe House. Still Alex couldn't feel too superior tonight, not when she'd been seconds from abandoning Michael Reyes to save her own ass.

Alex endured a long string of jokes about her spewed dinner of grilled chicken and Twizzlers, and stayed at the theater to make sure the remaining Bonesmen followed what she hoped was proper procedure for sanitizing the space.

She promised herself she'd return later to sprinkle the theater with bone dust. Reminders of death were the best way to keep Grays at bay. It was why cemeteries were some of the least haunted places in the world. She thought of the ghosts' open mouths, that horrible drone of insects. Something had been trying to slam its way into the chalk circle. At least that was how it had seemed. Grays—ghosts—were harmless. Mostly. It took a lot for them to take any kind of form in the mortal world. And to pass through the final Veil? To become physical, capable of touch? Capable of damage? They could. Alex knew they could. But it was close to impossible.

Even so, there had been hundreds of prognostications in this theater and she'd never heard of any Grays crossing over into physical form or interfering. Why had their behavior changed tonight?

If it had.

The greatest gift Lethe had given Alex was not the full ride to Yale, the new start that had scrubbed her past clean like a chemical burn. It was the knowledge, the certainty, that the things she saw were real and always had been. But she'd lived too long wondering if she was crazy to stop now. Darlington would have believed her. He always had. Except Darlington was gone.

Not for good, she told herself. In a week the new moon would rise and they would bring him home.

Alex touched her fingers to the cracked railing, already thinking about how to phrase her description of the prognostication for the Lethe House records. Dean Sandow reviewed all of them, and she wasn't anxious to draw his attention to anything out of the ordinary. Besides, if you set aside a helpless man having his guts rearranged, nothing bad had actually happened.

When Alex emerged from the passage into the hallway, Tripp Helmuth startled from his slouch. "They almost done in there?"

Alex nodded and took a deep breath of comparatively fresh air, eager to get outside.

"Pretty gross, huh?" Tripp asked with a smirk. "If you want I can slip you some of the tips when they get transcribed. Take the edge off those student loans."

"What the fuck would you know about student loans?" The words were out before she could stop them. Darlington would not approve. Alex was supposed to remain civil, distant, diplomatic. And anyway, she was a hypocrite. Lethe had made sure she would graduate without a cloud of debt hanging over her—if she actually made it through four years of exams and papers and nights like these.

Tripp held his hands up in surrender, laughing uneasily. "Hey, just tryin' to get by." Tripp was on the sailing team, a third-generation Bonesman, a gentleman and a scholar, a purebred golden retriever—dopey, glossy, and expensive. He was rumpled and rosy as a healthy infant, his hair sandy, his skin still tan from whichever island he'd spent winter break on. He had the ease of someone who had always been and would always be *just fine,* a boy of a thousand second chances. "We good?" he asked eagerly.

"We're good," she said, though she was not good at all. She could still feel the reverberation of that buzzing moan filling up her lungs, rattling the inside of her skull. "Just stuffy in there."

"Right?" Tripp said, ready to be pals. "Maybe getting stuck out here all night's not so bad." He didn't sound convinced.

"What happened to your arm?" Alex could see a bit of bandage peeking out from Tripp's windbreaker.

He shoved the sleeve up, revealing a patch of greasy cellophane taped over the inside of his forearm. "A bunch of us got tattoos today."

Alex looked closer: a strutting bulldog bursting through a big blue Y. The dudebro equivalent of *best friends forevah!*

"Nice," she lied.

"You got any ink?" His sleepy eyes roved over her, trying to peel back the winter layers, no different than the losers who had hung around Ground Zero, fingers brushing her clavicle, her biceps, tracing the shapes there. *So what does this one mean?*

"Nope. Not my thing." Alex wrapped her scarf around her neck. "I'll check in on Reyes on the ward tomorrow."

"Huh? Oh, right. Good. Where's Darlington anyway? He already sticking you with the shit jobs?"

Tripp tolerated Alex, tried to be friendly with her because he wanted his belly rubbed by everyone he encountered, but he genuinely liked Darlington.

"Spain," she said, because that was what she'd been instructed to say.

"Nice. Tell him *buenos días*."

If Alex could have told Darlington anything, it would have been, *Come back.* She would have said it in English and Spanish. She would have used the imperative.

"Adiós," she said to Tripp. "Enjoy the party."

Once she was clear of the building, Alex yanked off her gloves and unwrapped two sticky ginger candies, shoving them into her mouth. She was tired of thinking about Darlington, but the smell of the ginger, the heat it created at the back of her throat, brought him even more brightly alive. She saw his long body sprawled in front of the great stone fireplace at Black Elm. He'd taken his boots off, left his socks to dry on the hearth. He was on his back, eyes closed, head resting in the cradle of his arms, toes wiggling in time to the music floating around the room, something classical Alex didn't know, dense with French horns that left emphatic crescents of sound in the air.

Alex had been on the floor beside him, arms clasped around her knees, back pressed against the base of an old sofa, trying to seem relaxed and to stop staring at his feet. They just looked so *naked.* He'd cuffed his black jeans up, keeping the damp off his skin, and those slender white feet, hair dusting the toes, had made her feel a little obscene, like some sepia-toned pervert driven mad by a glimpse of ankle.

Fuck you, Darlington. She yanked her gloves back on.

For a moment she stood paralyzed. She should get back to Lethe House and write up her report for Dean Sandow to review, but what she really wanted was to flop down on the narrow bottom bunk of the room she shared with Mercy and cram in all the sleep she could before class. At this hour, she wouldn't have to make any excuses to curious roommates. But if she slept at Lethe, Mercy and Lauren would be clamoring to know where and with whom she'd spent the night.

Darlington had suggested making up a boyfriend to justify her long absences and late nights.

"If I do that, at some point I'll have to produce a boy-shaped human to gaze at me adoringly," Alex had replied in frustration. "How have you gotten away with this for the last three years?"

Darlington had just shrugged. "My roommates figured I was a player." If Alex's eyes had rolled back in her head any farther, she would have been facing the opposite direction.

"All right, all right. I told them I was in a band with some UConn guys and that we played out a lot."

"Do you even play an instrument?"

"Of course."

Cello, upright bass, guitar, piano, and something called an oud.

Hopefully, Mercy would be fast asleep when Alex got back to the room and she could slip inside to retrieve her basket of shower things and head down the hall without notice. It would be tricky. Anytime you tampered with the Veil between this world and the next, it left a stink that was something like the electrical crackle of ozone after a storm coupled with the rot of a pumpkin left too long on a windowsill. The first time she'd made the mistake of returning to the suite without showering, she'd actually had to lie about slipping in a pile of garbage to explain it. Mercy and Lauren had laughed about it for weeks.

Alex thought of the grimy shower waiting at her dorm . . . and then of sinking into the vast old claw-foot tub in Il Bastone's spotless bathroom, the four-poster bed so high she had to hoist herself onto it. Supposedly Lethe had safe houses and hidey-holes all over the Yale campus, but the two Alex had been introduced to were the Hutch and Il Bastone. The Hutch was closer to Alex's dorm and most of her classes, but it was just a shabby, comfortable set of rooms above a clothing store, always stocked with bags of chips and Darlington's protein bars, a place to stop in and take a quick nap on the badly sprung couch. Il Bastone was something special: a three-story mansion nearly a mile from the heart of campus that served as Lethe's main headquarters. Oculus would be waiting there tonight, the lamps lit, with a tray of tea, brandy, and sandwiches. It was tradition, even if Alex didn't show up to enjoy them. But the price of all that luxury would be dealing with Oculus, and she just couldn't handle Dawes's clenched-jaw silences tonight. Better to return to the dorms with the stink of the night's work on her.

Alex crossed the street and cut back through the rotunda. It was hard not to keep looking behind her, thinking of the Grays standing at the edge of the circle with their mouths stretched too wide, black pits humming that low insect sound. What would have happened if that railing had broken, if the chalk circle hadn't held? What had provoked them? Would she have had the strength or the knowledge to hold them off? *Pasa punto, pasa mundo.*

Alex pulled her coat tighter, tucking her face into her scarf, her breath humid against the wool, hurrying back past Beinecke Library.

"If you get locked in there during a fire, all of the oxygen gets sucked out," Lauren had claimed. "To protect the books."

Alex knew that was bullshit. Darlington had told her so. He'd known the truth of the building, all of its faces, that it had been built to the Platonic ideal (the building was a temple), employing the same ratios used by some typesetters for their pages (the building was a book), that its marble had been quarried in Vermont (the building was a monument). The entrance had been created so that only one person was permitted to enter at a time, passing through the rotating door like a supplicant. She remembered Darlington pulling on the white gloves worn to handle rare manuscripts, his long fingers resting reverently on the page. It was the same way Len handled cash.

There was a room in Beinecke, hidden on . . . she couldn't remember which floor. And even if she could have she wouldn't have gone. She didn't have the balls to descend into the patio, touch her fingers to the window in the secret pattern, enter in the dark.

This place had been dear to Darlington. There was no place more magical. There was no place on campus she felt more like a fraud.

Alex reached for her phone to check the time, hoping it wasn't much past three. If she could get washed up and into bed by four, she'd still be able to get three and a half solid hours before she had to be up and across campus again for Spanish. This was the math she ran every night, every moment. How much time to try to get the work done? How much time to rest? She could never quite make the numbers work. She was just scraping by, stretching the budget, always coming up a little short, and the panic clung to her, dogging her steps.

Alex looked at the glowing screen and swore. It was flooded with messages. She'd put the phone on silent for the prognostication and forgotten to switch it back on.

The texts were all from the same person: Oculus, Pamela Dawes, the grad student who maintained the Lethe residences and served as their research assistant. *Pammie,* though only Darlington called her that.

Call in.

Call in.

Call in.

The texts were all timed exactly fifteen minutes apart. Either Dawes was following some kind of protocol or she was even more uptight than Alex had thought.

Alex considered just ignoring the messages. But it was a Thursday night, the night the societies met, and that meant that some little shit had gotten up to something bad. For all she knew, the shapeshifting idiots at Wolf's Head had turned themselves into a herd of buffalo and trampled a bunch of students coming out of Branford.

She stepped behind one of the columns supporting the Beinecke cube to shelter from the wind and dialed.

Dawes picked up on the first ring. "Oculus speaking."

"Dante replies," Alex said, feeling like a jackass. She was Dante.

Darlington was Virgil. That was the way Lethe was supposed to work until Alex made it to her senior year and took on the title of Virgil to mentor an incoming freshman. She'd nodded and matched Darlington's small smile when he'd told her their code names—he'd referred to them as "offices"—pretending she got the joke. Later, she'd looked them up and discovered that Virgil had been Dante's guide as he descended into hell. More Lethe House humor wasted on her.

"There's a body at Payne Whitney," said Dawes. "Centurion is on site."

"A body," Alex repeated, wondering if fatigue had damaged her ability to understand basic human speech.

"Yes."

"Like a dead body?"

"Ye-es." Dawes was clearly trying to sound calm, but her breath caught, turning the single syllable into a musical hiccup.

Alex pressed her back against the column, the cold of the stone seeping through her coat, and felt a stab of angry adrenaline spike through her.

Are you messing with me? That was what she wanted to ask. That was what this felt like. Being fucked with. Being the weird kid who talked to herself, who was so desperate for friends she agreed when Sarah McKinney pleaded, "Can you meet me at Tres Muchachos after school? I want to see if you can talk to my grandma. We used to go there a lot and I miss her so much." The kid who stood outside the shittiest Mexican restaurant in the shittiest food court in the Valley by herself until she had to call her mom to ask her to pick her up because no one was coming. Of course no one was coming.

This is real, she reminded herself. And Pamela Dawes was a lot of things but she wasn't a Sarah McKinney–style asshole.

Which meant someone was dead.

And she was supposed to do something about it?

"Uh, was it an accident?"

"Possible homicide." Dawes sounded like she'd been waiting for just this question.

"Okay," Alex said, because she had no idea what else to say.

"Okay," Dawes replied awkwardly. She'd delivered her big line and now she was ready to get offstage.

Alex hung up and stood in the bleak, windswept silence of the empty plaza. She'd forgotten at least half of what Darlington had tried to teach her before he'd vanished, but he definitely hadn't covered murder.

She didn't know why. If you were going to hell together, murder seemed like a good place to start.

2

Last Fall

Daniel Arlington prided himself on being prepared for anything, but if he'd had to choose a way to describe Alex Stern, it would have been "an unwelcome surprise." He could think of a lot of other terms for her, but none of them were polite, and Darlington always endeavored to be polite. If he'd been brought up by his parents—his dilettante father, his glib but brilliant mother—he might have had different priorities, but he'd been raised by his grandfather, Daniel Tabor Arlington III, who believed that most problems could be solved with cask-strength scotch, plenty of ice, and impeccable manners.

His grandfather had never met Galaxy Stern.

Darlington sought out Alex's first-floor Vanderbilt dorm room on a sweating, miserable day in the first week of September. He could have waited for her to report to the house on Orange, but when he was a freshman, his own mentor, the inimitable Michelle Alameddine, who had served as his Virgil, had welcomed him to Yale and the mysteries of Lethe House by coming to meet him at the Old Campus freshman dorms. Darlington was determined to do things right, even if everything about the Stern situation had started out wrong.

He hadn't chosen Galaxy Stern as his Dante. In fact, she had, by sheer virtue of her existence, robbed him of something he'd been looking forward to for the entirety of his three-year tenure with Lethe: the moment when he would gift someone new with the job he loved, when he'd crack the ordinary world open for some worthy but barely suspecting soul. Only a few months before, he'd unloaded the boxes full of incoming freshman applications and stacked them in the great room at Black Elm, giddy with excitement, determined to read or at least skim through all eighteen hundred–plus files before he made his recommendations to the Lethe House alumni. He would be fair, open-minded, and thorough, and in the end he would choose twenty candidates for the role of Dante. Then Lethe would vet their backgrounds, check for health risks, signs of mental illness, and financial vulnerabilities, and a final decision would be made.

Darlington had created a plan for how many applications he'd have to tackle each day that would still free his mornings for work on the estate and his afternoons for his job at the Peabody Museum. He'd been ahead of schedule that day in July—on application number 324: Mackenzie Hoffer, 800 verbal, 720 math; nine APs her junior year; blog on the Bayeux Tapestry maintained in both English and French. She'd seemed promising until he'd gotten to her personal essay, in which she'd compared herself to Emily Dickinson. Darlington had just tossed her folder onto the *no* pile when Dean Sandow called to tell him their search was over. They'd found their candidate. The alumni were unanimous.

Darlington had wanted to protest. Hell, he'd wanted to break something. Instead, he'd straightened the stack of folders before him and said, "Who is it? I have all of the files right here."

"You don't have her file. She never applied. She didn't even finish high school." Before Darlington could sputter his indignation, Sandow added, "Daniel, she can see Grays."

Darlington had paused, his hand still atop Mackenzie Hoffer (two summers with Habitat for Humanity). It wasn't just the sound of his given name, something Sandow rarely used. *She can see Grays.* The only way for one of the living to see the dead was by ingesting the Orozcerio, an elixir of infinite complexity that required perfect skill and attention to detail to create. He'd attempted it himself when he was seventeen, before he'd ever heard of Lethe, when he'd only hoped there might be more to this world than he'd been led to believe. His efforts had landed him in the ER and he'd hemorrhaged blood from his ears and eyes for two days.

"She managed to brew an elixir?" he said, both thrilled and—he could admit it—a little jealous.

Silence followed, long enough for Darlington to switch off the light on his grandfather's desk and walk out to the back porch of Black Elm. From here he could see the gentle slope of houses leading down Edgewood to campus and, far beyond, the Long Island Sound. All of the land down to Central Avenue had once been a part of Black Elm but had been sold off in bits and pieces as the Arlington fortune dwindled. The house, its rose gardens, and the ruined mess of the maze at the edge of the wood were all that remained—and only he remained to tend and prune and coddle it back to life. Dusk was falling now, a long, slow summer twilight, thick with mosquitoes and the glint of fireflies. He could see the question mark of Cosmo's white tail as the cat wended his way through the high grass, stalking some small creature.

"No elixir," said Sandow. "She can just see them."

"Ah," said Darlington, watching a thrush peck half-heartedly at the broken base of what had once been the obelisk fountain. There was nothing else to say. Though Lethe had been created to monitor the activities of Yale's secret societies, its secondary mission was to unravel the mysteries of what lay beyond the Veil. For years they had documented stories of people who could actually see phantoms, some confirmed, some little more than rumor. So if the board had found a girl who could do these things and they could make her beholden to them . . . Well, that was that. He should be glad to meet her.

He wanted to get drunk.

"I'm not any happier about this than you are," said Sandow. "But you know the position we're in. This is an important year for

Lethe. We need everyone happy." Lethe was responsible for keeping watch over the Houses of the Veil, but it also relied on them for funding. This was a re-up year and the societies had gone so long without an incident, there were rumblings that perhaps they shouldn't dip into their coffers to continue supporting Lethe at all. "I'll send you her files. She's not . . . She's not the Dante we might have hoped for, but try to keep an open mind."

"Of course," said Darlington, because that was what a gentleman did. "Of course I will."

He'd tried to mean it. Even after he read her file, even after he'd watched the interview between her and Sandow recorded at a hospital in Van Nuys, California, heard the husky, broken woodwind sound of her voice, he'd tried. She'd been found naked and comatose at a crime scene, next to a girl who hadn't been lucky enough to survive the fentanyl they'd both taken. The details of it were all more sordid and sad than he could have fathomed, and he'd tried to feel sorry for her. His Dante, the girl he would gift with the keys to a secret world, was a criminal, a drug user, a dropout who cared about none of the things he did. But he'd tried.

And still nothing had prepared him for the shock of her presence in that shabby Vanderbilt common room. The room was small but high-ceilinged, with three tall windows that looked out onto the horseshoe-shaped courtyard and two narrow doors leading to the bedrooms. The space eddied with the easy chaos of a freshman year move-in: boxes on the floor, no proper furniture to be seen but a wobbly lamp and a battered recliner pushed up against the long-since-functional fireplace. A muscular blonde in running shorts—Lauren, he guessed (likely pre-med, solid test scores, field-hockey captain at her Philadelphia prep school)—was setting up a faux-vintage turntable on the ledge of the window seat, a plastic crate of records balanced beside it. The recliner was probably hers too, carted along in a moving truck from Bucks County to New Haven. Anna Breen (Huntsville, Texas; STEM scholarship; choir leader) sat on the floor trying to assemble what looked like a bookshelf. This was a girl who would never quite fit. She'd end up in a singing group or maybe get heavily into her church. She definitely wouldn't be partying with her other roommates.

Then the other two girls shuffled out of one of the bedrooms, awkwardly hefting a banged-up university-issued desk between them.

"Do you have to put that out here?" asked Anna glumly.

"We need more space," said a girl in a flowered sundress Darlington knew was Mercy Zhao (piano; 800 math, 800 verbal; prizewinning essays on Rabelais and a bizarre but compelling comparison of a passage in *The Sound and the Fury* to a bit about a pear tree in *The Canterbury Tales* that had garnered the notice of both the Yale and Princeton English departments).

And then Galaxy Stern (no high school diploma, no GED, no achievements to speak of other than surviving her own misery) emerged from the dark nook of the bedroom, dressed in a long-sleeved shirt and black jeans totally inappropriate to the heat and balancing one end of the desk in her skinny arms. The low quality of Sandow's video had caught the slick, straight sheaves of her black hair but not the severe precision of her center part, the hollow quality of her eyes but not the deep inkblot of their color. She looked malnourished, her clavicles sharp as exclamation points beneath the fabric of her shirt. She was too sleek, almost damp, less Undine rising from the waters than a dagger-toothed rusalka.

Or maybe she just needed a snack and a long nap.

All right, Stern. Let's begin.

Darlington rapped on the door, stepped into the room, smiled big, bright, welcoming, as they set the desk down in the common room corner. "Alex! Your mom told me I should check in on you. It's me, Darlington."

For a brief moment she looked utterly lost, even panicked, then she matched his smile. "Hey! I didn't recognize you."

Good. She was adaptable.

"Introductions, please," said Lauren, her gaze interested, assessing. She'd pulled a copy of Queen's *A Day at the Races* from the crate.

He extended his hand. "I'm Darlington, Alex's cousin."

"Are you in JE too?" Lauren asked.

Darlington remembered that unearned sense of loyalty. At the start of the year, all the incoming freshmen were sorted into residential colleges where they would eat most of their meals and where they would eventually sleep when they left Old Campus behind as sophomores. They would buy scarves striped in their residential college colors, learn the college's chants and mottos. Alex belonged to Lethe, just as Darlington had, but she'd been assigned to Jonathan Edwards, named for the fire and brimstone preacher.

"I'm in Davenport," Darlington said. "But I don't live on campus." He'd liked living in Davenport—the dining hall, the big grassy courtyard. But he didn't like Black Elm sitting empty, and the money he'd saved on his room and board had been enough to fix the water damage he'd found in the ballroom last spring. Besides, Cosmo liked the company.

"Do you have a car?" asked Lauren.

Mercy laughed. "Oh my God, you're ridiculous."

Lauren shrugged. "How else are we going to get to Ikea? We need a couch." She would be the leader of this crew, the one who'd suggest which parties to go to, who'd have them host a room for Liquor Treat at Halloween.

"Sorry," he said with an apologetic smile. "I can't drive you. At least not today." Or any day. "And I need to steal Alex away."

Alex wiped her palms on her jeans. "We're trying to get settled," she said hesitantly, hopefully even. He could see circles of sweat blooming beneath her arms.

"You made a promise," he said with a wink. "And you know how my mom gets about family stuff."

He saw a flash of rebellion in her oil-slick eyes, but all she said was, "Okay."

"Can you give us cash for the couch?" Lauren asked Alex, roughly shoving the Queen record back into the crate. He hoped it wasn't the original vinyl.

"You bet," said Alex. She turned to Darlington. "Aunt Eileen said she'd spring for a new couch, right?"

Darlington's mother's name was Harper, and he doubted she even knew the word *Ikea*. "Did she really?"

Alex crossed her arms. "Yup."

Darlington took his wallet from his back pocket and peeled off three hundred dollars in cash. He handed it to Alex, who passed it to Lauren. "Make sure you write her a thank-you note," he said.

"Oh, I will," said Alex. "I know she's a real stickler for that kind of thing."

When they were striding across the lawns of Old Campus, the red-brick towers and crenellations of Vanderbilt behind them, Darlington said, "You owe me three hundred dollars. I'm not buying you a couch."

"You can afford it," Alex said coolly. "I'm guessing you come from the good side of the family, cuz."

"You needed cover for why you're going to be off seeing me so much."

"Bullshit. You were testing me."

"It's my job to test you."

"I thought it was your job to teach me. That's not the same thing."

At least she wasn't stupid. "Fair enough. But visits to dear Aunt Eileen can cover a few of your late nights."

"How late are we talking about?"

He could hear the worry in her voice. Was it caution or laziness? "How much did Dean Sandow tell you?"

"Not much." She pulled the fabric of her shirt away from her stomach, trying to cool herself.

"Why are you dressed like that?" He hadn't meant to ask but she looked uncomfortable—her black Henley buttoned to the neck, sweat spreading in dark rings from her armpits—and completely out of place. A girl who managed lies so smoothly should have a better sense of protective cover.

Alex just slid him a sideways look. "I'm very modest."

Darlington had no reply to that, so he pointed to one of the two identical red-brick buildings bracketing the path. "This is the oldest building on campus."

"It doesn't look old."

"It's been well maintained. It almost didn't make it, though. People thought it ruined the look of Old Campus, so they wanted to knock it down."

"Why didn't they?"

"The books credit a preservation campaign, but the truth is Lethe discovered the building was lode-bearing."

"Huh?"

"Spiritually lode-bearing. It was part of an old binding ritual to keep the campus safe." They turned right, down a path that would lead them toward the ersatz-Medieval portcullis of Phelps Gate. "That's what the whole college used to look like. Little buildings of red bricks. Colonial. A lot like Harvard. Then after the Civil War, the walls went up. Now most of the campus is built that way, a series of fortresses, walled and gated, a castle keep."

Old Campus was a perfect example, a massive quadrangle of towering stone dorms surrounding a huge sun-dappled courtyard welcome to all—until night fell and the gates banged shut.

"Why?" Alex asked.

"To keep the rabble out. The soldiers came back to New Haven from the war wild, most of them unmarried, a lot of them messed up from the fighting. There was a wave of immigration too. Irish, Italians, freed slaves, everyone looking for manufacturing jobs. Yale didn't want any of it."

Alex laughed.

"Is something funny?" he asked.

She glanced back at her dorm. "Mercy's Chinese. A Nigerian

girl lives next door. Then there's my mongrel ass. We all got in anyway. Eventually."

"A long slow siege." The word *mongrel* felt like dangerous bait. He took in her black hair, her black eyes, the olive cast to her skin. She might have been Greek. Mexican. White. "Jewish mother, no mention of a father, but I assume you had one?"

"Never knew him."

There was more here but he wasn't going to push. "We all have spaces we keep blank." They'd reached Phelps Gate, the big echoing archway that led onto College Street and away from the relative safety of Old Campus. He didn't want to get sidetracked. They had too much literal and figurative ground to cover. "This is the New Haven Green," he said, as they strode down one of the stone paths. "When the colony was founded, this was where they built their meetinghouse. The town was meant to be a new Eden, founded between two rivers like the Tigris and the Euphrates."

Alex frowned. "Why so many churches?"

There were three on the green, two of them near-twins in their Federal design, the third a jewel of Gothic Revival.

"This town has a church for nearly every block. Or it used to. Some of them are closing now. People just don't go."

"Do you?" she asked.

"Do *you*?"

"Nope."

"Yes, I go," he said. "It's a family thing." He saw the flicker of judgment in her eyes, but he didn't need to explain. Church on Sunday, work on Monday. That was the Arlington way. When Darlington had turned thirteen and protested that he'd be happy to risk God's wrath if he could just sleep in, his grandfather seized him by the ear and dragged him out of bed despite his eighty years. "I don't care what you believe," he'd said. "The working man believes in God and expects us to do the same, so you will get your ass dressed and in a pew or I will tan it raw." Darlington had gone. And after his grandfather had died, he'd kept going.

"The green is the site of the city's first church and its first grave-yard. It's a source of tremendous power."

"Yeah . . . no shit."

He realized her shoulders had gone loose and easy. Her stride had changed. She looked a little less like someone gearing up to take a swing.

Darlington tried not to sound too eager. "What do you see?" She didn't answer. "I know about what you can do. It isn't a secret."

Alex's gaze was still distant, almost disinterested. "It's empty here, that's all. I never really see much around cemeteries and stuff."

And stuff. Darlington looked around, but all he saw was what everyone else would: students, people who worked at the court-house or the string of shops along Chapel, enjoying the sun on their lunch hour.

He knew the paths that seemed to bisect the green arbitrarily had been drawn by a group of Freemasons to try to appease and contain the dead when the cemetery had been moved a few blocks away. He knew that their compass lines—or a pentagram, depend-ing on whom you asked—could be seen from above. He knew the spot where the Lincoln Oak had toppled after Hurricane Sandy, revealing a human skeleton tangled in its roots, one of the many bodies never moved to Grove Street Cemetery. He saw the city dif-ferently because he knew it, and his knowledge was not casual. It was adoration. But no amount of love could make him see Grays. Not without Orozcerio, another hit from the Golden Bowl. He shuddered. Every time was a risk, another chance that his body would say *enough,* that one of his kidneys would simply fail.

"It makes sense you don't see them here," he said. "Certain things will draw them to graveyards and cemeteries, but as a rule, they steer clear."

Now he had her attention. Real interest sparked in her eyes, the first indication of something beyond watchful reserve. "Why?"

"Grays love life and anything that reminds them of being

alive. Salt, sugar, sweat. Fighting and fucking, tears and blood and human drama."

"I thought salt kept them out."

Darlington raised a brow. "Did you see that on television?"

"Would it make you happier if I say I learned it from an ancient book?"

"Actually, yes."

"Too bad."

"Salt is a purifier," he said, as they crossed Temple Street, "so it's good for banishing demons—though to my great sorrow I've never personally had the honor. But when it comes to Grays, making a salt circle is the equivalent of leaving a salt lick for deer."

"So what keeps them out?"

Her need crackled through the words. So this was where her interest lay.

"Bone dust. Graveyard dirt. The leavings of crematory ash. Memento mori." He glanced at her. "Any Latin?" She shook her head. Of course not. "They hate reminders of death. If you want to Gray-proof your room, hang a Holbein print." He'd meant it as a joke, but he could see she was chewing on what he'd said, committing the artist's name to memory. Darlington felt an acute twinge of guilt that he did not enjoy. He'd been so busy envying this girl's ability, he hadn't considered what it might be like if you could never close the door on the dead. "I can ward your room," he said by way of penance. "Your whole dorm if you like."

"You can do that?"

"Yes," he said. "And I can show you how to do it too."

"Tell me the rest," said Alex. Away from the dim cavern of the dorms, sweat had formed in a slick sheen over her nose and forehead, gathering in the divot above her upper lip. She was going to soak that shirt, and he could see she was self-conscious about it by the way she held her arms rigidly to her sides.

"Did you read *The Life of Lethe*?"

"Yes."

"Really?"

"I skimmed it."

"Read it," he said. "I've made you a list of other material that will help get you up to speed. Mostly histories of New Haven and our own compiled history of the societies."

Alex gave a sharp shake of her head. "I mean tell me what I'm in for here . . . with you."

That was a hard question to answer. Nothing. Everything. Lethe was meant to be a gift, but could it be to her? There was too much to tell.

They left the green and he saw tension snap back into her shoulders, though there was still nothing his eyes could see to warrant it. They passed the row of banks clustered along Elm, looming over Kebabian's, the little red rug store that had somehow thrived in New Haven for over one hundred years, then turned left up Orange. They were only a few blocks from campus proper now, but it felt like miles. The bustle of student life vanished, as if stepping into the city was like falling off a cliff. The streets were a mess of new and old: gently weathered townhouses, barren parking lots, a carefully restored concert hall, the gargantuan high rise of the Housing Authority.

"Why here?" Alex asked when Darlington didn't answer her previous question. "What is it about this place that draws them?"

The short answer was *Who knows?* But Darlington doubted that would cast him or Lethe in the most credible light.

"In the early eighteen hundreds, magic was moving from the old world to the new, leaving Europe along with its practitioners. They needed someplace to store their knowledge and preserve its practices. No one's certain why New Haven worked. They tried in other places too," Darlington said with some pride. "Cambridge. Princeton. New Haven was where the magic caught and held and took root. Some people think it's because the Veil is thinner here, easier to pierce. You can see why Lethe is happy to have you on board." *At least, some of Lethe.* "You may be able to offer us answers. There are Grays that have been here far longer than the university."

"And these practitioners thought it would be smart to teach all this magic to a bunch of college kids?"

"Contact with the uncanny takes a toll. The older you get, the harder it is to endure that contact. So each year, the societies replenish the supply with a new tap, a new delegation. Magic is quite literally a dying art, and New Haven is one of the few places in the world where it can still be brought to life."

She said nothing. Was she scared? Good. Maybe she would actually read the books he assigned instead of skimming them.

"There are over a hundred societies at Yale at this point, but we don't concern ourselves with most of them. They get together for dinners, tell their life stories, do a little community service. It's the Ancient Eight that matter. The landed societies. The Houses of the Veil. They're the ones that have held their tombs continuously."

"Tombs?"

"I'm betting you've already seen some of them. Clubhouses, though they look more like mausoleums."

"Why don't we care about the other societies?" she asked.

"We care about power, and power is linked to place. Each of the Houses of the Veil grew up around a branch of the arcane and is devoted to studying it, and each built their tomb over a nexus of power. Except for Berzelius, and no one cares about Berzelius." They'd founded their society in direct response to the growing magical presence in New Haven, claiming the other Houses were charlatans and superstitious dilettantes, dedicating themselves to investments in new technologies and the philosophy that the only true magic was science. They'd managed to survive the stock market crash of 1929 without the help of prognostication, and limped along until the crash of 1987 when they'd been all but wiped out. As it happened, the only true magic was magic.

"A *nexus*," Alex repeated. "They're all over campus? The . . . nexes—"

"Nexuses. Think of magic like a river. The nexuses are where the power eddies, and it's what allows the societies' rituals to function successfully. We've mapped twelve in the city. Tombs have been built on eight of them. The others are on sites where structures already exist, like the train station, and where it would be impossible to build. A few societies have lost their tombs over time. They can study all they want. Once that connection is broken, they don't accomplish much."

"And you're telling me this has all been going on for more than a hundred years and no one has figured it out?"

"The Ancient Eight have yielded some of the most powerful men and women in the world. People who literally steer governments, the wealth of nations, who forge the shape of culture. They've run everything from the United Nations to Congress to *The New York Times* to the World Bank. They've fixed nearly every World Series, six Super Bowls, the Academy Awards, and at least one presidential election. Hundreds of websites are dedicated to unraveling their connections to the Freemasons, the Illuminati, the Bilderberg Group—the list goes on."

"Maybe if they met at Denny's instead of giant mausoleums, they wouldn't have to worry about that."

They had arrived at Il Bastone, Lethe House, three stories of red brick and stained glass, built by John Anderson in 1882 for an outrageous sum and then abandoned barely a year later. He'd claimed he was being chased out by the city's high tax rates. Lethe's records told a different story, one that involved his father and the ghost of a dead cigar girl. Il Bastone didn't sprawl like Black Elm. It was a city house, bracketed closely on both sides by other properties, tall but contained in its grandeur.

"They're not worried," said Darlington. "They welcome all of the conspiracy theories and tinfoil-hat-wearing loons."

"Because they like feeling interesting?"

"Because what they're really doing is so much worse." Darlington pushed open the black wrought-iron gate and saw the porch of the old house straighten slightly, as if in anticipation. "After you."

As soon as the gate shut, darkness enveloped them. From somewhere beneath the house, a howl sounded, high and hungry. Galaxy Stern had asked what she was in for. It was time to show her.

3

Winter

Who *dies at the gym?* After her call with Dawes, Alex back-tracked across the plaza. She had been to Payne Whitney Gymnasium exactly once: when she'd let Mercy drag her to a salsa class, where a white girl snugly packed into taut black pants had told her to pivot, pivot, pivot.

Darlington had encouraged her to use the free weights and to "build up her cardio."

"For what?" Alex had asked.

"To better yourself."

Only Darlington could say something like that with a straight face. But, then again, he ran six miles every morning and swept into rooms on a cloud of physical perfection. Every time he showed up at the Vanderbilt suite, it was as if someone had run an electric current through the floor. Lauren, Mercy, even silent, frowning Anna, would sit up a little straighter, looking bright-eyed and slightly frantic as a bunch of well-groomed squirrels. Alex would have liked to be immune to it—the pretty face, his lean frame, the easy way he occupied space as if he owned it. He had a way of distractedly brushing the brown hair back from his forehead that made you want to do it for him. But Darlington's lure was offset by the healthy fear he instilled in her. At the end of the day, he was a rich boy in a nice coat who could capsize her without even meaning to.

That first day at the mansion on Orange, he'd set jackals on her. *Jackals.* He'd given a sharp whistle and they'd leapt from the bushes near the house, snarling and cackling. Alex had screamed. Her legs had tangled as she'd turned to run and she'd fallen to the grass, nearly impaling herself on the low iron fence. But early on in her time with Len she'd learned to always watch the person in charge. That changed from room to room, house to house, deal to deal, but it always paid to know who could make the big decisions. That was Darlington. And Darlington didn't look scared. He looked interested.

The jackals were stalking toward her, slavering, teeth bared and backs bent.

They looked like foxes. They looked like the coyotes that ran the Hollywood Hills. They looked like *hounds.*

We are the shepherds.

"Darlington," she said, forcing calm into her voice. "Call off your fucking dogs."

He'd spoken a series of words she didn't understand and the creatures had slunk back into the bushes, all of their aggression vanishing, bouncing on their paws and nipping at one another's heels. He'd had the gall to smile at her as he offered her an elegant hand. The Van Nuys girl inside her longed to slap it away, jab her fingers into his windpipe, and make him sorry. But she forced herself to take his hand, let him help her up. It had been the start of a very long day.

When Alex had finally returned home to the dorms, Lauren waited all of sixty seconds before pouncing with, "So does your cousin have a girlfriend?"

They were sitting around the new coffee table, trying to get its legs not to wobble as they pushed in little plastic screws. Anna had vanished off somewhere and Lauren had ordered pizza. The window was open, letting in the bare beginnings of a breeze as twilight fell, and Alex felt like she was watching herself from the courtyard—a happy girl, a normal girl, surrounded by people with futures who assumed she had a future too. She had wanted to hold on to that feeling, to keep it for herself.

"You know . . . I have no idea." She'd been so overwhelmed she hadn't had a chance to be curious.

"He smells like money," said Mercy.

Lauren threw an Allen wrench at her. "Tacky."

"Don't start dating my cousin," Alex said, because that was the kind of thing these girls said. "I don't need that mess."

On this night, with the wind clawing to get into her winter coat, Alex thought of that girl, illuminated in gold, sitting in that sacred circle. It was the last moment of peace she could remember. Only five months had passed but it felt much longer.

She cut left, shadowed by the white columns that ran along the south side of the vast dining hall that everyone still called Commons, though it was supposed to be the Schwarzman Center now. Schwarzman was a Bonesman, class of 1969, and had managed a notoriously successful private equity fund, the Blackstone Group. The center was the result of a one-hundred-fifty-million-dollar donation to the university, a gift and a kind of apology for stray magic that had escaped an unsanctioned ritual and caused bizarre behavior and seizures in half the members of the Yale Precision Marching Band during a football game with Dartmouth.

Alex thought of the Grays in the operating theater, mouths gaping. It had been a routine prognostication. Nothing should have gone wrong, but something most definitely had, even if she was the only one who knew it. And now she was supposed to contend with a murder? She knew Darlington and Dawes had kept an eye on homicides in the New Haven area, just to make sure there was no stink of the uncanny, no chance one of the societies had gotten overeager and stepped beyond the bounds of their rituals.

Ahead of her, Grays formed a thin gruel that shifted over the roof of the law school, spreading and curling like milk poured into coffee, drawn by the grind of fear and ambition. Book and Snake's towering white tomb loomed on her right. Of all the society buildings, it was the most like a crypt. "Greek pediment, Ionic columns. Pedestrian stuff," Darlington had said. He saved his admiration for the Moorish screens and scrollwork of Scroll and Key, the severe mid-century lines of Manuscript. But it was the fence surrounding Book and Snake that always drew Alex's eye: black iron crawling with snakes. "The symbol of Mercury, god of commerce," Darlington had said.

God of thieves. Even Alex knew that one. Mercury was the messenger.

Ahead of her lay Grove Street Cemetery. Alex glimpsed a cluster of Grays gathered by a grave near the entrance. Someone had probably left cookies for a lost relative or something sugary as a fan offering for one of the artists or architects buried there. But the rest of the cemetery, like all cemeteries at night, was empty of ghosts. During the day, Grays were called to the salt tears and fragrant flowers of mourners, gifts from the living left for the dead. She'd learned they loved anything that reminded them of life. The spilled beer and raucous laughter of frat parties; the libraries at exam time, dense with anxiety, coffee, and open cans of sweet, syrupy Coke; dorm rooms staticky with gossip, panting couples, mini-fridges stuffed with food going to rot, students tossing in their sleep, dreams full of sex and terror. *That's where I should be,* Alex thought, *in the dorm, showering in the grimy bathroom, not walking by a graveyard in the dead of night.*

The cemetery gates had been built to look like an Egyptian temple, their fat columns carved with lotus blossoms, the plinth emblazoned with giant letters: THE DEAD SHALL BE RAISED. Darlington called the period at the end of that sentence the most eloquent piece of punctuation in the English language. Another thing Alex had been forced to look up, another bit of code to decipher. It turned out the quote was from a Bible verse:

Behold, I show you a mystery: We shall not all sleep;
but we shall all be changed in a moment, in the

twinkling of an eye, at the last trumpet. For the
trumpet shall sound, and the dead shall be raised
incorruptible, and we shall be changed.

"Incorruptible." When she saw that word she understood Darlington's smirk. The dead would be raised, but as for incorrupt-
ibility, Grove Street Cemetery was making no promises. In New
Haven, it was best not to hope for guarantees.

The scene in front of Payne Whitney gym reminded Alex of
the operating theater, police floodlights illuminating the snow,
throwing the shadows of onlookers against the ground in stark
lines. It would have been beautiful, carved in white and black like
a lithograph, but the effect was ruined by barriers of yellow tape
and the lazy, rhythmic whirl of blue and red from patrol cars that
had been parked to block off the intersection where the two streets
conjoined. The activity seemed to be focused on the triangle of
orphaned land at its center.

Alex could see a coroner's van with its bay doors open; uniformed officers standing at attention along the perimeter; men
in blue jackets, who she thought might be forensics based on the
television she'd watched; students who had emerged from their
dorms to see what was happening despite the late hour.

Her time with Len had left her wary of cops. When she was
younger, he'd gotten a kick out of having her help with deliveries,
because no uniform—campus security or LAPD—was going to
stop a chubby kid in braids looking for her big sister on a high
school campus. But as she'd gotten older she'd lost the look of
someone who belonged in wholesome places.

Even when she wasn't carrying, she'd learned to keep well clear
of cops. Some of them just seemed to smell the trouble on her.
But now she was walking toward them, smoothing her hair with
a gloved hand, just another student.

Centurion wasn't hard to spot. Alex had met Detective Abel
Turner exactly once before. He'd been smiling, gracious, and she'd

known in an instant that he hated not only her but also Darlington and everything related to Lethe. She wasn't sure why he'd been
chosen as Centurion, the liaison between Lethe House and the
Chief of Police, but he clearly didn't want the job.

He stood speaking to another detective and a uniform. He was
a full half head taller than either of them, black, his head shaved
in a low fade. He wore a sharp navy suit and what was probably a
real Burberry overcoat, and ambition rolled off him like thunder.
Too pretty, her grandmother would have said. *Quien se prestado se
vestio, en medio de la calle se quito.* Estrea Stern didn't trust handsome men, particularly the well-dressed ones.

Alex hovered by the barricade. Centurion was on the scene just
as Dawes had promised, but Alex wasn't sure how to get his attention or what to do once she had it. The societies met on Thursdays and Sundays. No ritual of any real risk was allowed without
Lethe House delegates present, but that didn't mean someone
hadn't gone off script. Maybe word had spread that Darlington
was "in Spain" and someone at one of the societies had used the
opportunity to mess with something new. She didn't think they
had any real malice in mind, but the Tripps and Mirandas of the
world could do plenty of damage without ever meaning to. Their
mistakes never stuck.

The crowd around her had dispersed almost immediately and
Alex remembered how bad she must smell, but there was nothing
she could do about it now. She took out her phone and scrolled
through her few contacts. She'd gotten a new phone when she'd
accepted Lethe's offer, erasing everyone from her old life in a single
act of banishment, so it was a short list of numbers. Her roommates. Her mom, who texted every morning with a series of happy
faces, as if emoji were their own incantation. Turner was in there
too but Alex had never texted him, never had cause to.

I'm here, she typed, then added, *It's Dante*, on the very good
possibility that he hadn't bothered to add her to his contacts.

She watched as Turner drew his phone from his pocket, read the message. He didn't look around.

Her phone buzzed a second later.

I know.

Alex waited for ten minutes, twenty. She watched Turner finish his conversation, consult a woman in a blue jacket, walk back and forth near a marked-off area, where the body must have been found.

A cluster of Grays was milling around by the gym. Alex let her eyes skim over them, landing nowhere, barely focused. A few were local Grays who could always be found in the area, a rower who had drowned off the Florida Keys but who now returned to haunt the training tanks, a heavyset man who had clearly once been a football player. She thought she glimpsed the Bridegroom, the city's most notorious ghost and a favorite of murder nerds and *Haunted New England* guidebooks; he had reputedly killed his fiancée and himself in the offices of a factory that had once stood barely a mile from here. She didn't let her gaze linger to confirm it. Payne Whitney was always a beacon for Grays, steeped in sweat and endeavor, full of hunger and fast-beating hearts.

"When did you first see them?" Darlington had asked on the day they'd first met, the day he'd set the jackals on her. Darlington knew seven languages. He could fence. He knew Brazilian jujitsu and how to rewire an electrical box, could quote poetry and plays by people Alex had never heard of. But he always asked the wrong questions.

Alex checked her phone. She'd lost another hour. At this point she probably shouldn't even bother going to sleep. She knew she wasn't high on Turner's list of priorities, but she was in a bind.

She typed, *My next call is to Sandow.*

It was a bluff, one Alex almost hoped Turner wouldn't fall for. If he refused to speak to her, she'd happily snitch on him to the dean—but at a more civilized hour. First she'd go home and get two glorious hours of sleep.

Instead, she watched Turner take the phone from his pocket, shake his head, and then saunter over to where she stood. His nose wrinkled slightly, but all he said was, "Ms. Stern, how can I help you?"

Alex didn't really know, but he'd given her plenty of time to formulate a response. "I'm not here to make trouble for you. I'm here because I was told to be."

Turner gave a convincing chuckle. "We all have jobs to do, Ms. Stern."

Pretty sure you wish your job entailed wringing my neck right now. "I understand that, but it's Thursday night."

"Preceded by Wednesday, followed by Friday."

Go ahead and play dumb. Alex would have been happy to turn her back on him, but she needed something to put in her report. "Is there a cause of death?"

"Of course something caused her death."

This asshole. "I meant—"

"I know what you meant. Nothing definitive yet, but I'll be sure to write it up for the dean when we know more."

"If a society is involved—"

"There is no reason to think that." Like he was at a press conference, he added, "At this time."

"It's *Thursday*," she repeated. Though the societies met twice a week, rituals were only sanctioned on Thursday nights. Sundays were for "quiet study and inquiry," which usually meant a fancy meal served on expensive dishes, the occasional guest speaker, and plenty of alcohol.

"Were you out with the idiots tonight?" he said, voice still pleasant. "Is that why you smell like pan-warmed shit? Who were you with?"

That kick-me troublemaking part of her made her say, "You sound like a jealous boyfriend."

"I sound like a cop. Answer me."

"The Bonesmen are on tonight."

He looked bemused. "Tell them to return Geronimo's skull."

"They don't have it," Alex said truthfully. A few years back, Geronimo's heirs had brought suit against the society, but it had come to nothing. The Bonesmen did have his liver and small intestine in a jar, but she didn't feel this was the moment to point that out.

"Where's Darlington?" Turner asked.

"Spain."

"*Spain?*" For the first time, Turner's mild expression gave way.

"Study abroad."

"And he left you in charge?"

"Sure did."

"He must have a lot of faith in you."

"Sure does." Alex flashed him her most winning grin, and for a second she thought Detective Turner might smile back, because it took a con to know a con. But he didn't. He'd had to be careful for too long.

"Where are you from, Stern?"

"Why?"

"Look," he said. "You seem like a nice girl—"

"No," said Alex. "I don't."

Turner raised a brow, cocked his head to the side, assessing, then nodded, conceding the point. "All right," he said. "You have a job to do tonight and so do I. You did your part. You talked to me. You'll let Sandow know a girl died here—a white girl who's going to get plenty of attention without you getting in our way. We're going to keep this far from the university and . . . all the rest." He gave a wave of his hand as if he were distractedly swatting a fly instead of shooing away a century-old cabal of ancient magics. "You've done your bit and you can go home. That's what you want, isn't it?"

Hadn't Alex just thought that very thing? Even so, she hesitated, feeling Darlington's judgment heavy on her. "I do. But Dean Sandow will want—"

Turner's mask slipped, the fatigue of the night and his anger at her presence suddenly visible. "She's town, Stern. Back the fuck off."

She's town. Not a student. Not connected to the societies. *Let it go.*

"Yeah," Alex said. "That's fine."

Turner smiled, dimples appearing in his cheeks, boyish, pleased, almost a real smile. "There ya go."

He turned away from her, sauntered back to his people.

Alex glanced up at the gray, Gothic cathedral of Payne Whitney. It didn't look like a gym, but nothing here looked like what it was. *That's what you want, isn't it?*

Detective Abel Turner understood her in a way Darlington never had.

Good. Better. Best. That was the trajectory that got you to this place. What Darlington and probably all the rest of these eager, effortful children couldn't understand was that Alex would have happily settled for less than Yale. Darlington was all about the pursuit of perfection, something spectacular. He didn't know how precious a normal life could be, how easy it was to drift away from average. You started sleeping until noon, skipped one class, one day of school, lost one job, then another, forgot the way that normal people did things. You lost the language of ordinary life. And then, without meaning to, you crossed into a country from which you couldn't return. You lived in a state where the ground always seemed to be slipping from beneath your feet, with no way back to someplace solid.

It didn't matter that Alex had witnessed the delegates of Skull and Bones predict commodities futures using Michael Reyes's guts or that she'd once seen the captain of the lacrosse team turn himself into a vole. (He'd squealed and then—she could have sworn it— pumped his tiny pink fist.) Lethe was Alex's way back to normal. She didn't need to be exceptional. She didn't even need to be good, just good enough. Turner had given her permission. Go home. Go to sleep. Take a shower. Get back to the real work of trying to pass your classes and make it through the year. Her grades from first semester had been bad enough to land her in academic probation.

She's town.

Except the societies liked to shop town girls and boys for their experiments. It was the whole reason Lethe existed. Or a big part of it. And Alex had spent most of her life as *town*.

She eyed the coroner's van, parked half on and half off the sidewalk. Turner's back was still to her.

The mistake people made when they didn't want to get noticed was to try to look casual, so instead she strode toward the van with purpose, a girl who needed to get to the dorms. It was late, after all. When she rounded the back of the vehicle, she shot one quick glance in Turner's direction, then slipped into the wide V of the open van doors as a uniformed coroner turned to her.

"Hey," she said. He remained in a half crouch, face wary, body blocking the view behind him. Alex held up one of the two gold coins she kept tucked in the lining of her coat. "You dropped this."

He saw the glint and without thinking reached out to take it, his response part courtesy, part trained behavior. Someone offered you a boon, you accepted. But it was also a magpie impulse, the lure of something shiny. She felt a little like a troll in a fairy tale.

"I don't think . . ." he began. But as soon as his fingers closed over the coin, his face went slack, the compulsion taking hold.

"Show me the body," Alex said, half-expecting him to refuse. She'd seen Darlington flash one at a security guard before, but she'd never used a coin of compulsion herself.

The coroner didn't even blink, only backed farther into the van and offered her his hand. She clambered up behind him with a quick glance over her shoulder and shut the doors. They wouldn't have much time. All she needed was for the driver or, worse, Turner to come knocking on the door and find her there, having a chat over a corpse. She also wasn't sure how long the compulsion would last. This particular bit of magic had come from

Manuscript. They specialized in mirror magic, glamours, persuasion. Any object could be enchanted, the most famous being a condom that had convinced a philandering Swedish diplomat to hand over a cache of sensitive documents.

The coins took tremendous magic to generate, so they were kept in tight supply at Lethe, and Alex had been stingy with her allotted two. Why was she squandering one now?

As Alex joined the coroner in the enclosed space, she saw his nostrils flare at her smell, but his fingers were already on the zipper of the body bag, the coin clutched in his other hand. He was moving too quickly, as if in fast forward, and Alex had the urge to tell him to just stop for a second, but then the moment passed and he was pulling the body bag open, the black vinyl splitting like the skin of a fruit.

"Jesus," breathed Alex.

The girl's face was fragile, blue veined. She wore a white cotton camisole, torn and puckered where the knife had entered and retreated—again and again. The wounds were all centered on her heart, and she'd been struck with enough force that it looked as if her sternum had started to give way, the bones fracturing in a shallow, bloody crater. Alex was suddenly sorry she hadn't taken Turner's strongly worded advice and gone home. This didn't look like a ritual gone wrong. It looked personal.

She swallowed the bile that rose in her throat and forced herself to inhale deeply. If this girl had somehow been targeted by a society or was messing with the uncanny, the smell of the Veil should still be on her. But with Alex's own stink filling the ambulance, it was impossible to tell.

"It's the boyfriend."

Alex glanced at the coroner. Compulsions were supposed to make anyone under their power eager to please.

"How do you know?" she asked.

"Turner said so. They've already picked him up for questioning. He has priors."

"For what?"

"Dealing and possession. So does she."

Of course she did. The boyfriend was moving product, and this girl was too. But there was a good long leap from small-time dealing to murder. *Sometimes,* she reminded herself. *Sometimes it's not far at all.*

Alex looked again at the girl's face. She was blond, a little like Hellie.

The resemblance was superficial, at least on the outside. But underneath? In the cut-open places, they were all the same. Girls like Hellie, girls like Alex, girls like this one, had to keep running or eventually trouble caught up. This girl just hadn't run fast enough.

There were paper bags over her hands—to preserve the evidence, Alex realized. Maybe she'd scratched her attacker.

"What's her name?" It didn't matter, but Alex needed it for her report.

"Tara Hutchins."

Alex typed it into her phone so she wouldn't forget it. "Cover her up."

She was glad when she couldn't see that brutalized body anymore. This was nasty, ugly, but it didn't mean Tara was connected to the societies. People didn't need magic to be terrible to each other.

"Time of death?" she asked. That seemed like the kind of thing she should know.

"Sometime around eleven. Hard to pinpoint because of the cold."

She paused with her hand on the lever of the van doors. Sometime around eleven. Right around the time two docile Grays who had never given anyone any trouble had opened their jaws like they were trying to swallow the world and something had tried to slam its way into a chalk circle. What if that something had found its way to Tara instead?

Or what if her boyfriend got fucked up enough to think he could stab straight through to her heart? There were plenty of human monsters out there. Alex had met a few. For now she'd "done her part." More than done it.

Alex cracked the door to the van, scanned the street, then hopped down. "Forget you met me," she told the coroner.

A vague, confused expression crossed his face. Alex left him standing, dazed, beside Tara's body and strolled away, crossing the street and keeping to the dark sidewalk, away from the police lights. In a short while, the compulsion would wear off and he'd wonder how he'd ended up with a gold coin in his hand. He would put it in his pocket and forget about it or toss it in the trash without ever realizing the metal was real.

She glanced back at the Grays gathered around Payne Whitney. Was it her imagination or was there something in the bent of their shoulders, the way they huddled together by the gymnasium doors? Alex knew better than to look too closely, but in that fleeting moment she could have sworn they looked frightened. What did the dead have to fear?

She could hear Darlington's voice in her head: *When was the first time you saw them?* Low and halting, as if he wasn't sure whether the question was taboo. But the real question, the right question, was: *When was the first time you knew to be afraid?*

Alex was glad he'd never had the sense to ask.

Where do we begin to tell the story of Lethe? Does it begin in 1824 with Bathsheba Smith? Perhaps it should. But it would take another seventy years and many more disasters before Lethe would come to be. So instead we point to 1898, when Charlie Baxter, a man with no home and of no consequence, turned up dead with burns to his hands, feet, and scrotum, and a black scarab where his tongue should be. Accusations flew and the societies found themselves under threat from the university. To heal the rift and—let us speak frankly—to save themselves, Edward Harkness, a member of Wolf's Head, joined with William Payne Whitney of Skull and Bones, and Hiram Bingham III of the now-defunct Acacia Fraternity, to form the League of Lethe as an oversight body for the societies' occult activities.

From these earliest meetings rose our mission statement: We are charged with monitoring the rites and practices of any senior societies trafficking in magic, divination, or otherworldly discourse, with the express intent of keeping citizens and students safe from mental, physical, and spiritual harm and of fostering amicable relations between the societies and school administration.

Lethe was funded by an infusion of capital from Harkness and a mandatory contribution from the trusts of each of the Ancient Eight. When Harkness tapped James Gamble Rogers (Scroll and Key, 1889) to create a plan for Yale and design many of its structures, he ensured that safe houses and tunnels for Lethe would be built throughout the campus.

Harkness, Whitney, and Bingham drew on knowledge from each of the societies to create a storehouse of arcane magic for use by the deputies of Lethe. This was added to significantly in 1911, when Bingham traveled to Peru.

—*from* The Life of Lethe: Procedures
and Protocols of the Ninth House

4

Last Fall

"Come on," Darlington said, helping her to her feet. "The illusion will break any minute and you'll be lying in the front yard like a noon drinker." He half-dragged her up the stairs to the porch. She'd handled the jackals well enough, but her color wasn't good and she was breathing hard. "You're in terrible shape."

"And you're an asshole."

"Then we both have hardships to overcome. You asked me to tell you what you were getting into. Now you know."

She yanked her arm away. "Tell me. Not try to kill me."

He looked at her steadily. It was important she understand. "You were never in any danger. But I can't promise that will always be the case. If you don't take this seriously, you could get yourself or someone else hurt."

"Someone like you?"

"Yes," he said. "Most of the time nothing too bad happens at the Houses. You'll see things you'd like to forget. Miracles too. But no one completely understands what lies beyond the Veil or what might happen if it crosses over. *Death waits on black wings and we stand hoplite, hussar, dragoon.*"

She placed her hands on her thighs and peered up at him. "You make that up?"

"Cabot Collins. They called him the Poet of Lethe." Darlington reached for the door. "He lost both his hands when an interdimensional portal closed on them. He was reciting his latest work at the time."

Alex shuddered. "Okay, I get it. Bad poetry, serious business. Are those dogs real?"

"Real enough. They're spirit hounds, bound to serve the sons and daughters of Lethe. Why the long sleeves, Stern?"

"Track marks."

"Really?" He'd suspected that might be the issue, but he didn't quite believe her.

She straightened and cracked her back. "Sure. Are we going in or not?"

He bobbed his chin toward her wrist. "Show me."

Alex lifted her arm, but she didn't shove her sleeve back. She just held it out to him, like he was going to tap a vein for a blood drive.

A challenge. One that he suddenly didn't want to accept. It was none of his business. He should say that. Let it go.

Instead, he took hold of her wrist. The bones were narrow, sharp in his hand. With his other hand he pushed the fabric of her shirt up the slope of her forearm. It felt like a prelude.

No needle punctures. Her skin was covered in tattoos: the curling tail of a rattlesnake, the sunburst bloom of a peony, and . . .

"The Wheel." He resisted the urge to touch his thumb to the image below the crook of her elbow. Dawes would be interested in that bit of tarot. Maybe it would give them something to talk about. "Why hide tattoos? No one cares about that here." Half the student body had them. Not many had full sleeves, but they weren't unheard of.

Alex yanked her cuff back down. "Any other hoops to jump through?"

"Plenty." He pulled open the door and led her inside.

The entry was dark and cool, the stained glass throwing bright patterns onto the carpeted floor. Before them, the great staircase wound along the wall to the second story, dark wood carved in a thick sunflower motif. Michelle had told him the staircase alone was worth more than the rest of the house and the land it was built on.

Alex released a small sigh.

"Glad to be out of the sun?"

She made a soft humming noise. "It's quiet here."

It took him a moment to understand what she meant. "Il Bastone is warded. As are the rooms at the Hutch. . . . It's that bad?"

Alex shrugged.

"Well . . . they can't get to you here."

Alex looked around, her face impassive. Was she unimpressed by the soaring entry, the warm wood and stained glass, the scent of pine and cassis that always made stepping into the house feel a bit like Christmas? Or was she just trying to seem that way?

"Nice clubhouse," she said. "Not very tomblike."

"We're not a society and we don't run like one. This isn't a clubhouse; it's our headquarters, the heart of Lethe, and the storehouse of hundreds of years of knowledge on the occult." He knew he sounded like a horrible prig but he couldn't seem to stop himself. "The societies tap a new delegation of seniors every year, sixteen members—eight women, eight men. We tap a single new Dante—one freshman every *three* years."

"Guess that makes me pretty special."

"Let's hope so."

Alex frowned at that, then nodded at the marble bust propped on a table beneath the coat rack. "Who's that?"

"The patron saint of Lethe, Hiram Bingham the Third." Unfortunately, Bingham's boyish features and downturned mouth didn't lend themselves to immortalization in stone. He looked like a perturbed department store mannequin.

Dawes shuffled out of the parlor, her hands curled into the sleeves of her voluminous sweatshirt, her headphones snug around her neck, a vision in beige. Darlington could feel the discomfort radiating off her. Pammie hated new people. It had taken him the better part of his freshman year to win her over, and he still always had the sense that she might be one loud noise away from bolting into the library, never to be seen again.

"Pamela Dawes, meet our new Dante, Alex Stern."

With all the enthusiasm of someone greeting a cholera outbreak, Dawes offered her hand and said, "Welcome to Lethe."

"Dawes keeps everything running and ensures I don't make too big a fool of myself."

"So it's a full-time job?" asked Alex.

Dawes blinked. "Evenings and afternoons, but I can make myself available to you with enough notice." She glanced back at the parlor worriedly, as if her long-unfinished dissertation was a baby crying. Dawes had served as Oculus for nearly four years and she'd been hammering away on her dissertation—an examination of Mycenaean cult practices in early tarot iconography—all the while.

Darlington decided to put her out of her misery. "I'm giving Alex the tour and then I'll take her across campus to the Hutch."

"The Hutch?" asked Alex.

"Rooms we keep at the corner of York and Elm. It's not much, but it's convenient when you don't want to trek too far from your dorm. And it's warded too."

"It's stocked," Dawes said faintly, already scooting back into the parlor and safety.

Darlington gestured for Alex to follow him upstairs.

"Who was Bathsheba Smith?" Alex asked on his heels.

Then she had been reading her *Life of Lethe.* He was pleased she remembered the name, but, if memory served, Bathsheba appeared on the first page of the first chapter, so he wasn't going to get too excited. "The seventeen-year-old daughter of a local farmer. Her body was found in the basement of the Yale Medical School in 1824. She'd been dug up for study by the students."

"Jesus."

"It wasn't uncommon. Doctors needed to study anatomy and

they needed cadavers to do that. But we think Bathsheba was an early attempt to communicate with the dead. A medical assistant took the fall, and Yale's students learned to keep their activities more quiet. After the discovery of the girl's body, the locals nearly burned Yale to the ground."

"Maybe they should have," murmured Alex.

Maybe. They'd called it the Resurrection Riot, but it hadn't turned truly nasty. Boom or bust, New Haven was a town forever on the brink of things.

Darlington toured Alex around the rest of Il Bastone: the grand parlor, with the old map of New Haven above the fireplace; the kitchen and pantry; the downstairs training rooms; and the second-floor armory, with its wall of apothecary drawers, all of them stocked with herbs and sacred objects.

It was left to Dawes to make sure they were kept well supplied, that any perishable items were freshened or disposed of before they turned foul, and to maintain any artifacts that required it. Cuthbert's Pearls of Protection had to be worn for a few hours every month or they lost both their luster and their power to protect the wearer from lightning strikes. A Lethe alum named Lee De Forest, who had once been suspended as an undergrad for causing a campus-wide blackout, had left Lethe with countless inventions, including the Revolution Clock, which showed an accurate-to-the-minute countdown to armed revolt in countries around the globe. It had twenty-two faces and seventy-six hands and had to be wound regularly or it would simply begin screaming.

Darlington pointed out the stores of bone dust and graveyard dirt, with which they would provision themselves on Thursday nights, and the rare vials of Perdition Water, said to come from the seven rivers of hell and that were to be used only in case of emergency. Darlington had never had cause to tap into any of them, but he kept hoping.

At the center of the room sat Hiram's Crucible, or, as the delegates of Lethe liked to call it, "the Golden Bowl." It was the circumference of a tractor wheel and made of beaten twenty-two-karat gold.

"For years, Lethe knew there were ghosts in New Haven. There were hauntings, rumors of sightings, and some of the societies had managed to pierce the Veil through séances and summonings. But Lethe knew there was more, a secret world operating beside ours and frequently interfering with it."

"Interfering with it how?" Alex asked, and he could see the narrow line of her shoulders tighten, that slightly hunched fighter's stance.

"At the time, no one was sure. They suspected that the presence of Grays in sacred circles and temple halls was disrupting the spells and rituals of the societies. There were signs that stray magic loosed from rituals by the interference of Grays could cause anything from a sudden frost ten miles away to violent outbursts in schoolchildren. But Lethe had no proof and no way to prevent it. Year after year they attempted to perfect an elixir that would allow them to see spirits, experimenting on themselves through sometimes-deadly trial and error. Still, they had nothing to show for their work. Until Hiram's Crucible."

Alex ran her finger against the gilded edge of the basin. "It looks like a sun."

"Many of the structures in Machu Picchu were dedicated to the worship of the sun god."

"This thing came from Peru?" Alex asked. "You don't need to look so surprised. I know where Machu Picchu is. I can even find Texas on a map if you give me enough time."

"You'll have to forgive my lack of familiarity with the curriculum of the Los Angeles School District or your interest in same."

"Forgiven."

Maybe, thought Darlington. But Alex Stern looked like the type to hold a grudge.

"Hiram Bingham was one of the founding members of Lethe. He 'discovered' Machu Picchu in 1911, though that word tends

to ruffle feathers, since the locals were perfectly aware of its existence." When Alex said nothing, he added, "He was also rumored
to be the inspiration for Indiana Jones."

"Nice," said Alex.

Darlington held back a sigh. Of course that would be what
got her attention. "Bingham stole about forty thousand artifacts."

"And brought them back here?"

"Yes, to Yale, to be studied at the Peabody. He said they would
be returned after eighteen months. It took literally one hundred
years for Peru to get them back."

Alex flicked her finger against the crucible and it emitted a low
hum. "They forget this in the return shipment? It seems pretty
hard to miss."

"The crucible was never documented because it was never given
to Yale. It was brought to Lethe."

"Stolen goods."

"Very much so, I'm afraid. But it's the key to the Orozcerio.
The problem with Lethe's elixir wasn't the recipe; it was the vessel."

"So it's a magical mixing bowl?"

Such a little heathen. "I might not put it that way, but yes."

"And it's gold all the way through?"

"Before you think about trying to run off with it, keep in mind
that it weighs twice as much as you do and that the whole house
is warded against theft."

"If you say so."

With his luck she'd find a way to roll the crucible down the
stairs into the back of a truck and melt it down for earrings.

"The elixir has plenty of other names besides Orozcerio," he
said. "The Golden Trial. Hiram's Bullet. Every time a member of
Lethe drinks it, every time the crucible is used, he takes his life in
his hands. The mixture is toxic and the process incredibly painful.
But we do it. Again and again. For a glimpse behind the Veil."

"I get it," said Alex. "I've met users before."

It isn't like that, he wanted to protest. But maybe it was.

The rest of the tour was uneventful. Darlington showed her the storage and research rooms in the upper stories, how to use the library—though he warned her not to use it on her own until the house got to know her—and finally the bedroom and adjoining bath, tidied and readied for her as Lethe's new Dante. He'd moved his own things to Virgil's suite at the end of last year, back when he'd still believed he'd have a proper protégé. He'd felt embarrassingly sentimental about it all. Virgil's quarters were a floor above Dante's and twice as large. When he graduated, they would be left empty so that they would be available to him if he chose to visit. The vanity had belonged to Eleazar Wheelock. Half of the wall facing the bed was taken up by a stained-glass window depicting a hemlock wood, positioned so that as the sun rose and set throughout the day, the colors of the glass trees and the sky above it seemed to change as well. When he'd moved in, he discovered that Michelle had left him a bottle of brandy and a note on her last visit:

> *This is the forest primeval. The murmuring pines and the hemlocks,*
> *Bearded with moss, and in garment green, indistinct in the twilight,*
> *Stand like Druids of eld, with voices sad and prophetic . . .*
> There was a monastery that produced Armagnac so refined, its monks were forced to flee to Italy when Louis XIV joked about killing them to protect their secrets. This is the last bottle. Don't drink it on an empty stomach, and don't call unless you're dead. Good luck, Virgil!

He'd always thought Longfellow was tripe, but he'd treasured the note and the brandy anyway.

Now he watched Alex sweating amid the luxury of his old rooms, rooms that had been rarely used but much beloved—the dark blue walls, the canopied bed with its heavy teal covers, the armoire painted with white dogwood. The stained glass here was more modest, two elegant windows—clouds in shades of blue and violet set atop starry skies—bracketing a fireplace of painted tiles.

Alex stood at the center of it all, her arms wrapped around her middle, turning slowly. He thought again of Undine. But maybe she was just a girl lost at sea.

He had to ask. "When did you first see them?"

She glanced at him, then at the window above her, the moon waxing forever in a stained-glass sky. She picked up the Reuge music box from the desk, touched her finger to the lid, but then thought better of it, set it down.

Darlington was a good talker, but he was happiest when no one was speaking to him, when he didn't have to perform the ritual of himself and he could simply be left to watch others. Alex had a grainy quality to her, like an old film. He could tell she was making a choice. Whether to reveal her secrets? Whether to run?

She shrugged and he thought she would leave it at that, but then she picked up the music box again and said, "I don't know. I thought they were people for a while, and it's not like anyone pays attention to a kid talking to no one. I remember seeing a fat guy in nothing but socks and undershorts, holding a remote control in one hand like a teddy bear and standing in the middle of the street. I remember trying to tell my mom he was going to get hurt. On our trip to the Santa Monica Pier, I saw a woman lying in the water like a picture of . . ." She gestured as if stirring a pot. "With her hair and the flowers?"

"Ophelia."

"Ophelia. She followed me home, and when I cried and shouted at her to leave, she just tried to push closer."

"They like tears. The salt, the sadness, any strong emotion."

"Fear?" she asked. She was so still, as if she were posing for a portrait.

"Fear." Few Grays were malevolent, but they did love to startle and terrify.

"Why aren't there more of them? Shouldn't they be everywhere?"

"Only a few Grays can pass through the Veil. The vast majority remain in the afterlife."

"I'd see them at the supermarket, around the hot-foods case or those pink bakery boxes. They loved our school cafeteria. I didn't think about it much until Jacob Craig asked if I wanted to see his thing. I told him I'd seen plenty of them, and somehow it got back to his mom, and she called the school. So the teacher brings me in and asks, 'What do you mean you've seen lots of things?' I didn't know to lie." She plunked the music box down. "If you want to get Child Protective Services called fast, just start talking about ghost dick."

Darlington wasn't sure what he'd expected. A dead highwayman lurking romantically at the window? A banshee roaming the banks of the Los Angeles River like La Llorona? There was something so ordinary and awful about her story. About her. Someone had reported Alex's case to CPS, and one of Lethe's search algorithms or one of their many contacts in one of the many bureaus that they paid off had caught mention of those notable key words: *Delusions. Paranoia. Ghosts.* From that point on, she'd probably been watched. "And that night in the apartment on Cedros?"

She frowned and then said, "Oh, you mean Ground Zero. Don't tell me you haven't read the file."

"I have. I want to know how you survived."

Alex rubbed her thumb over the edge of the windowsill. "So do I."

Was that enough? Darlington had seen the crime-scene photos, video taken by officers arriving on scene. Five men dead, all of them beaten nearly unrecognizable, two of them staked through the heart like vampires. Despite the carnage, blood spatter indicated it was all the work of one perpetrator—arcs of red, every vicious blow struck from left to right.

Something was off about the whole thing, but Alex was never a suspect. For one thing, she was right-handed, and for another, she was far too small to have wielded a weapon with so much force. Besides, she had enough fentanyl in her system that she was lucky she hadn't died herself. Her hair had been wet and she'd been found naked as a newborn. Darlington had dug a little deeper, unable to shake his suspicions, but there had been no blood or remains in the drain—if she'd somehow been involved, she hadn't showered the proof away. So why had the attacker left the girls alone? If the police were right and this was some kind of beef with another dealer, why spare Alex and her friend? Drug dealers who beat people to death with bats didn't seem like the spare-the-women-and-children type. Maybe the attacker had believed they were dead already from the drugs. Or maybe Alex had tipped someone off. But she knew something more about what had happened than she'd told the police. He felt it in his bones.

"Hellie and I got high," she said quietly, still brushing her finger against the windowsill. "I woke up in the hospital. She didn't wake up at all."

She looked very small suddenly and Darlington felt a stab of shame. She was twenty, older than most freshmen, but she was still just a kid in a lot of ways, in over her head. And she'd lost friends that night, her boyfriend, everything familiar.

"Come with me," he said. He wasn't sure why. Maybe because he felt guilty for prying. Maybe because she didn't deserve to be punished for saying yes to a bargain no right-minded person would refuse.

He led her back to the gloom of the armory. It had no windows, and its walls were lined in shelves and drawers nearly two stories high. It took him a moment to find the cupboard he wanted. When he rested his hand on the door, the house paused, then let the lock give with a disapproving click.

Carefully, he removed the box—heavy, gleaming black wood, inlaid with mother-of-pearl.

"You'll probably need to remove your shirt," he said. "I'll give Dawes the box and she can—"

"Dawes doesn't like me."

"Dawes doesn't like anyone."

"Here," she said. She pulled the shirt over her head, revealing a black bra and ribs shadowed like the furrows of a tilled field. "Don't get Dawes."

Why was she so willing to put herself in his hands? Was she unafraid or just reckless? Neither trait boded well for her future at Lethe. But he had the sense that it was neither of those things. It felt like she was testing *him* now, like she'd laid down another challenge.

"Some propriety wouldn't kill you," he said.

"Why take the chance?"

"Usually when a woman takes her clothes off in front of me I have some warning."

Alex shrugged, and the shadows moved over her skin. "Next time, I'll light the signal fires."

"That would be best."

Tattoos covered her from wrist to shoulder and spread beneath her clavicles. They looked like armor.

He opened the box's lid.

Alex drew in a sudden breath and skittered backward.

"What's wrong?" he asked. She'd retreated nearly halfway across the room.

"I don't like butterflies."

"They're moths." They perched in even rows in the box, soft white wings fluttering.

"Whatever."

"I'll need you to stay still," he said. "Can you?"

"Why?"

"Just trust me. It will be worth it." He considered. "If it's not, I'll drive you and your roommates to Ikea."

Alex balled her shirt in her fists. "And take us for pizza after."

"Fine."

"And dear Aunt Eileen is going to buy me some new fall clothes."

"*Fine.* Now come here, you coward."

She crossed back to him in a kind of sideways shuffle, averting her eyes from the contents of the box.

One by one, he took out the moths and laid them gently on her skin. One at her right wrist, her right forearm, the crook of her elbow, her slender biceps, the knob of her shoulder. He repeated the process with her left arm, then placed two moths at the points of her collarbones where the heads of two black snakes curled, their tongues nearly meeting at the hollow of her throat.

"*Chabash,*" he murmured. The moths beat their wings in unison. "*Uverat.*" They flapped their wings again and began to turn gray. "*Memash.*"

With each beat of their wings, the moths grew darker and the tattoos started to fade.

Alex's chest rose and fell in jagged, rapid bursts. Her eyes were wide with fear, but as the moths darkened and the ink vanished from her skin, her expression changed, opened. Her lips parted.

She's seen the dead, he thought. *She's witnessed horrors. But she's never seen magic.*

This was why he had done it, not because of guilt or pride but because this was the moment he'd been waiting for: the chance to show someone else wonder, to watch them realize that they had not been lied to, that the world they'd been promised as children was not something that had to be abandoned, that there really was something lurking in the wood, beneath the stairs, between the stars, that everything was full of mystery.

The moths beat their wings again, again, until they were black, then blacker. One by one they tipped from her arms and dropped to the floor in a faint patter. Alex's arms were bare, stripped of all sign of the tattoos, though in places where the needle had gone deep, he could still discern faint ridges. Alex held her arms out, breath coming in gasps.

Darlington gathered the moths' fragile bodies, placing them gently in the box.

"Are they dead?" she whispered.

"Ink drunk." He shut the lid and placed the box back in the cupboard. This time the lock's click seemed more resigned. He and the house were going to have to have a discussion. "Address moths were originally used for transporting classified material. Once they drank a document, they could be sent anywhere in a coat pocket or a box of antiques. Then they'd be placed on a fresh sheet of paper and would recreate the document to the word. As long as the recipient knew the right incantation."

"So we could put my tattoos on you?"

"They might not fit quite right, but we could. Just be care-ful . . ." He waved a hand. "In the throes. Human saliva reverses the magic."

"Only human?"

"Yes. Feel free to let a dog lick your elbows."

Then she turned her gaze on him. In the shadows of the room, her eyes looked black, wild. "Is there more?"

He didn't have to ask what she meant. Would the world keep unraveling? Keep spilling its secrets?

"Yes. There's plenty more."

She hesitated. "Will you show me?"

"If you let me."

Alex smiled then, a small thing, a glimpse of the girl lurking inside her, a happy, less haunted girl. That was what magic did. It revealed the heart of who you'd been before life took away your belief in the possible. It gave back the world all lonely children longed for. That was what Lethe had done for him. Maybe it could do that for Alex as well.

Months later, he would remember the weight of the moths' bodies in his palm. He would think of that moment and how foolish he had been to think he knew her at all.

5

Winter

The sky was already fading into gray when Alex finally made it back to Old Campus. She'd stopped at the Hutch to shower with verbena soap beneath a hanging censer filled with cedar and palo santo—the only things that would counter the stink of the Veil.

She had spent so little time in Lethe places by herself. She had always been with Darlington, and she still expected to see him tucked into the window seat with a book, expected to hear him grumble that she'd used all of the hot water. He'd suggested leaving clothes there and at Il Bastone, but Alex already had so little to wear that she couldn't afford to stash an extra pair of jeans and one of her two bras somewhere other than her ugly school-issue dresser. So when she stepped out of the bathroom into the narrow dressing room, she had to opt for Lethe House sweats—the Lethe spirit hound embroidered at the left breast and right hip, a symbol meaningless to anyone but society members. Darlington's own clothes still hung there—a Barbour jacket, a striped Davenport College scarf, fresh jeans neatly folded and creased, perfectly broken-in engineer boots, and a pair of Sperry Top-Siders just waiting for Darlington to slip into them. She'd never seen him wear them, but maybe you had to have a pair in case your preppy card got pulled.

Alex left a green desk lamp burning at the Hutch. Dawes

wouldn't like it, but she couldn't quite bear to leave the rooms in darkness.

She was unlocking the door to the Vanderbilt entryway when a text arrived from Dean Sandow: *Have confabbed w Centurion. Rest easy.*

She wanted to throw her phone across the courtyard. Rest easy? If Sandow intended to handle the murder directly, why had she wasted her time—and her coin of compulsion—visiting the crime scene? She knew the dean didn't trust her. Why would he? He'd probably been up with a cup of chamomile tea when he got the news of Tara's death, his big dog asleep on his feet, waiting by the phone to make sure nothing went horribly wrong at the prognostication and Alex didn't humiliate herself or Lethe. Of course he wouldn't want her anywhere near a murder.

Rest easy. Everything else went unsaid: *I don't expect you to handle this. No one expects you to handle this. No one expects you to do anything but keep from drawing unwanted attention until we get Darlington back.*

If they could find him. If they could somehow bring him home from whatever dark place he'd gone. In less than a week they'd attempt the new-moon rite. Alex didn't understand the specifics, only that Dean Sandow believed it would work and that, until it did, her job was to make sure that no one asked too many questions about Lethe's missing golden boy. At least now she didn't have a homicide to worry about or a grumpy detective to deal with.

When she entered the common room to find Mercy already awake, Alex was glad she'd stopped to shower and change. She had thought college dorms would be like hotels, long hallways pocked with bedrooms, but Vanderbilt felt more like an old-fashioned apartment building, full of tinny music, people humming and laughing as they went in and out of the shared bathrooms, the slamming of doors echoing up and down the central staircase. The squat she'd shared with Len and Hellie and Betcha and the others had been noisy, but its sighs and moans had been different, defeated, like a dying body.

"You're awake," Alex said.

Mercy glanced up from her copy of *To the Lighthouse,* its pages thick with pastel sticky notes. Her hair was in an elaborate braid, and instead of bundling up in their ratty afghan, she'd thrown a silk robe patterned with blue hyacinths over her jeans. "Did you even come home last night?"

Alex took a chance. "Yeah. You were already snoring. I just got up to get a run in."

"You went to the gym? Are the showers even open this early?"

"For crew and stuff." Alex wasn't actually sure this was true, but she knew Mercy cared less about sports than just about anything. Besides, Alex didn't own running shoes or a sports bra, and Mercy never asked about that. People didn't go looking for lies that didn't have a reason, and why would anyone lie about going for a morning run?

"Psychos." Mercy tossed a stapled stack of pages at Alex, who caught them but couldn't quite bring herself to look. Her Milton essay. Mercy had offered to give it a read. Alex could already see the red pen all over it.

"How was it?" she asked, shuffling into their bedroom.

"Not terrible."

"But not good," Alex muttered as she entered their tiny cave of a room and stripped out of her sweats. Mercy had covered her side of the wall in posters, family photos, ticket stubs from Broadway shows, a poem written in Chinese characters that Mercy said her parents made her memorize for dinner parties when she was a kid but that she'd fallen in love with, a series of Alexander McQueen sketches, a starburst of red envelopes. Alex knew it was partially an act, a construction of the person Mercy wanted to be at Yale, but every item, every object connected her to something. Alex felt like someone had come along early and snipped all of her threads. Her grandmother had been her closest link to any kind of real past, but Estrea Stern had died when Alex was nine. And Mira Stern had grieved her but she'd had no interest in her mother's stories or songs, the way she cooked or prayed. She called herself an explorer—homeopathy, allopathy, healing gemstones, Kryon, spirit science, three months when she'd put spirulina in everything—each embraced with the same fierce optimism, dragging Alex along from one silver bullet to the next. As for Alex's father, Mira was hazy on the details, hazier when pushed. He was a question mark, Alex's phantom half. All she knew was that he loved the ocean, that he was a Gemini, and that he was brown—Mira couldn't tell her if he was Dominican or Guatemalan or Puerto Rican, but she did know he was Aquarius rising with his moon in Scorpio. Or something. Alex could never remember.

She'd brought few objects from home. She hadn't wanted to return to Ground Zero to pick up any of her old stuff, and the belongings in her mother's apartment were little-girl things—plastic ponies, rosettes made of colored ribbons, bubble-gum-scented erasers. In the end, she'd packed a hunk of smoky quartz that her mother had given her, her grandmother's nearly illegible recipe cards, an earring tree she'd had since she was eight, and a retro map of California, which she hung next to Mercy's poster of Coco Chanel. "I know she was a fascist," Mercy had said. "But I can't quit her."

Dean Sandow had suggested Alex purchase a few sketchbooks and charcoal too, and she'd dutifully placed them atop her half-empty dresser as cover.

Alex had tried to choose the easiest subjects possible—English lit, her Spanish requirement, an introductory sociology course, painting. She'd thought at least English would be easy because she liked to read. Even when things had been really bad in school, she'd still been able to fake her way through those classes. But this

English was an entirely different language. She'd gotten a D on her first paper, with a note that said, *This is a book report.* It had been just like high school except she'd actually been trying.

"I love you, but this essay is a mess," said Mercy from the common room. "It would probably be better if you spent less time working out and more time working." *No shit,* thought Alex. Mercy was going to be in for a real surprise if she ever asked Alex to jog somewhere or lift something heavy. "We can go through it over breakfast."

All Alex wanted was sleep, but going back to bed didn't seem to be the thing people did after a run, and Mercy had done her the courtesy of editing her awful English paper, so she definitely needed to say yes to breakfast. Lethe had provided Alex with a tutor, an American Studies grad student named Angus who spent most of their weekly sessions bent over Alex's work, snorting in exasperation and shaking his head like a horse plagued by flies. Mercy wasn't exactly gentle, but she was a lot more patient.

Alex yanked on jeans and a T-shirt, then the black cashmere sweater she'd prized so much when she'd picked it out at Target. It was only when she'd seen Lauren's lush lavender pullover and foolishly asked, "What is this made of?" that she'd understood there were as many kinds of cashmere as there were of cush, and that her own sad sweater pulled from the sale rack was strictly stems and seeds. At least it was warm.

She gave her coat another spray of cedar oil in case any Veil stink lingered, hefted up her bag, hesitated. She opened her dresser drawer and dug around in the back until she found the little bottle of what looked like ordinary eye drops. Before she could think too much about it, she tilted her head back and squeezed two drops of basso belladonna into each eye. It was a stimulant, a strong one, a bit like magical Adderall. The crash was brutal, but there was no way Alex was going to make it through the morning without a little help. The old boys of Lethe had all kept diaries of their time in the society, and they had plenty of tricks they used to cut corners. Alex had discovered this one after Darlington was gone.

Back into the morning cold with Mercy beside her. Alex always liked the walk from Old Campus to the JE dining hall, but the quad looked less beautiful with a gray day on it. At night, the grubby packs of snow gleamed vague and white, but now they were grimy and brown at the edges, heaps of dirty sheets ready for the wash. Harkness Tower loomed over it all like a melting candle, its chimes sounding the hour.

It had taken Alex a few weeks to realize why Yale looked wrong to her. It was the complete lack of glamour. In L.A., even in the Valley, even on its worst days, the city had style. Even Alex's mother in her purple eye shadow and chunks of turquoise, even their dumpy apartment with its shawls over the lamps, even her no-money friends, gathered at backyard barbecues, recovering from the night before, girls in tight shorts, midriffs bare, long hair swinging to the small of the back, boys with shaved heads or silky topknots or thick dreads. Everything, everybody, had a look.

But here the colors seemed to blur. There was a kind of uniform—jocks in backward baseball caps and long loose shorts they wore regardless of the chill, keys on lanyards that they swung like dandies; girls in jeans and quilted jackets; theater kids with crests of sink-dyed Kool-Aid-colored hair. Your clothes, your car, the music pumping from it, were supposed to tell people who you were. Here it was like someone had filed down all of the serial numbers, wiped away the fingerprints. *Who are you?* Alex would sometimes think, looking at another girl in a navy peacoat, pale face like a waning moon beneath a wool cap, ponytail lying like a dead animal over her shoulder. *Who are you?*

Mercy was an exception. She favored wild florals paired with a seemingly endless parade of eyeglasses that she wore on glittery strings around her neck and that Alex had yet to see her use. Today she'd opted for a brocade coat embroidered with poinsettias that made her look like the world's youngest eccentric grandma. When Alex had raised her brows, Mercy had just said, "I like loud."

They entered the Jonathan Edwards common room, warm air

closing over them in a gust. Winter light slatted over the leather couches in watery squares—all of it a coy, falsely humble prelude to the soaring rafters and stone alcoves of the dining hall.

Beside her, Mercy laughed. "I only see you smile like that when we're going to eat."

It was true. If Beinecke was Darlington's temple, then the dining hall was where Alex worshipped daily. At the squat in Van Nuys, they'd lived on Taco Bell and Subway when they were flush, cereal—sometimes dry, sometimes soaked in soda if she got desperate—when they were broke. She'd steal a bag of hot dog buns whenever they were invited to barbecues at Eitan's place so they had something to put peanut butter on, and once she'd tried to eat Loki's dry kibble, but her teeth couldn't manage it. Even when she'd lived with her mom, it had been all frozen food, boil-in-a-bag rice dishes, then weird shakes and nutrition bars after Mira got suckered into selling Herbalife. Alex had brought protein pudding mix to school for weeks.

The idea that there could be hot food just waiting for her three times a day was still shocking. But it made no difference what she ate or how much of it; it was as if her body, starved for so long, was ravenous now. Every hour her stomach would growl, chiming like the Harkness bells. Alex always took two sandwiches with her for the day and a stack of chocolate chip cookies wrapped in a napkin. The supply of food in her backpack was like a security blanket. If this all ended, if it all got taken away, she wouldn't go hungry for at least a couple of days.

"It's a good thing you work out so much," Mercy noted as Alex shoveled granola into her mouth. Except, of course, she didn't and eventually her metabolism would stop cooperating, but she just didn't care. "Do you think it's too much to wear a skirt to Omega Meltdown tomorrow night?"

"You're still committed to this frat thing?" Omega Meltdown was part of Mercy's Five Party Plan to get her and Alex to be more social.

"Some of us don't have a hot cousin to take us interesting

places, so until I'm offered a higher caliber of party, yes. This isn't high school. We don't have to be the losers waiting to get invited out. I've wasted too many good outfits on you."

"Okay, I'll wear a skirt if you wear a skirt," Alex said. "Also . . . I'm going to need to borrow a skirt." No one dressed up for frat parties, but if Mercy wanted to look cute for a bunch of guys in hazmat suits, then that was what they would do. "You should wear those boots you have with all the laces. I'm going back for seconds."

The basso belladonna kicked in just as she was stacking peanut butter pancakes onto her tray, and she drew in a sharp breath as she came wide awake. It felt a little like someone cracking an ice-cold egg on the nape of your neck. Of course, it was at that moment that Professor Belbalm waved her over from her table below the leaded windows in the corner of the dining room, her sleek white hair gleaming like a seal's head breaching a wave.

"Fuck," Alex said under her breath, and then cringed when Belbalm's mouth quirked as if she'd heard her.

"Gimme a minute," she told Mercy, and set down her tray at their table.

Marguerite Belbalm was French but spoke flawless English. Her hair was snow white and fell in a smooth, severe bob that looked like it had been carved from bone and set carefully on her head like a helmet, so little did it move. She wore asymmetrical black garments that hung in supremely chic folds, and she had a stillness that made Alex twitch. Alex had been in awe of her from the first glimpse of her slender, immaculate form at the Jonathan Edwards orientation, since the first whiff of her peppery perfume. She was a women's studies professor, the head of JE College, and one of the youngest people to ever achieve tenure. Alex didn't know exactly what tenure implied or if "young" meant thirty or forty or fifty. Belbalm might have been any of those, depending on the light. Right now, with the basso belladonna in Alex's system, Belbalm looked a dewy thirty and the light pinging off her white hair glittered like tiny shooting stars.

"Hi," Alex said, hovering behind one of the wooden chairs.

"Alexandra," Belbalm said, resting her chin on her folded hands. She always got Alex's name wrong, and Alex never corrected her. Admitting her name was Galaxy to this woman was unthinkable. "I know you're breakfasting with your friend, but I need to steal you away." *Breakfasting* had to be the classiest verb Alex had ever heard. Right up there with *summering*. "You have a moment?" Her questions never sounded like questions. "You'll come to the office, yes? So that we can talk."

"Of course." Alex said, when what she really wanted to ask was, *Am I in trouble?* When Alex was put on academic probation at the end of her first semester, Belbalm had given her the news sitting in her elegantly appointed office, three of Alex's papers laid out before her: one on *The Right Stuff*, for her sociology class on organizational disasters; one on Elizabeth Bishop's "Late Air," a poem she'd chosen for its meager length, only to realize she had nothing to say about it and couldn't even use up space with nice long quotes; and one for her class on Swift, which she'd thought would be fun because of *Gulliver's Travels*. As it turned out, the *Gulliver's Travels* she'd read had been for children and nothing like the impenetrable original.

At the time, Belbalm had smoothed her hand over the typed pages and gently said that Alex should have disclosed her learning disability. "You're dyslexic, yes?"

"Yes," Alex had lied, because she needed some reason for how very far behind everyone else she was. Alex had the sense she should be ashamed of failing to correct Belbalm, but she'd take all the help she could get.

So now what? They were too early in the semester for Alex to have screwed up all over again.

Belbalm winked and gave Alex's hand a squeeze. "It's nothing terrible. You needn't look quite so much like you're ready to flee." Her fingers were cool and bony, hard as marble; a single large stone glinted dark gray on her ring finger. Alex knew she was staring, but the drug in her system had made the ring a mountain, an altar, a planet in orbit. "I prefer singular pieces," Belbalm said. "Simplicity, hmm?"

Alex nodded, tearing her eyes away. She was wearing a pair of three-sets-for-five-dollars earrings that she'd boosted from the racks at Claire's in the Fashion Square Mall. Simplicity.

"Come," Belbalm said, rising and waving one elegant hand.

"Let me just get my bag," said Alex. She returned to Mercy and jammed a pancake into her mouth, chewing frantically.

"Did you see this?" Mercy said, turning her phone to Alex. "Some New Haven girl got killed last night. In front of Payne Whitney. You must have walked right by the crime scene this morning!"

"Damn," said Alex, casting cursory eyes over the screen of Mercy's phone. "I saw the lights. I just thought there was a car accident."

"So scary. She was only nineteen." Mercy rubbed her arms. "What does La Belle Belbalm want? I thought we were going to edit your paper."

The world glittered. She felt awake, able to do anything. Mercy was being generous and Alex wanted to work with her before the buzz began to fade, but there was nothing she could do about it.

"Belbalm has time now and I need to talk to her about my schedule. I'll meet you back in the room?"

That bitch can lie like she's breathing, Len had once said of Alex. He'd said a lot of things before he died.

Alex trailed the professor out of the dining hall and across the courtyard to her office. She felt shitty leaving Mercy behind. Mercy was from a wealthy suburb of Chicago. Her parents were both professors, and she'd written some kind of crazy paper that had impressed even Darlington. She and Alex had nothing in common. But they'd both been the kid with nobody to sit next to in the cafeteria and Mercy hadn't laughed when Alex had mispronounced Goethe. Around her and Lauren, it was easier to pretend to be the person she was supposed to be here. Still, if La Belle Belbalm demanded your presence, you didn't argue.

Belbalm had two assistants, who rotated at the desk outside of her office. This morning it was the very peppy, very pretty Colin Khatri. He was a member of Scroll and Key and some kind of chem prodigy.

"Alex!" he exclaimed, like she was a much anticipated guest at a party.

Colin's enthusiasm always seemed genuine, but sometimes its sheer wattage made her want to do something abruptly violent like put a pencil through his palm. Belbalm just draped her elegant coat on the rack and beckoned Alex into her sanctum.

"Tea, Colin?" Belbalm inquired.

"Of course," he said, beaming less like an assistant than an acolyte.

"Thank you, love."

Coat, mouthed Colin. Alex shucked off her jacket. She'd once asked Colin what Belbalm knew about the societies. "Nothing," he'd said. "She thinks it's all old-boy elitist bullshit."

She wasn't wrong. Alex had wondered what was so special about the seniors selected by the societies every year. She'd thought there must be something magical about them. But they were just favorites—legacies, high achievers, charisma queens, the editor of the *Daily News,* the quarterback for the football team, some kid who had staged a particularly edgy production of *Equus* that no one wanted to see. People who would go on to run hedge funds and start-ups and get executive producer credits.

Alex followed Belbalm inside, letting the calm of the office settle over her. The books lining the shelves, the carefully curated objects from Belbalm's travels—a blown-glass decanter that bulged like the body of a jellyfish, some kind of antique mirror, the herbs flowering on the window ledge in white ceramic containers like bits of geometric sculpture. Even the sunlight seemed more gentle here.

Alex took a deep breath.

"Too much perfume?" Belbalm asked with a smile.

"No!" Alex said loudly. "It's great."

Belbalm dropped gracefully into the chair behind her desk and gestured for Alex to seat herself on the green velvet couch across from her.

"Le Parfum de Thérèse," Belbalm said. "Edmond Roudnitska. He was one of the great noses of the twentieth century and he designed this fragrance for his wife. Only she was allowed to wear it. Romantic, no?"

"Then—"

"How do I come to wear it? Well, they both died and there was money to be made, so Frédéric Malle put it on the market for us peasants to buy."

Peasant was a word poor people didn't use. Just like *classy* was a word that classy people didn't use. But Belbalm smiled in a way that included Alex, so Alex smiled back in a way she hoped was just as knowing.

Colin appeared, balancing a tray laden with a tea set the color of red clay, and placed it on the edge of the desk. "Anything else?" he asked hopefully.

Belbalm shooed him away. "Go do important things." She poured out the tea and offered a cup to Alex. "Help yourself to cream and sugar if you like. Or there's fresh mint." She rose and broke a small sprig from the herbs on the sill.

"Mint please," Alex said, taking the sprig and echoing Belbalm's movements: crushing the leaves, dropping them into her own cup.

Belbalm sat back, took a sip. Alex did the same, then hid a flinch when it burned her tongue.

"I take it you heard the news about that poor girl?"

"Tara?"

Belbalm's slender brows rose. "Yes, Tara Hutchins. Did you know her?"

"No," Alex said, annoyed at her own stupidity. "I was just reading about her."

"A terrible thing. I will say a more terrible thing and admit that I'm grateful she was not a student. It does not diminish the loss in any way, of course."

"Of course." But Alex was fairly sure Belbalm was saying exactly that.

"Alex, what do you want from Yale?"

Money. Alex knew Marguerite Belbalm would find such an answer hopelessly crude. *When did you first see them?* Darlington had asked. Maybe all rich people asked the wrong questions. For people like Alex, it would never be *what do you want.* It was always just *how much can you get?* Enough to survive? Enough to help her take care of her mother when shit fell apart the way it always, always did?

Alex said nothing and Belbalm tried again. "Why come here and not to an art school?" Lethe had mocked up paintings for her, created a false trail of successes and glowing recommendations to excuse her academic lapses.

"I'm good, but I'm not good enough to make it." It was true. Magic could create competent painters, proficient musicians, but not genius. She had added art electives to her class schedule because it was expected, and they'd proven the easiest part of her academic life. Because it wasn't her hand that moved the brush. When she remembered to pick up the sketchbooks Sandow had suggested she buy, it was like letting a trivet skate over a Ouija board, though the images that emerged came from somewhere inside her—Betcha half naked and drinking from a hole; Hellie in profile, the wings of a monarch butterfly pushing from her back.

"I will not accuse you of false humility. I trust you to know your own talents." Belbalm took another sip of her tea. "The world is quite hard on artists who are good but not truly great. So. You wish what? Stability? A steady job?"

"Yes," Alex said, and despite her best intentions the word emerged with a petulant edge.

"You mistake me, Alexandra. There is no crime in wanting these things. Only people who have never lived without comfort deride it as bourgeois." She winked. "The purest Marxists are always men. Calamity comes too easily to women. Our lives can come apart in a single gesture, a rogue wave. And money? Money is the rock we cling to when the current would seize us."

"Yes," said Alex, leaning forward. This was what Alex's mother had never managed to grasp. Mira loved *art* and *truth* and *freedom.* She didn't want to be a *part of the machine.* But the machine didn't care. The machine went on grinding and catching her up in its gears.

Belbalm set her cup in its saucer. "So once you have money, once you can stop clinging to the rock and can climb atop it, what will you build there? When you stand upon the rock, what will you preach?"

Alex felt all of the interest go out of her. Was she really supposed to have something to say, some wisdom to impart? *Stay in school? Don't do drugs? Don't fuck the wrong guys? Don't let the wrong guys fuck with you? Be nice to your parents even if they don't deserve it, because they can afford to take you to the dentist? Dream smaller? Don't let the girl you love die?*

The silence stretched. Alex gazed at the mint leaves floating in her tea.

"Well," said Professor Belbalm on a sigh. "I ask you these things because I don't know how else to motivate you, Alex. Do you wonder why I care?"

Alex hadn't, actually. She'd just assumed Belbalm took her job as the head of JE seriously, that she looked out for all of the students under her care. But she nodded anyway.

"We all began somewhere, Alex. So many of these children have had too much handed to them. They've forgotten how to reach. You are hungry and I respect hunger." She tapped her desk with two fingers. "But hungry for *what*? You're improving; I see that. You've gotten some help, I think, and that's good. You're clearly a smart girl. The academic probation is worrisome, but what worries me more is that the classes you're choosing show no real pattern of interest other than ease. You cannot simply *get by* here."

Can and will, thought Alex. But all she said was, "I'm sorry." She meant it. Belbalm was looking for some secret potential to unlock and Alex was going to disappoint her.

Belbalm waved away the apology. "Think about what you want, Alex. It may not be something you can find here. But if it is, I will do what I can to help you stay."

This was what Alex wanted, the perfect peace of this office, the gentle light through the windows, the mint and basil and marjoram growing in lacy clusters.

"Have you given any thought to your summer plans?" asked Belbalm. "Would you consider staying here? Coming to work for me?"

Alex's head snapped up. "What could I possibly do for you?"

Belbalm laughed. "Do you think Isabel and Colin are performing complicated tasks? They maintain my calendar, do my filing, organize my life so I don't have to. I have no doubt you could manage it. There's a summer composition program that I think might get your writing where it needs to be to continue here. You could begin to think about what you might consider as a career path. I don't want to see you left behind, Alex."

A summer to catch up, to catch my breath. Alex was good at odds. She'd had to be. Before you walked into a deal, you had to know if you would walk out. And she knew the chance that she could bob and weave her way through four years of Yale was unlikely. With Darlington around, it had been different. His help had given her an edge, made this life manageable, possible. But Darlington was gone, who knew for how long, and she was so damn tired of treading water.

Belbalm was offering her three months to breathe, to recover, make a plan, gather her resources, to become a real Yale student, not just someone playing the part on Lethe's dime.

"How would that work?" Alex asked. She wanted to set down her cup, but her hand was shaking badly enough she was afraid it would clatter.

"Show me you can continue to improve. Finish the year strong. And the next time I ask you what you want, I expect an answer. You know about my salon? I had one last night but I'll have another next week. You can start by attending."

"I can do that," she said, though she wasn't at all sure she could. "I can do that. Thank you."

"Don't thank me, Alex." Belbalm looked at her over the red rim of her teacup. "Just do the work."

Alex felt light as she drifted out of the office and waved to Colin. She found herself in the silence of the courtyard. It was like this sometimes—all of the doors would close, no one passing through on their way to class or a meal, all the windows shut tight against the cold, and you'd be left in a pocket of silence. Alex let it pool around her, imagined that the buildings surrounding her had been abandoned.

What would the campus be like in the summer? Quiet like this? Humid and unpopulated, a city under glass. Alex had spent her winter break holed up at Il Bastone, watching movies on the laptop Lethe had bought for her, afraid Dawes would appear. She'd skyped with her mom and only ventured out for pizza and noodles. Even the Grays had vanished, as if without the students' excitement and anxiety, they had nothing to draw them to campus.

Alex thought of the stillness, the late mornings that summer might bring. She could sit behind that desk where Colin and Isabel sat, brew tea, update the JE website, do whatever had to be done. She could pick her courses, ones that had syllabi that didn't change much. She could do the reading ahead of time, take the composition course so she wouldn't have to lean on Mercy so much anymore—assuming Mercy wanted to room with her next year.

Next year. Magical words. Belbalm had built Alex a bridge to a possible future. She just had to cross it. Alex's mother would be disappointed when she didn't go home to California . . . Or would she? Maybe it was easier this way. When Alex had told her mother she was going to Yale, Mira had looked at her with such sadness that it had taken Alex a long moment to understand her mother thought she was high. Guiltily, Alex snapped a picture of the empty courtyard and texted it to her mom. *Cold morning!* Meaningless, but evidence that she was okay and *here,* proof of life.

She popped into the bathroom before she headed to class, ran her fingers through her hair. She and Hellie had loved wearing makeup, spending their rare bits of spare cash on glitter eyeliner and lip gloss. She missed it sometimes. Here, makeup meant something different; it sent a signal of effort that was unacceptable.

Alex endured an hour of Spanish II—dull but manageable because all it required of her was memorization. Everyone was chattering about Tara Hutchins, though no one called her by name. She was the dead girl, the murder victim, the townie who got stabbed. People were talking about crisis lines and emergency therapy for anyone triggered by the event. The TA who led her Spanish class reminded them to use the campus walking service after dark. *I was right near there. I was there like an hour before it happened. I walk by there every day.* Alex heard the same things repeated again and again. There was worry, some embarrassment—another bit of proof that, no matter how many chain stores moved in, New Haven would never be Cambridge. But no one seemed truly afraid. *Because Tara wasn't one of you,* Alex thought, as she packed up her bag. *You all still feel safe.*

Alex had two hours free after class and she meant to spend them hidden away in her dorm room, eating her pilfered sandwiches and writing her report for Sandow, then sleeping through the basso belladonna crash before she went to her English lecture.

Instead, she found her feet carrying her back to Payne Whitney. The intersection was no longer blocked off and the crowds were gone, but police tape still surrounded the triangular swath of barren ground across the street from the gym. The students who passed cast furtive glances at the scene and hurried along, as if mortified to be seen gawking at something so lurid in the cold gray sunlight. A police cruiser was parked half on the sidewalk, and a news van sat across the street.

She had to imagine Dean Sandow and the rest of the Yale administration were having plenty of harried meetings about damage control this morning. Alex hadn't understood the distinctions between Yale and Princeton and Harvard and the cities they occupied. They were all the same impossible place in the same imaginary town. But it was clear from the way that Lauren and Mercy laughed about New Haven that the city and its university were considered a little less Ivy than the others. A murder that close to campus, even if the victim hadn't been a student, couldn't be good PR.

Alex wondered if she was looking at the place where Tara had been murdered or if her body had simply been dumped in front of the gym. She should have asked the coroner while he was compelled. But she had to imagine it was the former. If you wanted to get rid of a body, you didn't drop it in the middle of a busy intersection.

An image of Hellie's shoe, that pink jelly sandal slipping from her painted toes, flashed through Alex's mind. Hellie's feet had been wide, the toes crammed together, the skin thick and callused—the only unbeautiful part of her.

What am I doing here? Alex didn't want to get any closer to where the body had been. *It was the boyfriend.* That's what the coroner had told her. He was a dealer. They'd gotten into some kind of argument. The wounds had been extreme, but if he'd been high, who knew what might have been going on in his head?

Still, there was something bothering her about the scene. Last night she'd approached from Grove Street, but now she was on the other side of the intersection, directly across from the Baker Hall dorms and the empty, icy ground where Tara had been found. From this angle there was something familiar about the way it all looked—the two streets, the stakes driven into the earth where Tara had died or been abandoned. Was it just seeing it in the daylight without the crowds that made it seem different? A false sense of déjà vu? Or maybe the basso belladonna was playing tricks on her as it left her system? The Lethe journals were full of warnings on just how powerful it was.

Alex thought of Hellie's shoe hanging for a brief moment from her toe, then dropping to the apartment floor with a thunk. Len turned to Alex, struggling with the weight of Hellie's limp body, his hands cupped beneath her armpits. Betcha had Hellie's knees tucked against his hip as if they were swing dancing. "Come on," Len said. "Open the door, Alex. Let us out."

Let us out.

She shook the memory away and glanced at the cluster of Grays in front of the gym. There were less of them today and their mood—if they'd ever really had a mood—had returned to normal. The Bridegroom was still there, though. Despite her best attempts to ignore him, the ghost was hard to miss—crisp trousers, shiny shoes, a handsome face like something out of an old movie, big dark eyes and black hair swept back from his brow in a soft wave, the effect spoiled only by the big bloody pockmark of a gunshot wound to his chest.

He was an actual haunter, a Gray who could pass through the layers of the Veil and make his presence felt, rattling windshields and setting off car alarms in the parking garage that stood where his family's carriage factory had once been—and where he'd killed his fiancée and then himself. It was a favorite stop on ghost tours of New England. Alex didn't let her gaze linger, but from the corner of her eye she saw him drift away from the group, sauntering toward her.

Time to get gone. She didn't want the interest of Grays, particularly Grays who could take any kind of real physical form. She turned her back on him and hurried toward the heart of campus.

By the time she got back to Vanderbilt, the crash had hold of her. She felt weak, exhausted, as if she'd just emerged from a week of the worst flu of her life. Her report for Sandow could wait. She didn't have much to say anyway. She would sleep. Maybe she would dream of summer. She could still smell crushed mint on her fingers.

She closed her eyes and saw Hellie's face, her pale brows bleached by the sun, vomit clinging to her lip. It was Tara Hutchins's fault. Blondes always made Alex think of Hellie. But why had the crime scene looked so familiar? What had she seen in that forlorn patch of dead earth bracketed by the flow of traffic?

Nothing. She'd just had too many late nights, too much Darlington whispering in her ear. Tara was nothing like Hellie. She was like a bad knockoff, generic to Hellie's name brand.

No, said a voice in her head—and it was Hellie, standing on a skateboard, rocking back and forth on those wide feet, her balance impeccable. Her skin was ashen. Her bikini top was spattered with clumps of her last meal. *She's me. She's you without a second chance.*

Alex fought her way back from the tide of sleep. The room was dark, little light filtering in from the single narrow window.

Hellie was long gone and so were the people who had hurt her. But someone had hurt Tara Hutchins too. Someone who hadn't been punished. Not yet.

Leave it to Detective Turner. That was what the survivor said. *Rest easy. Let it go. Focus on your grades. Think of the summer.*

Alex could see the bridge that Belbalm had built. She just had to cross it.

Alex reached into her dresser for the basso belladonna drops. One more afternoon. She could give Tara Hutchins that much before she buried her for good and moved on. The way she'd buried Hellie.

Aurelian, home to the would-be philosopher kings, the great uniters. Aurelian was founded to embrace ideals of leadership and, supposedly, to bring together the best of the societies. They modeled themselves as a kind of New Lethe, tapping members from every society to form a leadership council. That didn't last long. Lively debate gave way to raucous argument, new members were recruited, and they soon became as clannish as the other Houses of the Veil. In the end, their magic has a fundamental practicality best suited to the working professional, less a calling than a trade. That has made them the object of ridicule by some with more delicate sensibilities, but when Aurelian found themselves banned from their own "tomb" and without permanent address, they managed to survive where other Houses have foundered—by hiring themselves out to the highest bidder.

—*from* The Life of Lethe: Procedures
and Protocols of the Ninth House

They just lack any kind of *style*. Sure, they occasionally burp out a senator or an author of middling renown, but Aurelian nights always feel a bit like you've been handed the transcript to a juicy court case. You start out excited, and by page two you realize it's all a lot of words and not much drama.

—Lethe Days Diary of Michelle Alameddine
(Hopper College)

6

Last Fall

He started her small—with Aurelian. Darlington figured the big magics could wait for later in the semester, and he knew he'd made the right choice when he came downstairs at Il Bastone to find Alex perched on the edge of a velvet cushion, gnawing feverishly on a thumbnail. Dawes seemed oblivious, her attention focused on *A Companion to Linear B,* her noise-canceling headphones firmly in place.

"Ready?" he asked.

Alex stood and wiped her palms on her jeans. He had her run through the stock of protections in their bags, and Darlington was pleased to see she'd forgotten nothing.

"Good night, Dawes," he said as they unhooked their coats from the hall rack. "We won't be home late."

Dawes slid her headphones down to her neck. "We have smoked salmon and egg and dill sandwiches."

"Dare I ask?"

"And avgolemono."

"I'd say you're an angel, but you're so much more interesting."

Dawes clucked her tongue. "It's really not a fall soup."

"It's barely fall and there's nothing more fortifying." Besides, after a shot of Hiram's elixir it was tough to get warm.

Dawes smiled as she returned to her text. She liked being

praised for her cooking almost as much as she liked being acknowledged for her scholarship.

The air felt bright and cold against his skin as they walked down Orange, back toward the Green and campus. Spring came on slow in New England, but fall was like rounding a sharp turn. One moment you were sweating through summer cotton and the next you shivered beneath a sky gone hard enamel blue.

"Tell me about Aurelian."

Alex blew out a breath. "Founded in 1910. Rooms consecrated in Sheffield-Sterling-Strathcona Hall—"

"Save yourself the mouthful. Everyone calls it SSS."

"SSS. During the 1932 renovations."

"Around the same time Bones was sealing off their operating theater," Darlington added.

"Their what?"

"You'll learn during your first prognostication. But I thought we'd keep the training wheels on for our first journey out." Best that Alex Stern found her footing among the eager, generous Aurelians rather than in front of the Bonesmen. "The university gave those rooms to Aurelian as a gift for services rendered."

"Which services?"

"You tell me, Stern."

"Well, they specialize in logomancy, word magic. So something with a contract?"

"The purchase of Sachem's Wood in 1910. It was a huge acquisition of land and the university wanted to make sure the purchase could never be challenged. That land became Science Hill. What else?"

"People don't take them very seriously."

"People?"

"Lethe," she amended. "The other societies. Because they don't have a real tomb."

"But we're not like those people, Stern. We aren't snobs."

"You are most definitely a snob, Darlington."

"Well, I'm not that particular kind of snob. We have only two real concerns: Does their magic work and is it dangerous?"

"Does it?" asked Alex. "Is it?"

"The answer to both questions is sometimes. Aurelian specializes in unbreakable contracts, binding vows, stories that can literally put the reader to sleep. In 1989 a certain millionaire slipped into a coma in the cabin of his yacht. A copy of *God and Man at Yale* was found beside him, and if anyone had thought to look they would have found an introduction that exists in no other version—one composed by Aurelian. You may also be interested to know that Winston Churchill's last words were 'I'm bored with it all.'"

"You're saying Aurelian assassinated Winston Churchill?"

"That's mere speculation. But I can confirm that half of the dead in Grove Street Cemetery only stay in their graves because the inscriptions on their tombstones were crafted by members of Aurelian."

"Sounds pretty powerful to me."

"That was the old magic, when they were still considered a landed society. Aurelian was kicked out of their rooms when union contract negotiations with the university soured. The charge was serving alcohol to minors, but the fact is that Yale felt Aurelian had botched the initial contracts. They lost Room 405 and their work has been shaky ever since. These days, they mostly manage the occasional nondisclosure agreement or inspiration spell. That's what we'll be seeing tonight."

They passed the administrative offices of Woodbridge Hall and the glowing golden screens of Scroll and Key. The Locksmiths had canceled their next ritual. It wouldn't mean any less work for Lethe—Book and Snake had been happy to move into the Thursday night slot in their place—but Darlington wondered exactly what was going on at Keys. There had been rumors of weakening magic, portals that malfunctioned or didn't open at all. It might all be talk—the Houses of the Veil were secretive, competitive, and prone to petty gossip. But Darlington would take the delay as an opportunity to dig into what Scroll and Key might be contending with before he dragged his Dante into a possible mess.

"If Aurelian isn't dangerous, why do we need to be there?" Alex asked.

"To keep the proceedings from being interrupted. This particular ritual tends to draw a lot of Grays."

"Why?"

"All of the blood." Alex's steps slowed. "Please don't tell me you're squeamish. You won't make it through a semester if you can't handle a bit of gore."

Darlington immediately felt like an ass. After what Alex had survived back in California, of course she'd be wary. This girl had witnessed real trauma, not the theater of the macabre to which Darlington had become so accustomed.

"I'll be fine," she said, but she was gripping the strap of her satchel with clenched fists.

They entered the stark plateau of Beinecke Plaza, the library's windows glowing like chunks of amber.

"You will be," he promised. "This is a controlled environment and a simple spell. We're basically just serving as bouncers tonight."

"Okay."

She didn't *look* okay.

They pushed through the library's revolving door and into the high vault of the entry. Gordon Bunshaft had envisioned the library as a box within a box. Behind the empty security desk a vast glass wall rose to the ceiling, packed with shelves of books. This was the real library, the stacks, the paper-and-parchment heart of Beinecke, the outer structure that surrounded it acting as entry, shield, and false skin. Large windows on every side showed the empty plaza beyond.

A long table had been set up not far from the security desk, a comfortable distance away from the cases, where rotating exhibits from the library's collections were displayed and where the Gutenberg Bible was housed in its own little glass cube, lit from above. A single page of it was turned every day. God, he loved this place.

The Aurelians were milling around the table, already in their ivory robes, chatting nervously. That giddy energy alone was probably enough to start drawing Grays. Josh Zelinski, the delegation's current president, broke away from the group and hurried over to greet them. Darlington knew him from several American studies seminars. He had a Mohawk, favored oversize overalls, and talked a *lot*. A woman in her forties trailed him, tonight's Emperor—the alumna selected to supervise the ritual. Darlington recognized her from a rite Aurelian had conducted the previous year to draw up governing documents for her condo board.

"Amelia," he said, reaching for the name. "A pleasure to see you again."

She smiled and glanced at Alex. "Is this the new you?" It was the same thing they'd asked Michelle Alameddine when she'd taken him around his freshman year.

"Meet our new Dante. Alex is from Los Angeles."

"Nice," said Zelinski. "Do you know any movie stars?"

"I once swam naked in Oliver Stone's pool—does that count?"

"Was he there?"

"No."

Zelinski looked genuinely disappointed.

"We'll start at midnight," said Amelia.

That gave them plenty of time to set up a perimeter around the ritual table.

"For this rite, we can't block the Grays out completely," Darlington explained as he and Alex walked a wide circle around the table, choosing the path of the boundary they would create. "The magic requires that the channels with the Veil remain open. Now tell me first steps."

He'd assigned her excerpts from *Fowler's Bindings* and also a short treatise on portal magic from the early days of Scroll and Key.

"Bone dust or graveyard dirt or any memento mori to form the circle."

"Good," said Darlington. "We'll use this tonight." He handed her a stick of chalk made from compressed crematory ash. "It will allow us to be more precise in our markings. We'll leave channels open at each compass point."

"And then what?"

"Then we work the doors. The Grays can disrupt the ritual, and we don't want this kind of magic breaking loose. Magic needs resolution. Once this particular rite begins, it will be looking for blood, and if the spell gets free of the table, it could literally slice some nice law student studying a block away in two. One less lawyer to plague the world, but I'm told lawyer jokes are passé. So if a Gray tries to come through, you have two options: dust them or death words." Grays loathed any reminder of death or dying— lamentations, dirges, poems about grief or loss, even a particularly well-phrased mortuary ad could do the trick.

"How about both?" asked Alex.

"There's really no need. We don't waste power if we don't have to."

She looked skeptical. Her anxiety surprised him. Alex Stern might be graceless and uneducated, but she'd shown plenty of nerve—at least when anything but moths were concerned. Where was the steel he'd glimpsed in her before? And why did her fear disappoint him so acutely?

Just as they were finishing their markings to close the circle, a young man passed through the turnstile, his scarf pulled up nearly to his eyes. "The guest of honor," murmured Darlington.

"Who is he?"

"Zeb Yarrowman, wunderkind. Or former wunderkind. Surely the Germans have a name for prodigies who age out of enfant terrible."

"You would know, Darlington."

"Too cruel, Stern. I have time yet. Zeb Yarrowman wrote a novel his junior year at Yale, published it before he graduated, and was the darling of the New York literary scene for several years running."

"Good book?"

"It wasn't *bad*," Darlington said. "Malaise, madness, young love, the usual bildungsroman fare, all set against the background of Zeb working at his uncle's failing dairy. But the prose did impress."

"So he's here to mentor someone?"

"He's here because *The King of Small Places* was published almost eight years ago and Zeb Yarrowman hasn't written a word since." Darlington saw Zelinski signal to the Emperor. "It's time to start."

The Aurelians had assembled in two even lines, facing each other on either side of the long table. They wore white cloaks almost like choir robes, with pointed sleeves so long they brushed the tabletop. Josh Zelinski stood at one end, the Emperor at the other. They put on white gloves of the type used to handle archival manuscripts and unfurled a scroll down the table's length.

"Parchment," said Darlington. "Made from goatskin and soaked in elderflower. A gift for the muse. But that's not all she requires. Come on." He led Alex back to the first marks they'd made. "You'll watch the southern and eastern gates. Don't stand between the markings unless you absolutely have to. If you see a Gray approaching, just step into his path and use your graveyard dirt or speak the death words. I'll be monitoring the north and west."

"How?" Her voice held a nervous, truculent edge. "You can't even see them."

Darlington reached into his pocket and removed the vial of elixir. He couldn't put it off any longer. He broke the wax covering, unstopped the cork, and, before thoughts of self-preservation could intrude, downed the contents.

Darlington had never gotten used to it. He doubted he ever

would—the urge to gag, the bitter spike that drove through his soft palate and up into the back of his skull.

"Fuck," he gasped.

Alex blinked. "I think that's the first time I've heard you swear."

Chills shook him and he tried to control the tremors that quaked through his body. "I c-c-class p-p-profanity with declarations of love. Best used sparingly and only when wholeheartedly m-m-meant."

"Darlington . . . are your teeth supposed to chatter?"

He tried to nod, but of course he was already nodding—spasming, really.

The elixir was like dunking your head into the Great Cold, like stepping into a long, dark winter. Or as Michelle had once said, "It's like getting an icicle shoved up your ass."

"Less localized," Darlington had managed to joke at the time. But he'd wanted to pass out from the shuddering awful of it. It wasn't just the taste or the cold or the tremors. It was the feeling of having brushed up against something horrible. He hadn't been able to identify the sensation then, but months later he'd been driving on I-95 when a tractor trailer swayed into his lane, missing his car by the barest breath. His body had flooded with adrenaline, and the bitter tang of crushed aspirin had filled his mouth as he remembered the taste of Hiram's Bullet.

That was what it was like every time—and would be until the dose finally tried to kill him and his liver tipped into toxicity. You couldn't keep sidling up to death and dipping your toe in. Eventually it grabbed your ankle and tried to pull you under.

Well. If it happened, Lethe would find him a liver donor. He wouldn't be the first. And not everyone could be born gifted like Galaxy Stern.

Now the shaking passed, and for a brief moment the world went milky, as if he were seeing Beinecke's golden glow through a thick cataract of cobwebs. These were the layers of the Veil.

When they parted for him, the haze cleared. Beinecke's familiar columns, the cloaked members of Aurelian, and Alex's wary face came into ordinary focus once more—except he saw an old man in a houndstooth jacket hovering by the case that housed the Gutenberg Bible, then strolling past to examine the collection of James Baldwin memorabilia.

"I think . . . I think that's—" He caught himself before he spoke Frederic Prokosch's name. Names were intimate and risked forming a connection with the dead. "He wrote a novel that used to be famous, called *The Asiatics,* from a desk at Sterling Library. I wonder if Zeb's a fan." Prokosch had claimed to be unknowable, a mystery even to his closest friends. And yet here he was, moping around a college library in the afterlife. Maybe it was best that the elixir cost so much and tasted so bad. Otherwise Darlington would be downing it every other afternoon just for glimpses like this. But now it was time to work. "Send him on his way, Stern. But do not make eye contact."

Alex rolled her shoulders like a boxer stepping into the ring and approached Prokosch, keeping her gaze averted. She reached into her bag and pulled out the vial of graveyard dirt.

"What are you waiting for?"

"I can't get the lid off."

Prokosch looked up from the glass case and drifted toward Alex.

"Then say the *words,* Stern."

Alex took a step backward, still fumbling with the lid.

"He can't hurt you," said Darlington, putting himself between Prokosch and the entry to the circle. The ritual hadn't yet begun, but best to keep it clean. Darlington didn't love the idea of dispelling the Gray himself. He knew too much about the ghost as it was, and banishing him back behind the Veil risked creating a connection between them. "Go on, Stern."

Alex squeezed her eyes shut and shouted, "*Take courage! No one is immortal!*"

Prokosch shuddered in apprehension and lifted a hand as if to shoo Alex away. He bolted through the library's glass walls. Death words could be anything, really, as long as they spoke of the things Grays feared most—the finality of passing, a life without legacy, the emptiness of the hereafter. Darlington had given Alex some of the simplest to recall, from the Orphic lamellae found in Thessaly.

"See?" said Darlington. "Easy." He glanced at the Aurelians, a few of whom were giggling at Alex's ardent declaration. "Though you needn't shout."

But Alex didn't seem to care about the attention she'd drawn. Her eyes were alight, staring at the place where Prokosch had been moments before. "Easy!" she said. She frowned and looked at the vial of dirt in her hand. "So easy."

"At least crow a little, Stern. Don't deny me the enjoyment of putting you back in your place." When she didn't reply, he said, "Come on, they're ready to start."

Zeb Yarrowman stood at the head of the table. He had removed his shirt and was naked to the waist, his skin pale, his chest narrow, his arms tight to his sides like folded wings. Darlington had seen many men and women stand at the head of that table over the last three years. Some had been members of Aurelian. Some had simply paid the steep fee the society's trust charged. They came to speak their words, make their requests, hoping for something spectacular to happen. They came with different needs, and Aurelian moved locations depending on their requirement: Ironclad prenups could be fashioned beneath the entryway to the law school. Forgeries might be detected beneath the watchful eyes of poor, duped Benjamin West's *Cicero Discovering the Tomb of Archimedes* in the university art gallery. Land deeds and real estate deals were sealed high atop East Rock, the city glittering far below. Aurelian's magic may have been weaker than that of the other societies, but it was more portable and more practical.

Tonight's chants began in Latin, a soothing, gentle recitation that filled Beinecke, floating up, up, past shelf after shelf encased in the glass cube at the library's center. Darlington let himself listen with one ear as he scanned the perimeter of the circle and kept one eye on Alex. He supposed it was a good sign that she was so tense. It at least meant she cared about doing a good job.

The chants shifted, breaking from Latin and shifting into vernacular Italian, sliding from antiquity to modernity. Zeb's voice was the loudest, beseeching, echoing off the stone, and Darlington could feel his desperation. He would have to be desperate given what came next.

Zeb held out his arms. The Aurelians to his right and his left drew their knives and, as the chants continued, drew two long lines from Zeb's wrists up his forearms.

The blood ran slowly at first, welling to the surface in red slits like eyes opening.

Zeb settled his hands on the edge of the paper before him and his blood spread over it, staining the paper. As if the paper had a taste for it, the blood started to flow faster, a tide that crawled down the scroll as Zeb continued to chant in Italian.

As Darlington had known they would, the Grays began to appear, drifting through the walls, drawn by blood and hope.

When at last the blood tide reached the end of the parchment, the Aurelians each lowered their sleeves, letting them brush the soaked paper. Zeb's blood seemed to climb up the fabric as the sound of the chanting rose—not a single language now but all languages, words drawn from the books surrounding them, above them, tucked away in climate-controlled vaults beneath them. Thousands upon thousands of volumes. Memoirs and children's stories, postcards and menus, poetry and travelogues, soft, rounded Italian speared by the spiky sounds of English, the chugging of German, whispery threads of Cantonese.

As one, the Aurelians slammed their hands down on the blood-soaked parchment. The sound ruptured the air like thunder and black spread from their palms, a new tide as blood became ink and flowed back up the table, coursing along the paper to where

Zeb's hands rested. He screamed when the ink entered him, zig-zagging up his arms in a scrawl, line upon line, word upon word, a palimpsest that blackened his skin, slowly crawling in looping cursive up to his elbows. He wept and shuddered and wailed his anguish—but kept his hands flat to the paper.

The ink climbed higher, to his bent shoulders, up his neck, over his chest, and in the same instant entered his head and his heart.

This was the most dangerous part of the ritual, when all of Aurelian would be most vulnerable and the Grays would be most eager. They came faster through the walls and sealed windows, rounding the circle, looking for the gateways Alex and Darlington had left open, drawn by Yarrowman's need and the iron-filing pungence of fresh blood. Whatever worry had plagued Alex, she was enjoying herself now, hurling handfuls of graveyard dirt at Grays with unnecessarily elaborate gestures that made her look like a professional wrestler trying to psych up an invisible crowd. Darlington turned his attention to his own compass points, cast clouds of bone dust at approaching Grays, murmuring the old death words when one of them tried to rush past. His favorite Orphic hymn began *O spirit of the unripe fruit,* but it was almost too long to be worth diving into.

He heard Alex grunt and glanced over his shoulder, expecting to see her engaged in a particularly acrobatic banishing maneuver. Instead, she was on the ground, scrabbling backward, terror in her eyes—and Grays were walking straight through the circle of protection. It took him a bare moment to understand what had happened: The markings of the southern gateway were smudged. Alex had been so busy enjoying herself, she'd stepped on the mark-ings and ruptured the southern side of the circle. What had been a narrow door to allow the flow of magic had become a gaping hole with no barrier to entry. The Grays advanced, their attention focused on the pull of blood and longing, drawing nearer to the unsuspecting Aurelians.

Darlington threw himself into their path, barking the quickest, cruelest death words he knew: *"Unwept!"* he shouted. *"Unhonored, and unsung!"* Some checked their steps, some even fled. *"Unwept, unhonored, and unsung!"* he repeated. But they had momentum now, a mass of Grays that only he and Alex could see, dressed in clothes of every period, some young, some old, some wounded and maimed, others whole.

If they reached the table, the ritual would be disrupted. Yarrowman would certainly die and he might well take half of Aurelian with him. The magic would spring wild.

But if Beinecke was a living house of words, then it was one grand memorial to the end of everything. Thornton Wilder's death mask. Ezra Pound's teeth. Elegiac poems by the hundreds. Darlington reached for the words . . . Hart Crane on Melville, Ben Jonson on the death of his son. Robert Louis Stevenson's "Requiem." His mind scrambled for purchase. *Start somewhere. Start anywhere.*

"A wanton bone, I sing my song
and travel where the bone is blown."

Good Lord. When taxed with staving off the uncanny, how did he somehow resort to Foley's poem about a skeleton having sex?

A few of the Grays peeled off, but he needed something with some damn gravitas.

Horace.

"Winter will come on
And break the lower sea on the rocks
While we drink summer's wine."

Now they slowed, some covered their ears.

"See, in the white of the winter air," he cried. *"The day hangs like a rose. It droops down to the reaching hand. Take it before it goes!"*

He lifted his hands before him as if he could somehow push them back. Why couldn't he remember the first verse of the poem? Because it hadn't interested him. *Why try to know the future, which cannot be known?*

"Winter will come on!" he repeated. But even as Darlington pushed the Grays back through the ruptured gate and reached for the chalk, he looked through the glass walls of the library. A horde was assembling—a tide of Grays visible through the glass walls, surrounding the building. He was not going to be able to fix the markings in time.

Alex was still on the ground, shaking so hard he could see her trembling even from a distance. When the magic got free, it might kill them both first.

"Take courage," she said again and again. "Take courage."

"That's not enough!"

The Grays rushed toward the library.

"Mors vincit omnia!" Darlington cried, falling back on the words printed in every Lethe manual. The Emperor and the Aurelians had looked up from the table; only Zeb Yarrowman was still lost to the agonies of the ritual, deaf to the chaos that had entered the circle.

Then a voice pierced the air, high and wobbling, not speaking but singing . . . *"Pariome mi madre en una noche oscura."*

Alex was singing, the melody hitching on her sobs. *"Ponime por nombre niña y sin fortuna."*

My mother gave birth to me on a dark night and called me the girl with no fortune.

Spanish, but slanted. Some kind of dialect.

"Ya crecen las yerbas y dan amarillo triste mi corazón vive con suspiro."

He didn't know the song, but the words seemed to slow the Grays' steps.

The leaves are growing and turning gold.

My heavy heart beats and sighs.

"More!" said Darlington.

"I don't know the rest of the song!" Alex yelled. The Grays moved forward.

"Say something, Stern! We need more words."

"Quien no sabe de mar no sabe de mal!" She didn't sing these words; she shouted them, again and again.

He who knows nothing of the sea knows nothing of suffering.

The line of Grays outside stumbled, looked over their shoulders: Something was moving behind them.

"Keep going!" he told her.

"Quien no sabe de mar no sabe de mal!"

It was a wave, a massive wave, rising from nowhere over the plaza. But how? She wasn't even speaking death words. He who knows nothing of the sea knows nothing of suffering. Darlington wasn't even sure what the words meant.

The wave rose and new words came to Darlington from Virgil—the real Virgil. From the Eclogues. *"Let all become mid-ocean!"* he declared. The wave climbed higher, blotting out the buildings and the sky beyond. *"Farewell, ye woods! Headlong from some towering mountain peak I will throw myself into the waves; take this as my last dying gift!"*

The wave crashed and Grays were scattered over the stone tiles of the plaza. Darlington could see them through the glass, bobbing like chunks of ice in the moonlight.

Hastily, Darlington redrew the marks of protection, strengthening them with heaps of graveyard dirt.

"What was that?" he said.

Alex was staring out at the fallen Grays, her cheeks still wet with tears. "I . . . It was just something my grandmother used to say."

Ladino. She'd been speaking Spanish and Hebrew and he wasn't sure what else. It was the language of diaspora. The language of death. She'd gotten lucky. They both had.

He offered her his hand. "You're all right?" he asked. Her palm was cold, clammy in his, as she rose.

"Yes," she said, but she was still shaking. "Fine. I'm sorry, I—"

"Do not say another word until we're back at Il Bastone, and for God's sake don't apologize to anyone until we're out of here."

Zelinski was striding toward them, the Emperor close behind. The ritual had ended and they looked furious, though also a bit like Klan members who'd gone for a stroll and forgotten their hoods. "What the hell were you doing?" said Amelia. "You almost ruined the ritual with your shouting. What happened here?"

Darlington whirled on them, blocking their view of the smudged marks and summoning every bit of his grandfather's authority. "Why don't *you* tell me?"

Zelinski stopped short; his sleeves—now clean and white again—flapped gently as he dropped his arms. "What?"

"Have you performed this ritual before?"

"You know we have!" snapped Amelia.

"Exactly in this way?"

"Of course not! The ritual always changes a bit depending on the need. Every story is different."

Darlington knew he was on shaky ground but better to go on the offense than to make Lethe look like a bunch of amateurs. "Well, I don't know what Zeb has in mind for his new novel, but he almost unleashed a whole host of phantoms on your delegation."

Zelinski's eyes widened. "There were Grays here?"

"An army of them."

"But she was screaming—"

"You put my Dante and me at risk," said Darlington. "I'm going to have to report this to Dean Sandow. Aurelian shouldn't be tampering with forces—"

"No, no, please," Zelinski said, putting his palms up as if to tamp down a fire. "Please. This is our first ritual as a delegation. Things were bound to get a little tricky. We're campaigning to get our rooms in SSS back."

"She could have been hurt," said Darlington, bristling with blue-blood indignation. "Killed."

"This is a donation year, isn't it?" said Amelia. "We . . . we can make sure it's a generous one."

"Are you trying to bribe me?"

"No! Not at all! A negotiation, an understanding."

"Get out of my sight. You're just lucky no lasting damage was done to the collection."

"Thanks," Alex whispered as the Emperor and Zelinski hurried away.

Darlington cast her one angry glance and bent to begin the work of clearing the circle. "I did that for Lethe, not you."

They cleaned up the leavings of the markings, made sure the Aurelians had left no traces and that Zeb's arms were bandaged and his vitals were stable. He still had ink stains on his lips and all over his teeth and gums. It trickled from his ears and the inner corners of his eyes. He looked monstrous but he was grinning, gibbering to himself, already scribbling away in a notebook. He would continue that way until the story was out of him.

Darlington and Alex walked back to Il Bastone in strained silence. The night felt colder, not only because of the hour, but because of the lasting effects of Hiram's elixir. Usually he felt a sense of sadness when its magic was gone, but tonight he was perfectly happy for the Veil to fall back into place.

What had happened during the rite? How could Alex have been so incautious? She'd broken the most basic rules he'd set for her. The circle was inviolable. Guard the marks. Had he been too easygoing about the whole thing? Tried too hard to put her at ease?

When they entered Il Bastone, the entry lights flickered, as if the house could sense their mood. Dawes was exactly where they'd left her in front of the fireplace. She glanced up and

seemed to shrink more deeply into her sweatshirt, before returning to her array of index cards, happy to turn her back on human
conflict.

Darlington drew off his coat and hung it by the door, then
headed down the hall to the kitchen, not waiting to see if Alex
would follow. He turned on the burner to heat Dawes's soup and
took the sandwich platter from the refrigerator, setting it down
with a loud clatter. A bottle of Syrah had been decanted and
he poured himself a glass, then sat and watched Alex, who had
slumped into a chair at the kitchen table, her dark eyes trained on
the black-and-white tiles of the floor.

He made himself finish his glass of wine, poured another, and
at last said, "Well? What happened?"

"I don't know," she murmured, her voice barely audible.

"Not good enough. You are literally of no use to us if you can't
handle a few Grays."

"They weren't coming at you."

"They were. Two of those gates were mine to guard, remember?"
She rubbed her arms. "I just wasn't ready. I'll do better next
time."

"Next time will be different. And the next. And the next. There
are six functioning societies and each has different rituals."

"It wasn't the ritual."

"Was it the blood?"

"No. One of them grabbed me. You didn't say that was going
to happen. I—"

Darlington couldn't believe what he was hearing. "You're saying
one of them touched you?"

"More than one. I—"

"That isn't possible. I mean . . ." He set down his wine, ran his
hands through his hair. "Rarely. So rarely. *Sometimes* in the presence of blood or if the spirit is particularly moved. That's why true
hauntings are so rare."

Her voice was hard, distant. "It's possible."

Maybe. Unless she was lying. "You need to be ready next time. You weren't prepared—"

"And whose fault is that?"

Darlington sat up straighter. "I beg your pardon? I gave you two weeks to get up to speed. I sent you specific passages to read to keep it manageable."

"And what about all of the years before that?" Alex stood and shoved her chair back. She paced into the breakfast room, her black hair reflecting the lamplight, energy sparking off her. The house gave a warning groan. She wasn't sad or ashamed or worried. She was *mad*. "Where were you?" she demanded. "All you wise men of Lethe with your spells and your chalk and your books? Where were you when the dead were following me home? When they were barging into my classrooms? My bedroom? My damn bathtub? Sandow said you had been tracking me for years, since I was a kid. One of you couldn't have told me how to get rid of them? That all it would take was a few magic words to send them away?"

"They're harmless. It's only the rituals that—"

Alex grabbed Darlington's glass and threw it hard against the wall, sending glass and red wine flying. "They are not *harmless*. You talk as if you know, like you're some kind of expert." She struck her hands against the table, leaning toward him. "You have no idea what they can do."

"Are you done or would you like another glass to break?"

"Why didn't you help me?" said Alex, her voice nearly a growl.

"I did. You were about to be buried under a sea of Grays, if you recall."

"Not *you*." Alex waved her arm, indicating the house. "Sandow. Lethe. Someone." She covered her face with her hands. "*Take courage. No one is immortal.* Do you know what it would have meant to me to know those words when I was a kid? It would have taken so little to change everything. But no one bothered. Not until I could be useful to you."

Darlington did not like to think he had behaved badly. He did not like to think that Lethe had behaved badly. *We are the shepherds.* And yet they'd left Alex to face the wolves. She was right. They hadn't cared. She'd been someone for Lethe to study and observe from afar.

He'd told himself he was giving her a chance, being fair to this girl who had washed up on his shore. But he'd let himself think of her as someone who had made all of the wrong choices and stumbled down the wrong path. It hadn't occurred to him that she was being chased.

After a long moment, he said, "Would it help to break something else?"

She was breathing hard. "Maybe."

Darlington rose and opened a cupboard, then another, and another, revealing shelf after shelf of Lenox, Waterford, Limoges—glassware, plates, pitchers, platters, butter dishes, gravy boats, thousands of dollars' worth of crystal and china. He took down a glass, filled it with wine, and handed it to Alex.

"Where would you like to start?"

7

Winter

There had to be a Lethe protocol for murder, a series of steps she should follow, that Darlington would have known to follow.

He probably would have told her to enlist Dawes's help. But Alex and the grad student had never managed to do much more than politely ignore each other. Like almost everyone else, Dawes had loved shiny-penny Darlington. He'd been the only person who seemed totally at ease talking to her, who had managed it without any of the awkwardness that hung over Dawes like one of her bulky, indeterminately colored sweatshirts. Alex was pretty sure Dawes blamed her for what had happened at Rosenfeld Hall, and though Dawes had never said much to Alex, her silence had taken on a new hostility of slammed cupboards and suspicious glares. Alex didn't want to talk to Dawes any more than she had to.

So she would consult the Lethe library instead. *Or you could just leave this whole thing alone,* she thought as she climbed the steps to the mansion on Orange. A week from now, Darlington might be back beneath this very roof. He might emerge from the new-moon rite whole and happy and ready to turn his magnificent brain to the problem of Tara Hutchins's murder. Or maybe he'd have other things on his mind.

There was no key to get into Il Bastone. Alex had been introduced to the door the first day Darlington brought her to the house, and now it released a creaky sigh as she entered. It had always hummed happily when Darlington was with her. At least it hadn't sicced a pack of jackals on her. Alex hadn't seen the Lethe hounds since that first morning, but she thought about them every time she approached the house, wondering where they slept and if they were hungry, if spirit hounds even needed food.

In theory, Dawes had Fridays off, but she could almost always be counted on to be burrowed into the corner of the first-floor parlor with her laptop. That made her easy to avoid. Alex slipped down the hall to the kitchen, where she found the plate of last night's sandwiches Dawes had left covered with a damp towel on the top shelf of the fridge. She shoveled them into her mouth, feeling like a thief, but that just made the soft white bread, the cucumber coins, and thinly sliced salmon spiked with dill taste better.

The house on Orange had been acquired by Lethe in 1888, shortly after John Anderson abandoned it, supposedly trying to outrun the ghost of the cigar girl his father had murdered. Since then, Il Bastone had masqueraded as a private home, a school run by the Sisters of St. Mary's, a law office, and now as a private home perpetually awaiting renovation. But it had always been Lethe.

A bookcase stood in the second-floor hallway beside an antique secretary and a vase of dried hydrangea. This was the entry to the library. There was an old panel in the wall beside it that supposedly controlled a stereo system, but it only worked about half the time and sometimes the music coming through the speakers sounded so tinny and far away, it made the house feel more empty.

Alex drew the Albemarle Book from the third shelf. It looked like an ordinary ledger bound in stained cloth, but its pages crackled slightly as she opened it, and she swore when a low thrum of electricity jolted through her. The book retained echoes of a user's most recent request, and as Alex flipped to the last page of entries, she saw Darlington's scrawl and the words *Rosenfeld Hall schematics*. The date was December 10. The last night Daniel Arlington had been seen alive.

Alex took a pen from the top of the secretary, wrote out the date and then *Lethe House protocols. Homicide*. She slid the book back onto the shelf between *Stover at Yale* and a battered copy of *New England Cookery, Vol. 2*. She'd never seen any sign of volume one.

The house gave a disapproving groan and the shelf shook slightly. Alex wondered if Dawes was too deep in her work to notice or if she would be turning her eyes to the ceiling, speculating on what Alex might be up to.

When the bookcase stopped rattling, Alex gripped its right side and pulled. It swung out from the wall like a door, revealing a two-story circular chamber lined with bookshelves. Though it was still afternoon, the sky through the glass dome above her glowed the luminous blue of early dusk. The air felt slightly balmy and she could smell orange blossoms on the air.

Lethe had a limited amount of room, so the library had been rigged with a telescope portal, using magic borrowed from Scroll and Key and deployed by the late Lethe delegate Richard Albemarle when he was still only a Dante. You wrote down the subject you sought in the Albemarle Book, placed it in the bookcase, and the library would kindly retrieve a selection of volumes from the Lethe House collection, which would be waiting for you when you swung open the secret door. The full collection was located in an underground bunker beneath an estate in Greenwich and was heavily weighted toward the history of the occult, New Haven, and New England. It had an original printing of Heinrich Kramer's *Malleus Maleficarum* and fifty-two different translations of its text, the complete works of Paracelsus, the secret diaries of Aleister Crowley and Francis Bacon, a spell book from the Zoroastrian Fire Temple in Chak Chak, a signed photo of Calvin Hill, and a first edition of William F. Buckley's *God and Man at Yale* along with a spell written on a Yankee Doodle napkin that revealed the book's secret chapters. But good luck finding a copy of *Pride and Prejudice* or a basic history of the Cold War that didn't focus entirely on the faulty magic used in the wording of the Eisenhower Doctrine.

The library was also a little temperamental. If you weren't specific enough in your request or if it couldn't find books on your desired subject, the shelf would just keep shaking and eventually start to give off heat and emit a high, frantic whine, until you snatched the Albemarle Book and murmured a soothing incantation over its pages while gently caressing its spine. The portal magic also had to be maintained through a series of elaborate rites conducted every six years.

"What happens if you guys miss a year?" Alex had asked when Darlington first showed her how the library worked.

"It happened in 1928."

"And?"

"All of the books from the collection crowded into the library at once and the floor collapsed on Chester Vance, Oculus."

"Jesus, that's horrible."

"I don't know," Darlington had said meditatively. "Suffocating beneath a pile of books seems an appropriate way to go for a research assistant."

Alex always approached the library with caution and didn't get near the bookcase when it was shaking. It was too easy to imagine some future Darlington joking about the delicious irony of ignorant Galaxy Stern being fatally clocked in the jaw by rogue knowledge.

She set her bag down on the circular table at the room's center, the wood inlaid with a map of constellations she didn't recognize. It was strange to Alex that the smell of books was always the same. The ancient documents in the climate-controlled stacks and glass cases of Beinecke. The research rooms at Sterling. The changeable library of Lethe House. They all had the same scent as the fluorescent-lit reading rooms full of cheap paperbacks she'd lived in as a kid.

Most of the shelves were empty. There were some heavy old books on New Haven history and a glossy paperback titled *New Haven Mayhem!* that had probably been sold in tourist shops. It took Alex a minute to realize that one shelf was packed with reprints of the same slender volume—*The Life of Lethe: Procedures and Protocols of the Ninth House*, initially hardbound and then stapled together more cheaply when Lethe lost some of its pretensions and began watching its budget.

Alex reached for the most recent edition, the year 1987 stamped on its cover. It had no table of contents, just pages reproduced crookedly on a copier with the occasional note in the margin, and a ticket stub for Squeeze playing the New Haven Coliseum. The Coliseum was long gone, demolished for apartments and a community-college campus that had failed to materialize. Alex had seen a teen Gray in an R.E.M. T-shirt roaming around the parking lot that had taken the Coliseum's place, moving in aimless circles as if still hoping to score tickets.

The entry for *murder* was frustratingly short:

In the event of violent death associated with the activities of the landed societies, a colloquy will be called between the dean, the university president, the active members of Lethe House, the acting Centurion, and the president of the Lethe Trust to decide a course of action. (See "Meeting Protocols.")

Alex flipped to "Meeting Protocols," but all she found was a diagram of the Lethe House dining room, along with a guide to seating according to precedence, a reminder of the need for minutes to be kept by the residing Oculus, and suggested menus. Apparently, light fare was prescribed, alcohol to be served only upon request. There was even a recipe for something called minted slush punch.

"Big help, fellas," Alex muttered. They talked about death like it was a breach of manners. And she had no idea how to pronounce "colloquy" but it was obviously a big-ass meeting she had no intention of calling. Was she really supposed to hit up the president of the university and invite him over for cold meats? Sandow had told her to rest easy. He hadn't said anything about a colloquy. Why? *Because this is a funding year. Because Tara Hutchins is town. Because there's no indication the societies are involved at all. So let it go.*

Instead, Alex returned to the hallway, shut the door to the library, and reopened the Albemarle Book. This time the scent of cigars puffed up from the pages and she heard the clinking of dishes. That was the Lethe memory of murder—not blood or suffering, but men gathered around a table, drinking minted slush punch. She hesitated, trying to think of the right words to guide the library, then she inscribed a new entry: *How to speak to the dead.*

She slid the book into place and the bookcase shuddered violently. This time when she entered the library, the shelves were packed.

It was hard not to feel that Darlington was somehow looking over her shoulder, the eager scholar restraining himself from interfering in her clumsy attempts at research.

When did you first see them? Alex had told Darlington the truth. She simply couldn't remember the first time she'd seen the dead. She'd never even called them that in her head. The blue-lipped girl in a bikini by the pool; the naked man standing behind the chain-link fence at the schoolyard, toying lazily with himself as her class ran suicides; the two boys in bloody sweatshirts seated at a booth at the In-N-Out who never ordered. They were just the Quiet Ones, and if she didn't pay them too much attention, they left her alone.

That had all changed in a Goleta bathroom when she was twelve years old.

By then she'd learned to keep her mouth shut about the things she saw, and she'd been doing pretty well. When it was time to start junior high, she asked her mother to start calling her Alex instead of Galaxy and to fill out her school forms that way. At her old school, everyone had known her as the twitchy kid who talked to herself and flinched at things that weren't there, who didn't have a dad and who didn't look like her mom. One counselor thought she had ADD; another thought she needed a more regular sleep schedule. Then there was the vice principal, who had taken her mother aside and murmured that Alex might just be a little slow. "Some things can't be fixed with therapy or a pill, you know? Some kids are below average, and there's room for them in the classroom too."

But a new school meant a fresh start, a chance to remake herself into someone ordinary.

"You shouldn't be ashamed to be different," her mother had said when Alex had summoned the courage to ask for the name change. "I called you Galaxy for a reason."

Alex didn't disagree. Most of the books she read and the TV shows she watched told her different was okay. Different was great! Except no one was different quite like her. Besides, she thought, as she looked around their tiny apartment laden with dream catchers and silk scarves and paintings of fairies dancing under the moon, it wasn't like she was ever really going to be like everyone else.

"Maybe I can work up to it."

"All right," Mira said. "That is your choice and I respect it." Then she'd yanked her daughter into her arms and blown a raspberry on her forehead. "But you're still my little star."

Alex had squirmed away, laughing, nearly woozy with relief and anticipation, then started thinking about how she could get her mom to buy her new jeans.

Seventh grade started and Alex wondered if her new name was some kind of magic word. It didn't fix everything. She still didn't have the right sneakers or the right scrunchie or bring the right things for lunch. It couldn't make her blond or tall or prune her thick eyebrows, which had to be vigilantly kept from joining forces to create a unified eyebrow front. The white kids still thought she was Mexican and the Mexican kids still thought she was white. But she was doing okay in class. She had people to eat with at lunchtime. She had a friend named Meagan, who invited her over to watch movies and eat bowls of sugary name-brand cereals shimmering with artificial colors.

On the morning of the Goleta trip, when Ms. Rosales told them to buddy up and Meagan seized Alex's hand, Alex felt a gratitude so overwhelming, she thought she might vomit the tiny blueberry muffins the teachers had provided. They spent the morning drinking hot chocolate from foam cups, pressed together on the green vinyl seat of the bus. Both of their moms liked Fleetwood Mac, and when "Go Your Own Way" came on the bus driver's radio, they sang along with it, mostly shouting, giggling and breathless as Cody Morgan pressed his hands to his ears and yelled at them to *SHUT UP.*

It took nearly three hours to get to the butterfly reserve, and Alex savored every minute of the drive. The grove itself was nothing special: a pretty sprawl of eucalyptus trees lined by dusty paths, and a guide who talked about the eating habits and migration patterns of monarchs. Alex glimpsed a slender woman walking through the grove, her arm hanging from her body by the barest scrap of tendon, and quickly looked away, just in time to see a blanket of orange wings gust up from the trees as the monarchs took flight. She and Meagan ate their lunches shoulder to shoulder on picnic tables near the entrance, and before they got back on the buses, everyone went to use the bathrooms. They were low slab buildings with damp concrete floors, and both Meagan and Alex gagged when they entered.

"Forget it," said Meagan. "I can hold it until we get back."

But Alex had to go. She chose the cleanest metal stall, laid toilet paper carefully on the seat, pulled down her jean shorts, and froze. For a long moment, she wasn't sure what she was looking at. The blood was nearly dry and so brown that she had trouble understanding it was blood. She'd gotten her period. Wasn't she supposed to have cramps or something? Meagan had gotten hers over the summer and had lots of thoughts about tampons and pads and the importance of ibuprofen.

The only important thing was that the blood hadn't soaked through to her shorts. But how was she supposed to make it through the bus ride home?

"Meagan!" she shouted. But if anyone else was in the bathroom they'd already cleared out. Alex felt her panic rise. She needed to get to Ms. Rosales before everyone was seated and ready to go. She would know what to do.

Alex wound a bunch of toilet paper around her hand and tucked the makeshift pad into her ruined underwear, then pulled up her shorts and shoved out of the stall.

She yelped. A man was standing there, his face a mottled mess of bruises. She was relieved when she realized he was dead. A dead man in the girls' bathroom was a lot less scary than a living one. She balled her fists and pushed through him. She *hated* going through them. Sometimes she got flashes of memory, but this time she just felt a blast of cold. She hurried to the sinks and quickly washed her hands. Alex could sense he was still there, but she refused to meet his gaze in the mirror.

She felt something brush the small of her back.

In the next second her face was jammed up against the mirror. Something shoved her hips against the porcelain ledge of the sink. She felt cold fingers tugging on the waistband of her shorts.

Alex screamed, she kicked out, struck solid flesh and bone, felt the grip on her shorts loosen. She tried to shove back from the sink, glimpsed her face in the mirror, a blue barrette sliding from her hair, saw the man—the thing—that had hold of her. *You can't do that*, she thought. *You can't touch me.* It wasn't possible. It wasn't allowed. None of the Quiet Ones could touch her.

Then she was facedown on the concrete floor. She felt her hips jerked backward, her panties yanked down, something nudging against her, pushing *into* her. She saw a butterfly lying in a puddle beneath the sink, one wing flapping listlessly as if it were waving to her. She screamed and screamed.

That was how Meagan and Ms. Rosales found her, on the bathroom floor, shorts crumpled around her ankles, panties at her knees, blood smeared over her thighs and a lump of blood-soaked toilet paper wadded between her legs, as she sobbed and thrashed, hips humped up and shuddering. Alone.

Ms. Rosales was beside her, saying, "Alex! Sweetheart!" and the thing that had been trying to get inside her was gone. She never knew why he stopped, why he fled, but she'd clung to Ms. Rosales, warm and alive and smelling of lavender soap.

Ms. Rosales sent Meagan out of the bathroom. She dried Alex's tears and helped her clean up. She had a tampon in her purse and told Alex how to put it in. Alex followed her instructions, still shaking and crying. She didn't want to touch down there. She didn't want to think about him trying to push in. Ms. Rosales sat beside her on the bus, gave her a juice box. Alex listened to the sounds of the other kids laughing and singing, but she was afraid to turn around. She was afraid to look at Meagan.

On that long bus ride back to school, in the long wait at the nurse's office, all she had wanted was her mother, to be wrapped up in her arms and taken home, to be safe in their apartment, bundled in blankets on the couch, watching cartoons. By the time her mother arrived and finished her whispered conversation with the principal and the school counselor and Ms. Rosales, the halls had cleared and the school was empty. As Mira led her out to the parking lot through the echoing quiet, Alex wished she were still small enough to be carried.

When they got home, Alex showered as quickly as possible. She felt too vulnerable, too naked. What if he came back? What if something else came for her? What was to stop him, to stop any of them, from finding her? She'd seen them walk through walls. Where could she ever be safe again?

She left the shower running and slipped into the kitchen to

burrow through their junk drawer. She could hear her mother murmuring on the phone in her bedroom.

"They think she may have been molested," Mira said. She was crying. "That she's acting out now because of it . . . I don't know. I don't know. There was that swim coach at the Y. He always seemed a little off and Alex didn't like going to the pool. Maybe something happened?"

Alex had hated the pool because there was a Quiet kid with the left side of his skull caved in who liked to hang around the rusted podium where the diving board had once been.

She rooted around in the drawer until she found the little red pocketknife. She took it with her into the shower, setting it on the soap dish. She didn't know if it would do any good against one of the Quiet Ones, but it made her feel a little better. She washed quickly, dried off, and changed into pajamas, then went out into the living room to curl up on the couch, her wet hair wrapped in a towel. Her mother must have heard the shower turn off, because she emerged from her bedroom a few moments later.

"Hey, baby," she said softly. Her eyes were red. "Are you hungry?"

Alex kept her eyes on the TV screen. "Can we have real pizza?"

"I can make you pizza here. Don't you want almond cheese?"

Alex said nothing. A few minutes later, she heard her mother on the phone, ordering from Amici's. They ate watching TV, Mira pretending not to watch Alex.

Alex ate until her stomach hurt, then ate some more. It was too late for cartoons, and the shows had switched to the bright sitcom stories of teenage wizards and twins living in lofts, that everyone at school pretended they were too old for. *Who are these people?* Alex wondered. *Who are these happy, frantic, funny people? How are they so unafraid?*

Her mother nibbled on a piece of crust. Then at last she reached for the remote and hit mute.

"Baby," she said. "Galaxy."

"Alex."

"Alex, can you talk to me? Can we talk about what happened?"

Alex felt a hard burble of laughter pushing at her throat, making it ache. If it got free, would she laugh or cry? *Can we talk about what happened?* What was she supposed to say? *A ghost tried to rape me? Maybe he did rape me?* She wasn't sure when it counted, how far inside he had to be. But it didn't matter, because no one would believe her anyway.

Alex clutched the pocketknife in her pajama pocket. Her heart was suddenly racing. What could she say? *Help me. Protect me.* Except no one could. No one could see the things hurting her.

They might not even be real. That was the worst of it. What if she'd imagined it all? She might just be crazy, and then what? She wanted to start screaming and never stop.

"Baby?" Her mother's eyes were filling with tears again. "Whatever happened, it's not your fault. You know that, right? You—"

"I can't go back to school."

"Galaxy—"

"Mama," Alex said, turning to her mother, grabbing her wrist, needing her to listen. "*Mama,* don't make me go."

Mira tried to draw Alex into her arms. "Oh, my little star."

Alex did scream then. She kicked at her mom to keep her away. *"You're a fucking loser,"* she shrieked again and again, until her mother was the one crying and Alex locked herself in her room, sick with shame.

Mira let Alex stay home for the rest of the week. She'd found a therapist to take Alex in for a session, but Alex had nothing to say.

Mira pleaded with Alex, tried to bribe her with junk food and TV hours, then at last said, "You talk to the therapist or you go back to school."

So the following Monday, Alex had gone back to school. No one spoke to her. They barely looked at her, and when she found spaghetti sauce smeared on her gym locker, she knew that Meagan had told.

Alex got the nickname Bloody Mary. She ate lunch by herself.

She was never picked for lab partner or field-trip buddy and had to be foisted on people. In desperation, Alex made the mistake of trying to tell Meagan what had really happened, of trying to explain. She knew it was stupid, even as she'd reeled off the things she'd seen, the things she knew, as she'd watched Meagan shift farther away from her, her eyes going distant, twirling a long curl of glossy brown hair around her forefinger. But the more Meagan drew away, the longer her silence stretched, the more Alex talked, as if somewhere in all of those words was a secret code, a key that would get back the glimmer of what she'd lost.

In the end, all Meagan said was, "Okay, I have to go now." Then she'd done what Alex knew she would and repeated it all.

So when Sarah McKinney begged Alex to meet her at Tres Muchachos to talk to the ghost of her grandmother, Alex had known it was probably a setup, one big joke. But she went anyway, still hoping, and found herself sitting in the food court, trying not to cry.

That's when Mosh had looked over from the counter at Hot Dog on a Stick and taken pity on her. Mosh was a senior with dyed black hair and a thousand silver rings on her corpse-white hands. She knew all about mean girls, and she invited Alex to hang out with her friends in the parking lot of the mall.

Alex hadn't been sure how to act, so she stood with her hands in her pockets until Mosh's boyfriend offered her the bong they were passing around.

"She's twelve years old!" Mosh had said.

"She's stressed, I can see it. And she's cool, right?"

Alex had seen older kids at her school take drags on joints and cigarettes. She and Meagan had pretended to smoke, so she at least knew you weren't supposed to blow it out like a cigarette.

She clamped her lips on the bong and drew in the smoke, tried to hold it, coughed loud and hard.

Mosh and her friends broke into applause.

"See?" said Mosh's boyfriend. "This kid is cool. Pretty too."

"Don't be a creep," said Mosh. "She's just a kid."

"I didn't say I wanted to fuck her. What's your name anyway?"

"Alex."

Mosh's boyfriend held his hand out; he had leather bracelets on both wrists, a smattering of dark hair on his forearms. He didn't look like the boys in her grade.

She shook his hand and he gave her a wink. "Nice to meet you, Alex. I'm Len."

Hours later, crawling into bed, feeling both sleepy and invincible, she realized she hadn't seen a single dead anything since the smoke first hit her lungs.

Alex learned it was a balance. Alcohol worked, oxy, anything that unwound her focus. Valium was the best. It made everything soft and wrapped her in cotton. Speed was a huge mistake, Adderall especially, but Molly was the worst of all. The one time Alex made that mistake, she not only saw Grays, she could *feel* them, their sadness and their hunger oozing toward her from every direction. Nothing like the incident in the grove bathroom had happened again. None of the Quiet Ones had been able to touch her, but she didn't know why. And they were still everywhere.

The beautiful thing was that around her new friends, her high friends, she could freak out and they didn't care. They thought it was hilarious. She was the youngest kid who got to hang with them, their mascot, and they all laughed when she talked to things that weren't there. Mosh called girls like Meagan "the blond bitches" and "Mutant Cutes." She said they were all "sad little fishes drinking their own piss in the mainstream." She said she'd kill for Alex's black hair, and when Alex said the world was full of ghosts trying to get in, Mosh just shook her head and said, "You should write this stuff down, Alex. I swear."

Alex got held back a year. She got suspended. She took cash from her mom's purse, then little things from around the house, then finally her grandfather's silver kiddush cup. Mira cried and shouted and set new house rules. Alex broke them all, felt guilty for making her mom sad, felt furious at feeling guilty. It all made her tired, so eventually she stopped coming home.

When Alex turned fifteen, her mother used the last of her savings to try to send her to a scared-straight rehab for troubled teens. By then Mosh was long gone, off at art school, and she didn't hang with Alex or Len or any of the other kids when she came home for the holidays. Alex had run into her at the beauty supply, still buying black hair dye. Mosh asked how school was, and when Alex just laughed, Mosh had started to offer her an apology.

"What are you talking about?" Alex said. "You saved me."

Mosh had looked so sad and ashamed that Alex practically ran out of the store. She'd gone home that night, wanting to see her mom and sleep in her own bed. But she woke up to a pair of beefy men shining a flashlight in her eyes and dragging her out of her room as her mom looked on and cried, saying, "I'm sorry, baby. I don't know what else to do." Apparently it was a big day for apologies.

They bound her wrists with zip ties, tossed her in the back of an SUV, barefoot in pajamas. They screamed at her about respect and breaking her mother's heart and that she was going to Idaho to learn the right way to live and she had a lesson coming. But Len had shown Alex how to snap zip ties and it only took her two tries to get herself free, quietly open the back door, and vanish between two apartment buildings before the meatheads in the front seat realized she was gone. She walked seven miles to where Len was working at Baskin-Robbins. After his shift, they put Alex's blistered feet in a tub of bubble gum ice cream and got high and had sex on the storeroom floor.

She worked at a TGI Fridays, then a Mexican restaurant that scraped the beans off the customers' plates and reused them every night, then a laser tag place, and a Mail Boxes Etc. One afternoon when she was standing at the shipping desk, a pretty girl with chestnut curls came in with her mother and a stack of manila envelopes. It took Alex a solid minute to realize it was Meagan. Standing there in her maroon apron, watching Meagan chat with the other clerk, Alex had the sudden sensation that she was among the Quiet Ones, that she had died in that bathroom all of those years ago, and that people had been looking straight through her ever since. She'd just been too high to notice. Then Meagan glanced over her shoulder and the skittery, tense look in her eye had been enough for Alex to come back to her body. *You see me,* she thought. *You wish you didn't, but you do.*

The years slid by. Sometimes Alex would put her head up, think about staying sober, think about a book or school or her mom. She'd fall into a fantasy of clean sheets and someone to tuck her in at night. Then she'd catch a glimpse of a biker, the skin scraped from the side of his face, the pulp beneath studded with gravel, or an old woman with her housecoat half open, standing unnoticed in front of the window of an electronics store, and she'd go back under. If she couldn't see them, somehow they couldn't see her.

She'd gone on that way until Hellie—golden Hellie, the girl Len had expected her to hate, maybe hoped she would, the girl she'd loved instead—until that night at Ground Zero when everything had gone so very wrong, until the morning she'd woken up to Dean Sandow in her hospital room.

He'd taken some papers out of his briefcase, an old essay she'd written when she still bothered going to school. She didn't remember writing it, but the title read, *A Day in My Life.* A big red F was scrawled over the top, beside the words *The assignment was not fiction.*

Sandow had perched on a chair by the side of her bed and asked, "The things you describe in this essay, do you still see them?"

The night of the Aurelian ritual, when the Grays had flowed into the protective circle, taken on form, drawn by blood and longing, it had all come flooding back to her. She'd almost lost everything before she'd begun, but somehow she'd held on, and with a little help—like a summer job learning to brew the perfect cup of tea in Professor Belbalm's office, for starters—she thought she could hold on a little longer. She just had to lay Tara Hutchins to rest.

By the time Alex finished in the Lethe library, the sun had set and her brain felt numb. She'd made the initial mistake of not limiting the retrieved books to English, and even after she'd reset the library, there were a baffling number of hard-to-parse texts on the shelf, academic papers and treatises that were simply too dense for her to pull apart. In a way, it made things easier. There were only so many rituals Alex could understand, and that narrowed her options. Then there were the rites that required a particular alignment of the planets or an equinox or a bright day in October, one that demanded the foreskin of a *yonge, hende man of ful corage,* and another that called for the less disturbing but equally hard to procure feathers of one hundred golden ospreys.

"The satisfaction of a job well done" was one of those phrases Alex's mom liked. "Hard work tires the soul. Good works feed the soul!" Alex wasn't sure that what she intended qualified as "good" work at all, but it was better than doing nothing. She copied the text—since her phone wouldn't work in the annex, even to take a photo—then sealed up the library and trudged down the stairs to the parlor.

"Hey, Dawes," Alex said awkwardly. No response. "Pamela."

She was in her usual spot, huddled on the floor by the grand piano, a highlighter shoved between her teeth. Her laptop was set off to one side, and she was surrounded by stacks of books and rows of index cards with what Alex thought might be chapter titles for her dissertation.

"Hey," she tried again, "I need you to go with me on an errand."

Dawes shuffled *From Eleusis to Empoli* under *Mimesis and the Chariot's Wheel.*

"I have work to do," she mumbled around the highlighter.

"I need you to go with me to the morgue."

Now Dawes glanced up, brow furrowed, blinking like someone newly exposed to sunlight. She always looked a little put out when you spoke to her, as if she'd been on the brink of the revelation that would finally help her finish the dissertation she'd been writing for six years.

She removed the highlighter from her mouth, wiping it unceremoniously on her nubbly sweatshirt, which might have been gray or navy, depending on the light. Her red hair was twisted into a bun, and Alex could see the pink halo of a zit forming on her chin.

"Why?" asked Dawes.

"Tara Hutchins."

"Does Dean Sandow want you to go?"

"I need more information," Alex said. "For my report." That was a problem dear Dawes should be able to sympathize with.

"Then you should call Centurion."

"Turner isn't going to talk to me."

Dawes ran a finger over the edge of one of her index cards. *Heretical Hermeneutics: Josephus and the influence of the trickster on the Fool.* Her nails were bitten down to the quick.

"Aren't they charging her boyfriend?" asked Dawes, pulling at her fuzzy sleeve. "What does this have to do with us?"

"Probably nothing. But it was a Thursday night and I think we should make sure. It's what we're here for, right?"

Alex hadn't actually said, *Darlington would do it,* but she might as well have.

Dawes shifted uncomfortably. "But if Detective Turner—"

"Turner can go fuck himself," Alex said. She was tired. She'd missed dinner. She'd wasted hours on Tara Hutchins and she was about to waste a few more.

Dawes worried her lip as if she was legitimately trying to visualize the mechanics. "I don't know."

"Do you have a car?"

"No. Darlington does. Did. Fuck." For a moment, he was there in the room with them, gilded and capable. Dawes rose and unzipped her backpack, removed a set of keys. She stood in the fading light, weighing them in her palm. "I don't know," she said again.

She might have been referring to a hundred different things. *I don't know if this is a good idea. I don't know if you can be trusted. I don't know how to finish my dissertation. I don't know if you robbed me of our golden, destined for glory, perfect boy.*

"How are we going to get in?" Dawes asked.

"I'll get us in."

"And then what?"

Alex handed her the sheet of notes she'd transcribed in the library. "We have all this stuff, right?"

Dawes scanned the page. Her surprise was obvious when she said, "This isn't bad."

Don't apologize. Just do the work.

Dawes gnawed on her lower lip. Her mouth was as colorless as the rest of her. Maybe her thesis was draining the life right out of her. "Couldn't we call a car instead?"

"We may need to leave in a hurry."

Dawes sighed and reached for her parka. "I'm driving."

8

Winter

Dawes had parked Darlington's car a little ways up the block. It was an old wine-colored Mercedes, maybe from the eighties—Alex had never asked. The seats were upholstered in caramel leather, worn in some places, the stitching a bit threadbare. Darlington had always kept the car clean, but now it was immaculate. Dawes's hand no doubt.

As if asking for permission, Dawes paused before she turned the key in the ignition. Then the car rumbled to life and they were moving away from campus and out onto the highway.

They rode in silence. The Office of the Chief Medical Examiner was actually in Farmington, almost forty miles outside New Haven. *The morgue,* thought Alex. *I'm going to the morgue. In a Mercedes.* Alex thought about turning on the radio—the old kind with a red line that glided through the stations like a finger seeking the right spot on a page. Then she thought of Darlington's voice floating out of the speakers—*Get out of my car, Stern*—and decided she was fine with the silence.

It took them the better part of the hour to find their way to the OCME. Alex wasn't sure what she'd expected, but when they got there she was grateful for the bright lights, the big lot, the office-park feel of it all.

"Now what?" said Dawes.

Alex took the plastic baggie and the tin they'd prepared from her satchel and wedged them into the back pockets of her jeans. She opened her door, shrugged off her coat and scarf, and tossed them onto the passenger seat.

"What are you doing?" asked Dawes.

"I don't want to look like a student. Give me your sweat-shirt." Alex's peacoat was thin wool with a polyester lining, but it screamed *college.* That was exactly why she'd bought it.

Dawes seemed like she wanted to object, but she unzipped her parka, shucked off her sweatshirt, and tossed it over to Alex, shivering in her T-shirt. "I'm not sure this is a good idea."

"Of course it isn't. Let's go."

Through the glass doors, Alex saw that the waiting room had a few people in it, all trying to get their business done before closing. A woman sat at a desk near the back of the room. She had fluffy brown hair that showed a red rinse beneath the office lights.

Alex sent a quick text to Turner: *We need to talk.* Then she told Dawes, "Wait five minutes and then come in, sit down, pretend you're waiting for someone. If that woman leaves her desk, text me right away, okay?"

"What are you going to do?"

"Talk to her."

Alex wished she hadn't wasted her coin of compulsion on the coroner. She had only one left and she couldn't afford to use it to get past the front desk, not if the plan went the way she hoped.

She tucked her hair behind her ears and bustled into the waiting room, rubbing her arms. A poster had been hung behind the desk: SYMPATHY AND RESPECT. A small sign read, *My name is Moira Adams and I'm glad to help.* Glad, not happy. You weren't supposed to be happy in a building full of dead people.

Moira looked up and smiled. She had some hard-living lines around her eyes and a cross around her neck.

"Hi," Alex said. She made a show of taking a deep, shuddering breath. "Um, a detective said I could come here to see my cousin."

"Okay, hon. Of course. What's your cousin's name?"

"Tara Anne Hutchins." The middle name had been easy enough to come by online. The woman's face grew wary. Tara Hutchins had been in the news. She was a homicide victim, the kind that could draw crazies. "Detective Turner sent me here."

Moira's expression was still cautious. He was the lead detective on the case and his name had most likely been in the media.

"You can have a seat while I try to reach him," said Moira.

Alex held up her phone. "He gave me his information." She sent another quick text: *Pick up NOW, Turner.* Then she slid to the call screen and dialed on speaker. "Here," she said, holding out her cell.

Moira sputtered, "I can't . . ." But the faint sound of the phone ringing and Alex's expectant expression did the trick. Moira pressed her lips together and took the cell from Alex.

The call went to Turner's voicemail, just as Alex had known it would. Detective Abel Turner would pick up when he damn well felt like it, not when some pissy undergrad told him to, especially not when she demanded it.

Alex hoped Moira would just hang up, but instead she cleared her throat and said, "Detective Turner, this is Moira Adams, public outreach at OCME. If you could give us a call back . . ." She gave the number. All Alex could hope was that Turner wouldn't check a voicemail from her number anytime too soon. Maybe he'd be really petty and delete it.

"Tara was a good girl, y'know?" she said when Moira handed her phone back. "She didn't deserve any of this."

Moira made sympathetic sounds. "I'm so sorry for your loss." Like she was reading from a script.

"I just need to pray over her, say my goodbyes."

Moira's fingers touched her cross. "Of course."

"She had a lot of problems, but who doesn't? We got her going to church every weekend. You can bet that boyfriend of hers didn't like it." At this Moira gave a little huff of agreement. "You think Detective Turner'll call back soon?"

"As soon as he can. He may be tied up."

"But you guys close in an hour, right?"

"To the public, yes. But you can come back on Mon—"

"I can't, though." Alex's eyes scanned the photos taped below the ledge of Moira's desk and spotted a woman in Winnie-the-Pooh scrubs. "I'm in nursing school."

"At Albertus Magnus?"

"Yeah!"

"My niece is there. Alison Adams?"

"Real pretty girl with red hair?"

"That's her," Moira said with a smile.

"I can't miss class. They're so tough. I don't think I've ever been this tired."

"I know," Moira said ruefully. "They're running Allie ragged."

"I just . . . I need to be able to tell my mama I said goodbye to her. Tara's mom and dad were . . . They all weren't close." Alex was flat out guessing now, but she suspected Moira Adams had her own story about girls like Tara Hutchins. "If I could just see her face, say goodbye."

Moira hesitated, then reached forward and gave her hand a squeeze. "I can have someone take you down to see her. Just have your ID ready and . . . It can be hard, but prayer helps."

"It always does," said Alex fervently.

Moira pressed a button, and a few minutes later an exhausted-looking coroner in blue scrubs appeared and waved Alex through.

It was cold on the other side of the double doors, the floors tiled in heathered gray, the walls a melted cream. "Sign in here," he said, gesturing to the clipboard on the wall. "I'll need photo ID. Cell phones, cameras, and all recording devices in the bin. You can retrieve them when you return."

"Sure," said Alex. Then she held out her hand, gold glinting beneath the fluorescents. "I think you dropped this."

The room was larger than she'd expected and ice-cold. It was also unexpectedly noisy—the dripping of a faucet, the hum of the freezers, the rush of the air conditioner—though it was silent in another way. This was the last place Grays would come. To hell with Belbalm. She should intern at the morgue this summer.

The tables were metal, as were the basins and the hoses coiled above them, and the drawers—flat squares slotted into two of the walls like filing cabinets. Had Hellie been cut up in a place like this? It wasn't like the cause of death had been a mystery.

Alex wished she had her coat. Or Dawes's parka. Or a shot of vodka.

She needed to work fast. The compulsion would give her about thirty minutes to get her work done and get out. But it didn't take her long to find Tara, and though the drawer was heavier than she'd expected, it slid out smoothly.

There was something worse about seeing her like this a second time, as if they knew each other. Looking at Tara now, Alex could see it had only been the blond hair that made her think of Hellie. Hellie had been strong. Her body remembered the soccer and softball she'd played in high school, and she could surf and skateboard like a girl out of *Seventeen* magazine. This girl was built like Alex, ropy, but weak.

Tara's knees looked brownish gray. There was stubble near her bikini area, red razor bumps like a rash. She had a tattoo of a parrot at her hip and below it was written *Key West* in looping scrawl. Her right arm had an ugly realistic portrait of a young girl on it. A daughter? A niece? Her own face as a child? There was a pirate flag and a ship on cresting waves, a Bettie Page zombie girl in heels and black lingerie. The cameo on Tara's inner arm looked newer, the ink fresh and dark, though the text was nearly illegible in that tired

Gothic font: *Rather die than doubt.* Song lyrics, but Alex couldn't remember what they were from.

She wondered if her own tattoos would reappear if she died or if the art would live inside the address moths forever.

Enough stalling. Alex took out her notes. The first part of the ritual was easy, a chant. *Sanguis saltido*—but you couldn't just say the words; you had to sing them. It felt utterly obscene to do in that empty, echoing room, but she made herself sing the chant: *Sanguis saltido! Salire! Saltare!* No tune was specified, only *allegro.* It was on her second round through that she realized she was singing the words to the tune of the Twizzlers jingle. *So chewy. So fruity. So happy and oh so juicy.* But if that's what it took to make the blood dance . . . She knew it was working when Tara's lips began to pink.

Now things were going to get worse. The blood chant was only intended to start Tara's circulation and loosen rigor so that Alex could get her mouth open. Alex took hold of Tara's chin, trying to ignore the newly warm, pliant feel of her skin, and wiggled the girl's jaw open.

She took the scarab from the plastic bag in her back pocket and placed it gently on Tara's tongue. Then she took the tin from her other pocket and began to trace waxy patterns over Tara's body with the balm inside, trying to think about anything but the dead skin beneath her fingertips. Feet, shins, thighs, stomach, breasts, collarbone, down Tara's arms to her wrists and middle fingers. Finally, starting at the navel, she drew a line bisecting Tara's torso up to her throat, her chin, and to the crown of her head.

Alex realized she'd forgotten to bring a lighter. She needed fire. There was a desk next to the door, beneath a messy whiteboard. The big drawers were locked, but the narrow top drawer slid open. A pink plastic lighter lay beside a pack of Marlboros.

Alex took the lighter and held the flame just above the places she'd applied the balm, retracing her path up Tara's body. As she did, a faint haze appeared over the skin, like heat rising off blacktop, the air seeming to wave and shimmer. The effect was denser in certain spots, so thick it blurred and vibrated as if seen through the spinning spokes of a wheel.

Alex put the lighter back in the drawer. She reached out to the blur above Tara's elbow, ran her hand through the shimmer. In a rush, she was racing down the street on a bicycle. In front of her, a car door flew open in her path. She hit the brakes, failed to stop, struck the door at an angle, clipping her arm. Pain shot through her. Alex hissed and drew back her hand, cradling her arm as if the broken bone had been hers and not Tara's.

The haze above Tara was a map of all the harm done to her body—flickers over her tattoos and where her ears had been pierced, dense clumping above her broken arm, a tiny dim spiral over a pockmark left by a BB on her cheek, the murky darkness that hung suspended over the wounds in her chest.

In Lethe's books, Alex had found no way to make Tara talk or any way to reach her on the other side of the Veil—at least, nothing that was achievable without the help of one of the societies. Even if Alex could have managed it, many of the rituals she'd found made it clear that speaking to the newly dead usually risked raising them, and that was always a dangerous proposition. No one could be brought back from beyond the Veil permanently, and hauling a reluctant soul back into its body could be wildly unpredictable. Book and Snake specialized in necromancy and had created numerous safeguards for their rituals, but even they sometimes lost control once a Gray found its way to a body. In the late seventies, they'd tried to summon the spirit of Jennie Cramer, the legendary Belle of New Haven, into the body of a teenage girl from Camden, who had frozen to death when she'd passed out drunk in her car during a blizzard. Instead, it was the Camden girl who had returned, shivering with cold and possessed of the ferocious strength of the newly dead.

She'd broken through the Book and Snake gates and walked to Yorkside Pizza, where she'd eaten two pies and then lain down in one of the ovens in an attempt to get warm. A Lethe delegate had been present and was able to quickly quarantine the area and, through a serious of compulsions, convince the customers the girl was part of a performance-art piece. The owner was Greek and less easily swayed. He had long carried a *gouri* given to him by his mother—specifically the blue "evil eye" or *mati,* which stymied any attempts at compulsion. Cash proved far more effective. At the owner's request, Lethe also stepped in to make sure Yorkside retained its lease when the majority of other businesses were forced out of Yale's premiere shopping district by rising rents designed to bring in upscale retailers. The local businesses along Elm and Broadway had vanished, making way for prestige brands and chain stores, but Yorkside Pizza remained.

So since Tara couldn't talk, her body would have to. Alex had discovered a ritual to reveal harm, something simpler, lighter, used for diagnosis or for when a patient or witness was unable to speak. It had been invented by Girolamo Fracastoro to discover who had poisoned an Italian countess after she'd keeled over, foaming at the mouth, at her own wedding feast.

Alex didn't want to put her hand into the haze above the gruesome wounds on Tara's chest. But that was what she'd come here to do. She took a breath and thrust her fingers forward.

She was on the ground, a boy's face above her—Lance. Sometimes she loved him, but lately things had been . . . The thought left her. She felt herself open her mouth, tasted something acrid on her tongue. Lance was smiling. They were on their way . . . where? She felt only excitement, anticipation, the world beginning to blur.

"I'm sorry," Lance said.

She was on her back, staring up at the sky. The streetlights seemed far away; everything was moving, and the cathedral beside her melted into a building that blotted out the few stars. It was quiet but she could hear something, like a boot squelching in mud. *Thunk squelch, thunk squelch.* She saw a body looming above her, saw the knife, understood the sound was her own blood and bone breaking open as the blade sawed away at her. Why didn't she feel it? What was real and what wasn't?

"Close your eyes," said an unfamiliar voice. She did and was gone.

Alex stumbled backward, clutching her chest. She could still hear that horrible squelching sound, feel the warm wet spreading over her chest. But no pain? How had there been no pain? Had she been high? High enough not to feel being stabbed? Lance had drugged her first. He'd told her he was sorry. He must have been high too.

So there was her answer. Tara and Lance had clearly been messing with something other than weed. No doubt by now Turner had been through their apartment, found whatever weird shit they were using and selling. Alex had no way of knowing what Lance had been thinking that night, but if he'd been taking some kind of hallucinogen it could be anything.

Alex looked down at Tara's body. She'd been frightened in those last moments, but she hadn't been hurting. That had to count for something.

Lance would go to prison. There would be evidence. That amount of blood . . . Well, you couldn't hide it. Alex knew.

The map still glowed above Tara. Little injuries. Big ones. What would Alex's map show? She'd never broken a bone, had surgery. But the worst damage didn't leave a mark. When Hellie died, it was as if someone had cut into Alex's chest, cracked her open like balsa wood. What if it really had been like that and she'd had to walk down the street bleeding, trying to hold her ribs together, her heart and her lungs and every part of her open to the world? Instead, the thing that had broken her had left no mark, no scar for her to point to and say, *This is where I ended.*

No doubt that was true for Tara too. There was more pain locked inside her that no glowing map would reveal. But though her wounds were grotesque, there were no organs taken, no blood marks or indications of magical harm. Tara had died because she'd been as stupid as Alex and no one had come to rescue her in time. She hadn't found Jesus or yoga, and no one had offered her a scholarship to Yale.

It was time to leave. She had her answers. This should be enough to appease Hellie's memory and Darlington's judgment too. But something was still tugging at her, that sense of familiarity she'd felt at the crime scene that had nothing to do with Tara's blond hair or the sad, parallel tracks of their lives.

"Should we go?" she asked the coroner standing in the corner in his scrubs, looking vaguely at nothing.

"Whatever you like," he said.

Alex closed the drawer.

"I think I'd like to sleep for eighteen hours," Alex said on a sigh. "Walk me out and tell Moira everything went fine."

She opened the door and strolled straight into Detective Abel Turner.

He seized her arm and drove her backward into the room, slamming the door behind him. "What the living fuck do you think you're doing?"

"Hey!" Alex said cheerfully. "You made it."

The coroner hovered behind him. "Are we going?" he asked.

"Stay there a minute," said Alex. "Turner, you're gonna want to let go of me."

"You don't tell me what I want. And what the hell is wrong with him?"

"He's having a good night," said Alex, her heart pounding in her chest. Abel Turner did not lose his cool. He was always smiling, always calm. But something in Alex liked him better this way.

"Did you lay hands on that girl?" he said, fingers digging into her skin. "Her body is evidence and you are tampering with it. That's a crime."

Alex thought about kneeing Turner in the nuts, but that wasn't what you did with a cop, so she went limp. Completely limp. It was a strategy she'd learned to use with Len.

"What the hell?" He tried to hold her up as she slumped against him, then released her. "What is wrong with you?" He wiped his hand on his arm as if her weakness were catching.

"Plenty," Alex said. She managed to right herself before she actually fell, making sure to stay out of his reach. "What kind of stuff were Tara and Lance getting into?"

"I beg your pardon?"

She thought of Lance's face floating above her. *I'm sorry.* What had they been using that final night together? "What were they dealing? Acid? Molly? I know it wasn't just pot."

Turner's eyes narrowed, his old, smooth demeanor slipping back into place. "Like everything else related to this case, that is none of your business."

"Were they dealing to students? To the societies?"

"They had a long roster."

"Who?"

Turner shook his head. "Let's go. *Now.*"

He reached for her arm but she sidestepped him. "You can stay here," Alex told the coroner. "The handsome Detective Turner will see me out."

"What did you do to him?" Turner muttered as they stepped into the hall.

"Freaky shit."

"This isn't a joke, Ms. Stern."

As he hustled her down the hall, Alex said, "I'm not doing this for fun either, you get that? I don't like being Dante. You don't like being Centurion, but these are our jobs and you're screwing it up for both of us."

Turner looked slightly put out by that. Of course, it wasn't really true. Sandow had told her to stand down. *Rest easy.*

They stepped into the waiting room. Dawes was nowhere to be

seen. "I told your friend to wait in the car," said Turner. "At least she has the sense to know when she fucks up."

And not a single warning. Dawes was a crap lookout.

Moira Adams smiled from the desk. "You get your moment, hon?"

Alex nodded. "I did. Thank you."

"I'll have your family in my prayers. Good night, Detective Turner."

"You do some freaky shit to her too?" Turner asked as they stepped into the cold.

Alex rubbed her arms miserably. She wanted her coat. "Didn't have to."

"I told Sandow I'd keep him up-to-date. If I thought any of the young psychopaths under your care were connected, I would be pursuing it."

Alex believed that. "There could be things you're not seeing."

"There's nothing to see. Her boyfriend was arrested near the scene. Their neighbors heard some ugly arguments the last few weeks. There's blood evidence linking him to the crime. He had powerful hallucinogens in his system—"

"What exactly?"

"We're not sure yet."

Alex had stayed away from any kind of hallucinogen after she realized they just made the Grays more terrifying, but she'd held plenty of hands during good and bad trips and she had yet to meet the mushroom that could make you feel like you weren't being stabbed to death.

"Do you want him to get away with it?" Turner said.

"What?" The question startled her.

"You tampered with a corpse. Tara's body is evidence. If you mess around with this case enough, it could mean Lance Gressang doesn't go away for this. Do you want that?"

"No," Alex said. "He doesn't get away with it."

Turner nodded. "Good." They stood in the cold. Alex could see the old Mercedes idling in the lot, one of the only remaining cars. Dawes's face was a dim smudge behind the windshield. She raised her hand in what Alex realized was a limp wave. *Thanks, Pammie.* It was long past time to let this go. Why couldn't she?

She tried one last play. "Just give me a name. Lethe will find out eventually. If the societies are messing around with illegal substances, we should know." And then we can move on to kidnapping, insider trading, and—did cutting someone open to read their innards fall under assault? They'd need a whole new section of the penal code to cover what the societies dabbled in. "We can investigate without stepping on your murder case."

Turner sighed, his breath pluming white in the cold. "There was only one society name in her contacts. Tripp Helmuth. We're in the process of clearing him—"

"I saw him last night. He's a Bonesman. He was working the door at a prognostication."

"That's what he said. Was he there the whole night?"

"I don't know," she admitted. Tripp had been banished to the hallway to stand guard. It was true that once a ritual started, people rarely went in or out, only when someone got faint or sick or if something had to be fetched for the Haruspex. Alex thought she remembered the door opening and closing a few times, but she couldn't be certain. She'd been worrying about the chalk circle and trying not to vomit. But it was hard to believe Tripp could have skipped out on the ritual, gotten all the way to Payne Whitney, murdered Tara, and gotten back on duty without anyone knowing. Besides, what homicidal beef could he have with Tara? Tripp was rich enough to buy himself out of any kind of trouble Tara or her boyfriend might have tried to make for him, and it wasn't Tripp's face Alex had seen hovering above Tara with a knife. It was Lance's.

"Do not talk to him," Turner said. "I'll send you and the dean the info once we lock in his alibi. You stay away from my case."

"And away from your career?"

"That's right. The next time I find you anywhere you're not supposed to be, I'll arrest you on the spot."

Alex couldn't help the dark bubble of laughter that burst from her.

"You're not going to arrest me, *Detective* Turner. The last place you want me is in a police station, making noise. I'm messy and Lethe is messy and all you want is to get through this without our mess getting on those expensive shoes."

Turner gave her a long, steady look. "I don't know how you ended up here, Ms. Stern, but I know the difference between quality goods and what I find on the bottom of my shoe, and you are most definitely not quality."

"Thanks for the talk, Turner." Alex leaned in, knowing the stink of the uncanny was radiating off her in heavy waves. She gave him her sweetest, warmest smile. "And don't grab me like that again. I may be shit, but I'm the kind that sticks."

9

Winter

Alex parted with Dawes near the divinity school, at a sad horseshoe-shaped apartment building in the grad school ghetto. Dawes hadn't wanted to leave the car in Alex's care, but she had papers to grade that were already late, so Alex said she would return the Mercedes to Darlington's home. She could tell Dawes wanted to refuse, papers be damned.

"Be careful and don't . . . You shouldn't . . ." But Dawes just trailed off, and Alex had the startling realization that Dawes had to defer to her in this situation. Dante served Virgil, but Oculus served them both. And they all served Lethe. Dawes nodded, kept nodding, nodded all the way out of the car and up the walkway to her apartment, as if she was affirming every step.

Darlington's house was out in Westville, just a few miles from campus. This was the Connecticut Alex had dreamed of—farmhouses without farms, sturdy red-brick colonials with black doors and tidy white trim, a neighborhood full of wood-burning fireplaces, gently tended lawns, windows glowing golden in the night like passageways to a better life, kitchens where something good bubbled on the stove, breakfast tables scattered with crayons. No one drew their curtains; light and heat and good fortune spilled out into the dark as if these foolish people didn't know what such bounty might attract, as if they'd left these shining doorways open for any hungry girl to walk through.

Alex hadn't driven much since she'd left Los Angeles and it felt good to be back in a car, even one she was terrified of leaving a scratch on. Despite the map on her phone, she missed the turn into Darlington's driveway and had to double back twice before she spotted the thick stone columns that marked the entry to Black Elm. The lamps that lined the drive were lit, bright halos that made the bare-branched trees look soft and friendly like a winter postcard. The bulky shape of the house came into view, and Alex slammed her foot down on the brakes.

A light glowed in the kitchen window, bright as a beacon, another up in the high tower—Darlington's bedroom. She remembered his body curled against hers, the cloudy panes of the narrow window, the sea of black branches below, the dark woods separating Black Elm from the world outside.

Hurriedly, Alex turned off the headlights and the engine. If someone was here, if *something* was here, she didn't want to scare it away.

Her boots on the gravel drive sounded impossibly loud but she wasn't sneaking—no, she wasn't sneaking; she was just walking up to the kitchen door. She had the keys in her hand. She was welcome here.

It could be his mom or dad, she told herself. She didn't know much about Darlington's family, but he had to have one. *Another relative. Someone else Sandow had hired to look after the place when Dawes was busy.*

All of those things were more likely, but . . . *He's here,* her heart insisted, pounding so hard in her chest she had to pause at the door, make herself breathe more steadily. *He's here.* The thought pulled her along like a child who had hold of her sleeve.

She peered in through the window, safe in the dark. The kitchen was all warm wood and patterned blue tiles—*the tiles are Delft*—a big brick hearth and copper pots gleaming from their hooks. Mail was stacked on the kitchen island, as if someone had been in the middle of sorting it. *He's here.*

Alex thought of knocking, fumbled with the keys instead. The second one turned in the lock. She entered, gently shut the door behind her. The merry light of the kitchen was warm, welcoming, reflected back in flat copper pans, caught in the creamy green enamel of the stove that someone had installed in the fifties.

"Hello?" she said, her voice a breath.

The sound of the keys dropping onto the counter made an unexpectedly loud jangle. Alex stood guiltily in the middle of the kitchen, waiting for someone to chastise her, maybe even the house. But this was not the mansion on Orange with its hopeful creaks and disapproving sighs. Darlington had been the life of this place, and without him the house felt huge and empty, a shipwreck hull.

Ever since that night at Rosenfeld Hall, Alex would catch herself hoping that maybe this was all a test, one given to every Lethe House apprentice, and that Dawes and Sandow and Turner were all in on it. Darlington was in his third-floor bedroom hiding out right now. He'd heard the car in the driveway. He'd raced up the stairs and was huddling there, in the dark, waiting for her to leave. The murder could be part of it too. There was no dead girl. Tara Hutchins would come waltzing down the stairs herself when this was all over. They just had to be sure Alex could handle something serious on her own.

It was absurd. Even so, that voice persisted: *He's here.*

Sandow had said he might still be alive, that they could bring him back. He'd said all they needed was a new moon, the right magic, and everything would be the way it had been before. But maybe Darlington had found his own way back. He could do anything. He could do this.

She drifted farther into the house. The lights from the driveway cast a yellowy dimness over the rooms—the butler's pantry, with its white cupboards full of dishes and glasses; the big walk-in freezer, with its metal door so like the one at the morgue; the formal dining room, with its mirror-shine table like a dark lake in a silent glade; and then the vast living room, with its big black window looking out over the dim shapes of the garden, the humps of hedges and skeletal trees. There was another, smaller room off the main living room, full of big couches, a TV, gaming consoles. Len would have wet himself over the size of the screen. It was very much a room he would have loved, maybe the only thing he and Darlington had in common. *Well, not the only thing.*

Most of the rooms on the second floor were closed up. "This was where I ran out of money," he'd told her, his arm slung across her shoulders, as she'd tried to move him along. The house was like a body that had cut off circulation to all but the most vital parts of itself in order to survive. An old ballroom had been turned into a kind of makeshift gym. A speed bag hung from the ceiling on a rack. Big metal weights, medicine balls, and fencing foils were stacked on the wall, and heavy machines loomed against the windows like bulky insects.

She followed the stairs to the top floor and wound her way down the hall. The door to Darlington's room was open.

He's here. Again, the certainty came at her, but worse this time. He'd left the light on for her. He wanted her to find him. He would be sitting in his bed, long legs crossed, bent over a book, dark hair falling over his forehead. He would look up, cross his arms. *It's about time.*

She wanted to run toward that square of light, but she forced herself to take measured steps, a bride approaching an altar, her certainty draining away, the refrain of *He's here* shifting from one step to the next until she realized she was praying: *Be here, be here, be here.*

The room was empty. It was small compared to the lodgings at Il Bastone, a strange round room that had clearly never been meant to be a bedroom and somehow reminded her of a monk's chamber. It looked exactly as she had last seen it: the desk pushed against one curved wall, a yellowing newspaper clipping of an old roller coaster taped above it, as if it had been forgotten there; a mini-fridge—because of course Darlington wouldn't want to stop reading or working to go downstairs for sustenance; a high-backed chair placed by the window for reading. There were no book-shelves, only stacks and stacks of books piled at varying heights, as if he had been in the process of walling himself in with colored bricks. The desk lamp cast a circle of light over an open book: *Meditations on the Tarot: A Journey into Christian Hermeticism.*

Dawes. Dawes had come to see to the house, to sort the mail, to take the car out. Dawes had come to this room to study. To be closer to him. Maybe to wait for him. She'd been called away suddenly, left the lights on, assumed she'd be back that evening to take care of it. But Alex had been the one to return the car. It was that simple.

Darlington was not in Spain. He was not home. He was never coming home. And it was all Alex's fault.

A white shape cut through the dark from the corner of her vision. She leapt backward, knocking over a pile of books, and swore. But it was just Cosmo, Darlington's cat.

He prowled the edge of the desk, nudging up against the warmth of the desk lamp. Alex always thought of him as Bowie Cat because of his marked-up eye and streaky white fur that looked like one of the wigs Bowie had worn in *Labyrinth*. He was stupid affectionate—all you had to do was hold your hand out and he would nuzzle your knuckles.

Alex sat down on the edge of Darlington's narrow bed. It was neatly made, probably by Dawes. Had she sat here too? Slept here?

Alex remembered Darlington's delicate feet, his scream as he'd vanished. She held her hand down, beckoning to the cat. "Hey, Cosmo."

He stared at her with his mismatched eyes, the pupil of the left like an inkblot.

"Come on, Cosmo. I didn't mean for it to happen. Not really."

Cosmo padded across the room. As soon as his small sleek head touched Alex's fingers, she began to cry.

Alex slept in Darlington's bed and dreamed that he was curled behind her on the narrow mattress.

He pulled her close, his fingers digging into her abdomen, and she could feel claws at their tips. He whispered in her ear, "I will serve you 'til the end of days."

"And love me," she said with a laugh, bold in the dream, unafraid.

But all he said was, "It is not the same."

Alex woke with a start, flopped over, gazed at the sharp pitch of the roof, the trees beyond the window striping the ceiling in shadow and hard winter sun. She'd been scared to try fiddling with the thermostat, so she'd bundled herself in three of Darlington's sweaters and an ugly brown hat she'd found on top of his dresser but that she'd never seen him wear. She remade the bed, then headed downstairs to fill Cosmo's water dish and eat some fancy nuts-and-twigs dry cereal from a box in the pantry.

Alex took her laptop from her bag and went to the dusty sunroom that ran the length of the first floor. She gazed out at the backyard. The slope of the hill led to a hedge maze overgrown with brambles, and she could see some kind of statue or fountain at its center. She wasn't sure where the grounds left off, and she wondered just how much of this particular hill the Arlington family owned.

It took her nearly two hours to write up her report on the Tara Hutchins murder. Cause of death. Time of death. The behavior of the Grays at the Skull and Bones prognostication. She'd hesitated over that last, but Lethe had brought her here for what she could see and there was no reason for her to lie about it. She mentioned the information she'd gleaned from the coroner and from Turner in his capacity as Centurion, noting Tripp's name coming up and also Turner's belief that the Bonesman was not involved. She hoped Turner wouldn't mention her visit to the morgue.

At the end of the incident report, there was a section titled "Findings." Alex thought for a long time, her hand idly stroking Cosmo's fur as he purred beside her on the old wicker love seat. In the end, she said nothing about the strange feeling she'd had at the crime scene or that she suspected Tara and Lance were probably dealing to other members of the other societies. *Centurion will update Dante on his findings, but at this time all evidence suggests this was a crime committed by Tara's boyfriend while under the influence of powerful hallucinogenics and that there is no connection to Lethe or the Houses of the Veil.* She read through twice more for punctuation and to try to make her answers sound as Darlingtonish as possible, then she sent the report to Sandow with Dawes cc'd.

Cosmo meowed plaintively as Alex slipped out the kitchen door, but it felt good to leave the house behind her, breathe the icy air. The sky was bright blue, scrubbed clean of clouds, and the gravel of the drive glittered. She put the Mercedes in the garage, then walked to the end of the driveway and called a car. She could return the keys to Dawes later.

If her roommates asked where she had been, she would just say she'd spent the night at Darlington's. Family emergency. The excuse had long since worn thin, but there would be fewer late nights and unexplained absences from now on. She'd done right by Tara. Lance would be punished and Alex's conscience was off the hook, for this at least. Tonight she'd nurse a beer while her roommate got shitfaced on peppermint schnapps via ice luge at Omega Meltdown, and tomorrow she'd spend all day catching up on her reading.

She had the driver drop her in front of the fancy mini-mart on Elm. It wasn't until she was already inside the store that she realized she was still wearing Darlington's hat. She slid it off her head, then jammed it back on. It was cold. She didn't need to be sentimental about a hat.

Alex filled her basket with Chex Mix, Twizzlers, sour gummy worms. She shouldn't be spending so much money, but she craved the comfort of junk food. She reached into the drinks case, rooting back for a chocolate milk with a better expiration date, and felt something brush her hand—fingertips caressing her knuckles.

Alex yanked her arm back, cradling her hand to her chest as if it had been burned, and slammed the case door closed with a rattle, heart pounding. She stepped back from the case, waiting for something to come crashing through, but nothing happened. She looked around, embarrassed.

A guy sporting little round glasses and a navy Yale sweatshirt glanced at her. She bent to pick up her shopping basket, using the chance to shut her eyes and take a deep breath. Imagination. Sleep deprivation. Just general jumpiness. Hell, maybe even a rat. But she'd pop in at the Hutch. It was right across the street. She could slip behind the wards to gather her thoughts in a Gray-less environment.

She grabbed her basket and stood. The guy with the little glasses had come up next to her and was standing far too close. She couldn't see his eyes, just the light reflecting off the lenses. He smiled and something moved at the corner of his mouth. Alex realized it was the waving black feeler of an insect. A beetle crawled from the pocket of his cheek as if he'd been keeping it there like chewing tobacco. It dropped from his lips. Alex leapt back, stifling a scream.

Too slow. The thing in the blue sweatshirt seized the back of her neck and slammed her head into the door of the refrigerator case. The glass shattered. Alex felt the shards slice into her skin, warm blood trickling down her cheeks. He yanked her back, threw her to the ground. *You can't touch me. It isn't allowed.* Still, after all these years and all these horrors, that stupid, childish response.

She staggered away. The woman behind the register was shouting, her husband emerging from the back room with wide eyes. The man in glasses advanced. Not a man. A Gray. But what had drawn him and helped him cross over? And why didn't he seem like any Gray she'd ever seen? His skin no longer looked human. It had a sheer, glasslike quality through which she could see his veins and the shadows of his bones. He stank of the Veil.

Alex dug in her pockets, but she hadn't replenished her supplies of graveyard dirt. She almost always had some on her—just in case.

"Take courage!" she cried. *"No one is immortal!"* The death words she'd repeated to herself every day since Darlington had taught them to her.

But the thing showed no sign of distress or distraction.

The shop owners were yelling; one of them had a phone in his hand. *Yes, call the police.* But they were screaming at her, not at him. They couldn't see him. All they saw was a girl smashing their drinks case and tearing up their store.

Alex launched to her feet. She had to get to the Hutch. She slammed through the door and out onto the sidewalk.

"Hey!" cried a girl with a green coat as Alex smacked into her. The store owner followed, bellowing for someone to stop her.

Alex glanced back. The thing with glasses glided around the owner and then seemed to *leap* over the crowd. His hand latched on to Alex's throat. She stumbled off the lip of the curb, into the street. Horns blared. She heard the screech of tires. She couldn't breathe.

She saw Jonas Reed on the corner, staring. He was in her English section. She remembered Meagan's startled face, the surprise giving way to disgust. She could hear Ms. Rosales gasp, *Alex! Sweetheart!* She was going to get choked out in the middle of the street and no one could see it, no one could stop it.

"Take courage," she tried to say, but only a rasp emerged. Alex looked around desperately, eyes watering, face suffused with blood. *They can't get to you now,* Darlington had promised. She'd known it wasn't true, but she'd let herself believe that she could be protected, because it had made everything bearable.

Her hands scrabbled against the thing's skin; it was hard and slippery as glass. She saw something burble up from the clear flesh of its throat, cloudy, dark red. His lips parted. He released her neck and, before she could stop herself, she inhaled sharply, just as he blew a stream of red dust into her face. Pain exploded through her chest in sharp bursts as the dust entered her lungs. She tried to cough, but the thing sat with his knees pressing down on her shoulders as she struggled to buck free.

People were yelling. She heard a siren wail, but she knew the ambulance would be too late. She would die here in Darlington's stupid hat. Maybe he'd be waiting on the other side of the Veil with Hellie. And Len. And all of the others.

The world fluttered black—and then suddenly she could move. The weight vanished from her shoulders. She released a grunt and shoved to her feet, clutching her chest, trying to find her breath. Where had the monster gone? She looked up.

High above the intersection, the thing with the glasses was grappling with something. No, *someone*. A Gray. The Bridegroom, New Haven's favorite murder-suicide, with his fancy suit and silent-movie-star hair. The thing in glasses had hold of his lapels and he flickered slightly in the sun as they careened through the air, slammed into a streetlight that sparked to life and then dimmed, passed through the walls of a building and back out. The whole street seemed to shake as if rumbling with thunder, but Alex knew only she could hear it.

The squeal of brakes cut through the noise. A black-and-white was pulling up on York, followed by an ambulance. Alex took a last look at the Bridegroom's face, his mouth pulled back in a grimace as he launched his fist at his opponent. She bolted across the intersection.

The pain in her chest continued to unfurl in popping bursts like fireworks. Something had happened to her, something bad, and she didn't know how much longer she'd be able to stay conscious. She only knew she had to get to the Hutch, upstairs to the safety of Lethe's hidden rooms. There might be other Grays coming, other monsters. What could they do? What couldn't they do? She needed to get behind the wards.

She glanced over her shoulder and saw an EMT running toward her. She leapt up on the sidewalk around the corner and then into the alley. He was right behind, but he couldn't protect her. She would die in his care. She knew this. She dodged left, toward the doorway, out of view.

"It's me!" she cried out to the Hutch, praying it would know her. The door blew open and the steps rolled toward her, pulling her inside.

She tried to take the stairs on her feet but slid to her knees. Usually the smell of the hall was comforting, a winter smell of burning wood, cranberries cooking slowly, mulled wine. Now it made her stomach churn. *It's the uncanny,* she realized. The garbage stink of the alley outside had at least been real. These false smells of comfort were too much. Her system couldn't handle any more magic. She fastened one hand around the iron railing, the other braced against the lip of the stone step, and pushed herself up. She saw spots on the concrete, black stars blooming in lichen clusters on the stairs. Her blood, dripping from her lips.

Panic reeled through her. She was on the floor in that public bathroom. The broken monarch flapped its one able wing.

Get up. Blood can draw them. Darlington's voice in her head. *Grays can cross the line if they want something badly enough.* What if the wards didn't hold? What if they weren't built to keep something like that monster out? The Bridegroom had seemed to be winning. And if he won? Who said he'd be any gentler than the thing in glasses? He hadn't looked gentle at all.

She tapped a message into her phone to Dawes. *SOS. 911.* There was probably some code she was supposed to use for bleeding from the mouth, but Dawes would just have to make do.

If Dawes was at Il Bastone and not here at the Hutch, Alex

was going to die on these stairs. She could see the grad student clearly, sitting in the parlor of the house on Orange, those index cards she used to organize chapters spread out like the tarot before her, all of them reading disaster, failure. The Queen of Pointlessness, a girl with a cleaver over her head. The Debtor, a boy crushed beneath a rock. The Student, Dawes herself in a cage of her own making. All while Alex bled to death a mile away.

Alex dragged herself up another step. She had to get behind the doors. The safe houses were a matryoshka doll of safety. The Hutch. Where small animals went to ground.

A wave of nausea rolled through her. She retched and a gout of black bile poured from her mouth. It was moving on the stairs. She saw the wet, shiny backs of beetles. *Scarabs.* Bits of iridescent carapace glinting in whatever blood and sludge had erupted from her. She shoved past the mess she'd made, retching again, even as her mind tried to make sense of what was happening to her. What had that thing wanted from her? Had someone sent it after her? If she died, her petty heart wanted to know who to haunt. The stairwell was fading in and out now. She was not going to make it.

She heard a metallic clang and a moment later understood it was the door banging open somewhere above her. Alex tried to cry out for help, but the sound from her mouth was a small, wet whimper. The smack of Dawes's Tevas echoed down the stairs—a pause, then her footsteps, faster now, punctuated by "Fuck fuck fuck fuck fuck fuck."

Alex felt a solid arm beneath her, yanking her upward. "Jesus. *Jesus.* What happened?"

"Help me, Pammie." Dawes flinched. Why had Alex used that name? Only Darlington called Dawes that.

Her legs felt heavy as Dawes hauled her up the stairs. Her skin itched as if something was crawling beneath it. She thought of the beetles pouring from her mouth and retched again.

"Don't vomit on me," said Dawes. "If you vomit, I'll vomit."

Alex thought of Hellie holding her hair back. They'd gotten

drunk on Jäger and then sat on the bathroom floor at Ground Zero, laughing and puking and brushing their teeth, then doing it all over again.

"Move your legs, Alex," Hellie said. She was pushing Alex's knees aside, slumping down next to her in the big basket chair. She smelled like coconut and her body was warm, always warm, like the sun loved her, like it wanted to cling to her golden skin as long as possible.

"Move your stupid legs, Alex!" Not Hellie. Dawes, shouting in her ear.

"I am."

"You're *not*. Come on, give me three more steps."

Alex wanted to warn Dawes that the thing was coming. The death words hadn't affected it; maybe the wards wouldn't stop it either. She opened her mouth and vomited again.

Dawes heaved in response. Then they were on the landing, through the door, toppling forward. Alex found herself falling. She was on the floor of the Hutch, face pressed to the threadbare carpet.

"What happened?" Dawes asked, but Alex was too tired to reply. She felt herself rolled onto her back, a sharp slap across her face. "Tell me what happened, Alex, or I can't fix it."

Alex made herself look at Dawes. She didn't want to. She wanted to go back to the basket chair, Hellie like a glowing slice of sun beside her.

"A Gray, I don't know. Like glass. I could see through him."

"Shit, that's a *gluma*."

Alex needed her flash cards. The word was there, though, somewhere in her memory. A *gluma* was a husk, a spirit raised from the recently dead to pass through the world, go-betweens who could travel across the Veil. They were messengers. For Book and Snake.

"There was red smoke. I breathed it in." She heaved again.

"Corpse beetles. They'll eat you from the inside out."

Of course. Of course they would. Because magic was never good or kind.

She heard bustling and then felt a cup pressed to her lips. "Drink," said Dawes. "It's going to hurt like hell and blister the skin right off your throat, but I can heal that."

Dawes was tipping Alex's chin up, forcing her mouth open. Alex's throat caught fire. She had a vision of prairies lit by blue flame. The pain seared through her and she grabbed Dawes by the hand.

"Jesus, Alex, why are you smiling?"

The *gluma*. The husk. Someone had sent something after her and there could only be one reason why: Alex was onto something. They knew she had gone to see Tara's body. But who? Book and Snake? Skull and Bones? Whoever it was had no reason to think she would stop with a visit to the morgue. They didn't know the choice she'd made, that the report had already been filed. Alex had been right. There was something wrong with Tara's death, some connection to the societies, the Houses of the Veil. But that wasn't why she was smiling.

"They tried to kill me, Hellie," she rasped as she slid into the dark. *That means I get to try to kill them.*

Manuscript, the young upstart among the Houses of the Veil but arguably the society that has weathered modernity best. It is easy to point to its Oscar winners and television personalities, but their alumni also include advisers to presidents, the curator of the Metropolitan Museum of Art, and, perhaps most tellingly, some of the greatest minds in neuroscience. When we speak of Manuscript, we talk of mirror magic, illusions, great glamours of the type that can make a star, but we would do well to remember that all of their workings derive from the manipulation of our own perception.

—*from* The Life of Lethe: Procedures
and Protocols of the Ninth House

Don't go to a Manuscript party. Just don't.
—Lethe Days Diary of Daniel Arlington
(Davenport College)

10

Last Fall

The night of the Manuscript party, Darlington spent the early-evening hours with the windows of Black Elm lit, handing out candy, jack-o'-lanterns lining the driveway. He loved this part of Halloween, the ritual of it, the tide of happy strangers arriving on his shores, hands outstretched. Most times Black Elm felt like a dark island, one that had somehow ceased to appear on any chart. Not on Halloween night.

The house lay in the gentle swell of a hill not far from the lands that had once belonged to Donald Grant Mitchell, and its library was stocked with multiple copies of Mitchell's books: *Reveries of a Bachelor, Dream Life,* and the only title his grandfather had deemed worth reading, *My Farm of Edgewood.* As a boy, Darlington had been drawn in by the mysterious sound of Mitchell's pen name, Ik Marvel, and woefully disappointed by the lack of anything magical or marvelous in his books.

But that had been his feeling about everything. There should be more magic. Not the creased-greasepaint performances of clowns and hack illusionists. Not card tricks. The magic he'd been promised would be found at the backs of wardrobes, under bridges, through mirrors. It was dangerous and alluring and it did not seek to entertain. Maybe if he'd been raised in an ordinary house with quality insulation and a neatly mowed front yard, instead of beneath Black Elm's crumbling towers, with its lakes of moss, its sudden, sinister spikes of foxglove, its seeping mist that crawled up through the trees in the autumn dusk, maybe then he would have stood a chance. Maybe if he'd been from somewhere like Phoenix instead of cursed New Haven.

The moment that doomed him hadn't even really belonged to him. He was eleven years old, at a picnic organized by the Knights of Columbus, which their housekeeper Bernadette had insisted on bringing him to because "boys need fresh air." Once they'd arrived at Lighthouse Point, she sequestered herself beneath a tent with her friends and a plate of deviled eggs and told him to go play.

Darlington had found a group of boys around his age, or they'd found him, and they spent the afternoon running races and competing in carnival games, then inventing their own games when those got boring. A tall boy named Mason, with buzzed hair and buck teeth, had somehow become the day's decision maker—when to eat, when to swim, when a game got dull—and Darlington was happy to follow in his wake. When they tired of riding the old carousel, they walked down to the edge of the park that looked out over the Long Island Sound and the New Haven Harbor in the distance.

"They should have boats," said Mason.

"Like a speedboat. Or a Jet Ski," said a boy named Liam. "That would be cool."

"Yeah," said another kid. "We could go across to the roller coaster." He'd been tagging along with them all afternoon. He was small, his face dense with sand-colored freckles and now sunburned across the nose.

"What roller coaster?" Mason asked.

The freckled kid had pointed across the sound. "With all the lights on it. Next to the pier."

Darlington had looked into the distance but seen nothing there, just the fading day and a flat spit of land.

Mason stared, then said, "What the fuck are you talking about?"

Even in the growing twilight, Darlington had seen red spreading hot across the freckled kid's face. The kid laughed. "Nothing. I was just fucking with you."

"Tool."

They'd walked down to the thin sliver of beach to run back and forth in the waves, and the moment had been forgotten. Until months later, when Darlington's grandfather opened his paper at the breakfast table and Darlington saw the headline: REMEMBERING SAVIN ROCK. Beneath it was a picture of a big wooden roller coaster jutting into the waters of the Long Island Sound. The caption read: *The legendary Thunderbolt, a favorite at Savin Rock amusement park, destroyed by a hurricane in 1938.*

Darlington had cut the picture from the paper and taped it above his desk. That day at Lighthouse Point, that sunburned, freckled boy had *seen* the old roller coaster. He'd believed they could all see it. He hadn't been pretending or joking around. He'd been surprised and embarrassed, and then he'd shut up quick. As if he'd had something like that happen before. Darlington had tried to remember his name. He'd asked Bernadette if they could go to the Knights of Columbus for bingo, potluck dinners, anything that might put him back in that kid's path. Eventually his grandfather had put a stop to it with a growled "Stop trying to turn him into a goddamn Catholic."

Darlington had grown older. The memory of Lighthouse Point had grown dimmer. But he never took the picture of the Thunderbolt from his wall. He would forget about it for weeks, sometimes months at a time, but he could never shake the thought that he was seeing only one world when there might be many, that there were lost places, maybe even lost people who might come to life for him if he just squinted hard enough or found the right magic words. Books, with their promises of enchanted doorways and secret places, only made it worse.

The feeling should have ebbed away with time, worn down by the constant, gentle disappointments of growing up. But at sixteen, with his brand-new provisional driver's license tucked into his wallet, the first place Darlington had taken his grandfather's old Mercedes was Lighthouse Point. He'd stood at the edge of the water and waited for the world to reveal itself. Years later, when he met Alex Stern, he had to resist the urge to bring her there too, to see if the Thunderbolt might appear to her like any other Gray, a rumbling ghost of joy and giddy terror.

When full dark fell and the stream of children in their goblin masks slowed to a trickle, Darlington put on his own costume, the same one he wore every year—a black coat and a pair of cheap plastic fangs that made him look like he'd just had dental surgery.

He parked in the alley behind the Hutch, where Alex was waiting, shivering in a long black coat that he'd never seen before.

"Can't we drive?" she asked. "It's freezing."

Californians. "It's fifty degrees and we're walking three blocks. Somehow you'll manage this journey through the tundra. I pray you're not wearing a skimpy cat ensemble underneath that. We're supposed to project some measure of authority."

"I can do my job in hot pants. I can probably do it better." She executed a half-hearted karate kick. "More room to move." At least she'd worn practical boots.

In the light from the streetlamp, he could see she'd heavily lined her eyes and had big gold earrings on. Hopefully she hadn't worn anything too provocative or appropriative. He didn't want to spend the evening fielding judgmental snipes from Manuscript because Alex had felt the urge to dress as sexy Pocahontas.

He led them up the alley and onto Elm. She seemed alert, ready. She'd done well since the incident at Aurelian, since they'd smashed a few thousand dollars' worth of glass and china on Il Bastone's kitchen floor. Maybe Darlington had done a little better too. They'd watched a series of first transformations at Wolf's Head that had gone without incident—though Shane Mackay had trouble coming down and they had to pen him in the kitchen while he shook off his rooster form. He'd bloodied his nose trying to peck the table and one of his friends had spent an hour dutifully plucking tiny white feathers from his body. The cock jokes had been interminable. They'd monitored a raising at Book and Snake, where, with the help of a translator, a desiccated corpse had relayed the final accounts of recently dead soldiers in the Ukraine in a bizarre game of macabre telephone. Darlington didn't know who in the state department had requested the information, but he assumed it would be dutifully passed along. They'd observed an unsuccessful portal opening at Scroll and Key—a botched attempt to send someone to Hungary, which had resulted in nothing but the whole tomb smelling like goulash—and an equally unimpressive storm summoning by St. Elmo at their dump of an apartment on Lynwood, which had left the delegation president and attending alumni sheepish and ashamed.

"They all have the look a guy gets when he's too drunk to get it up," Alex had whispered.

"Must you be so vulgar, Stern?"

"Tell me I'm wrong, Darlington."

"I certainly wouldn't know."

Tonight would be a bit different. They would draw no circles of protection, only make their presence known, monitor the power being gathered at the Manuscript nexus, and then write up a report.

"How long will we be at this thing?" Alex asked as the street forked left.

"After midnight, maybe a little later."

"I told Mercy and Lauren I'd meet them at the Pierson Inferno."

"They'll be so wasted by then they're not going to notice if you're late. Now focus: Manuscript looks harmless, but they're not."

Alex cut him a glance. There was some kind of glitter on her cheeks. "You actually sound nervous."

Of all the societies, the one that made Darlington most wary was Manuscript. He could see the skepticism on Alex's face as they stopped in front of a grubby white brick wall.

"Here?" she asked, drawing her coat tighter. The thump of bass and murmur of conversation floated back to them from somewhere down the narrow walkway.

Darlington understood Alex's disbelief. The other tombs had been built to look like *tombs*—the flat neo-Egyptian plinths of Bones, the soaring white columns of Book and Snake, the delicate screens and Moorish arches of Scroll and Key, Darlington's favorite crypt. Even Wolf's Head, who had claimed they wanted to shake off the trappings of the arcane and establish a more egalitarian house, had built themselves an English country estate in miniature. Darlington had read the descriptions of each tomb in Pinnell's guide to Yale and felt that, somehow, the analysis of their parts had fallen short of the mystery they evoked. Of course, Pinnell hadn't known about the tunnel beneath Grove Street that led directly from Book and Snake to the heart of the cemetery, or the enchanted orange trees taken from the Alhambra that bore fruit year-round in the Scroll and Key courtyard.

But the exterior of Manuscript just looked like a squat brick lump with a bunch of recycling bins stacked along its side.

"This is it?" Alex asked. "This is sadder than that place on Lynwood."

Actually, nothing was sadder than the St. Elmo house on Lynwood, with its stained carpet and sagging stairs and roof spiked with tilting weather vanes.

"Don't judge a book, Stern. This crypt is eight stories deep and houses one of the best collections of contemporary art in the world."

Alex's brows shot up. "So they're Cali rich."

"Cali rich?"

"In L.A., the really loaded guys dress like bums, like they need everyone to know they live at the beach."

"I suspect Manuscript was aiming for understated elegance, not

I bang models at my Malibu manse, but who can say?" The tomb had been finished in the early sixties by King-lui Wu. Darlington had never managed more than a grudging respect for mid-century architecture. Despite his best attempts to admire its severe lines, its clean execution, it always fell flat for him. His father had openly mocked his son's bourgeois taste for turrets and gabled roofs.

"Here," Darlington said, taking Alex by the shoulders and walking her a little to the left. "Look."

It pleased him when she exclaimed, "Oh!"

At this angle, the circular pattern hidden in the white bricks emerged. Most people thought it represented a sun, but Darlington knew better.

"It can't be seen head-on," said Darlington. "Nothing here can. This is the house of illusions and lies. Keep in mind just how charismatic some of these people can be. Our job is to make sure that no one gets too out of line and no one gets hurt. There was an incident in 1982."

"What kind of incident?"

"A girl ate something at one of these parties and decided she was a tiger."

Alex shrugged. "I watched Salome Nils pull feathers out of a guy's butt in the Wolf's Head kitchen. Pretty sure it could be worse."

"She never *stopped* thinking she was a tiger."

"What?"

"Wolf's Head is all about changing the physical, relinquishing human form but retaining human awareness. Manuscript specializes in altering consciousness."

"Messing with your head."

"That girl's parents still have her in a cage in upstate New York. It's a pretty nice setup. Acres to run on. Raw meat twice a day. She got out once and tried to maul their mailman."

"Hell on a manicure."

"She had him down on the ground and was chewing on his

calf. We covered it up as a mental breakdown. Manuscript paid for all of her care and was suspended from activity for a semester."

"Harsh justice."

"I didn't say it was fair, Stern. Not much is. But I'm telling you, you cannot trust your own perception tonight. Manuscript's magics are all about tricking the senses. Don't eat or drink *anything*. Keep your wits about you. I don't want to have to send you upstate with your own ball of yarn."

They followed a cluster of girls dressed in corsets and zombie makeup down the narrow alley and in through the side door. Henry VIII's wives. Anne Boleyn's neck was covered in sticky-looking fake blood.

Kate Masters perched on a stool by the door with a hand stamp, but Darlington snatched Alex's wrist before she could offer it up. "You don't know what's in the stamp dye," he murmured. "You can just let us through, Kate."

"Coatroom to the left." She winked, red glitter sparkling on her lids. She was dressed as Poison Ivy, construction-paper leaves stapled onto a green bustier.

Inside, the music thumped and wailed, the heat of bodies washing over them in a gust of perfume and moist air. The big square room was dimly lit, packed with people circling skull-shaped vats of punch, the back garden strewn with strings of twinkling lights beyond. Darlington was already starting to sweat.

"Doesn't look so bad," said Alex.

"Remember what I said? The real party is down below."

"So nine levels total? Nine circles of hell?"

"No, it's based around Chinese mythology. Eight is considered the luckiest number, so eight secret levels. The staircase represents a divine spiral."

Alex shucked off her coat. Beneath it she wore a black sheath dress. Her shoulders were strewn with a cascade of silver stars. "What are you supposed to be?" he asked.

"A girl in black with a lot of eye makeup on?" She pulled a

crown of plastic flowers sprayed with silver paint from her coat pocket and settled it on her head. "Queen Mab."

"You didn't strike me as a Shakespeare fan."

"I'm not. Lauren got a Puck costume from the Dramat closet. Mercy's going as Titania, so she shoved me in this and said I could be Mab."

"You know Shakespeare called Mab the faeries' midwife."

Alex frowned. "I thought she was the Queen of the Night."

"That too. It suits you."

Darlington had meant it to be a compliment, but Alex scowled. "It's just a dress."

"What have I been trying to tell you?" Darlington said. "Nothing is ever *just* anything." And maybe he wanted her to be the kind of girl who dressed as Queen Mab, who loved words and had stars in her blood. "Let's walk the first floor before we tackle what lies beneath."

It didn't take them long. Manuscript had been built on the open floor plans popular in the fifties and sixties, so there were few rooms or passages to investigate. At least on this level.

"I don't get it," Alex murmured as they glanced around the scrubby backyard. It was too crowded for comfort, but nothing out of the ordinary seemed to be happening. "If tonight is so special to Manuscript, why perform a rite with so many people around?"

"It's not a rite precisely. It's a culling. But that's the problem with their magic. It can't be practiced in seclusion. Mirror magic is all about reflection and perception. A lie isn't a lie until someone believes it. It doesn't matter how charming you are if there's no one to charm. Everybody on this floor is powering what happens below."

"Just by having a good time?"

"By *trying* to. Look around. What do you see? People in costumes, horns, false jewels, adorning themselves in tiny layers of illusion. They stand up straighter, suck in their stomachs, say things they don't mean, indulge in flattery. They commit a thousand small acts of deception, lying to each other, lying to themselves, drinking to the point of delusion to make it easier. This is a night of compacts, between the seers and the seen, a night when people enter false bargains willingly, hoping to be duped and to dupe in turn for the pleasure of feeling brave or sexy or beautiful or simply wanted—no matter how fleetingly."

"Darlington, are you telling me Manuscript is powered by beer goggles?"

"You do have a way of cutting straight to it, Stern. Every weekend night, every party is a series of these bargains, but Halloween compounds it all. These people enter the pact when they walk through that door, full of anticipation. Even before that, when they put on their wings and horns"—he shot her a glance—"and glitter. Didn't someone say love is a shared delusion?"

"Cynical, Darlington. Doesn't suit you at all."

"Call it magic if you prefer. Two people reciting the same spell."

"Well, I like it," said Alex. "It looks like a party from a movie. But the Grays are all over it."

He knew that and yet it still surprised him. After so long, he felt he should be able to sense their presence in some way. Darlington tried to step back, see this place as Alex did, but it just looked like a party. Halloween was a night when the dead came alive because the living were more alive: happy children high on candy, angry teenagers with eggs and shaving cream tucked into their hoodies, drunk college students in masks and wings and horns giving themselves permission to be something else—angel, demon, devil, good doctor, bad nurse. The sweat and excitement, the over-sugared punches loaded with fruit and grain alcohol. The Grays could not resist.

"Who's here?" he asked.

Her dark brows shot up. "You want specifics?"

"I'm not asking you to endanger yourself for the sake of my curiosity. Just . . . an overview."

"Two by the sliding glass door, five or six in the yard, one by the entry right behind that girl working the door, a whole herd of them clumped by the punch. Impossible to tell how many."

She hadn't missed a beat. She was aware of them because she was afraid of them.

"The lower floors are all warded. You don't have to worry about that tonight." He led her to the top of the stairs, where Doug Far was leaning against the banister, making sure no one without an invite proceeded below. "Blood magic is strictly regulated on Halloween. It's too appealing to the dead. But tonight Manuscript will siphon off all the desire and abandon of the holiday to power their rites for the rest of the year."

"Partying is that powerful?"

"Anderson Cooper is actually five foot four inches tall, weighs two bills, and talks with a knee-deep Long Island accent." Alex's eyes widened. "Just be careful."

"Darlington!" Doug said. "The gentleman of Lethe!"

"You stuck here all night?"

"Just the next hour and then I'm gonna go get high as fuck."

"Nice," said Darlington, and glimpsed Alex rolling her eyes. Other than the night they'd gotten drunk after the disastrous Aurelian ritual, he'd never seen her take even a sip of wine. He wondered if she partied with her roommates or if she'd chosen to stay mostly clean after what had happened to her friends in Los Angeles.

"Who's this?" Doug said, and Darlington found himself annoyed by Doug's lazy perusal of Alex's costume. "Your date or your Dante?"

"Alex Stern. She's the new me. She'll be watching over all you dullards when I finally get out of here." He said it because they expected him to, but Darlington would never leave this city. He'd fought too hard to remain here, to hold on to Black Elm. He would take a few months to travel, visit the remnants of the library cave in Dunhuang, make a pilgrimage to the monastery at Mont Sainte-Odile. He knew Lethe expected him to apply to graduate school, maybe take a research position in the New York office. But that wasn't what he really wanted. New Haven needed a new map, a map of the unseen, and Darlington wanted to be the one to draw it, and maybe, in the lines of its streets, the quiet of its gardens, the deep shadow of East Rock, there would be an answer to why New Haven had never become a Manhattan or a Cambridge, why, despite every opportunity and every hope for prosperity, it had always foundered. Was it merely chance? Bad luck? Or had the magic that lived here somehow stunted the town even as it continued to flourish?

"So what are you?" Doug asked Alex. "A vampire? Gonna suck my blood?"

"If you're lucky," said Alex, and disappeared down the stairs.

"Stay safe tonight, Doug," Darlington said as he followed her. She was already out of sight, vanishing down the spiral, and she shouldn't be on her own tonight.

Doug laughed. "That's your job."

The blast of a fog machine struck him full in the face, and he nearly stumbled. He waved the mist away, annoyed. Why couldn't people just have a quality drink and a conversation? Why all of this desperate pretense? And was some part of him jealous of Doug, of everyone who managed to be reckless for a night? Maybe. He'd felt disconnected from everything since he'd moved back to Black Elm. Freshmen and sophomores were required to live in the dorms, and though he'd visited Black Elm religiously, he'd liked the feeling of being pulled into other orbits, yanked forcibly from his shell by his well-meaning roommates, drawn into a world that had nothing to do with Lethe or the uncanny. He'd liked Jordan and E.J. enough to room with them both years, and he was grateful that they'd felt the same. He kept intending to call them, to invite them out. But another day would go by and he'd find it lost to books, to Black Elm, to Lethe, and now to Alex Stern.

"You should stay behind me," he said when he caught up to her, vexed by the petulant edge to his own voice. She was already on the next level, looking around with eager eyes. This floor resembled the VIP section of a nightclub, the lights dimmer, the bass muted, but there was a dreamy quality to it all, as if every person and every item in the room was limned in golden light.

"It looks like a music video," Alex said.

"With an infinite budget. It's a glamour."

"Why did he call you the gentleman of Lethe?"

"Because people who can't be bothered with manners pretend to be amused by them. Onward, Stern."

They continued down the next flight of stairs. "Are we going all the way down?"

"No. The lowest levels are where the rites are performed and maintained. At any given time they have five to ten magics working internationally. Charisma spells and glamours need constant maintenance. But they won't be performing any rites tonight, just culling power from the party and the city to store in the vault."

"Do you smell that?" asked Alex. "It smells like—"

Forest. The next landing brought them to a verdant wood. The previous year it had been a high desert mesa. Sunlight filtered through the leaves of a copse of trees and the horizon seemed to stretch on for miles. Partyers dressed in white lolled on picnic blankets that had been laid out over the lush grass, and hummingbirds bobbed and hovered in the warm air. From this level on, only alumni and the current members who attended them were permitted.

"Is that a real horse?" Alex whispered.

"As real as it has to be." This was magic, wasteful, joyous magic, and Darlington couldn't deny that some part of him wanted to linger here. But that was exactly why they had to press on. "Next floor."

The stairs curved again, but this time the walls seemed to bend with them. The building somehow took on a different shape, the ceiling high as a cathedral, painted the bright blue and gold of a

Giotto sky; the floor was covered in poppies. It was a church but it was not a church. The music here was otherworldly, something that might have been bells and drums or the heartbeat of a great beast lulling them with every deep thud. On the pews and in the aisles, bodies lay entwined, surrounded by crushed red petals.

"Now this is more like what I expected," said Alex.

"An orgy in a flower-filled cathedral?"

"Excess."

"That's what this night is all about."

The next level was a mountaintop arbor, which didn't even bother trying to look real. It was all hazy peach clouds, wisteria hanging in thick clusters from pale pink columns, women in sheer gowns lazing on sun-warmed stone, their hair caught in an impossible breeze, a golden hour that would never end. They'd walked into a Maxfield Parrish painting.

Finally, they arrived in a quiet room, a long banquet table set against one wall and lit by fireflies. The murmur of conversation was low and civilized. A vast circular mirror nearly two stories high took up the north-facing wall. Its surface seemed to swirl. It was like looking into a huge cauldron being stirred by an invisible hand, but it was wiser to understand the mirror as a vault, a repository of magic fed by desire and delusion. This level of Manuscript, the fifth level, marked the central point between the culling rooms above and the ritual rooms below. It was far larger than the others, stretching under the street and beneath the surrounding houses. Darlington knew the ventilation system was fine, but he struggled not to think about being crushed.

Many of the partygoers here were masked, most likely celebrities and prominent alums. Some wore fanciful gowns, others jeans and T-shirts.

"Do you see the purple tongues?" Darlington asked, bobbing his chin toward a boy covered in glitter pouring wine and a girl in cat ears and little else carrying a tray. "They've taken Merity, the drug of service. It's taken by acolytes to give up their will."

"Why would anyone do that?"

"To serve me," said a soft voice.

Darlington bowed to the figure dressed in celadon silk robes and a golden headdress that also served as a half-mask.

"How may we address you this night?" Darlington inquired.

The wearer of the mask represented Lan Caihe, one of the eight immortals of Chinese myth, who could move amongst genders at will. At each gathering of Manuscript, a different Caihe was chosen.

"Tonight I am she." Her eyes were entirely white behind her mask. She would see all things this night and be deceived by no glamour.

"We thank you for the invitation," said Darlington.

"We always welcome the officers of Lethe, though we regret you never accept our hospitality. A glass of wine perhaps?" She raised a smooth hand, the nails curled like claws but smooth and polished as glass, and one of the acolytes stepped forward with a pitcher.

Darlington gave Alex a warning shake of his head. "Thank you," he said apologetically. He knew some members of Manuscript took personal offense that Lethe members never sampled the society's pleasures. "But we're bound by protocol."

"None of our suggestions for the freshman tap were accepted," said Lan Caihe, her white eyes on Alex. "Very disappointing."

Darlington bristled. But Alex said, "At least you won't expect much from me."

"Careful now," said Caihe. "I like to be disarmed. You may raise my expectations yet. Who glamoured your arms?"

"Darlington."

"Are you ashamed of the tattoos?"

"Sometimes."

Darlington glanced at Alex, surprised. Was she under persuasion? But when he saw Lan Caihe's pleased smile, he realized Alex was just playing the game. Caihe liked surprises and candor was surprising.

Caihe reached out and ran a fingernail up the smooth skin of Alex's bare arm.

"We could erase them entirely," said Caihe. "Forever."

"For a small price?" asked Alex.

"For a *fair* price."

"My lady," said Darlington in warning.

Caihe shrugged. "This is a night of culling, when the stores are replenished and the casks are made full. No bargain will be made. Descend, boy, if you wish to know what's next. Descend and see what awaits you, if you dare."

"I just want to know if Jodie Foster is here," Alex murmured as Lan Caihe returned to the banquet table. She was one of Manuscript's most famous alums.

"For all you know that *was* Jodie Foster," said Darlington, but his head felt heavy. His tongue felt too big for his mouth. Everything around him seemed to shimmer.

Lan Caihe turned to him from her place at the head of the banquet table. "Descend." Darlington shouldn't have been able to hear the word at this distance, but it seemed to echo through his head. He felt the floor drop away and he was falling. He stood in a vast cavern carved into the earth, the rock slick with moisture, the air rich with the smell of turned soil. A hum filled his ears and Darlington realized it was coming from the mirror, the vault that still somehow hung on the cave wall. He was in the same room but he was not. He looked into the mirror's swirling surface and the mists within it parted, the hum rising, vibrating through his bones.

He shouldn't look. He knew that. You should never look into the face of the uncanny, but had he ever been able to turn away? No, he'd courted it, begged for it. He had to know. He wanted to know everything. He saw the banquet table reflected in the mirror, the food upon it going to rot, the people around it still shoveling spoiled fruit and meat into their mouths along with the swirling flies. They were old, some barely strong enough to lift a cup of wine or a withering peach to their cracked lips. All but Lan Caihe, who stood illumined by fire, the golden headdress a flame, her gown glowing ember red, the features of her face changing with each breath, high priestess, hermit, hierophant. For a moment, Darlington thought he glimpsed his grandfather there.

He could feel his body quaking, felt dampness on his lips, touched his hand to his face and realized his nose had started to bleed.

"Darlington?" Alex's voice, and in the mirror he saw her. But she looked the same. She was still Queen Mab. No . . . This time she really was Queen Mab. Night ebbed and flowed around her in a cape of glittering stars; above the oil-black sheaf of her hair, a constellation glowed—a wheel, a crown. Her eyes were black, her mouth the dark red of overripe cherries. He could feel power churning around her, through her.

"What are you?" he whispered. But he didn't care. He went to his knees. This was what he'd been waiting for.

"Ah," said Lan Caihe, approaching. "An acolyte at heart."

In the mirror, he saw himself, a knight with bowed head, offering his service, a sword in his hand, a sword in his back. He felt no pain, only the ache in his heart. *Choose me.* There were tears on his cheeks, even as he felt the shame of it. She was no one, a girl who had lucked into a gift, who had done nothing to earn it. She was his queen.

"Darlington," she said. But that was not his true name any more than Alex was hers.

If only she would choose him. If only she would let him . . .

She touched her fingers to his face, lifted his chin. Her lips brushed his ear. He didn't understand it. He only wanted her to do it again. Stars poured through him, a cold and billowing wave of night. He saw everything. He saw their bodies entwined. She was above him and beneath him all at once, her body splayed and white as a lotus flower. She bit his ear—hard.

Darlington yelped and flinched back, sense flooding through him.

"Darlington," she snarled. "Get your shit together."

And then he saw himself. He'd hiked up her skirt. His hands were braced on her white thighs. He saw the masked faces around them, sensed their eagerness as they leaned forward, eyes glittering. Alex was looking down at him, gripping his shoulders, trying to shove him away. The cavern was gone. They were in the banquet room.

He fell backward, letting her skirt drop, his erection throbbing valiantly in his jeans before humiliation washed over him. What the hell had they done to him? And how?

"The mist," he said, feeling like the worst kind of fool, his mind still spinning, his body buzzing with whatever he had inhaled. He'd walked straight through the blast of that fog machine and hadn't thought twice about it.

Lan Caihe grinned. "You can't blame a god for trying."

Darlington used the wall to push to his feet, keeping clear of the mirror. He could still feel its hum vibrating through him. He wanted to rage at these people. Interfering with representatives of Lethe was strictly prohibited, a violation of every code of the societies, but he also just wanted to get clear of Manuscript before he humiliated himself further. Everywhere he looked he saw masked and painted faces.

"Come on," said Alex, taking his arm and leading him up the stairs, forcing him to walk ahead of her.

He knew they should stay. See the night past the witching hour, make sure nothing got past the forbidden floors or interfered with the culling. He couldn't. He needed to get free. *Now.*

The stairs seemed to go on forever, turning and turning until Darlington had no idea how long they'd been climbing. He wanted to look back to make sure that Alex was still there, but he'd read enough stories to know you never looked back on your way out of hell.

The upper floor of Manuscript felt like a wild blaze of color and light. He could smell the fruit fermenting in the punch, the yeasty tang of sweat. The air felt sticky and warm against his skin.

Alex shook his arm and pulled him along by his elbow. All he could do was stumble after. They burst into the cold night air as if they'd slid through a membrane. Darlington inhaled deeply, feeling his head clear a little. He heard voices and realized Alex was talking to Mike Awolowo, the Manuscript delegation president. Kate Masters was beside him. She was covered in flowering vines. They were going to consume her—*no*. She was just dressed as Poison Ivy, for God's sake.

"Unacceptable," Darlington said. His lips felt fuzzy.

Alex kept one hand on his arm. "I'll handle it. Stay here."

They'd made it down the street to the Hutch. Darlington leaned his head against the Mercedes. He should pay attention to what Alex was saying to Kate and Mike, but the metal felt cool and forgiving against his face.

Moments later they were getting into his car and he was mumbling the address for Black Elm.

Mike and Kate peered through the passenger window as the car drove off.

"They're afraid you're going to report them," Alex said.

"Damn right I will. They're going to eat a huge fine. A suspension."

"I told him I'd handle the write-up."

"You will not."

"You can't be objective about this."

No, he couldn't. In his head, he was kneeling again, face pressed to her thighs, desperate to get closer. The thought of it made him instantly hard again, and he was grateful for the dark.

"What do you want me to say in the report?" Alex asked.

"All of it," Darlington muttered miserably.

"It isn't a big deal," she said.

It had been a big deal, though. He had felt . . . "desire" wasn't even the right word for it. He could still feel her skin under his palms, the heat of her against his lips through the thin fabric of her panties. What the hell was wrong with him?

"I'm sorry," he said. "That was unforgivable."

"You got wasted and acted a fool at a party. Relax."

"If you don't want to continue working with me—"

"Shut up, Darlington," Alex said. "I'm not doing this job without you."

She got him back to Black Elm and put him to bed. The house was ice-cold and he realized his teeth were chattering. Alex lay down beside him with the covers pulled tight between them, and his heart hurt for the wanting of someone.

"Mike said the drug should be out of your system in about twelve hours."

Darlington lay in his narrow bed, writing and rewriting angry emails in his head to the Manuscript alumni and the Lethe board, losing the thread, overwhelmed by images of Alex lit by stars, the thought of that black dress sliding from her shoulders, then returning to his rant and a demand for action. The words tangled together, caught on the spokes of a wheel, the points of a crown. But one thought returned again and again as he tossed and turned, fell in and out of dreams, morning light beginning its slow bleed through the high tower window: Alex Stern was not what she seemed.

11

Winter

Alex woke abruptly. She was asleep and then she was conscious and terrified, batting at the hands she could still feel around her neck.

Her throat felt raw and red. She was on the couch of the common room at the Hutch. Night had fallen and the lights burned low in their sconces, casting yellow half-moons against framed paintings of rolling meadows dotted with sheep and shepherds playing their pipes.

"Here," Dawes said, perching on the cushions, holding a glass full of what looked like eggnog with a little green food coloring in it up to Alex's lips. A musty smell emanated from the rim. Alex recoiled and opened her mouth to ask what it was, but all that emerged was a faint rasp that made her throat feel like someone had touched a lit match to it.

"I'll tell you after you drink it," said Dawes. "Trust me."

Alex shook her head. The last thing Dawes had given her to drink had set her insides on fire.

"You're alive, aren't you?" Dawes asked.

Yes, but right now she wished she were dead.

Alex pinched her nose, took the glass, and gulped. The taste was stale and powdery, the liquid so thick it almost choked her going down, but as soon as it touched her throat, the burning eased, leaving only a faint ache.

She handed the glass back and wiped a hand over her mouth, shuddering slightly at the aftertaste.

"Goat's milk and mustard seed thickened with spider eggs," Dawes said.

Alex pressed her knuckles to her lips and tried not to gag. "*Trust* you?"

Her throat was sore, but she could at least talk and the raging fire inside her seemed to have banked.

"I had to use brimstone to burn the beetles out of you. I'd say the cure was worse than the disease, but given that those things eat you from the inside out, I think that would be lying. They were used to clean corpses in ancient times, to empty bodies so that they could be stuffed with fragrant herbs."

That crawling sensation returned, and Alex had to clench her fists to keep from scratching at her skin. "What did they do to me? Will there be lasting damage?"

Dawes rubbed her thumb against the glass. "I honestly don't know."

Alex pushed up from the pillows that Dawes had placed beneath her neck. *She likes taking care of people,* Alex realized. Was that why she and Dawes had never gotten along? Because Alex had refused her mothering? "How did you know what to do?"

Dawes frowned. "It's my job to know."

And Dawes was good at her job. Simple as that. She seemed calm enough, but if she gripped that glass any harder it was going to break in her hands. Her fingers were stained with rainbow splotches that Alex realized were the pale remnants of highlighter.

"Did anything try to . . . get in?" Alex wasn't even sure what that would look like.

"I'm not sure. The chimes have been ringing off and on. Something's been brushing up against the wards."

Alex rose and felt the room spin. She stumbled and made herself take Dawes's solicitous hand.

Alex wasn't sure what she expected to see waiting outside. The *gluma's* face looking back at her, light glinting off its glasses?

Something worse? She touched her fingers to her throat and yanked the curtain back.

The street to the left was dark and empty. She must have slept through the entire day. In the alley she saw the Bridegroom, pacing back and forth in the yellow light of the streetlamp.

"What is it?" asked Dawes nervously. "What's there?" She sounded almost breathless.

"Just a Gray. The Bridegroom." He looked up at the window. Alex drew the curtain closed.

"You can really see him? I've only seen photos."

Alex nodded. "He's very tousled. Very mournful. Very . . . Morrissey."

Dawes surprised her by singing, *"And I wonder, does anybody feel the same way I do?"*

"And is evil," sang Alex quietly, *"just something you are or something you do?"* She'd meant it as a joke, a way to solidify the bare threads of camaraderie forming between them, but in the eerie lamplit quiet, the words sounded menacing. "I think he saved my life. He attacked that thing."

"The *gluma*?"

"Yeah." Alex shuddered. It had been so strong and seemingly immune to everything she'd thrown at it—which admittedly hadn't been much. "I need to know how to stop one of those things."

"I'll pull whatever we have on them," said Dawes. "But you shouldn't form ties with Grays, especially a violent one."

"We don't have a tie."

"Then why did he help you?"

"Maybe he wasn't helping me. Maybe he was trying to hurt the *gluma*. I didn't exactly have time to ask."

"I'm just saying—"

"I know what you're saying," said Alex, then flinched when a low gong sounded. Someone had entered the stairwell.

"It's okay," Dawes said. "It's only Dean Sandow."

"You called Sandow?"

"Of course," Dawes said, straightening. "You were nearly killed."

"I'm fine."

"Because a Gray interceded on your behalf."

"Don't tell him that," Alex snarled before she could tame her response.

Dawes drew back. "He needs to know what happened!"

"Don't tell him anything." Alex wasn't sure why she was so afraid of Sandow knowing what had gone down. Maybe it was just old habit. You didn't talk. You didn't tell. That was how CPS got called. That was how you got locked up "for observation."

Dawes planted her hands on her hips. "What would I tell him? I don't know what happened to you any more than I know what happened to Darlington. I'm just here to clean up your messes."

"Isn't that what they pay you for?" Empty the fridge. A little light dusting. *Save my worthless life.* Damn it. "Dawes—"

But Sandow was already pushing open the door. He startled when he saw Alex by the window. "You're up. Dawes said you were unconscious."

Alex wondered what else Dawes had said. "She took good care of me."

"Excellent," Sandow said, draping his overcoat on a bronze post shaped like a jackal's head and striding across the room to where the old-fashioned samovar sat in a corner. Sandow had been a Lethe delegate in the late seventies and a very good one, according to Darlington. *Brilliant on theory, but just as good on fieldwork. He fashioned some original rites that are still on the books today.* Sandow had returned to campus as an associate professor ten years later, and since then he had served as Lethe's liaison with the university president. Excluding a few alums who had been taps themselves, the rest of the administration and faculty knew nothing about Lethe or the societies' true activities.

Alex could imagine Sandow happily working away in the Lethe

library or fastidiously marking a chalk circle. He was a small, tidy man with the trim build of a jogger and silvery brows that steepled at the center of his forehead, giving him a permanent look of concern. She'd seen little of him since she'd begun her education at Lethe. He'd sent her his contact information and an "open invitation to office hours" that she'd never taken him up on. Sometime in late September, he'd come to a long, awkward lunch at Il Bastone, during which he and Darlington discussed a new book on women and manufacturing in New Haven and Alex hid her white asparagus beneath a bread roll.

And, of course, he was the one Alex texted the night Darlington disappeared.

Sandow had come to Il Bastone that night with his old yellow Labrador, Honey. He made a fire in the parlor grate and asked Dawes for tea and brandy as Alex tried to explain—not what had happened. She didn't *know* what had happened. She only knew what she'd seen. She was shaking by the time she finished, remembering the cold of the basement, the crackling smell of electricity on the air.

Sandow had patted her knee gently and set a steaming mug before her.

"Drink," he'd said. "It will help. That must have been very frightening." The words took Alex by surprise. Her life had been a series of terrifying things she'd been expected to take in stride. "It sounds like portal magic. Someone playing with something they shouldn't."

"But he said it wasn't a portal. He said—"

"He was scared, Alex," Sandow had said gently. "Probably panicked. For Darlington to disappear that way, a portal must have been involved. It may have been a kind of anomaly created by the nexus beneath Rosenfeld Hall." Dawes had drifted into the room, hovering behind the couch with her arms crossed tight, barely holding herself together while Sandow murmured about retrieval spells and the likelihood that Darlington simply had to be pulled back from wherever he'd gone. "We'll need a new-moon night," Sandow had said. "And then we'll just call our boy home."

Dawes burst out crying.

"Is he . . . *where* is he?" Alex had asked. *Is he suffering? Is he scared?*

"I don't know," said the dean. "That will be part of the challenge for us." He'd sounded almost eager, as if presented with a delicious problem. "A portal of the size and shape you described, stable enough to be maintained without practitioners present, can't have gone anywhere interesting. Darlington was probably transported to a pocket realm. It's like dropping a coin between the cushions of a couch."

"But he's trapped there—"

"He probably isn't even aware he's gone. Darlington will come back to us thinking he was just in Rosenfeld and furious that he'll have to repeat the semester."

There had been emails and text chains since then—Sandow's updates on who and what would be needed for the rite, the creation of the Spain cover story, a flurry of apologetic and frustrated messages when the January new moon had to be scrapped due to Michelle Alameddine's schedule, followed by profound silence from Dawes. But that night, the night when Darlington had gone from the world, was the last time they'd all been in a room together. Sandow was the fire alarm they weren't supposed to pull without good cause. Alex was tempted to think of him as the nuclear option, but really, he was just a parent. A proper adult.

Now the dean stirred sugar into his cup. "I appreciate your quick thinking, Pamela. We can't afford another . . ." He trailed off. "We just need to see the year out and . . ." Again he let his sentence dissolve as if he'd dunked it into his tea.

"And what?" Alex nudged. Because she really did wonder what was supposed to come next. Dawes was standing with her hands clasped as if about to sing a choir solo, waiting, waiting.

"I've been thinking about that," said Sandow at last. He sank down into a wing-backed chair. "We're ready for the new moon. I'll pick up Michelle Alameddine from the train station Wednesday night and bring her directly to Black Elm. I have every hope that the rite will work and that Darlington will be back with us soon. But we also need to be prepared for the alternative."

"The alternative?" said Dawes. She sat down abruptly. Her face was tight, angry even.

Alex couldn't pretend to understand the mechanics of what Dean Sandow had planned, but she would have bet Dawes did. *It's my job.* She was there to clean up the messes that invariably got made, and this was a big one.

"Michelle is at Columbia, working on her master's. She'll be with us for the new-moon rite. Alex, I think she could be persuaded to come up on the weekends and continue your education and training. That will reassure the alumni if we have to"— he brushed his finger over his graying mustache—"bring them up-to-date."

"What about his parents? His family?"

"The Arlingtons are estranged from their son. As far as anyone knows, Daniel Arlington is studying the nexus beneath San Juan de Gaztelugatxe. If the rite fails—"

"If the rite fails, we try again," said Dawes.

"Well, of course," said Sandow, and he seemed genuinely distressed. "Of course. We try every avenue. We exhaust every possibility. Pamela, I'm not trying to be callous." He held out a hand to her. "Darlington would do everything he could to bring one of us home. We'll do the same."

But if the rite failed, if Darlington couldn't be brought back, then what? Would Sandow tell the alumni the truth? Or would he and the board invent a tale that didn't sound like *We sent two college kids into situations we knew they couldn't handle and one died.*

Either way, Alex didn't like that it would be so easy for Lethe to close Darlington's chapter. He had been a lot of things, most of them annoying, but he had loved his job and Lethe House. It was cruel that Lethe couldn't love him back. This was the first time Sandow had even broached the possibility that Darlington wouldn't return, that he couldn't just be yanked from between the interdimensional cushions of a cosmic couch. Was it because they were only days away from trying?

Sandow picked up the empty glass coated in film from the vile green milk drink.

"Axtapta? You were attacked by a *gluma*?"

His voice had been smooth, diplomatic, pensive, while he discussed Darlington—his dean voice. But at the thought of a *gluma*, a deep crease appeared between his worried brows.

"That's right," Alex said solidly, though she still wasn't entirely sure what that implied. Then she made the leap. "I think someone sent it after me. Maybe Book and Snake."

Sandow huffed a disbelieving laugh. "Why would they ever have cause to do something like that?"

"Because Tara Hutchins is dead and I think they had something to do with it."

Sandow blinked rapidly, as if his eyes were defective camera lenses. "Detective Turner says—"

"This is what I think, not Turner."

Sandow's gaze snapped to hers, and she knew he was surprised by the surety in her voice. But she couldn't afford the deferential dance she knew he would prefer.

"You've been investigating?"

"I have."

"That isn't safe, Alex. You aren't equipped to—"

"Someone had to." And Darlington was far away.

"Do you have evidence a society was involved?"

"Book and Snake raises the dead. They use *glumas*—"

"*Glumae*," murmured Dawes.

"*Glumae* as messengers to talk to the dead. One of them attacked me. Seems like a solid theory."

"Alex," he said gently, a faint scold in his voice. "We knew when you came here that someone of your abilities had never been in such a position. It's possible, likely even, that simply being here has disrupted systems we can only guess at."

"You're saying I triggered the *gluma* attack?" She hated the defensive edge in her voice.

"I'm not saying you *did* anything," said Sandow mildly. "I'm just saying by dint of what you are, you may have brought this on."

Dawes crossed her arms. "That sounds a lot like *She was asking for it,* Dean Sandow."

Alex couldn't quite believe what she was hearing. Pamela Dawes disagreeing with Dean Sandow. On her behalf.

Sandow set his mug down with a clatter. "That's certainly not what I meant to imply."

"But that *is* the implication," said Dawes in a voice Alex had never heard her use before, clear and incisive. Her eyes were cold. "Alex has indicated her own concerns regarding her assault, and instead of hearing her out, you've chosen to question her credibility. You may not have meant to imply anything, but the intent and the effect were to silence her, so it's hard not to think this stinks of victim blaming. It's the semantic equivalent of saying her skirt was too short."

Alex tried not to smile. Dawes had leaned back in her chair, legs and arms crossed, head cocked to one side, somehow both angry and at ease. Sandow's face was flushed. He put his palms up as if trying to gentle a beast—*easy now.* "Pamela, I hope you know me better than that." Alex had never seen him so flustered. So Dawes knew how to speak the dean's language, the threats that counted.

"Someone sent that monster after me," Alex said, pushing the advantage Dawes had given her. "And it isn't a coincidence that a girl died just days before. Tara's phone log showed calls to Tripp Helmuth. That points to Bones. A *gluma* just tried to murder me in the street. That might point to Book and Snake. Tara was killed on a Thursday night, a ritual night, and if you read my report, you know that at the same time someone was carving her up, I saw two formerly docile Grays completely lose their shit." Sandow's brows pinched further together, as if such language pained him. "You—*Lethe*—brought me here for a reason, and I'm telling you that a girl is dead and there's a connection to the societies. For a minute just pretend I'm Darlington and try to take me seriously."

Sandow studied her, and Alex wondered if maybe she'd gotten through to him. Then he shifted his gaze to Dawes. "Pamela, I believe we have a camera facing the intersection at Elm and York."

Alex saw the way Dawes's shoulders softened, her head lowering, as if Sandow had spoken the words to break whatever spell she had been under. She rose and retrieved her laptop. Alex felt something twist in her gut.

Dawes struck a few keys on her computer, and the mirror on the far wall brightened. A moment later, the screen showed Elm Street teeming with cars and people, a sea of gray and darker gray. The time stamp in the corner read 11:50 a.m. Alex searched the tide of people moving along the sidewalk, but everyone just looked like a bulky lump in a coat. Then a flash of movement outside the Good Nature Market caught her eye. She watched the crowd part and ripple, instinctively moving away from violence. There she was, fleeing the store, the owner shouting at her, a girl with black hair in a woolly hat—Darlington's hat. She must have lost it in the fight.

The girl on the screen stepped off the sidewalk and into traffic, all of it in cold silence, a pantomime.

Alex remembered the *gluma*'s furious grip as it had dragged her into the street, but there was no *gluma* on the screen. Instead, she saw the dark-haired girl throw herself into the flow of cars, stumbling and wild, screaming and clawing at nothing. Then she was on her back. Alex's memory said the *gluma* was on top of her, but the screen showed nothing at all, just her lying at the center of the street as cars swerved to avoid her, her back bowing and flexing, her mouth wide, her hands clawing at nothing, convulsing.

A moment later she was on her feet, lurching toward the alley that ran behind the Hutch. She saw herself look back once, eyes wide, face streaked with blood, mouth open in horror, the corners pulled down like the corners of a sail pulled taut. *I was seeing the Bridegroom fight the* gluma. *Or was I?* It was the face of a mad-woman. She was back on that bathroom floor, shorts around her ankles, screaming and alone.

"Alex, everything you say may be true. But there is no proof of what attacked you, let alone who might be responsible. If I show this to the alumni . . . It's essential that they see you as stable, re-liable, particularly given . . . well, given how precarious things are now."

Given that Darlington had disappeared. Given that it had hap-pened when she was supposed to be watching his back.

"Isn't this why we're here?" asked Alex, a last try, an appeal on behalf of something bigger than herself, something Sandow might value more. "To protect girls like Tara? To make sure the societies don't just . . . do whatever they want?"

"Absolutely. But do you really believe you're equipped to in-vestigate a homicide by yourself? There's a reason I told you to stand down. I'm trying to keep things as normal as they can be in a world where monsters live. The police are investigating the Hutchins murder. The girl's boyfriend has been arrested and is awaiting trial. Do you honestly think that if Turner found a con-nection to one of the societies, he wouldn't pursue it?"

"No," admitted Alex. "I know he would." Whatever she thought of him, Turner was a bloodhound with a conscience that never took the day off.

"If he does, we will absolutely be there to lend him support, and I promise to pass along everything you've learned. But right now I need you to focus on getting well and staying safe. Dawes and I will both put our minds to what might have triggered the *gluma* attack and if there may be other disruptions caused by your ability. Your presence here on campus is an unknown factor, a disruptor. The behavior of those Grays during the prognostication, Darlington's disappearance, a violent death near campus, now a *gluma*—"

"Wait," said Alex. "You think my being here had something to do with Tara getting killed?"

"Of course not," said the dean. "But I don't want to give the Lethe board reasons to start drawing those kinds of conclusions. And I cannot afford to let you play amateur detective in a matter this serious. Our funding is up for review this year. We exist by the university's good graces and we keep our lights on through the continued support of the other societies. We need their good will." He released a long breath. "Alex, I don't mean to sound cold. The Hutchins murder is gruesome and tragic and I am absolutely going to monitor this situation, but we have to tread cautiously. The end of last semester . . . What happened at Rosenfeld changed everything. Pamela, do you want to see Lethe's funding pulled?"

"No," Dawes whispered. If she spoke Sandow's language, Sandow was also fluent in Dawes. Lethe was her hiding place, her bunker. There was no way she was going to risk losing it.

But Alex was only half paying attention to the dean's speech. She was staring at the old map of New Haven that hung above the mantel. It showed the original nine-square plan for the New Haven colony. She remembered what Darlington had said that first day as they crossed the green: *The town was meant to be a new Eden, founded between two rivers like the Tigris and the Euphrates.*

Alex looked at the shape of the colony—a wedge of land bracketed by West River and the Farmington Canal, two slender channels of water rushing to meet each other at the harbor. She finally understood why the crime scene had looked so familiar. The intersection where Tara Hutchins's body had been found looked just like the map: That slab of empty land in front of Baker Hall was like the colony in miniature. The streets that framed that plot of

land were the rivers, flowing with traffic, joining at Tower Park-
way. And Tara Hutchins had been found in the middle of it all, as
if her punctured body lay at the heart of a new Eden. Her body
hadn't just been dumped there. It had been placed there deliberately.

"Honestly, Alex," Sandow was saying, "what possible motive
could any of these people have for hurting a girl like that?"

She didn't really know. She just knew that they had.

Then someone had found out Alex visited the morgue. Whoever it was thought Alex knew Tara's secrets—at least some of
them—and that she had enough magic at her disposal to learn
more. They'd decided to do something about it. Maybe they'd
been trying to kill her, or maybe discrediting her was enough.

And the Bridegroom? Why had he chosen to help her? Was he
part of this somehow?

"Alex, I want you to thrive here," said Sandow. "I want us to get
through this difficult year and I want all of our attention focused
on the new-moon rite and bringing Darlington home. Let's get
through this and then take stock."

Alex wanted that too. She needed Yale. She needed her place
here. But the dean was wrong. Tara's death hadn't been the easy
ugly thing that Sandow wanted it to be. Someone from the societies was involved, and whoever it was wanted to silence her.

I'm in danger, she wanted to say. *Someone hurt me and I don't
think they're finished. Help me.* But what good had that ever done?
Somehow Alex had thought this place was different, with all of its
rules and rituals and Dean Sandow watching over them. *We are the
shepherds.* But they were children at play. Alex looked at Sandow
sipping his tea, one leg crossed over the other, light glinting off
his shiny loafer as his knee bounced, and she understood that at
some level he truly did not care what harm came to her. He might
even be hoping for it. If Alex got hurt, if she vanished, she would
take with her all the blame for what had happened to Darlington,
and her short, disastrous tenure at Yale would be written off as an

unfortunate mistake in judgment, an ambitious experiment gone wrong. He'd get his golden boy back at the new moon and make everything right. He wanted to be comfortable. And wasn't Alex the same? Dreaming of a peaceful summer and mint in her tea while Tara Hutchins lay cold in a drawer?

Rest easy. She'd been ready to do just that. But someone had tried to hurt her.

Alex felt something dark inside her uncoil. "You're a flat beast," Hellie had once said to her. "Got a little viper lurking in there, ready to strike. A rattler probably." She'd said it with a grin, but she'd been right. All this winter weather and polite conversation had put the serpent to sleep, its heartbeat slowing as it grew lazy and still, like any cold-blooded thing.

"I want us to get through this too," said Alex, and she smiled for him, a cowed smile, an eager smile. His relief gusted through the room like a warm front, the kind that New Englanders welcome and that Angelenos know means wildfires.

"Good, Alex. Then we will." He rose and put on his coat, his striped scarf. "I'll submit your report to the alumni, and I'll see you and Dawes Wednesday night at Black Elm." He gave her shoulder a squeeze. "Just a few more days and everything will be back to normal."

Not for Tara Hutchins, you ass. She smiled again. "See you Wednesday."

"Pamela, I'll send you an email on refreshments. Nothing fancy. We're expecting two representatives from Aurelian along with Michelle. " He gave Alex a wink. "You're going to love Michelle Alameddine. She was Darlington's Virgil. An absolute genius."

"Can't wait," said Alex, returning the dean's wave as he saw himself out. When the door shut, she said, "Dawes, how tough is it to talk to the dead?"

"Not difficult at all if you're in Book and Snake."

"They're last on my list. I try not to ask for help from people who might want to kill me."

"Limits your options," Dawes muttered to the floor.

"Aw, Dawes, I like you bitchy." Dawes shifted uncomfortably and tugged at her murky gray sweatshirt. She closed the laptop. "Thanks for backing me with the dean. And for saving my life." Dawes nodded at the carpet. "So what are my other options if I need to talk to someone on the other side of the Veil?"

"The only one I can think of is Wolf's Head."

"The shapeshifters?"

"Do *not* call them that. Not if you're looking for favors."

Alex crossed to the window, pulled open the curtain.

"Is he still there?" Dawes said from behind her.

"He's there."

"Alex, what are you doing? Once you let him in . . . You know the stories about him, what he did to that girl."

Open the door, Alex.

"I know he saved my life and he wants my attention. Relationships have been built on less."

The rules of Lethe House were opaque and convoluted. *Catholic,* Darlington had said. *Byzantine.* Still, the big stuff wasn't tough to remember. Leave the dead to the dead. Turn your eyes to the living. But Alex needed allies, and Dawes wasn't going to be enough.

She knocked on the window.

Below, on the street, the Bridegroom looked up. His dark eyes met hers in the light from the streetlamp. She did not look away.

Wolf's Head, fourth of the Houses of the Veil, though Berzelius would argue the point. Members practice therianthropy and consider simple shapeshifting to be base magic. They focus instead on the ability to retain human consciousness and characteristics while in animal form. Primarily used for intelligence gathering, corporate espionage, and political sabotage. Wolf's Head was a major recruitment ground for the CIA in the 1950s and '60s. It can take days for someone to shake off the traits of an animal after a shifting ritual. Keep discussions of an important or sensitive nature around animals to a minimum.

—*from* The Life of Lethe: Procedures
and Protocols of the Ninth House

I'm tired and my heart won't stop racing. My eyes look pink. Not the whites. The irises. When Rogers said we were going to fuck like rabbits, I didn't think he meant actual rabbits.

—Lethe Days Diary of Charles "Chase"
MacMahon *(Saybrook College '88)*

12

Winter

Alex knew she couldn't go to Wolf's Head empty-handed. If she wanted their help, she had a stop to make at Scroll and Key first to retrieve a statue of Romulus and Remus. Wolf's Head had been badgering Lethe to orchestrate its return since it went missing during their Valentine's Day party the year before, when they'd opened their doors to other society members, as was tradition. Though Alex had since spotted the statue sitting on a shelf in the Locksmiths' tomb, with a plastic tiara slung over it, Darlington had refused to get involved. "Lethe doesn't concern itself with petty squabbles," he'd said. "These kinds of pranks are beneath us."

But Alex needed a way into the temple room at the heart of the Wolf's Head tomb, and she knew exactly what their delegation president, Salome Nils, would demand in payment.

Alex drank one of Darlington's disgusting protein shakes from the fridge. She was hungry, which Dawes claimed was a good sign, but her throat couldn't tolerate anything solid yet. She wasn't eager to leave the safety of the wards when she didn't know exactly what had happened to the *gluma*, but she couldn't just sit still. Besides, whoever had sent the *gluma* thought she was laid up somewhere being consumed by corpse beetles from the inside out. As for her public fit in the middle of Elm Street, at least there hadn't been too many witnesses, and aside from Jonas Reed, it was unikely any of them knew her. If someone did, she'd probably be getting a call from a concerned therapist at the health center.

Alex had known the Bridegroom would be waiting as soon as she and Dawes stepped out into the alley. It was almost dawn and the streets were quiet. Her "protector" followed them all the way to Scroll and Key, where she found a harried Locksmith writing a paper and convinced him to let her into the tomb to look for a scarf Darlington had left behind during the last rite they'd observed. Lethe was usually permitted entry to the tombs only on ritual nights and during sanctioned inspections. "Gets chilly in Andalusia," she told him.

The Locksmith hovered in the doorway, eyes on his phone as Alex pretended to search. He swore when the bell beside the front door rang again. *Thank you, Dawes.* Alex nabbed the statue and shoved it into her satchel. She glanced at the round stone table where the delegation gathered to work their rites—or try to. A quote was carved into the table's edge, one she'd always liked: *Have power on this dark land to lighten it, and power on this dead world to make it live.* Something about those words rang a bell but she couldn't pry the memory loose. She heard the front door slam and hurried out of the room, thanking the Locksmith—now muttering about drunk partyers who couldn't find their damn dorms—on her way out.

There was a very good chance Scroll and Key would point the finger at her once they noticed the statue was missing, but she would just have to deal with that later. Dawes was waiting around the corner by the Gothic folly that served as an entrance to the Bass Library. Darlington had told her that the stone swords carved into its decoration were signs of warding.

"This is a bad idea," Dawes said, bundled into her parka and radiating disapproval.

"At least I'm consistent."

Dawes's head swiveled on her neck like a searchlight. "Is he here?"

Alex knew she meant the Bridegroom, and though she would never admit it, she was unnerved by how easy it had been to secure his attention. She doubted it would be that easy to shake it. She glanced over her shoulder, where he trailed them by what could only be called a respectful distance. "Half a block away."

"He's a *murderer*," Dawes whispered.

Well, then we have something in common, thought Alex. But all she said was, "Beggars can't be choosers."

She didn't like the idea of letting a Gray get close to her, but she'd made her choice and she wasn't going to rethink it now. If someone from the societies was responsible for slapping a target on her back, she was going to find out who, and then she was going to make sure they didn't have a chance to hurt her again. Even so . . .

"Dawes," she murmured. "When we get back, let's start looking for ways to break the link between people and Grays. I don't want to spend the rest of my life with Morrissey peering over my shoulder."

"The easiest way is not to form a bond to begin with."

"Really?" said Alex. "Let me write that down."

The Wolf's Head tomb was only a few doors away from the Hutch, a grand gray manor house, fronted by a scrubby garden and surrounded by a high stone wall. It was one of the most magical places on campus. The alley that horseshoed around it was bordered by old fraternity houses, sturdy brick structures long ago ceded to the university, ancient symbols of channeling carved into the stone above their doorways beside unremarkable clusters of Greek letters. The alley acted as a kind of moat where power gathered in a thick, crackling haze. Passing through, most people wrote off the shiver that seized them to a shift in weather or a bad mood, then forgot as soon as they had moved on to the Yale Cabaret or the Af-Am Center. Wolf's Head's members took great pride in the fact that they'd housed protesters during the Black Panther trials, but they'd also been the last of the Ancient Eight to let in women, so Alex considered it a wash. On ritual nights, she regularly saw a Gray standing in the courtyard, mooning the offices of the *Yale Daily News* next door.

Alex had to ring the bell at the gate twice before Salome Nils finally answered and let them inside.

"Who's this?" Salome asked. For a second, Alex thought she could see the Bridegroom. He had drawn closer, matching Alex step for step, a small smile quirking his lips, as if he could hear the hummingbird beat of her heart. Then she realized Salome was talking about Dawes. Most people in the societies probably had no idea Pamela Dawes even existed.

"She's assisting me," said Alex.

But Salome was already leading them into the dark foyer. The Bridegroom followed. The tombs were kept unwarded to allow the easy flow of magic, but that meant Grays could come and go as they pleased. It was what made Lethe's protections necessary during rites.

"Do you have it?" Salome asked. The interior was nondescript: slate floors, dark wood, leaded windows overlooking a small interior courtyard where an ash tree grew. It had been there long before the university and would probably still be stretching its roots when the stones around it crumbled to dust. A magnetic board by the door showed which delegation members were currently at the tomb, a necessity given the size of the place. They were listed by their Egyptian god names, and only Salome's ankh, labeled *Chefren,* had been moved to the *At home* column.

"Got it," said Alex, pulling the statue from her bag.

Salome seized it with a happy shriek. "Perfect! Keys is going to be so pissed when they realize we got it back."

"What does it do?" Alex asked as Salome led them back into another dark room, this one with an elongated lozenge of a table at its center, surrounded by low chairs. The walls were lined with glass cases full of Egyptian curios and depictions of wolves.

"It doesn't *do* anything," Salome said with a withering look. She set the statue back in the case. "It's the principle of the thing. We invited them into our house and they shat on our hospitality."

"Right," said Alex. "That's awful." But she felt that angry rattle inside her twitch, vibrating against her sternum. Someone had just tried to kill her and this princess was playing stupid games. "Let's get this started."

Salome shifted her weight. "Listen, I really can't open up the temple without approval from the delegation. Not even alumni are allowed in."

Dawes released a small humming sigh. She was clearly relieved at the prospect of turning right around to go home. That wasn't going to happen.

"We had a deal. Are you actually trying to run game on me?" Alex asked.

Salome grinned. She didn't feel the least bit bad about it. And why would she? Alex was a freshman, an apprentice, clearly out of her element. She'd been nothing but quiet and deferential around Salome and the Wolf's Head delegation, always letting Darlington, the real presence, the gentleman of Lethe, do the talking. Maybe if Lethe had rescued her from her life sooner, she could have been that girl. Maybe if the *gluma* hadn't attacked and Dean Sandow hadn't ignored her she could have kept pretending to be her.

"I got your stupid figurine," said Alex. "You owe me."

"Except you weren't really supposed to do that, were you? So."

Most drug deals were done on credit. You got your supply from someone with the real connections, you proved you could move it for a good price, maybe next time you got the chance at a bigger bite. "You know why your boy is amateur and will stay amateur?" Eitan had asked Alex in his heavy accent once. He'd hiked a thumb at Len, who was giggling over a bong while Betcha played Halo beside him. "He's too busy smoking my product to make anyone but me rich." Len was always scraping by, always coming up a little short.

When Alex was fifteen she'd come back to Len without his money, confused and flustered by the investment banker she'd met in the parking lot of the Sherman Oaks Sports Authority. Len usually handled him, leaving sweet-faced Alex to do runs at the colleges and malls. But Len had been too hungover that morning, so he'd given her bus fare and she'd ridden the RTD down to Ventura Boulevard. Alex didn't know what to say when the banker told her he was short on cash, that he didn't have the money right then but he was good for it. She'd never had someone flat-out refuse to pay. The college kids she dealt with called her "little sis," and sometimes they even invited her to smoke up with them.

Alex had expected Len to be pissed, but he'd been furious in a way she'd never seen before, frightened, screaming it was on her and she was going to have to answer to Eitan. So she'd found a way to pay back the money. She'd gone home for the weekend and stolen her grandmother's garnet earrings to hock, had gotten a shift at Club Joy—the worst of the strip clubs, full of losers who barely tipped and owned by a tiny guy called King King, who wouldn't let you out of the dressing room without copping a feel first. It was the only place willing to take her on with no ID and nothing to fill her bikini. "Some guys like that," King King had said before shoving his hand in her top. "But not me."

She'd never come back short again.

Now she looked at Salome Nils, lean and smooth-faced, a Connecticut girl who rode horses and played tennis, her heavy bronze ponytail tucked over one shoulder like an expensive pelt. "Salome, how about you rethink your position?"

"How about you and your spinster aunt run home?"

Salome was taller than Alex, so Alex grabbed her by the lower lip, hard, and yanked. The girl squeaked and bent at the waist, flailing her arms.

"Alex!" Dawes yelped, hands pressed to her chest like a woman pretending to be a corpse.

Alex wrapped her arm around Salome's neck, looping her into a choke hold, a grip she'd learned from Minki, who was only four foot five and the one girl at Club Joy who King King never messed with. Alex fastened her fingers around the pear-shaped diamond drop that hung from Salome's ear.

She was aware of Dawes's shocked presence, of the Bridegroom stepping forward as if chivalry demanded he do so, the way the very air around them was shifting, changing, the haze dissipating so that Salome and Dawes and maybe even the Gray could see her clearly for the first time. Alex knew it was probably a mistake. Better not to be noticed, to keep your head down, remain the quiet girl, in over her head but no threat to anyone. But, like most mistakes, it felt good.

"I really like these earrings," she said softly. "How much did they cost?"

"Alex!" Dawes protested again. Salome scrabbled at Alex's forearm. She was strong from sports like squash and sailing, but she'd never had anyone lay hands on her, probably never seen a fight outside of a movie theater. "You don't know, right? They were a present from your dad on your sweet sixteen or on graduation or some shit like that?" Alex jostled her and Salome squeaked again. "Here's what's going to happen: You're going to let me into that room or I'm going to tear these things out of your ears and shove them both down your throat and you can choke on them." It was an empty threat. Alex wasn't in the business of wasting a nice pair of diamonds. But Salome didn't know that. She started crying. "Better," Alex said. "We understand each other?"

Salome gave a frantic nod of her head, the sweaty skin of her throat bobbing against Alex's arm.

Alex released her. Salome backed away, hands held out in front of her. Dawes had pressed her fingers to her mouth, and even the Bridegroom looked disturbed. She'd managed to scandalize a murderer.

"You're insane," said Salome, touching her fingertips to her throat. "You can't just—"

The snake inside Alex stopped twitching and uncoiled. She curled her hand into the sleeve of her coat and slammed it through the glass case where they kept their little trinkets. Salome and Dawes shrieked. They both took another step back.

"I know you're used to dealing with people who *can't just,* but I can, so give me the key to the temple room and let's get square so we can forget all about this."

Salome hovered, poised on the tips of her toes, framed by the doorway. She looked so light, so impossibly slender, as if she might simply lose contact with the ground and float up to the ceiling to bob there like a party balloon. Then something shifted in her eyes, all of that Puritan pragmatism seeping back into her bones. She settled on her heels.

"Whatever," she muttered, and fished her keys from her pocket, slipping one from the ring and setting it on the table.

"Thank you." Alex winked. "Now we can be friends again."

"Psycho."

"So I hear," said Alex. But crazy survived. Alex snatched up the key. "After you, Dawes." Dawes passed through to the hallway, keeping a wide distance between herself and Alex, eyes on the floor. Alex turned back to Salome.

"I know you're thinking that as soon as I'm in the temple you're going to start making calls, try to get me jammed up." Salome folded her arms. "I think you should do that. Then I'll come back and use that wolf statue to knock your front teeth in."

The Bridegroom shook his head.

"You can't just—"

"Salome," Alex said, shaking her finger. "Those words again."

But Salome clenched her fists. "You can't just do things like that. You'll go to jail."

"Probably," said Alex. "But you'll still look like a brother-fucking hillbilly."

"What is wrong with you?" Dawes spat as Alex joined her at the nondescript door that led to the temple room, the Bridegroom trailing behind.

"I'm a bad dancer and I don't floss. What's wrong with *you*?"

Now that the wave of adrenaline had passed, remorse was setting in. Once a mask was off you couldn't just slide it back into place. Salome wouldn't be calling the cavalry, Alex felt pretty sure of that. But she felt equally certain that the girl would talk. *Psycho. Crazy bitch.* Whether she would be believed was another thing entirely. Salome had said it herself: *You can't just.* People here didn't behave the way that Alex had.

The more pressing concern was how good Alex felt, like she was breathing easy for the first time in months, free from the suffocating weight of the new Alex she'd tried to construct.

But Dawes was breathing hard. As if she'd done all the work.

Alex flipped a light switch and flames flared to life in the gas lanterns along the red and gold walls, illuminating an Egyptian temple built into the heart of the English manor house. An altar was laden with skulls, taxidermied animals, and a leather ledger signed by each of the delegation's members before the start of a ritual. At the center of the back wall was a sarcophagus topped with glass, a desiccated mummy pilfered from a Nile Valley dig inside. It was all almost too expected. The ceiling was painted to look like a vaulted sky, acanthus leaves and stylized palms at the corners, and a stream cut through the center of the room, fed by a sheet of water that toppled from the edge of the balcony above, the echo overwhelming. The Bridegroom drifted across the stream, as far from the sarcophagus as he could get.

"I'm leaving," Salome shouted from down the hall. "I don't want to be here if something goes wrong."

"Nothing's going to go wrong!" Alex called back. They heard the front door slam. "Dawes, what did she mean if something goes wrong?"

"Did you read the ritual?" Dawes asked as she walked the perimeter of the room, studying its details.

"Parts of it." Enough to know it could put her in touch with the Bridegroom.

"You have to cross into the borderland between life and death."

"Wait . . . I'm going to have to die?" She really should start doing the reading.

"Yes."

"And come back?"

"I mean, that's the idea."

"And you're going to have to kill me?" Timid Dawes who, at the first sign of violence, had curled into a corner like a hedgehog in a sweatshirt? "You okay with that? It's not going to look good for you if I don't make it back."

Dawes expelled a long breath. "So make it back."

The Bridegroom's face was bleak, but that was sort of his look.

Alex contemplated the altar. "So the afterlife is Egypt? Of all the religions, the ancient Egyptians got it right?"

"We don't really know what the afterlife is like. This is one way into one borderland. There are others. They're always marked by rivers."

"Like Lethe to the Greeks."

"Actually, to the Greeks, Styx is the border river. Lethe is the final boundary the dead must cross. The Egyptians believed the sun died on the western banks of the Nile every day, so to journey from its eastern bank to the west is to leave the world of the living behind."

And that was the journey Alex would have to make.

The "river" bisecting the temple was symbolic, hewn of stone mined from the ancient limestone tunnels beneath Tura, hieroglyphs from the Book of Emerging Forth into Night carved into the sides and base of the channel.

Alex hesitated. Was this the crossroads? Was this the last foolish thing she would do? And who would be there to greet her in the beyond? Hellie. Maybe Darlington. Len and Betcha, their skulls crushed in, that cartoonish look of surprise still stuck on Len's face. Or maybe they'd be made whole somewhere on that other shore. If she died, would she be able to cross back through the Veil and spend an eternity flitting around campus? Would she end up back home, doomed to haunt some dump in Van Nuys? *So make it back.* Make it back or leave Dawes holding her dead body and Salome Nils to share the blame. The last thought wasn't entirely unpleasant.

"All I have to do is drown?"

"That's all," said Dawes without a hint of a smile.

Alex unbuttoned her coat and drew off her sweater, while Dawes shed her parka, drawing two slender green reeds from her pockets. "Where is he?" she whispered.

"The Bridegroom? Right behind you." Dawes flinched. "Kidding. He's by the altar, doing his brooding thing." The Bridegroom's scowl deepened.

"Have him stand opposite you on the western shore."

"He can hear you fine, Dawes."

"Oh, yes, of course." Dawes made an awkward gesture and the Bridegoom drifted to the other side of the stream. It was narrow enough that he crossed it with a single long step. "Now you both kneel."

Alex wasn't sure if the Bridegroom would be so quick to follow instructions, but he did. They knelt. He seemed to want this little talk as much as Alex did.

She could feel the cold of the floor through her jeans. She realized she was wearing a white T-shirt and it was going to get soaked. *You're about to die,* she scolded herself. *Maybe now isn't the time to worry about giving a ghost a look at your boobs.*

"Put your hands behind your back," said Dawes.

"Why?"

Dawes held up the reeds and recited: *"Let his wrists be bound with stalks of papyrus."*

Alex put her hands behind her back. It was like getting arrested. She half-expected Dawes to slide a zip tie around her wrists. Instead, she felt Dawes drop something into her left pocket.

"It's a carob pod. When you want to come back, put it in your mouth and bite down. Ready?"

"Go slow," said Alex.

Alex bent forward. It was awkward with her hands behind her back. Dawes braced her head and neck and helped her fall forward. Alex hovered for a moment above the surface, raised her eyes, met the Bridegroom's gaze. "Do it," she said. She took a deep breath and tried not to panic as Dawes shoved her head underwater.

Silence filled her ears. She opened her eyes but could see nothing but black stone. She waited, breath leaking from her in reluctant bubbles as her chest tightened.

Her lungs ached. She couldn't do this, not this way. They'd have to come up with something else.

She tried to push up, but Dawes's fingers were claws on the back of Alex's skull. It was impossible to break her grip in this position. Dawes's knee pressed into her back. Her fingers felt like spikes digging into Alex's scalp.

The pressure in Alex's chest was unbearable. Panic came at her like a dog slipped free of its leash, and she knew she'd made a very bad mistake. Dawes had been working with Book and Snake. Or Skull and Bones. Or Sandow. Or whoever wanted her gone. Dawes was finishing what the *gluma* had started. Dawes was punishing her for what had happened to Darlington. She'd known the truth of what had gone down that night at Rosenfeld all along, and this was her revenge on Alex for stealing away her golden boy.

Alex bucked and thrashed in silence. She had to breathe. *Don't.* But her body wouldn't listen. Her mouth opened on a gasp. Water rushed into her nose, her mouth, filled her lungs. Her mind was screaming in terror, but there was no way out. She thought of her mother, the silver bangles stacked on her forearms like gauntlets. Her grandmother whispered, *Somos almicas sin pecado.* Her gnarled hands gripped the skin of a pomegranate, spilling the seeds into a bowl. *We are little souls without sin.*

Then the pressure on the back of her neck was gone. Alex hurled herself backward, chest heaving. A rush of gritty water spewed from her mouth as her body convulsed. She realized her wrists were free and pushed up to her hands and knees. Deep, rattling coughs shook her body. Her lungs burned as she gulped at the air. *Screw Dawes. Screw everyone.* She was sobbing, unable to stop. Her arms gave way and she fell to the floor, flopped onto her back, sucking in breath, and wiped a wet sleeve over her face, trailing snot and tears—and blood. She'd bitten her tongue.

She squinted up at the painted ceiling. There were clouds moving across it, gray against the indigo sky. Stars glinted above her in strange formations. They were not her constellations.

Alex forced herself to sit up. She touched her hand to her chest, rubbing it gently, still coughing, trying to get her bearings. Dawes was gone. Everything was gone—the walls, the altar, the stone floors. She sat on the banks of a great river that flowed black beneath the stars, the sound of the water a long exhalation. A warm wind moved through the reeds. *Death is cold,* thought Alex. *Shouldn't it be cold here?*

Far across the water, she could see a man's shape moving toward her from the opposite shore. The water parted around the Bridegroom's body. So he had true physical form here. Had she stepped behind the Veil, then? Was she truly dead? Despite the balmy air, Alex felt a chill creep through her as the figure drew closer. He had no reason to harm her; he'd saved her. *But he's a killer,* she reminded herself. *Maybe he just misses murdering women.*

Alex didn't want to go back into the water, not when her chest still rattled with the memory of that violent pressure and her throat was raw from coughing. But she had come here with a purpose. She rose, scrubbed the sand from her palms, and waded into the shallows, her boots squelching in the mud. The river rose, warm against her calves, the current pulling gently at her knees, then her thighs, then her waist. She drifted past the spiky bowls of lotus flowers resting gently on the surface, still as a table setting. The water tugged at her hips, the current strong. She could feel the silt shift beneath her feet.

Something brushed against her in the water and she glimpsed starlight glinting off a shiny, ridged back. She flinched backward as the crocodile passed, a single golden eye rolling toward her as it submerged. To her left, another black tail flicked through the water.

"They cannot harm you." The Bridegroom stood only a few yards away. "But you must come to me, Miss Stern." To the center of the river. Where the dead and the living might meet.

She didn't like that he knew her name. His voice was low and pleasant, the accent almost English but broader in the vowels, a little like someone imitating a Kennedy.

Alex waded in farther, until she stood directly in front of the Bridegroom. He looked just as he had in the living world, silver light clinging to the sharp lines of his elegant face, caught in his dark mussed hair—except here she was close enough to see the creases of the knot in his necktie, the sheen of his coat. The bits of bone and gore that had splattered the white fabric of his shirt were gone. He was clean here, free of blood or wound. A boat slid past, a slim craft topped by a pavilion of billowing silks. Shadows moved behind the fabric, dim shapes that were men one moment and jackals the next. A great cat lay at the edge of the boat, its paw playing with the water. It looked at her with huge diamond eyes, then yawned, revealing a long pink tongue.

"Where are we?" she asked the Bridegroom.

"At the center of the river, the place of Ma'at, divine order. In Egypt all gods are the gods of death and life as well. We don't have much time, Miss Stern. Unless you wish to join us here permanently. The current is strong and inevitably we all succumb."

Alex looked over his shoulder to the shore beyond, west to the setting sun, to the dark lands, and the next world.

Not yet.

"I need you to look for someone on the other side of the Veil," she said.

"The murdered girl."

"That's right. Her name is Tara Hutchins."

"No small feat. This is a crowded place."

"But I'm betting you're up to the task. And I'm guessing that you want something in return. That's why you came to my rescue, isn't it?"

The Bridegroom didn't answer. His face remained very still, as if waiting for an audience to quiet. In the starlight, his eyes looked almost purple. "If I'm to find the girl, I'll need something personal of hers, a beloved possession. Preferably something that retains her effluvia."

"Her what?"

"Saliva, blood, perspiration."

"I'll get it," Alex said, though she had no idea how she was going to manage that. No chance was she going to be able to talk her way back into the morgue, and she was all out of coins of compulsion. Besides, Tara might be underground or ashes by now for all she knew.

"You'll need to bring it to the borderlands."

"I doubt I can come back here. Salome and I aren't exactly on friendly terms."

"I can't imagine why." The Bridegroom's lips pursed slightly, and in that moment, he reminded her so much of Darlington, she felt a tremor pass through her. On the western shore, she could see dark shapes moving, some human, some less so. A murmur rose from them, but she couldn't tell if there was reason in the noise, if it was language or just sounds.

"I need to know who murdered Tara," she said. "A name."

"And if she doesn't know her attacker?"

"Then find out what she was doing with Tripp Helmuth. He's in Skull and Bones. And if she knew anyone in Book and Snake. I need to know how she's connected to the societies." If she was connected at all, if it wasn't just coincidence. "Find out why the hell—" A bolt of lightning flashed overhead. Thunder cracked and the river suddenly seemed alive with restless reptilian bodies.

The Bridegroom raised a brow. "They don't like that word here."

Who? Alex wanted to ask. *The dead? The gods?* Alex dug her boots into the sand as the current tugged at her knees, urging her west into darkness. She could ponder the mechanics of the afterlife later.

"Just find out why someone wanted Tara dead. She has to know something."

"Then let us come to terms," said the Bridegroom. "You shall have your information, and in return I wish to know who murdered my fiancée."

"This is awkward. I was under the impression you did."

The Bridegroom's lips pursed again. He looked so prim, so put out, Alex almost laughed. "I'm aware."

"Murder-suicide? Shot her, then yourself?"

"I did not. Whoever killed her was responsible for my death as well. I don't know who it was. Just as Tara Hutchins may not know who harmed her."

"All right," Alex said dubiously. "Then why not ask your fiancée what she saw?"

His eyes slid away. "I can't find her. I've been searching for her on both sides of the Veil for over a hundred and fifty years."

"Maybe she doesn't want to be found."

He nodded stiffly. "If a spirit doesn't wish to be found, there's an eternity to hide in."

"She blames you," Alex said, fitting the pieces together.

"Possibly."

"And you think she'll stop blaming you if you find out who really did this?"

"Hopefully."

"Or you could just leave her be."

"I was responsible for Daisy's death, even if I didn't deal her the blow. I failed to protect her. I owe her justice."

"Justice? It's not like you can seek revenge. Whoever killed you is long since dead."

"Then I will find him on this side."

"And do what? Kill him real good?"

The Bridegroom smiled then, the corners of his mouth pulling back to reveal an even, predatory set of teeth. Alex felt a chill settle over her. She remembered the way he'd looked wrestling with the *gluma*. Like something that wasn't quite human. Something even the dead should fear.

"There are worse things than death, Miss Stern."

Again the murmuring rose from the banks of the western shore, and this time Alex thought she could pick out the sound of what might have been French. *Jean Du Monde?* It might be a man's name or just nonsense syllables her mind was trying to shape into meaning.

"You've had over a hundred years to try to find this mystery killer," Alex said. "Why do you think I'm going to have any better luck?"

"Your associate Daniel Arlington was looking into the case."

"I don't think so." An old murder that headlined Haunted New England tours wasn't Darlington's style at all.

"He visited the . . . place where we fell. He had a notebook with him. He took photos. I highly doubt he was just sightseeing. I can't get past the wards of the house on Orange Street. I want to know why he went there and what he found."

"And Darlington isn't . . . he isn't *there*? With you?"

"Even the dead don't know where Daniel Arlington is."

If the Bridegroom hadn't found Darlington on the other side, then Sandow had to be right. He was just missing, and that meant he could be found. Alex needed to believe that.

"Find Tara," Alex said, eager to be out of the water and back to the world of the living. "I'll see what work Darlington left behind. But I need to know something. Tell me you didn't send that thing, the *gluma*, after me."

"Why would I—"

"To form a connection between us. To make me indebted to you and lay the groundwork for this little partnership."

"I didn't send that thing after you and I don't know who did. How am I to convince you?"

Alex wasn't sure. She'd hoped she'd somehow be able to tell, that there was some vow she could force him to make, but she supposed she'd know soon enough. Assuming she could figure out what Darlington had discovered—if anything. The factory that had been the murder site was a parking garage now. Knowing Darlington, he'd probably gone there to take notes on the history of New Haven concrete.

"Just find Tara," she said. "Get me my answers and I'll get yours."

"This is not the pact I would have chosen, nor are you the partner I would have sought, but we will both make the best of it."

"You're quite the charmer. Daisy like that way with words?" The Bridegroom's eyes turned black. Alex had to force herself not to take a step backward. "Quick temper. Just the type of guy to off a lady who got sick of his shit. Did you?"

"I loved her. I loved her more than life."

"That isn't an answer."

He took a deep breath, summoning his composure, and his eyes returned to their normal state. He held out his hand to her. "Speak your true name, Miss Stern, and let us make our bargain."

There was power in names. It was why the names of Grays were blacked from the pages of Lethe's records. It was why she would rather think of the thing before her as the Bridegroom. The danger lay in connection, in the moment when you bound your life to someone else's.

Alex fingered the carob pod in her pocket. Best to be ready in case . . . what? He tried to drag her under? But why would he? He needed her and she needed him. That was how most disasters began.

She took his hand in hers. His grip was firm, his palm damp and ice-cold against hers. What was she touching? A body? A thought?

"Bertram Boyce North," he said.

"That's a terrible name."

"It's a family name," he said indignantly.

"Galaxy Stern," she said, but when she tried to pull her hand back, his fingers closed tighter.

"I have waited a long time for this moment."

Alex popped the carob pod into her mouth. "Moments pass," she said, letting it rest between her teeth.

"You thought me sleeping, but I heard you say, I heard you say, that you were no true wife." Again, Alex tried to pull away. His hand stayed closed hard around hers. *"I swear I will not ask your meaning in it: I do believe yourself against yourself, and will henceforward rather die than doubt."*

Rather die than doubt. Tara's tattoo. The quote wasn't from some metal band.

"Idylls of the King," she said.

"You remember now."

She'd had to read the whole long sprawl of Tennyson's poem as part of the preparation for Darlington's and her first visit to Scroll and Key. There were quotes from it all over their tomb, tributes to King Arthur and his knights—and a vault full of treasures plundered during the Crusades. *Have power on this dark land to lighten it, and power on this dead world to make it live.* She remembered the words etched into the stone table at the Locksmiths' tomb.

Alex shook free of the Bridegroom's grip. So Tara's death was potentially connected to *three* societies. Tara was tied to Skull and

Bones through Tripp Helmuth, to Book and Snake by the *gluma* attack, and—unless Tara had a secret taste for Victorian poetry—she was linked to Scroll and Key by her Tennyson tattoo.

North bowed slightly. "When you find something that belonged to Tara, bring it to any body of water and I will come to you. They are all crossing places for us now."

Alex flexed her fingers, wanting to be free of the feel of the Bridegroom's hand in hers. "I'll do that." She turned from him, biting down on the carob pod, her mouth flooding with a bitter, chalky taste.

She tried to push toward the eastern bank, but the river yanked at her knees and she stumbled. She felt herself pulled backward as she lost her footing, her boots seeking purchase on the riverbed as she was dragged toward the host of dark shapes on the western shore. North had his back to her and he already seemed impossibly far away. The shapes did not look quite human anymore. They were too tall, too lean, their arms long and bent at wrong angles, like insects. She could see their heads silhouetted against the indigo sky, noses lifted as if scenting her, jaws opening and closing.

"North!" she shouted.

But North did not break his stride. "The current claims us all in the end," he called without turning. "If you want to live, you have to fight."

Alex gave up trying to find the bottom. She wrenched her body toward the east and swam, kicking hard, fighting the current as she plunged her arms into the water. She turned her head to gasp for breath, the weight of her shoes drawing her down, her shoulders aching. Something heavy and muscular bumped her, driving her back; a tail lashed her leg. Maybe the crocodiles couldn't harm her, but they could do the river's work. Fatigue sat leaden in her muscles. She felt her pace slow.

The sky had gone dark. She couldn't see the shore any longer, wasn't even sure she was swimming in the right direction. *If you want to live.*

And wasn't that the worst of it? She did. She did want to live and always had.

"Hell!" she shouted. "Goddamn hell!" The sky exploded with forked lightning. A little blasphemy to light the way. For a long, horrible moment, there was only black water, and then she spotted the eastern shore.

She drove forward, plowing her hands through the water, until at last she let her legs drop. The bottom was there, closer than she'd thought. She crawled through the shallows, crushing lotus blossoms beneath her sodden body, and slumped down on the sand. She could hear the crocodiles behind her, the low engine rumble of their open mouths. Would they nudge her back to the river's grasp? She dragged herself a few more feet, but she was too heavy. Her body was sinking into the sand, the grains weighing her down, filling her mouth, her nose, drifting beneath her eyelids.

Something hard struck Alex's head again, then again. She forced her eyes open. She was on her back on the floor of the temple room, choking up mud and staring at Dawes's frightened face framed by the painted sky—mercifully static and free of clouds. Her body was shaking so hard she could hear the thump of her own skull on the stone floor.

Dawes seized her, wrapped her up tight, and, slowly, Alex's muscles stopped spasming. Her breathing returned to normal, though she could still taste silt and the bitter remnants of carob in her mouth. "You're all right," said Dawes. "You're all right."

And Alex had to laugh, because the last thing she would ever be was all right.

"Let's get out of here," she managed.

Dawes slung Alex's arm around her shoulders with surprising strength and pulled her to her feet. Alex's clothes were bone dry, but her legs and arms felt wobbly, as if she'd tried to swim a mile. She could still smell the river, and her throat had the raw, fish-slick feel of water going up her nose.

"Where do I leave the key?" asked Dawes.

"By the door," said Alex. "I'll text Salome."

"That seems so civil."

"Never mind. Let's break a window and pee on the pool table."

Dawes released a breathy giggle.

"It's okay, Dawes. I didn't die. Much. I went to the borderlands. I made a deal."

"Oh, Alex. What did you do?"

"What I set out to do." But she wasn't sure how she felt about it. "The Bridegroom is going to find Tara for us. That's the easiest way to figure out who hurt her."

"And what does he want?"

"He wants me to clear his name." She hesitated. "He claims Darlington was looking into the murder-suicide."

Dawes's brows shot up. "That doesn't sound right. Darlington hated popular cases like that. He thought they were . . . ghoulish."

"Tawdry," said Alex.

A faint smile touched Dawes's lips. "Exactly. Wait . . . then the Bridegroom *didn't* kill his fiancée?"

"He says he didn't. That's not quite the same thing."

Maybe he was innocent, maybe he wanted to make peace with Daisy, maybe he just wanted to find his way back to the girl he had murdered. It didn't matter. Alex would hold up her end of the bargain. Whether you made a deal with the living or the dead, best not to come up short.

We may wish to pass more quickly over Book and Snake, and who could blame us? There is an element of the unsavory to the art of necromancy, and this natural revulsion can be nothing but increased by the way the Lettermen have chosen to present themselves. When entering their giant mausoleum, one can hardly forget one is entering a house of the dead. But it is perhaps best to put aside fear and superstition and instead contemplate a certain beauty in their motto: *Everything changes; nothing perishes.* In truth, the dead are rarely raised beneath their showy pediments. No, the bread and butter of the Lettermen is intelligence, gathered from a network of dead informants, who traffic in all manner of gossip and who needn't listen at keyholes when they can simply walk unseen through walls.

—*from* The Life of Lethe: Procedures
and Protocols of the Ninth House

Tonight Bobbie Woodward coaxed the location of an abandoned speakeasy from what looked like little more than the remnants of a spine, a broken jawbone, and a hunk of hair. There is no amount of Jazz Age bourbon that can make me forget that sight.

—Lethe Days Diary of Butler Romano
(Saybrook College '65)

13

Last Fall

Darlington had woken from the Manuscript party with the worst shame hangover of his life. Alex showed him a copy of the report she'd sent. She'd kept the details murky, and though he wanted to be the kind of person who demanded a strict adherence to the truth, he really wasn't sure he could look Dean Sandow in the eye if the specifics of his humiliation were known.

He'd showered, made Alex breakfast, then called a car to take them both back to the Hutch so he could pick up the Mercedes. He returned to Black Elm in the old car, the images of the previous night a blur in his head. He collected the pumpkins along the drive and put them in the compost pile, raked the leaves from the back lawn. It felt good to work. The house suddenly seemed very empty, in a way it hadn't in a long time.

He'd brought few people to Black Elm. When he'd invited Michelle Alameddine to see the place his freshman year, she'd said, "This place is crazy. How much do you think it's worth?" He hadn't known how to answer.

Black Elm was an old dream, its romantic towers raised by a fortune made on the soles of vulcanized rubber boots. The first Daniel Tabor Arlington, Darlington's great-great-great-grandfather, had employed thirty thousand people in his New Haven plant. He'd bought up art and iffy antiquities, purchased a six-thousand-square-foot vacation "cabin" on a New Hampshire lake, given out turkeys at Thanksgiving.

The hard times had begun with a series of factory fires and ended with the discovery of a process to successfully waterproof leather. Arlington rubber boots were sturdy and easy to mass-manufacture but miserably uncomfortable. When Danny was ten, he'd found a heap of them in the Black Elm attic, shoved into a corner as if they'd misbehaved. He'd dug through until he found a matched pair and used his T-shirt to wipe the dust off them. Years later, when he took his first hit of Hiram's elixir and saw his first Gray, pale and leached of color as if still shrouded in the Veil, he would remember the look of those boots covered in dust.

He'd intended to wear the boots all day, stomping around Black Elm and mucking about in the gardens, but he only lasted an hour before he pulled them off and shoved them back into their pile. They'd given him a keen understanding of why, as soon as people had been offered another option for keeping the wet off their feet, they'd taken it. The boot factory had closed and stood empty for years, like the Smoothie Girdle factory, the Winchester and Remington plants, the Blake Brothers and Rooster Carriages before them. As he grew older, Darlington learned that this was always the way with New Haven. It bled industry but stumbled on, bleary and anemic, through corrupt mayors and daft city planners, through misguided government programs and hopeful but brief infusions of capital.

"This town, Danny," his grandfather liked to say, a common refrain, sometimes bitter, sometimes fond. *This town.*

Black Elm had been built to look like an English manor house, one of the many affectations adopted by Daniel Tabor Arlington when he made his fortune. But it was only in old age that the house really became convincing, the slow creep of time and ivy accomplishing what money could not.

Danny's parents came and went from Black Elm. They sometimes brought presents, but more often they ignored him. He didn't feel unwanted or unloved. His world was his grandfather, the housekeeper Bernadette, and the mysterious gloom of Black Elm. An endless stream of tutors buttressed his public school education—fencing, world languages, boxing, mathematics, piano. "You're learning to be a citizen in the world," his grandfather said. "Manners, might, and know-how. One will always do the trick." There wasn't much to do at Black Elm besides practice and Danny liked being good at things, not just the praise he received, but the feeling of a new door unlocking and swinging wide. He excelled at each new subject, always with the sense that he was preparing for something, though he didn't know what.

His grandfather prided himself on being as much blue collar as blue blood. He smoked Chesterfield cigarettes, the brand he'd first been given on the factory floor, where his own father had insisted he spend his summers, and he ate at the counter at Clark's Luncheonette, where he was known as the Old Man. He had a taste for both Marty Robbins and what Danny's mother described as "the histrionics of Puccini." She called it his "man-of-the-people act."

There was little warning when Danny's parents came to town. His grandfather would just say, "Set the table for four tomorrow, Bernadette. The Layabouts are gracing us with their presence." His mother was a professor of Renaissance art. He wasn't entirely sure what his father did—micro-investing, portfolio building, foreign-market hedges. It seemed to change with every visit and it never seemed to be going well. What Danny did know was that his parents lived off his grandfather's money and that the need for more of it was the thing that lured them back to New Haven. "The only thing," his grandfather would say, and Danny did not quite have the heart to argue.

The conversations around the big dinner table were always about selling Black Elm and became more urgent as the neighborhood around the old house began to come back to life. A sculptor from New York had bought up a run-down old home for a dollar, demolished it, and built a vast open-space studio for her work.

She'd convinced her friends to follow, and Westville had suddenly started to feel fashionable.

"This is the time to sell," his father would say. "When the land is finally worth something."

"You know what this town is like," his mother said. *This town.* "It won't last."

"We don't need this much space. It's going to waste; the upkeep alone costs a fortune. Come to New York. We could see you more often. We could get you into a doorman building or you could move someplace warm. Danny could go to Dalton or board at Exeter."

His grandfather would say, "Private schools turn out pussies. I'm not making that mistake again."

Danny's father had gone to Exeter.

Sometimes Danny thought his grandfather liked toying with the Layabouts. He would examine the scotch in his glass, lean back, prop his feet by the fire if it was winter, contemplate the green cloud formations of the elm trees that loomed over the back garden in the summer. He would seem to think on it. He would debate the better places to live, the upside to Westport, the downside to Manhattan. He'd expound on the new condominiums going up by the old brewery, and Danny's parents would follow wherever his fancies led, eagerly, hopefully, trying to build a new rapport with the old fellow.

The first night of their visits always ended with *I'll think on it,* his father's cheeks rosy with liquor, his mother gamely clutching her cocoon of plush cashmere around her shoulders. But by the close of day two the Layabouts would start to get restless, irritable. They'd push a little harder and his grandfather would start to push back. By the third night, they were arguing, the fire in the grate sparking and smoking when no one remembered to add another log.

For a long time Danny wondered why his grandfather kept playing this game. It wasn't until he was much older, when his grandfather was gone, and Danny was alone in the dark towers of Black Elm, that he realized his grandfather had been lonely, that his routine of the diner and collecting rents and reading Kipling might not be enough to fill the dark at the end of the day, that he might miss his foolish son. It was only then, lying on his side in the empty house, surrounded by a nest of books, that Darlington understood how much Black Elm demanded and how little it gave back.

The Layabouts' visits always ended the same way: his parents departing in a flurry of indignation and the scent of his mother's perfume—Caron Poivre, Darlington had learned on a fateful night in Paris the summer after sophomore year, when he'd finally worked up the courage to ask Angelique Brun for a date and arrived at her door to her looking glorious in black satin, her pulse points daubed with the expensive stink of his miserable youth. He'd claimed a migraine and cut the evening short.

Danny's parents had insisted they would take Danny away, that they'd enroll him in private school, that they'd bring him back to New York with them. At first Danny had been thrilled and panicked by these threats. But soon he'd come to understand they were empty blows aimed at his grandfather. His parents couldn't afford expensive schools without Arlington money, and they didn't want a child interfering with their freedom.

Once the Layabouts had gone, Danny and his grandfather would go to dinner at Clark's and his grandfather would sit and talk with Tony about his kids and look at family photos and they'd extoll the value of "good, honest work" and then his grandfather would grab Danny's wrist.

"Listen," he would say, his eyes rheumy and wet when you looked this close. "Listen. They'll try to take the house when I die. They'll try to take it all. You don't let them."

"You're not going to die," Danny would say.

And his grandfather would wink and laugh and reply, "Not yet."

Once, installed in a red booth, the smell of hash browns and steak sauce thick in the air, Danny had dared to ask, "Why did they even have me?"

"They liked the idea of being parents," his grandfather said, waving his hand over the leavings of his dinner. "Showing you off to their friends."

"And then they just dumped me here?"

"I didn't want you raised by nannies. I told them I'd buy them an apartment in New York City if they left you with me."

That had seemed okay to Danny at the time, because his grandfather *knew best,* because his grandfather had *worked for a living.* And if maybe some part of him wondered if the old man had just wanted another shot at raising a son, had cared more about the Arlington line than what might be best for a lonely little boy, the rest of him knew better than to walk down that dark hall.

As Danny got older, he made it a point to be out of the house when the Layabouts came to town. He was embarrassed by the idea of hanging around, hoping for a gift or a sign of interest in his life. He'd grown tired of watching them play out the same drama with his grandfather and seeing them indulged.

"Why don't you leave the old man alone and go back to wasting your time and his money?" he sneered at them on his way out of the house.

"When did the little prince become so pious?" his father had retorted. "You'll know what it's like when you fall out of favor."

But Darlington never had the chance. His grandfather got sick. His doctor told him to stop smoking, change the way he ate, said he could buy himself a few more months, maybe even a year. Danny's grandfather refused. He would have things his way or not at all. A nurse was hired to live in the house. Daniel Tabor Arlington grew grayer and more frail.

The Layabouts came to stay, and suddenly Black Elm felt like enemy territory. The kitchen was full of his mother's special foods, stacks of plastic containers, little bags of grains and nuts that crowded the counters. His father was constantly pacing through the ground-floor rooms, talking on his cell phone—about getting the house assessed, probate law, tax law. Bernadette was banished in favor of a cleaning crew that appeared twice a week in a dark green van and used only organic products.

Danny spent most of his time at the museum or in his room with the door locked, lost in books he consumed like a flame eating air, trying to stay alight. He practiced his Greek, started teaching himself Portuguese.

His grandfather's bedroom was crowded with equipment—IVs to keep him hydrated, oxygen to keep him breathing, a hospital bed beside the huge four-poster to keep him elevated. It looked like a time traveler from the future had taken over the dim space.

Whenever Danny tried to talk to his grandfather about what his parents were doing, about the real estate agent who had come to walk the property, his grandfather would seize his wrist and glance meaningfully at the nurse. "She listens," he hissed.

And maybe she did. Darlington was fifteen years old. He didn't know how much of what his grandfather said was true, if the cancer was speaking or the drugs.

"They're keeping me alive so they can control the estate, Danny."

"But your lawyer—"

"You think they can't make him promises? Let me die, Danny. They'll bleed Black Elm dry."

Danny went out alone to sit at the counter at Clark's, and when Leona had set a dish of ice cream in front of him, he'd had to press the heels of his hands against his eyes to keep from crying. He'd sat there until they needed to close and only then taken the bus home.

The next day, they found his grandfather cold in his bed. He'd slipped into a coma and could not be revived. There were furious, whispered conversations, closed doors, his father yelling at the nurse.

Danny had spent his days at the Peabody Museum. The staff didn't mind. There was a whole herd of kids who got dumped there during the summers. He'd walked through the mineral room; communed with the mummy, and the giant squid, and

Crichton's raptor; tried to redraw the reptile mural. He walked the Yale campus, spent hours deciphering the different languages above the Sterling Library doors, was drawn again and again to the Beinecke's collection of tarot cards, to the impenetrable Voynich Manuscript. Staring at its pages was like standing at Lighthouse Point all over again, waiting for the world to reveal itself.

When it started to get dark, he took the bus home and crept in through the garden doors, moving silently through the house, retreating to his bedroom and his books. Ordinary subjects weren't enough anymore. He was too old to believe in magic, but he needed to believe that there was something more to the world than living and dying. So he called his need an interest in the occult, the arcane, sacred objects. He spent his time hunting down the work of alchemists and spiritualists who had promised ways of looking into the unseen. All he needed was a glimpse, something to sustain him.

Danny had been curled up in his high tower room, reading Paracelsus beside Waite's translation, when his grandfather's attorney had knocked on the door. "You're going to have to make some choices," he'd said. "I know you want to honor your grandfather's memory, but you should do what's best for you."

It wasn't bad advice, but Danny had no idea what might be best for him.

His grandfather had lived off the Arlington money, doling it out as he saw fit, but the estate prohibited him from leaving it to anyone but his son. The house was another story. It would be held in trust for Danny until he was eighteen.

Danny was surprised when his mother appeared at his bedroom door. "The university wants the house," she said, then looked around the circular turret room. "If we all sign off, then the profits can be shared. You can come to New York."

"I don't want to live in New York."

"You can't begin to imagine the opportunities that will open for you there."

Nearly a year before, he'd taken the Metro-North to the city, spent hours walking Central Park, sitting in the Temple of Dendur at the Met. He'd gone to his parents' apartment building, thought about ringing the bell, lost his nerve. "I don't want to leave Black Elm."

His mother sat down on the edge of the bed. "Only the land is valuable, Danny. You have to understand that this house is worthless. Worse than worthless. It will drain every dollar we have."

"I'm not selling Black Elm."

"You have no idea what the world is like, Daniel. You're still a child, and I envy that."

"That's not what you envy."

The words emerged low and cold, exactly the way Danny wanted them to sound, but his mother just laughed. "What do you think is going to happen here? There's less than thirty thousand dollars in the trust for your college education, so unless you think you'd like to make some friends at UConn, it's time to start reevaluating. Your grandfather sold you a false bill of goods. He led you on just as he led us on. You think you'll be some Lord of Black Elm? You don't rule this place. It rules you. Take what you can from it now."

This town.

Danny stayed in his room. He locked the door. He ate granola bars and drank water from the sink in his bathroom. He supposed it was a kind of mourning, but he also just didn't know what to do. There was a stash of one thousand dollars tucked into a copy of McCullough's *1776* in the library. When he was eighteen he'd have access to his college fund. Beyond that, he had nothing. But he couldn't let go of Black Elm, he wouldn't, not so someone could put a wrecking ball through its walls. Not for anything. This was his place. Who would he be untethered from this house? From its wild gardens and gray stone, from the birds that sang in its hedges, from the bare branches of its trees. He'd lost the person who knew him best, who loved him most. What else was there to cling to?

And then one day he realized the house had gone silent, that he'd heard his parents' car rumble down the drive but never heard them return. He opened his door and crept down the stairs to find Black Elm completely empty. It hadn't occurred to him that his parents might simply leave. Had he secretly been holding them hostage, forcing them to stay in New Haven, to pay attention to him for the first time in his life?

At first he was elated. He turned on all of the lights, the television in his bedroom and the one in the den downstairs. He ate leftover food from the fridge and fed the white cat that sometimes prowled the grounds at dusk.

The next day, he did what he always did: He got up and went to the Peabody. He came home, ate beef jerky, went to bed. He did it again and again. When the school year started, he went to school. He answered all of the mail that came to Black Elm. He lived off Gatorade and chicken rolls from 7-Eleven. He was ashamed that sometimes he missed Bernadette more than he missed his grandfather.

One day he came home and flipped the switch in the kitchen, only to discover the electricity had been turned off. He pulled all of the blankets and his grandfather's old fur coat down from the attic and slept buried beneath them. He watched his breath plume in the quiet of the house. For six long weeks he lived in the cold and dark, doing his homework by candlelight, sleeping in the old ski clothes he discovered in a trunk.

When Christmas came, his parents appeared at the front door of Black Elm, rosy-cheeked and smiling, laden with presents and bags from Dean & DeLuca, Jaguar idling in the drive. Danny bolted the doors and refused to let them in. They'd made the mistake of teaching him he could survive.

Danny worked at the luncheonette. He got a job laying out manure and seed at Edgerton Park. He took tickets at Lyric Hall. He sold off clothes and pieces of furniture from the attic. It was enough to keep him fed and keep the lights on. His few friends were never invited over. He didn't want inquiries about his parents or about what a teenage boy was doing alone in a big, empty house. The answer he couldn't give was simple: He was caring for it. He was keeping Black Elm alive. If he left, the house would die.

A year passed, another. Danny got by. But he didn't know how long he could keep just making do. He wasn't sure what came next. He wasn't even sure if he could afford to apply to college with his friends. He would take a year off. He would work, wait for the money from his trust. And then? He didn't know. He didn't know and he was scared, because he was seventeen and already weary. He'd never thought of life as long, but now it seemed impossibly so.

Later, looking back on what happened, Danny could never be sure what he'd intended that night in early July. He'd been in and out of the Beinecke and the Peabody for weeks, researching elixirs. He'd spent long nights gathering ingredients and sending away for what he couldn't scavenge or steal. Then he'd begun the brew. For thirty-six hours straight he'd worked in the kitchen, dozing when he could, setting his alarm to wake him for the next stage in the recipe. When at last he'd looked down at the thick, tarlike syrup at the bottom of Bernadette's ruined Le Creuset, he'd hesitated. He knew what he was attempting was dangerous. But he'd run out of things to believe in. Magic was all he had left. He was a boy on an adventure, not a boy swallowing poison.

The UPS man had found him lying on the steps the next morning, blood streaming from his eyes and mouth. He'd made it out of the kitchen door before he'd collapsed.

Danny woke in a hospital bed. A man in a tweed jacket and a striped scarf sat beside his bed.

"My name is Elliot Sandow," he said. "I have an offer for you."

Magic had almost killed him, but in the end it had saved him. Just like in stories.

14

Winter

Alex curled into the window seat at the Hutch, and Dawes brought her a cup of hot chocolate. She'd placed a gourmet marshmallow at the top, the kind that looked like a rough-hewn stone yanked from a quarry.

"You went to the underworld," said Dawes. "You earned a treat."

"Not all the way to the underworld."

"Then give the marshmallow back." She said it shyly, as if afraid to make the joke, and Alex cradled her cup close to show she was playing along. She liked this Dawes, and she thought maybe this Dawes liked her.

"What was it like?"

Alex looked out over the rooftops in the late-morning light. From here she could see the gray gables of Wolf's Head and part of the ivy-tangle backyard, a blue recycling bin leaning tipsily against the wall. It looked so ordinary.

She set aside her bacon and egg sandwich. Usually she could eat at least two herself, but she could still feel the water pulling her under and it was messing with her appetite. Had she really crossed over? How much was illusion and how much was real? She described what she could and what the Bridegroom required.

When she finished, Dawes said, "You can't go to Tara Hutchins's apartment."

Alex picked at her sandwich. "I just told you about communing with the dead in a river full of golden-eyed crocodiles and that's what you have to say?"

But apparently a taste of adventure had been enough for Dawes. "If Dean Sandow finds out what you did to Salome to get us into the temple—"

"Salome may bitch to her friends, but she's not going to bring in the big guns. Offering us access to the temple, stealing from Scroll and Key, it's all too messy."

"And if she does?"

"I'll deny it."

"And you want me to deny it too?"

"I want you to think about what's important."

"And are you going to threaten me?" Dawes kept her eyes on her cup of cocoa, her spoon circling around and around.

"No, Dawes. Are you afraid I will?"

The spoon stopped. Dawes looked up. Her eyes were a warm, dark coffee, and sunlight caught in her messy bun making the red in her hair glow brighter. "I don't think I am," she said, as if she was surprised by the fact herself. "Your reaction was . . . extreme. But Salome *was* in the wrong." Dawes with the ruthless streak. "Still, if the dean learns you made a deal with a Gray . . ."

"He won't."

"But if he does—"

"You're afraid he'll call you out for helping me. Don't worry. I won't snitch. But Salome saw you. You might have to keep her quiet too."

Dawes's eyes widened and then she realized Alex was kidding. "Oh. Right. It's just . . . I really need this job."

"I get it," said Alex. Maybe better than anyone else who had ever sat beneath this roof. "But I need something that belonged to Tara. I'm going to her apartment."

"Do you even know where she lived?"

"No," Alex admitted.

"If Detective Turner figures out—"

"What's Turner going to find out? That I went halfway to the underworld to talk to a ghost? I'm pretty sure that doesn't count as witness tampering."

"But going to Tara's apartment, going through her stuff—that's breaking and entering. It's interfering with an active police investigation. You could be arrested."

"Only if I get caught."

Dawes gave a decisive shake of her head. "You're crossing a line. And I can't follow if you're going to put both of us and Lethe at risk. Detective Turner doesn't want you involved and he'll do whatever he has to do to protect his case."

"Good point," Alex said, considering. So maybe instead of going around Turner, she should just go through him.

Alex wanted to hide at the Hutch and let Dawes make her cups of cocoa. She wouldn't have minded a little mothering. But she needed to go back to Old Campus, to renew her grasp on the ordinary world before the things that really mattered slipped away.

She left Dawes in front of the Dramat, but not before she'd asked about the name she'd heard—or thought she'd heard—spoken in the borderlands. "Jean Du Monde? Or maybe Jonathan Desmond?"

"It doesn't ring a bell," said Dawes. "But I'll do a few searches and see what the library has to say once I'm back at Il Bastone."

Alex hesitated, then said, "Be careful, Dawes. Keep your eyes open."

Dawes blinked. "Why?" she said. "I'm nobody."

"You're Lethe and you're alive. You're somebody."

Dawes blinked again, like clockwork waiting for a cog to turn, for the right wheel to click so she could continue moving. Then her vision cleared and her brows knitted together. "Did you see him?" she said in a rush, staring at her feet. "On the other side?"

Alex shook her head. "North claims he isn't there."

"That's got to be a good sign," said Dawes. "On Wednesday we'll call him back. We'll bring him home. Darlington will know what to do about everything."

Maybe. But Alex wasn't going to bet her life on waiting.

"Do you know much about the Bridegroom murders?" Alex asked. Just because she knew North's name, she didn't have to make a habit of using it. It would only strengthen their bond.

Dawes shrugged. "It's on all of those Haunted Connecticut tours along with Jennie Cramer and that house in Southington."

"Where did it go down?"

"I'm not sure. I don't like reading about that kind of stuff."

"You chose the wrong line of work, Dawes." She cocked her head. "Or did it choose you?" She remembered Darlington's story about waking in the hospital at age seventeen, with an IV in his arm and Dean Sandow's card in his hand. It was something they had in common, though it had never really felt that way.

"They approached me because of the topic for my dissertation. I was well suited to research. It was boring work until—" She broke off. Her shoulders hitched like someone had yanked on her strings. Until Darlington. Dawes brushed at her eyes with her mittened hands. "I'll let you know if I learn anything."

"Dawes—" Alex began.

But Dawes was already hurrying back toward the Hutch.

Alex looked around, hoping to see the Bridegroom, wondering if the *gluma* or its master knew she had survived, if an ambush would be waiting around the next corner. She needed to get back to the dorm.

Alex thought of the passage the Bridegroom had quoted from *Idylls of the King,* the sinister weight of the words. If she remembered right, that passage was about Geraint's romance with Enid, a man driven mad by jealousy though his wife had remained faithful. It didn't exactly inspire confidence. *Rather die than doubt.* Why had Tara chosen those lines for her tattoo? Had she related to Enid or had she just liked the sound of the words? And why would someone from Scroll and Key share them with her? Alex couldn't imagine one of the Locksmiths saying thank you for a particularly sweet high with a tour of the tomb and an education in its mythology. And even if Alex wasn't making something out of nothing, how had dealing weed to a few undergrads turned into murder? There had to be something more at play here.

Alex remembered lying on her back at that intersection, seeing through Tara's eyes in her last moments, seeing Lance's face above her. But what if hadn't been Lance at all? What if it had been some kind of glamour?

She swerved down High Street toward the Hopper College dining hall. She longed for the safety of her dorm room, but answers could protect her better than any ward. Even though Turner had warned her off Tripp, it was the only name she had and the only direct connection between the societies and Tara.

It was early yet, but sure enough, there he was, seated at a long table with a few of his buddies, all of them in loose shorts and baseball caps and fleeces, all of them rosy-cheeked and wind-buffed despite the fact she knew they must be nursing hangovers. Apparently wealth was better than vitamin injections. Darlington had been cut from the same moneyed cloth, but he'd had a real face, one with a little hardness in it.

As she approached, she saw Tripp's friends turn their eyes to her, assess her, discard her. She'd showered at the Hutch, changed into a pair of Lethe sweats, and combed her hair. After being shoved into traffic and drowning, it was all the effort she owed anyone.

"Hey, Tripp," she said easily. "You got a minute?"

He turned her way. "You want to ask me to prom, Stern?"

"Depends. Gonna be a good little slut for me and put out?" Tripp's friends whooped and one of them let out a long *Ohhhh shit*. Now they were looking at her. "I need to talk to you about that problem set."

Tripp's cheeks pinked, but then his shoulders squared and he rose. "Sure."

"Bring him home early," said one of his buddies.

"Why?" she asked. "You want seconds?"

They whooped again and clapped their hands as if she'd landed an impressive put.

"You're kinda nasty, Stern," Tripp said over his shoulder as she trailed him out of the dining hall. "I like it."

"Come here," she said. She led him up the stairs, past the stained-glass windows of plantation life that had survived the name change of the college from "slavery is a positive good" Calhoun to Hopper. A few years back a black janitor had smashed one of them to bits.

Tripp's face changed, eager mischief pulling at his mouth. "What's up, Stern?" he said as they entered the reading room. It was empty.

She closed the door behind her and his grinned widened—like he actually thought she was about to make a move.

"How do you know Tara Hutchins?"

"What?"

"How do you know her? I've seen her phone logs," she lied. "I know just how often you were in touch."

He scowled and leaned on the back of a leather couch, folding his arms. The sulk didn't suit him. It pushed his round features from boyish sweetness to angry infant. "You a cop now?"

She walked toward him and she saw him stiffen, tell himself not to back up. His world was all about deferral, moving in sideways patterns. You didn't step to someone directly. You didn't look them in the eye. You were cool. You were fine with it. You could take a joke.

"Don't make me say I'm the law, Tripp. I'll have trouble keeping a straight face."

His eyes narrowed. "What is this about?"

"How stupid are you?" His mouth fell open. His lower lip looked wet. Had anyone ever spoken to Tripp Helmuth this way? "It's about a dead girl. I want to know what she was to you."

"I already talked to the police."

"And now you're talking to me. About a dead girl."

"I don't have to—"

She leaned in. "You know how this works, right? My job—the job of Lethe House—is to keep entitled little shits like you from making trouble for the administration."

"Why are you being such a hard-ass? I thought we were friends."

Because of all the beer pong we played and the summer we spent in Biarritz? Did he really not know the difference between friends and friendly?

"We *are* friends, Tripp. If I wasn't your friend I'd have taken this to Dean Sandow already, but I don't want hassle and I don't want to make trouble for you or for Bones if I don't have to."

His big shoulders shrugged. "It was just a hookup."

"Tara doesn't seem like your type."

"You don't know my type." Was he really trying to flirt his way out of this? She held his gaze and his eyes slid away. "She was fun," he muttered.

For the first time, Alex had the sense he was being honest.

"I bet she was," Alex said gently. "Always had a smile, always glad to see you." That's what dealing was about. Tripp probably didn't understand that he was just a customer, that he was a pal as long as he had cash on hand.

"She was nice." Did he care that she was dead? Was there something more haunted than a hangover in his eyes or did Alex just want to believe he gave a damn? "I swear all we ever did was fuck around and smoke a couple of bowls."

"You ever meet at her place?"

He shook his head. "She always came to me."

Of course figuring out her address couldn't be that easy. "You ever see her with anyone from another society?"

Another shrug. "I don't know. Look, Lance and T were deal-ers; they got the best weed I've ever had, like the lushest, greenest shit you've ever seen. But I didn't keep track of who she hung out with."

"I asked if you saw her with anyone."

He lowered his head more. "Why are you being like this?"

"Hey," she said softly. She squeezed his shoulder. "You know you're not in trouble, right? You're going to be fine." She felt some of the tension ease out of him.

"You're being so mean."

She was torn between wanting to slap him or put him to bed with his favorite binky and a cup of warm milk.

"I'm just trying to get some answers, Tripp. You know how it is. Just trying to do my job."

"I feel you, I feel you." She doubted that, but he knew the script. Regular guy, Tripp Helmuth. Working hard or hardly working.

She gripped his shoulder more firmly. "But you need to under-stand this situation. A girl died. And these people she ran with? They aren't your friends and you aren't going to stay hard or not rat or any of that crap you've seen in movies, because this isn't a movie, this is your life, and you have a good life, and you don't want to mess it up, yeah?"

Tripp kept his eyes on his shoes. "Yeah, okay. Yeah." She thought he might cry.

"So who did you see with Tara?"

When Tripp was done talking, Alex leaned back. "Tripp?"

"Yeah?" He kept staring at his shoes—ridiculous plastic san-dals, as if summer never stopped for Tripp Helmuth.

"Tripp," she repeated, and waited for him to raise his head and meet her eyes. She smiled. "That's it. We're done. It's over." *You don't ever have to think about that girl again. How you fucked her and forgot her. How you thought she might give you a good deal if you made her come. How it got you off to be with someone who felt a little dangerous.* "We good?" she asked. This was the language he understood.

"Yeah."

"I'm not going to let this go any further, I promise."

And then he said it and she knew he wouldn't tell anyone about this conversation—not his friends, not the Bonesmen. "Thank you."

That was the trick of it: to make him believe he had more to lose than she did.

"One last thing, Tripp," she said as he made to scurry back toward the dining hall. "Do you have a bike?"

Alex pedaled across the green, past the three churches, then down to State Street and under the highway. She had about two hundred pages of reading to do if she didn't want to fall behind this week, and possibly a monster hunting her, but right now she needed to talk to Detective Abel Turner.

Once you were off campus, New Haven lost its pretensions in fits and starts—dollar stores and grimy sports bars shared space with gourmet markets and sleek coffee spots; cheap nail salons and cell-phone hubs sat next to upscale noodle shops and boutiques selling small, useless soaps. It left Alex uneasy, as if the city's identity kept shifting in front of her.

State Street was just a long stretch of nothing—parking lots, power lines, the train tracks to the east—and the police station was just as bad, an ugly, muscular building of oatmeal-colored slabs. There were dead spaces like this all over the city, entire blocks of massive concrete monoliths looming over empty plazas like a drawing of the future from the past.

"*Brutalist,*" Darlington had called them, and Alex had said, "It does sort of feel like the buildings are ganging up on you."

"No," he'd corrected. "It's from the French, *brut.* As in *raw,* because they used bare concrete. But, yes, it does feel like that."

There had been slums here before, and then money had poured into New Haven from the Model Cities program. "It was supposed to clean everything up, but they built places no one wanted to be. And then the money ran out and New Haven just has these . . . gaps."

Wounds, Alex had thought at the time. *He was about to say "wounds," because the city is alive to him.*

Alex looked down at her phone. Turner hadn't replied to her texts. She hadn't worked up the nerve to call, but now she was here and there was nothing else to do. When he didn't answer, she hung up and dialed back again, and then again. Alex hadn't been anywhere near a police station since after Hellie died. *Not only Hellie died that night.* But to think of it in any other terms, to think of the blood, the pale pudding of Len's brain clinging to the lip of the kitchen counter, set her mind rabbiting around her skull in panic.

At last Turner answered.

"What can I do for you, Alex?" His voice was pleasant, solicitous, as if there were no one else he'd rather speak to.

Reply to my goddamn texts. She cleared her throat. "Hi, Detective Turner. I'd like to speak to you about Tara Hutchins."

Turner chuckled—there was no other word for it; it was the indulgent laugh of a seventy-year-old grandfather, though Turner couldn't have been much over thirty. Was he always like this at the office? "Alex, you know I can't talk about an active investigation."

"I'm outside the police station."

A pause. Turner's voice was different when he answered, a bit of that jolly warmth gone. "Where?"

"Right across the street."

Another long pause. "Train station in five."

Alex walked Tripp's bike the rest of the way up the block to Union Station. The air was soft, moist with the promise of snow. She wasn't sure if she was sweaty from the ride or because she was never going to get used to talking to cops.

She propped the bike against a wall by the parking lot and sat down on a low concrete bench to wait. A Gray hurried past in his undershorts, checking his watch and bustling along as if afraid he was going to miss his train. *You're not going to make that one, buddy. Or any of the rest.*

She scrolled through her phone, keeping one eye on the street as she searched Bertram Boyce North's name. She wanted a little context before she went asking the Lethe library questions.

Luckily, there was plenty online. North and his fiancée were celebrities of a kind. In 1854, he and his betrothed, the young Daisy Fanning Whitlock, had been found dead in the offices of the North & Sons Carriage Company, long since demolished. Their portraits were the first link under *New Haven* on the Connecticut Haunts site. North looked handsome and serious, his hair more tidily arranged than it had been in death. The only other difference was his clean white shirt, unmarred by bloodstains. Something cold slithered up her spine. Sometimes, despite her best efforts, she forgot she was seeing the dead, even with the gore splattered all over his fancy coat and shirt. Seeing this stiff, still black-and-white photo was different. *He is moldering in a grave. He is a skeleton gone to dust.* She could have what was left of him dug up. They could stand by the edge of his tomb together and marvel at his bones. Alex tried to shake off the image.

Daisy Whitlock was beautiful in that dark-haired stony-eyed way that girls of that time were. Her head was tilted slightly, only the barest hint of a smile on her lips, her curls parted in the middle and arranged in soft loops that left her neck bare. Her waist was tiny and her white shoulders emerged from a froth of ruffles, a posy of mums and roses clutched in her delicate hands.

As for the factory where the murder had taken place, parts of it hadn't yet been finished at the time of North's murder and it was never completed. North & Sons moved their operations to Boston and continued to do business until the early 1900s. There were no photographs of the crime scene, only lurid descriptions of blood and horror, the gun—a pistol North had kept in his new offices in case of intruders—still gripped in his hand.

The bodies had been discovered by Daisy's maid, a woman named Gladys O'Donaghue, who had gone screaming into the streets. She'd been found nearly a half mile away, hysterical, at the corner of Chapel and High. Even after a calming dose of brandy, she'd had little information to offer the authorities. The crime seemed an obvious one; only the motive offered any kind of intrigue. There were theories that Daisy had been pregnant by another man but her family had hushed it up in the wake of the murders to avoid further scandal. One commenter suggested that North had been driven mad by mercury poisoning because of the time he'd spent near Danbury's hat factories. The simplest theory was that Daisy wanted to break off the engagement and North wouldn't have it. His family wanted an infusion of capital from the Whitlocks—and North wanted Daisy. She'd been a favorite of the local society columns and known as flirtatious, bold, and sometimes inappropriate.

"I like you already," murmured Alex.

Alex scrolled past maps to both Daisy's and North's graves and was trying to zoom in on an old newspaper article when Turner arrived at the station.

He hadn't bothered with an overcoat. Apparently he didn't intend to stay long. Even so, the man could dress. He wore a simple, staid charcoal suit, but the lines were sharp, and Alex saw the careful touches—the pocket square, the thin lavender stripe on the tie. Darlington had always looked good, but effortlessly so. Turner wasn't afraid to look like he tried.

His jaw was set, his mouth a pinched seam. It was only when he spotted Alex that his mask of diplomacy dropped into place. His whole bearing changed, not just his expression. His body went loose and easy, unthreatening, as if actively discharging the current of tension that animated his form.

He sat down beside her on the bench and rested his elbows on his knees. "I need to ask you not to show up at my place of work."

"You didn't answer my texts."

"There's a lot going on. I'm in the middle of a homicide investigation as you know."

"It was that or go to your house."

That live-wire tension sprang back into his body, and Alex felt a jolt of gratification at being able to rile him.

"I suppose Lethe has all of my particulars on file," he said. Lethe most likely did know everything from Turner's Social Security number to his tastes in porn, but no one had ever offered Alex a look at the file. She didn't even know if Turner lived in New Haven proper. Turner checked his phone. "I have about ten minutes to give you."

"I'd like you to let me talk to Lance Gressang."

"Sure. Maybe you'd like to run his prosecution too."

"Tara wasn't just connected to Tripp Helmuth. She and Lance were dealing to members of Scroll and Key and Manuscript. I have names."

"Go on."

"They're not something I can disclose."

Turner's face was still impassive, but she could feel his resentment building with each moment he was forced to indulge her. Good.

"You come to me for information but you're not willing to share yours?" he asked.

"Let me talk to Gressang."

"He is the chief suspect in a murder investigation. You understand that, right?" A disbelieving smile had crept up his lips. He really thought she was stupid. No, entitled. Another Tripp. Maybe another Darlington. And he would like this version of her better than the one he'd met at the morgue. Because this version could be intimidated.

"All I need is a few minutes," she said, adding a whiny note to her voice. "I don't actually need your permission. I can make the request through his lawyer, say I knew Tara."

Turner shook his head. "Nope. As soon as I leave this meeting I'm calling him and letting him know there's a crazy girl trying to insert herself into this case. Maybe I'll give him a look at the video of you running around Elm Street like some kind of fool."

A bolt of shame shook Alex as she thought of herself writhing in the middle of the road, cars swerving around her. So Sandow had shared the video with Turner. Had he shared it with anyone else? The thought of Professor Belbalm seeing it made her stomach churn. No wonder the detective was doubly smug with her today. He didn't just think she was stupid. He thought she was unhinged. Even better.

"What's the big deal?" Alex said.

Turner's fingers flexed on the immaculately pressed legs of his suit. "The *big deal*? I can't just sneak you in there. All visitors to a jail are logged. I have to have a good official reason to bring you there. His attorneys have to be there. The whole thing will have to be recorded."

"You're telling me cops always follow the rules?"

"*Police*. And if I bent the rules and the defense found out, Lance Gressang would get away with murder and I'd lose my job."

"Look, when I went up to Tara's place—"

Turner's gaze snapped to her, eyes blazing, all pretense of diplomacy gone. "You went to her house? If you crossed that tape—"

"I needed to know if—"

He shot to his feet. This was the real Turner: young, ambitious, forced to dance to make his way in the world and sick of it. He paced back and forth in front of the bench, then pointed a finger at her. "Stay the fuck away from my case."

"Turner—"

"*Detective* Turner. You are not going to mess with my case. I see you anywhere near Woodland, I will fuck your life so hard, you'll never walk straight again."

"Why are you being such a hard-ass?" she whined, cribbing a line from Tripp.

"This isn't a *game* for you to play. You need to understand how easy it would be for me to take your life apart, to find a little stash of weed or pills on you or in your dorm room. Get that."

"You can't just—" Alex began, eyes wide, lip wobbling.

"I'll do whatever I have to do. Now get out of here. You have no idea the line you're walking, so do not press me."

"I get it, okay?" Alex said meekly. "I'm sorry."

"Who did Tripp say he saw with Tara?"

Alex didn't mind sharing the names. She'd meant to from the start. Turner needed to know that Tara had been dealing to students who weren't in her phone logs, using a burner or a phone Lance had hidden or destroyed. She looked down at her gloved hands and said quietly, "Kate Masters and Colin Khatri."

Kate was in Manuscript but Alex barely knew her. The last time she'd spoken to her had been the night of the Halloween party, when she and Mike Awolowo had begged her not to tattle to Lethe about drugging Darlington. She'd been dressed as Poison Ivy. But Colin she knew. Colin worked for Belbalm and he was in Scroll and Key. He was cute, tidy, as preppy as they came. She could imagine him relaxing with an outrageously expensive bottle of wine, not hotboxing with town goods. But she knew from her time at Ground Zero, appearances could be deceiving.

Turner smoothed his lapels, his cuffs, ran his hands over the clean sides of his head. She watched him put himself back together, and when he smiled and winked it was as if the angry, hungry Turner had never been there. "Glad we had this chat, Alex. You let me know if there's anything at all I can do to help you out in the future."

He turned and marched back toward the hulking form of the police station. She hadn't liked whimpering in front of Turner. She hadn't liked being called crazy. But now she knew what street Tara had lived on, and the rest would be easy.

Alex was tempted to go directly to Woodland and find Tara's apartment, but she didn't want to try to do her snooping on a Sunday, when people would be home from work. It would have to wait until tomorrow. She hoped that whoever had sent the *gluma* after her thought she was still laid up at the Hutch—or dead. But if they were watching her, she hoped they'd seen her talking to Turner. Then they'd think the police knew what she knew, and there'd be no point to shutting her up. *Unless somehow Turner is in on all of it.*

Alex shook the thought from her mind as she pedaled back toward the Hopper gates. Cautious was helpful; paranoid was just another word for distracted.

She texted Tripp to let him know where she'd dumped his bike inside the gate and headed across Old Campus, turning over Tara's ties to the societies. The *gluma* suggested the involvement of Book and Snake, but so far it didn't look like Tara had been dealing to anyone in that society. Tripp connected her to Skull and Bones, Colin and that weird tattoo connected her to Scroll and Key, Kate Masters tied her to Manuscript—and Manuscript specialized in glamours. If someone had been dressed in magic that night, pretending to be Lance, Manuscript was probably involved. That could explain why Alex had seen Lance's face in Tara's memory of the murder.

But all of that also assumed Tripp's information was good. When you were scared you'd say anything to get yourself out of a bad situation. She should know. And Alex had no doubt that Tripp would happily sell out whoever first came to mind to get himself out of trouble. She supposed she could take those names to Sandow, explain that Turner would now be hunting down their alibis, try to make him reconsider Lethe's involvement in the investigation. But then she'd have to explain that she'd badgered the information out of a Bonesman.

Alex had to be honest with herself too. Something in her had shaken loose when the *gluma* attacked—the real Alex coiled like a serpent in the false skin of who she pretended to be. That Alex had snapped her jaws closed on Salome, bullied Tripp, manipulated Turner. But she had to be careful. *It's essential that they see you as stable, reliable.* She didn't want to give Sandow any more excuses to sever her from Lethe and her only hope of staying at Yale.

Alex felt a rush of relief as she climbed the steps to Vanderbilt. She wanted to be behind the wards, to see Lauren and Mercy and talk about work and boys. She wanted to sleep in her own narrow bed. But when Alex entered the suite, the first thing she heard was crying. Lauren and Mercy were on the couch. Lauren had her arm around Mercy and was rubbing her back as Mercy sobbed.

"What happened?" Alex said.

Mercy didn't look up and Lauren's face was harsh.

"Where have you been?" she snapped.

"Darlington's mom needed help with something."

Lauren rolled her eyes. Apparently the family-emergency excuse was past retirement.

Alex sat down on the battered coffee table, her knees bumping Mercy's. Mercy had her head buried in her hands. "Tell me what's going on."

"Can I show her?" said Lauren.

Mercy released another sob. "Why not?"

Lauren handed over Mercy's phone. Alex slid unlock on the screen and saw a text string with someone named Blake.

"Blake Keely?" He was a lacrosse player, if she remembered right. There was a story about him kicking a kid from a rival team in the head during a game in high school. The player had been on the ground at the time. Every college had revoked his scholarship—every college but Yale. The lacrosse team had been Ivy League champs four years running, and Blake had landed a modeling gig with Abercrombie & Fitch. His posters were plastered all over the store's windows on Broadway, giant black-and-white images of him emerging shirtless from a mountain lake, hauling a Christmas tree through a snowy wood, snuggling a bulldog puppy by a roaring fire.

You were hot last night. All the brothers agree. Come by again tonight. There was a video attached.

Alex didn't want to press play, but she did. The sound of raucous laughter blared from the phone, the thump of a bass track. Blake said, "Heyyyyy hey, we have such a pretty girl, something exotic on the menu tonight, right?"

He turned the camera on Mercy, who laughed. She was sitting in another boy's lap, her velvet skirt hiked high on her thighs, a red Solo cup in her hand. *Shit. Omega Meltdown.* Alex had promised Mercy she'd go with her, but she'd completely forgotten.

"Take it in the other room," said Lauren as Mercy wept.

Hurriedly, Alex entered her bedroom and shut the door. Mercy's bed was unmade. That, even more than her sobbing, was a sure sign of distress.

In the video Mercy's skirt was pushed up to her waist, her panties pulled down. "Jesus, look at all that bush!" Blake giggled, a high, giddy sound, his eyes tearing with laughter. "It's so straight. You doing good, hon?"

Mercy nodded.

"Haven't had too much to drink? You're sober and consensual as they say?"

"You bet."

Mercy's eyes were bright, lively, alert, not glazed or heavy lidded. She didn't look drunk or like she'd been roofied.

"On your knees, hon. Time for Chinese takeout."

Mercy knelt, her dark eyes wide and wet. She opened her mouth. Her tongue was stained purple from the punch. Alex paused the video. No, not the punch. She knew that color. That was how those servants had looked that night at Manuscript. That was Merity, the drug of service, taken by acolytes to give up their will.

The door opened and Lauren slipped inside. "She won't let me take her to the health center."

"They're rapists. We should be going to the cops." They should be good for that at least.

"You saw the video. She told me she barely drank."

"She was drugged."

"I thought so too, but she isn't acting like it. She doesn't look like it. Did you watch it?"

"Part of it. How bad does it get?"

"Bad."

"How many guys?"

"Just the two. She thinks he's going to send it around to his boys if he hasn't already. Why weren't you with her?"

I forgot. Alex didn't want to say it. Because, yes, a girl had been murdered and Alex had been attacked, but at the end of the day, Alex hadn't spared a second thought for Mercy, and Mercy deserved better. She deserved a night out to have fun and flirt and maybe meet a cute boy she could kiss and take to a formal. That was why Alex had agreed to go to Omega Meltdown with her. She owed Mercy, who had been kind to her and helped with Alex's papers and never pitied, just pushed her to do better. But she'd forgotten all about the party after the *gluma* attack. She'd gotten caught up in her fear and desperation and her desire to know why she was being hunted.

"Who did she go with?" Alex asked.

"Charlotte and that crew from upstairs." Lauren's voice was an angry growl. "They just left her there."

If Mercy was under the influence of Merity, then she would have said she was fine, that they should leave, and they wouldn't have known her well enough to argue with her. But if Alex had been there, she would have seen Mercy's purple tongue. She could have stopped this.

Alex put her coat back on. She took a screenshot of the video and sent it to her own phone showing Mercy's mouth open, her purple tongue out.

"Where are you going?" Lauren whispered furiously. "Does Darlington's mom need some more help?"

"To fix this."

"She doesn't want us talking to the police."

"I don't need the police. Where does Blake live?"

"The Omega house."

Up on Lynwood, in the filthy frat row that had sprung up when the university had kicked the fraternities off campus years ago.

"Alex—" said Lauren.

"Just try to keep her calm and don't leave her alone."

Alex strode back out of Vanderbilt and across Old Campus. She wanted to go straight to Blake, but that would do no good. A group of Grays flickered in the corner of her vision. *"Orare las di Korach,"* she spat. Her grandmother's curse felt good on her tongue. *Let them be swallowed alive.* All of her anger must have gathered in the words. The Grays scattered like birds.

And what about the *gluma*? If it was out there hunting, would it go running? She would have been glad for a glimpse of the Bridegroom, but she hadn't seen him since their encounter in the borderlands.

Alex knew she shouldn't have riled Detective Turner. He might have been willing to help if she hadn't messed with him. It was possible he still would. Part of her believed he really was one of the good guys. But she didn't want to rely on Turner or the law or the administration to fix this. Because the video would still be out there, and Blake Keely was rich and beautiful and beloved, and there was a big difference between things being fair and things being set right.

15

Winter

Alex hadn't been back to Manuscript since the Halloween party. That night, she'd stayed with Darlington at Black Elm, trying to keep warm in his narrow bed. She'd woken to dawn light trickling through the room and Darlington curled behind her, asleep. He was hard again, the ridge of him tucked against the curves of her ass. One of his hands was cupped over her breast, his thumb moving back and forth over her nipple with the lazy rhythmic sway of a cat's tail. Alex felt her whole body flush.

"Darlington," she had snapped.

"Mmm?" he murmured against the back of her neck.

"Wake up and fuck me or *cut that out.*"

He froze and she felt him wake. He rolled off the bed, stumbling, tangled in covers. "I didn't . . . I'm sorry. Did we?"

She rolled her eyes. "No."

"Those assholes."

A rare swear but a deserved one. His eyes had been bloodshot, his face haggard. It would have been worse if he'd known that the report she showed him over breakfast bore no resemblance to the one she'd actually sent to Dean Sandow.

The Manuscript tomb looked even uglier beneath a noon sun, the circle hidden in its brickwork seeming to appear then disappear as Alex approached the front door. Mike Awolowo waved her inside. The big room and the yard beyond looked airy, safe, all signs of the arcane buried deep beneath the surface.

"I'm glad you reached out," he said, though Alex doubted that was true. He was an international studies major and had the intense, friendly poise of a daytime talk-show host.

Alex glanced over his shoulder and was happy to see the place seemed empty. Now that Kate Masters was on Alex's suspect list, she didn't want to complicate things.

"Time to settle up."

Mike's expression was resigned, the look of someone sitting in a dentist's chair. "What do you need?"

"A way to call back something. A video."

"If it's gone viral, there's nothing we can do."

"I don't think it has, not yet, but it could tip any minute."

"How many people have seen it?"

"I'm not sure. Right now maybe a handful."

"That's a big ritual, Alex. And I'm not even sure it would work."

Alex held his gaze. "The only reason you're even up and functioning is because of the report I filed on Halloween."

The night of the party, she and Darlington had stormed out of the tomb, or done their best to, Mike and Kate trailing after in their Batman and Poison Ivy costumes. Darlington was wobbly on his feet, blinking at everything as if it was too bright, clinging hard to her arm.

"Please," Awolowo had begged. "This wasn't sanctioned by the delegation. One of the alumni had a bug up his ass about Darlington. It was supposed to be a joke."

"Nothing happened," said Kate.

"That wasn't nothing," Alex retorted, dragging Darlington farther down the block. But Awolowo and Masters had followed, arguing and then making offers. So Alex had propped Darlington against the Mercedes and made a deal, a favor for a softening of the report. She'd described the drugging as an accident and Manuscript had faced nothing but a fine, when otherwise they would have been suspended. She'd known eventually Darlington would find out, when harsher sanctions never materialized. If nothing else, she'd get a stern lecture on the difference between morals and ethics. But then Darlington had disappeared, and the report had never been an issue. She knew it was a punk move, but if she survived her freshman year, Lethe would be her show to run. She had to do things her way.

Awolowo crossed his arms. "I thought you did that to save Darlington's pride."

"I did it because the world runs on favors." Alex rubbed a hand over her face, trying to shake a sudden wave of fatigue. She held up her phone. "Look at her tongue. Someone's using one of your drugs to mess with girls."

Mike took the phone in hand and frowned at the screenshot. "Merity? Impossible. Our supplies are locked down."

"Someone could be sharing the recipe."

"We know what the stakes are. And we all have strong prohibitions placed on us. We can't just walk around talking about what we do here. Besides, it's not a question of knowing a formula. Merity only grows in the Greater Khingan Mountains. There's literally one supplier, and we pay him a very steep fee to only sell to us."

Then where had Blake and his friends gotten it? Another mystery.

"I'll look into it," Alex said. "But right now I need to fix this."

Mike studied Alex. "This isn't Lethe business, is it?" Alex didn't answer. "There's a threshold for media. It varies for music, celebrity, memes. But if you pass it, no ritual can call it back. I guess we could try to reverse the Full Cup. We use it to build momentum for projects. That's what we did for Micha's single last September."

Alex remembered Darlington's description of the society members gathered naked in a huge copper vat, chanting as it filled gradually with wine that bubbled up from some invisible place beneath their feet. The Full Cup. It had been enough to get a very mediocre single to number two on the dance charts.

"How many people would you need for it?"

"At least three others. I know who to talk to. But it will take a while to prepare. You'll need to do everything you can to stanch the bleeding in the meantime or none of it will matter."

"Okay. Call your people. As fast as you can." She didn't like the idea of Kate Masters being involved, but mentioning her name would only raise questions.

"You're sure?"

Alex knew what Mike was asking. This was a violation of every Lethe protocol. "I'm sure."

She was already at the door when Mike said, "Wait."

He crossed to a wall of decorative urns and opened one, then drew a small plastic envelope from a drawer and measured out a tiny portion of silver powder. He sealed the envelope and handed it to Alex.

"What is it?"

"Starpower. Astrumsalinas. It's salt skimmed from a cursed lake where countless men drowned, in love with their own reflections."

"Like Narcissus?"

"The lake bed is covered in their bones. It's going to make you really convincing for about twenty-five to forty minutes. Just promise me you'll find out where that creep got the Merity."

"Do I snort it? Sprinkle it over my head?"

"Swallow. It tastes awful, so you may have trouble keeping it down. You're going to have a brutal headache after it wears off, and so will everyone you came in contact with."

Alex shook her head. So much power just left on the mantel for anyone to seize. What was in the rest of those urns?

"You shouldn't have these things," she said, thinking of Darlington's wild eyes, of Mercy on her knees. "You shouldn't be able to do this to people."

Mike's brows rose. "You don't want it?"

"I didn't say that." Alex folded the envelope into her pocket. "But if I ever find out you used something like this on me, I'll burn this building down."

The house on Lynwood was two stories of white wood and a porch sagging beneath the weight of a moldy couch. Darlington had told her that Omega once had a house in the alley behind Wolf's Head, a sturdy stone cottage full of glowing brown wood and leaded glass. Their letters were still worked into the stone, but Alex found it hard to imagine parties like Omega Meltdown and Sex on the Beach in what looked like a cozy tea room for Scottish spinsters.

"Fraternity culture wasn't quite the same then," Darlington had said. "They dressed better, dined formally, took the 'gentlemen and scholars' bit seriously."

"'Gentleman scholar' seems like a good description for you."

"A true gentleman doesn't boast of the title, and a true scholar has better uses for his time than downing flaming Dr Pepper shots."

But when Alex had asked why the frat had been kicked off campus, he'd only shrugged and underlined something in the book he was reading. "Times changed. The university wanted the property and not the liability."

"Maybe they should have kept them on campus."

"You surprise me, Stern. Sympathy for the brotherhood of keg stands and misplaced aggression?"

Alex thought of the squat on Cedros. "Make people live like animals, they start acting like animals."

But "animal" was too kind a term for Blake Keely.

Alex took the plastic packet from her pocket and downed the powder inside. She gagged instantly and had to pinch her nose shut, covering her mouth with her fingers to keep from spewing the substance back up. The taste was fetid and salty and she desperately wanted to rinse her mouth out, but she forced herself to swallow.

She didn't feel any different. Jesus, what if Mike had been messing with her?

Alex spat once in the muddy yard, then climbed the stairs and tried the front door. It was unlocked. The living room stank of old beer. Another busted couch and a La-Z-Boy recliner were arranged around a chipped coffee table covered in red Solo cups, and a banner with the house's letters had been hung above a makeshift bar with two mismatched stools in front of it. A shirtless guy in a backward baseball cap and pajama pants was picking up scattered cups and shoving them into a big black garbage bag.

He startled when he saw her.

"I'm looking for Blake Keely."

He frowned. "Uh . . . You a friend of his?"

Alex wished she'd been in less of a hurry back at Manuscript. Just how was the Starpower supposed to work? She took a breath and gave him a big smile. "I'd really appreciate your help."

The guy took a step backward. He touched his hand to his heart as if he'd been punched in the chest. "Of course," he said earnestly. "*Of course.* Whatever I can do." He returned her smile and Alex felt a little ill. And a little wonderful.

"Blake!" he called up the stairs, gesturing for her to follow. He had a bounce in his step. Twice on the way up he turned to look at her over his shoulder, grinning.

They reached the second floor and Alex heard music, the thunderous rattle of a video game being played at full volume. Here, the beer smell receded and Alex detected the distant whiff of some very bad weed, microwave popcorn, and boy. It was just like the place she'd shared with Len in Van Nuys. Shabby in a different way maybe, the architecture older, dimmer without the clean gilding of a Southern California sun.

"Blake!" the shirtless boy called again. He reached back and took Alex's hand with an utterly open smile.

A giant poked his head out of a doorway. "Gio, you fuck," he said. He wore shorts and was shirtless too, cap backward like it was some kind of uniform. "You were supposed to clean the toilet." So Gio was a pledge or some other kind of lackey.

"I was cleaning downstairs," he explained. "Do you want to meet . . . Oh God, I can't remember your name."

Because she hadn't said it. Alex just winked.

"Clean the fucking toilet first," the giant complained. "You cockshiners can't just keep shitting on top of shit! And who the hell is—"

"Hi," said Alex, and—because she never had—she tossed her hair.

"I. Hey. Hi. How are you?" He tugged his shorts up then down, removed his cap, ran a hand through his tufty hair, set the cap back in place. "Hi."

"I'm looking for Blake."

"Why?" His voice was mournful.

"Help me find him?"

"Absolutely. Blake!" the giant bellowed.

"What?" demanded an irritated voice from a bedroom down the hall.

Alex didn't know how much time she had left. She shook off Gio the Lackey's hand and forged ahead, making sure *not* to look into the bathroom as she passed.

Blake Keely was slouched on a futon, sipping from a big bottle of Gatorade and playing Call of Duty. He was at least wearing a shirt.

She could sense the other boys hovering behind her.

"Where's your phone?" Alex asked.

"Who the fuck are you?" Blake said, tipping his head back and assessing her with a single arrogant glance.

For a moment, Alex panicked. Had Mike's magic powder worn off so fast? Was Blake somehow immune? Then she remembered the way the powder had burned her throat. She yanked the cord from the wall and the game went silent.

"What the—"

"I'm soooo sorry," Alex said.

Blake blinked, then gave her a lazy, easy smile. *That's his panty-dropper grin,* thought Alex, and considered knocking his teeth in. "No worries at all," he said. "I'm Blake."

"I know."

His grin widened. "Have we met? I was pretty wasted last night, but—"

Alex shut the door and his eyes widened. He looked almost flustered but utterly delighted. A kid on Christmas. A rich kid on Christmas.

"Can I see your phone?"

He stood and handed it over, offering her his spot on the futon. "Do you want to sit?"

"No, I want you to stand there looking like an asshole."

He should have reacted, but instead he just stood smiling obediently.

"You're a natural." She gave the phone a shake. "Unlock it."

He obliged and she found his gallery, pressed play on the first video. Mercy's face appeared, smiling and eager. Blake stroked the wet head of his penis against her cheek and she laughed. He turned the camera back on himself and gave his stupid, shit-eating grin again, nodding as if to the viewers at home.

Alex held up the phone. "Who did you send this video to?"

"Just a couple of the brothers. Jason and Rodriguez."

"Get them in here; make them bring their phones."

"I'm here!" said the giant from behind the door. She pulled it open. "I'm Jason!" He was actually raising his hand.

While Blake scampered off to find Rodriguez and Jason the Giant waited patiently, Alex found the texts he'd sent, deleted them, then deleted the rest of his messages for good measure. He'd obligingly named one of his photo albums *Pussy Vault*. It was full of videos of different girls. Some of them were bright eyed and had purple tongues, some just looked wasted, drunk girls with glazed eyes, their tops off or pushed to the side. One girl was so far gone only the whites of her eyes were visible, appearing and disappearing like slivers of moon as Blake fucked her, another with vomit in her hair, her face pressed into a pool of sick as Blake took her from behind. And always he turned the camera back on himself, as if he couldn't resist showing off that star-worthy smile.

Alex wiped the photo and video files clean, though she couldn't be sure they weren't backed up somewhere. Jason's phone was next. Either he had a shred of a conscience or he'd been too hungover to send the video to anyone yet.

She heard panting from down the hall and saw Blake dragging Rodriguez along the filthy carpet. "What are you doing?"

"You said to get him," said Blake.

"Just give me his phone."

Another quick check. Rodriguez had sent the video to two friends, and there was no way of knowing who they'd passed it along to. *Damn it.* Alex could only hope that Mike had succeeded in gathering enough members of Manuscript and that reversing the Full Cup would work.

"Did they know?" Alex asked Blake. "Did they know about the Merity? That Mercy was drugged?"

"No," Blake said, still smiling. "They just know I don't have a problem getting laid."

"Where did you get the Merity?"

"A guy from the forestry school."

The forestry school? There were greenhouses up there with regulated temperature gauges and moisture control, designed to recreate environments from all over the world—maybe one just like the Greater Khingan Mountains. What had Tripp said? *Lance and T had the lushest, greenest shit you've ever seen.*

"What about Lance Gressang and Tara Hutchins?" she asked.

"Yeah! That's them. You know Lance?"

"Did you hurt Tara? Did you kill Tara Hutchins?"

Blake looked confused. "No! I would never do something like that."

Alex really wondered where he thought he was drawing a line. An ache had started to throb in her right temple. That had to mean the Starpower was going to wear off soon. And she just wanted to get out of here. The house made her skin crawl, as if it had absorbed every sad, sordid thing that had happened within its walls.

She looked down at the phone in her hand, thought of Blake's girls lined up in their galleries. She wasn't done just yet.

"Come on," she said, glancing back down the hall to the open door of the bathroom.

"Where we going?" Blake asked, his lazy grin spreading like a broken yolk.

"We're going to make a little movie."

16

Winter

Lauren had given Mercy an Ambien and put her to bed. Alex stayed with her, dozing in the darkened room, waking in the late evening to Mercy's snuffling tears.

"The video is gone," Alex told her, reaching down to clasp her hand.

"I don't believe you. It can't just be gone."

"If it was going to break it would have broken."

"Maybe he wants to hold it over my head so that I come back and . . . do things."

"It's gone," said Alex. There was no real way of knowing if Mike's ritual had worked. The Full Cup was meant to build momentum, not drain it, but she had to hope.

"Why would he pick me?" Mercy asked again and again, searching for logic, for some equation that would make this all add up to something she'd said or done. "He could have any girl he wanted. Why would he do that to me?"

Because he doesn't want girls that want him. Because he grew weary of desire and developed a taste for causing shame. Alex didn't know what lived in boys like Blake. Beautiful boys who should be happy, who wanted for nothing but still found things to take.

When night fell, she climbed down from her bunk and pulled on a sweater and jeans.

"Come to dinner," she begged Mercy, squatting by their beds

to turn on a lamp. Mercy's face was puffy from crying. Her hair gleamed in a black slash against the pillow. She had the same thick, dark, impossible-to-curl hair as Alex.

"I'm not hungry."

"Mercy, you have to eat."

Mercy buried her face in her pillow. "I can't."

"Mercy." Alex shook her shoulder. "Mercy, you're not dropping out of school over this."

"I never said I was."

"You don't have to say it. I know you're thinking it."

"You don't understand."

"I do," said Alex. "I had something like this happen to me back in California. When I was younger."

"And it all blew over?"

"No, it sucked. And I kind of let it wreck my life."

"You seem all right."

"I'm not. But I feel all right when I'm here with you and Lauren, so no one gets to take that away."

Mercy wiped her hand across her nose. "So this is all about you?"

Alex smiled. "Exactly."

"If anyone says anything—"

"If anyone even looks at you wrong, I'll take his eye out with a fork."

Mercy put on jeans and a high-necked sweater to cover her hickeys, the outfit so restrained she almost looked like a stranger. She splashed water on her face and dabbed concealer under her eyes. She still looked pale and her eyes were red, but no one looked great on a Sunday night in the dead of a New Haven winter.

Alex and Lauren bracketed her, looping their arms through hers as they entered the dining hall. It was noisy as always, filled with the clink of dishes and the warm rise and fall of conversation, but there were no hiccups in the tide of sound as they entered. Maybe, just maybe, Mike and Manuscript had succeeded.

They were seated with their trays, Mercy pushing listlessly at her fried cod as Alex guiltily bit into her second cheeseburger, when the laughter started. It was a particular kind of laughter Alex recognized—sneering, too bright, cut short by a hand placed to a mouth in false embarrassment. Lauren went utterly still. Mercy shrank deep into the neck of her sweater, her whole body shaking. Alex tensed, waiting.

"Let's get out of here," said Lauren.

But Evan Wiley swooped down into the seat beside her. "Oh my God, I am dying."

"It's okay," Lauren said to Mercy, and then muttered angrily, "What is your problem?"

"I knew Blake was gross, but I didn't know he was that gross."

Lauren's phone buzzed, then Alex's. But no one was looking at Mercy; people were just shrieking and gagging at their tables, faces glued to their own screens.

"Just look," said Mercy, her face in her hands. "Tell me."

Lauren took a deep breath and picked up her phone. She frowned.

"Gross," she gasped.

"I *know*," said Evan.

There on the screen was Blake Keely, bent over a filthy toilet. Alex felt the snake inside her unwind, warm and gratified, as if it had found the perfect sunbaked rock to warm its belly.

"Are you serious?" Blake said, giggling in exactly the same wild, high-pitched way he had when he'd said, *Look at all that bush!*

"Okay, okay," he went on in the video. "You're so crazy!" But whoever he was talking to couldn't be seen.

"No," said Lauren.

"Oh my God," said Mercy.

"I *know*," repeated Evan.

And as they watched, Blake Keely dipped his cupped hand into the clogged toilet, scooped up a handful of shit, and took a big bite.

He chewed and swallowed, still giggling, and then, brown smearing his even white teeth and caking his lips, Blake looked at whoever was holding the camera and gave his famous, lazy, shit-eating smile.

Alex's phone buzzed again. Awolowo.

WTF IS WRONG WITH YOU.

Alex kept her reply simple: *xoxoxo*

You had no right. I trusted you.

We all make mistakes.

Mike wasn't going to complain to Sandow. He'd have to explain that his delegation had somehow let the secret to Merity slip free *and* that he'd handed Alex a dose of Starpower. Alex had used Blake's own phone to send the new video to all of his contacts, and no one at Omega knew her name.

"Alex," whispered Lauren. "What is this?"

Around them, the dining hall had exploded into pockets of heated conversation, people cackling and pushing their food away in disgust, others demanding to know what was happening. Evan had already moved on to the next table. But Lauren and Mercy were staring at Alex, quiet, their phones placed facedown on the table.

"How did you do it?" asked Lauren.

"Do what?"

"You said you would fix it," Mercy said. She tapped her phone. "So?"

"So," said Alex.

The silence eddied around them for a long moment.

Then Mercy dragged her finger over the table and said, "You know how people say two wrongs don't make a right?"

"Yeah."

Mercy pulled Alex's plate toward her and took a huge bite of her remaining cheeseburger. "They're full of shit."

Whether the magic of Scroll and Key was learned or stolen from Middle Eastern sorcerers during the Crusades is not really a matter of debate—fashions change, thieves become curators—though the Locksmiths still like to protest that their mastery of portal magic was gotten by strictly honest means. The exterior of the Scroll and Key tomb pays homage to the origins of their power, but the interior of the tomb is nonsensically devoted to Arthurian legend, complete with a round table at its heart. There are some who claim the stone comes from Avalon itself, others who swear it comes from the Temple of Solomon, and still others who whisper it was quarried down the road in Stony Creek. Regardless of its origins, everyone from Dean Acheson to Cole Porter to James Gamble Rogers—the architect responsible for Yale's very bones—has jostled elbows at it.

—*from* The Life of Lethe: Procedures
and Protocols of the Ninth House

Sunburn keeping me awake. Andy said we'd be in Miami in time for kickoff no problem, all of it on the books and approved by the S&K board and the alumni. But whatever magic they got cooking went wobbly fast. At least now I've seen Haiti?

—Lethe Days Diary of Naomi Farwell
(Timothy Dwight College '89)

17

Winter

Alex had spent the rest of Sunday night in the common room with Mercy and Lauren, Rimsky-Korsakov on Lauren's turntable, and a copy of *The Good Soldier* in her lap. The dorm seemed particularly raucous that night, and there were repeated knocks at the suite door—all of which they ignored. Eventually Anna came home looking glum and somnolent as ever. She gave them a flat "hey" and vanished into her bedroom. A minute later, they heard her on the phone to her family in Texas and had to cover their mouths, shoulders heaving and tears squeezing from their eyes when they heard her say, "I'm pretty sure they're witches."

If you only knew.

Alex slept dreamlessly but woke in the night to find the Bridegroom hovering outside her bedroom window, the wards keeping him at bay. His face was expectant.

"Tomorrow," she promised. Less than twenty-four hours had passed since her journey to the borderlands. She would get to Tara, but Mercy had needed her first. She owed more to the living than to the dead.

I'm handling this, she thought, as she downed two more aspirin and fell back into bed. *Maybe not the way Darlington would have, but I'm managing.*

Her first stop on Monday morning was Il Bastone, to pack her pockets with graveyard dirt and to spend an hour skimming the information she could find on *glumae*. If Book and Snake—or whoever had sent that thing after her—wanted to try again, this was the perfect time to do it. She'd freaked out in public; she was under the gun academically. If she suddenly threw herself in a river or off a building or into traffic, there would be plenty of warning signs to point to.

Did she seem depressed? She was distant. She didn't make many friends. She was struggling in her classes. All true. But would it have mattered if she'd been someone else? If she'd been a social butterfly, they would have said she liked to drink away her pain. If she'd been a straight-A student, they would have said she'd been eaten alive by her perfectionism. There were always excuses for why girls died.

And yet Alex was weirdly comforted by how different her story would be now from what it might have been a year ago. Dying of hypothermia after getting wasted and breaking into a public pool. Overdosing when she tried something new or went too far. Or just vanishing. Losing Len's protection and disappearing into the long sprawl of the San Fernando Valley, the rows of little houses like stucco mausoleums in their tiny plots.

But if she could avoid dying right now, that would be nice. *It's the principle of the thing,* as Darlington would say. After arguing with the library for a few hours, she found two passages on how to combat *glumae*, one in English, one in Hebrew, which required a translation stone and turned out to be less about *glumae* than golems. But since both sources mentioned the use of a wrist or pocket watch, the advice seemed sound.

Wind your timepiece tight. The steady tick of a watch confuses any creature made, not born. They perceive a heartbeat in simple clockwork and will look to find a body where there is none.

It wasn't exactly protection, but distraction would have to do.

Darlington had worn a wristwatch with a wide black leather band and mother-of-pearl face. She'd assumed it was an heirloom or affectation. But maybe it had a purpose too.

Alex entered the armory, where they kept Hiram's Crucible; the Golden Bowl looked almost bereft for lack of use. She found a pocket watch tangled up in a drawer with a collection of pendulums used for hypnotism, wound it, and tucked it into her pocket. But she had to open a lot of drawers before she found the mirrored compact she wanted, wrapped in cotton batting. A card in the drawer explained the mirror's provenance: the glass originally fashioned in China, then set into the compact by members of Manuscript for a still-classified Cold War op run by the CIA. How it had made its way from Langley to the Lethe mansion on Orange, the card didn't say. The glass was smudged, and Alex wiped it clean with a puff of breath and her sweatshirt.

Despite the events of the weekend, she made it through Spanish without her usual sense of blurriness or panic, spent two hours in Sterling powering through the last of her reading for her Shakespeare section, and then ate her usual double-serving lunch. She felt awake, focused the way she was on basso belladonna but without the heart-twitching jitters. And to think, all it had taken was an attempt on her life and a visit to the borderlands of hell. If only she'd known sooner.

That morning, North had been hovering in the Vanderbilt courtyard, and she'd muttered that she wouldn't be free until after lunch. Sure enough, he was waiting when she emerged from the dining hall, and they set out together up College to Prospect. They were nearly to Ingalls Rink when she realized she hadn't seen a single Gray—no, that wasn't quite true. She saw them behind columns, darting into alleys. *They're afraid of him,* she realized. She remembered him standing in the river, smiling. *There are worse things than death, Miss Stern.*

Alex had to keep consulting her phone as she cut down to Mansfield. She still couldn't quite hold the map of New Haven in her head. She knew the main arteries of the Yale campus, the routes she walked each week to class, but the rest of the body was vague and shapeless to her. She was headed toward a neighborhood she'd driven with Darlington once in his old battered Mercedes. He'd shown her the old Winchester Repeating Arms factory, which had been partially turned into fancy lofts, the line running straight down the building where the paint gave way to raw brick—the exact moment when the developer had run out of money. He'd gestured to the sad grid of Science Park—Yale's bid for medical-tech investment in the nineties.

"I guess it didn't work," Alex had said, noting the boarded-up windows and empty parking lot.

"In the words of my grandfather, this town has been fucked from the start." Darlington had leaned on the gas, as if Alex had witnessed some embarrassing family spat at the Thanksgiving table. They'd passed the cheap row houses and apartment buildings where workmen had lived during the Winchester days, then, farther up the slope of Science Hill, the homes that had belonged to the company's foremen, their houses built of brick instead of wood, their lawns wider and trimmed by hedges. Up the hill, farther and farther, solid homes giving way to grand mansions and, at last, the imposing, wooded sprawl of the Marsh Botanical Garden, as if a spell had been lifted.

But today, Alex wouldn't go to the top of the hill. She kept to the shallows, the weathered row houses, barren yards, liquor stores notched into the corners. Detective Turner had said Tara lived on Woodland, and even without the uniform posted at the door, Alex would have had no trouble picking out the dead girl's place. Across the street, a woman leaned against the fence bordering her yard, arms draped over the chain links as if caught in a slow-motion dive, gazing at the ugly apartment building as if it might start speaking. Two guys in tracksuits stood talking on the sidewalk, their bodies turned toward the scrubby front lawn of Tara's building but keeping a coy distance. Alex couldn't blame them. Trouble had a way of catching.

"Most cities are palimpsests," Darlington had once told her.

When she'd searched for the word's meaning, it had taken her three starts to find the right spelling. "Built over and over again so you can't remember what went where. But New Haven wears its scars. The big highways that run the wrong way, the dead office parks, the vistas that stretch into nothing but power lines. No one realizes how much life happens between the wounds, how much it has to offer. It's a city built to make you want to keep driving away from it."

Tara had lived in the ridges of one of those scars.

Alex hadn't worn her peacoat, hadn't pulled her hair back. It was easy for her to fit in here and she didn't want to draw notice.

She set a slow pace, stopped well down the block as if waiting for someone, checked her phone, glanced at North just long enough to detect his frustrated expression.

"Relax," she muttered. *I don't answer to you, buddy. At least I don't think I do.*

At last a man exited Tara's building. He was tall, thin, wearing a Patriots jacket and light-wash jeans. He nodded a hello to the officer and popped his headphones in as he made his way down the brick steps. Alex trailed him around the corner. When they were out of view, she tapped him on the shoulder. He turned and she held up the mirror in her hand. It flashed bright sunlight over his face and he threw his hand up to block the glare, stepping back.

"What the hell?"

Alex snapped the mirror shut. "Oh my gosh, I'm so sorry," she said. "I thought you were Tom Brady."

The guy shot her an ugly look and strode off.

Alex jogged back to the apartment building. When she approached the officer at the door, she held up the mirror like a badge. The light fell on his face.

"Back already?" asked the cop, seeing nothing but the captured image of the guy in the Patriots jacket. Manuscript might have the worst tomb, but they had some of the best tricks.

"Forgot my wallet," Alex said, making her voice as gruff as possible.

The cop nodded and she vanished inside the front door.

Alex pocketed the mirror and headed down the hall, moving quickly. She found Tara's apartment on the second floor, the threshold marked by police tape.

Alex thought she might have to pick the lock—she'd had to learn the basics after her mom had gone all tough love and barred her from the apartment. There had been something eerie about breaking into her own home, slipping inside like she was herself a phantom, standing in a space that might have belonged to anyone. But the lock on Tara's door was missing entirely. It looked like the cops had removed it.

Alex nudged the door forward and ducked beneath the tape. It was clear no one had been back to try to straighten up Tara's apartment after the police had been through it. Who would? One of its occupants was in police custody, the other dead on a slab.

Drawers were pulled open, cushions removed from the couches, some cut open by the police looking for contraband. The floor was littered with debris: a framed poster that had been yanked out of its frame, a discarded golf club, makeup brushes. Even so, Alex could see Tara had tried to make it a nice place to live. There were colorful quilts pinned to the walls, all purples and blues. *Calming colors,* Alex's mom would have said. *Oceanic.* A dream catcher hung in the window above a collection of succulents. Alex picked up one of the small pots, touching her fingers to the fat, waxy leaves of the plant inside. She'd bought one almost exactly like it at a farmers' market. They required almost no care or water. Little survivors. She knew her plant had probably been thrown into the garbage or bagged as evidence, but she liked to think of it still sitting on the windowsill at Ground Zero, gathering sun.

Alex walked down the narrow hall to the bedroom. It was in a similar state of disarray. A heap of pillows and stuffed animals lay by the bed. The back of the dresser had been taken apart. From the window, Alex could just make out the peaked tower of the old Marsh mansion. It was part of the forestry school, its long, sloping backyard full of greenhouses—and all just a few minutes walk from Tara's place. *What did you get up to, girl?*

North had paused in the hall by the bathroom, hovering. Something with *effluvia,* he'd told her.

The bathroom was long and skinny, with little room to move between the standing sink and the battered shower-tub combination. Alex eyed the items on the sink, in the wastebasket. A toothbrush or used tissues weren't going to do it. North had said the item should be personal. Alex opened the medicine cabinet. There was barely anything left inside, but perched on the top shelf was a blue plastic box. A sticker on the lid read: *Change your smile, change your life.*

Alex popped it open. Tara's retainer. North looked skeptical.

"Do you even know what this is?" Alex asked. "Do you know you're looking at the miracle of modern orthodonture?" He crossed his arms. "Didn't think so."

North was a century and a half short of getting it, but most of the kids on campus probably wouldn't have given it a second thought either. A retainer was the kind of thing people's parents bought them, that kids never knew the cost of, that got lost on school trips or forgotten in a drawer. But for Tara this was important. Something she would have saved for months to get, that she would have worn every night and would have taken care not to lose. *Change your smile, change your life.*

Alex tore off a piece of toilet paper and plucked the retainer from the case. "It mattered to her. Trust me." And hopefully still had some quality effluvia on it.

Alex stoppered the sink and filled it. Would this count as a body of water? She hoped so.

She dropped the retainer into the water. Before it could sink to the bottom, she saw a pale hand emerge beside the drain, as if it had bloomed from the cracked basin. As soon as the fingers closed, both hand and retainer vanished. When she looked up, North held it in his dripping palm, his mouth curled in distaste.

Alex shrugged. "You wanted effluvia." She pushed the stopper down, dropped the tissue in the basket, and turned to go.

A man was standing in the doorway. He was huge, his head nearly brushing the frame, his shoulders filling the space. He wore a mechanic's gray coverall, the top unzipped and hanging loose. His white T-shirt revealed muscled arms covered in ink.

"I—" Alex began. But he was already charging.

He barreled into her, slamming her backward against the wall. Her head cracked against the window ledge and he grabbed her by the throat. She clawed at his arms.

North's eyes had gone black. He threw himself at her attacker but passed right through him.

This was not a *gluma*. Not a ghost. This wasn't something from beyond the Veil. He was flesh and blood and trying to kill her. North couldn't help her now.

Alex slammed her palm into his throat. His breath caught on a gulp and his grip loosened. She brought her knee up between his legs. Not a direct hit, but close enough. He doubled over.

Alex shoved past him, tearing the shower curtain off its rings as she passed, stumbling over the plastic. She hurtled into the hallway, North on her heels, and was reaching for the door when suddenly the mechanic was in front of her. He hadn't opened the door—he'd simply appeared through it—just like a Gray might. Portal magic? For the briefest moment Alex glimpsed what looked like a barren yard behind him, then he was striding toward her.

She backed up through the cluttered living room, wrapping an arm around her middle, trying to think. She was bleeding and it hurt to breathe. He'd broken her ribs. She wasn't sure how many. She could feel something warm and wet trickling down the back of her neck from where she'd hit her head. Could she make it to the kitchen? Grab a knife?

"Who are you?" the mechanic growled. His voice was low and raspy, maybe from Alex's chop to his windpipe. "Who hurt Tara?"

"Her shitbag boyfriend," Alex spat.

He roared and rushed at her.

Alex lurched left toward the mantel, dodging him narrowly, but he was still between her and the door, bouncing on his heels, as if this were some kind of boxing match.

He smiled. "Nowhere to run, bitch."

Before she could slip past him, he had his hands around her throat again. Black spots filled her vision. North was shouting, gesturing wildly, powerless to help. No, not powerless. That wasn't right. *Let me in, Alex.*

No one knew who she was. Not North. Not this monster in front of her. Not Dawes or Mercy or Sandow or any of them.

Only Darlington had guessed.

18

Last Fall

Darlington knew Alex resented the call. He could hardly blame her. It wasn't a Thursday, when rituals took place, or a Sunday, when she was expected to prepare for the next week's work, and he knew she was struggling to keep up with her classes and the demands of Lethe. He'd been concerned about how the incident at Manuscript might impact their work, but she'd shrugged it off more easily than he had, handling the report so that he wouldn't have to relive the embarrassment and going right back to complaining about Lethe's demands. The ease with which she let go of that night, the casual forgiveness she'd offered, unnerved him and made him wonder again at the grim march of the life she'd lived before. She'd even made it smoothly through her second rite with Aurelian—a patent application at the Peabody's ugly, fluorescent-lit satellite campus—and her first prognostication for Skull and Bones. There'd been a rocky moment when she turned distinctly green and looked like she might vomit all over the Haruspex. But she'd managed, and he could hardly fault her for wavering. He'd been through twelve prognostications and they still left him feeling shaken.

"It will be quick, Stern," he promised her as they set out from Il Bastone on Tuesday night. "Rosenfeld is causing trouble with the grid."

"Who's Rosenfeld?"

"It's a what. Rosenfeld Hall. You should know the rest."

She adjusted the strap on her satchel. "I don't remember."

"St. Elmo," he prompted her.

"Right. The electrocuted guy."

He'd give her the point. St. Erasmus had supposedly survived electrocution and drowning. He was the namesake for St. Elmo's fire and for the society that had once been housed in Rosenfeld Hall's Elizabethan towers. The red-brick building was used for offices and annex space now and was locked at night, but Darlington had a key.

"Put these on," he said, handing her rubber gloves and rubber overboots not unlike the kind once made in his family's factory.

Alex obliged and followed him into the foyer. "Why couldn't this wait until tomorrow?"

"Because the last time Lethe let trouble at Rosenfeld go, we had a campus-wide blackout." As if chiming in, the lights in the upper stories flickered. The building hummed softly. "This is all in *The Life of Lethe.*"

"Remember how you said we don't concern ourselves with the non-landed societies?" Alex asked.

"I do," said Darlington, though he knew what was coming.

"I took your teachings to heart."

Darlington sighed and used his key to open another door, this one to a huge storage room packed with battered dorm furniture and discarded mattresses. "This is the old dining hall of St. Elmo." He shone his flashlight over the soaring Gothic arches and cunning stone details. "When the society was cash poor in the sixties, the university purchased the building from them and promised to keep leasing the crypt rooms to St. Elmo to use for their rituals. But instead of a proper contract built by Aurelian to secure the terms, the parties opted for a gentleman's agreement."

"Did the gentlemen change their minds?"

"They died, and less gentle men took over. Yale refused to renew the society's lease and St. Elmo's ended up in that grubby little house on Lynwood."

"Home is where the heart is, you snob."

"Precisely, Stern. And the heart of St. Elmo was here, in their original tomb. They've been broke and all but magicless since they lost this place. Help me move these."

They shoved two old bed frames out of the way, revealing another locked door. The society had been known for weather magic, *artium tempestate*, which they had used for everything from manipulating commodities to swaying the outcome of essential field goals. Since the move to Lynwood they hadn't managed so much as a swift breeze. All of the societies' houses were built at nexuses of magical power. No one was sure what created them, but it was why new tombs couldn't simply be built. There were places in this world that magic avoided, like the bleak lunar planes of the National Mall in Washington, D.C., and places it was drawn to, like Rockefeller Center in Manhattan and the French Quarter in New Orleans. New Haven had an extremely high concentration of sites where magic seemed to catch and build, like cotton candy on a spool.

The staircase they were descending wound down through three subterranean floors, the hum growing louder with every downward step. There was little left to actually see in the lower levels: the dusty stuffed bodies of retired New Haven zoo animals—acquired on a lark by J. P. Morgan in his wilder days; old electrical conductors with pointed metal spires, straight out of a classic monster movie; empty vats and cracked glass tanks.

"Aquariums?" asked Alex.

"Teapots for tempests." This was where the students of St. Elmo had brewed weather. Blizzards that raised utility prices, droughts that burned away crops, winds high and strong enough to sink a battleship.

The hum was louder here, a relentless electrical moan that raised the hair on Darlington's arms and reverberated over his teeth.

"What *is* that?" Alex asked over the noise, pressing her hands to her ears. Darlington knew from experience that would do no good. The hum was in the floor, in the air. Stay in it long enough and you'd start to go mad.

"St. Elmo's spent years here, summoning storms. For some reason the weather likes to return."

"And when it does, we get the call?"

He led her back to the old fuse box. It was long since out of use but mostly free of dust. Darlington took the silver weather vane from his bag.

"Hold out your hand," he said. He set it in Alex's palm. "Breathe on it."

Alex gave him a skeptical look, then huffed a breath over the spindly silver arms. It shot upright like a sleepwalker in a cartoon.

"Again," he instructed.

The weather vane turned slowly, catching the wind, then began to whir in Alex's palm as if caught in a gale. She leaned back slightly. In the beam of his flashlight, her hair rose around her head, a halo of wind and electricity that made her look as if her face were wreathed in dark snakes. He remembered her at the Manuscript party, shrouded in night, and had to blink twice to shake the image from his mind. It wasn't the first time the memory had come back to him, and he was always left uneasy, unsure of whether it was the shame of that night that lingered or if he'd seen something real, something he should have had the sense to look away from.

"Set the vane spinning," he instructed. "Then hit the switches." He flipped them in rapid succession, all the way down the line. "And always wear gloves."

His finger hooked the last switch and the hum escalated to a high whine that clawed at his skull, the piercing, frustrated shriek of a cranky child that did not want to be sent to bed. Alex grimaced. A trickle of blood flowed from her nose. He felt wetness on his lip and knew his nose was bleeding too. Then, *crack,* the room flared with bright light. The weather vane went flying and pinged against the wall in a clatter, and the whole building seemed to sigh as the hum vanished to nothing.

Alex shuddered with relief and Darlington handed her a clean handkerchief to wipe her nose.

"We have to do this every time the weather gets antsy?" she asked.

Darlington dabbed at his own nose. "Once or twice a year. Sometimes less. The energy has to go somewhere and if we don't give it direction, it will create a power surge."

Alex picked up the mangled weather vane. The tips of its silver arrows had melted slightly and its spine was bent. "What about this thing?"

"We'll put it in the crucible with some flux. It should restore itself in forty-eight hours or so."

"And that's it? That's all we have to do?"

"That's it. Lethe has sensors on all of the lower levels of Rosenfeld. If the weather returns, Dawes will get an alert. Always bring the vane. Always wear gloves and boots. No big deal. And now you can get back to . . . what are you getting back to?"

"*The Faerie Queene.*"

Darlington rolled his eyes, steering them toward the door. "My condolences. Spenser is a wretched bore. What's your paper on?" He was only half paying attention. He wanted to keep Alex calm. He wanted to keep himself calm. Because in the silence left in the wake of the weather hum, he could hear something breathing.

He led Alex back through the aisles of dusty glass and broken machinery, listening, listening.

Dimly, he was aware of Alex talking about Queen Elizabeth and how a kid in her section had wasted a solid fifteen minutes talking about how all of the great poets were left-handed.

"That's patently false," said Darlington. The breathing was deep and even, like a creature at rest, so steady it might be mistaken for just another sound in the ventilation system of the building.

"That's what our TA said, but I guess this guy is left-handed, so he went off on how people used to force lefties to write with their right hands."

"Being left-handed was seen as a sign of demonic influence. The sinister hand and all that."

"Was it?"

"Was it what?"

"A sign of demonic influence."

"Not at all. Demons are ambidextrous."

"Do we ever have to fight demons?"

"Absolutely not. Demons are confined to some kind of hell-scape behind the Veil, and the ones that do manage to push through are far above our pay grade."

"What pay grade?"

"Precisely."

There, in the corner, the dark looked deeper than it should—a shadow that was not a shadow. A portal. In the basement of Rosenfeld Hall. Where it had no business being.

Darlington felt relieved. What he'd thought was breathing must be the rush of air through the portal, and though its presence here was a mystery, it was one he could solve. Someone had clearly been in the basement trying to capture the power of the old St. Elmo's nexus for some kind of magic. The obvious culprit was Scroll and Key. They'd canceled their last rite, and if their previous attempt to open a portal to Hungary had been any indication, the magic at their own tomb was on the wane. But he wasn't going to go making accusations without evidence. He would cast a containment and warding spell to render the portal unusable, and then they'd have to return to Il Bastone to get the tools he'd need to close this thing permanently. Alex wouldn't like that.

"I don't know," she was saying. "Maybe they just tried to curb all those lefty devil kids because it's messy as hell. I could always tell when Hellie had been journaling, because she had ink all over her wrist."

He supposed he could manage closing the portal on his own. Give her a break so she could go write some tiresome paper about tiresome Spenser. *Modes of Travel and Models of Transgression in The Faerie Queene.*

"Who's Hellie?" he asked. But the moment he did, the name clicked into place for him. Helen Watson. The dead girl who overdosed, the one Alex had been found beside. Something in him stuttered like a flashbulb. He remembered the ferocious pattern of blood spatter, repeated again and again over the walls of that miserable apartment, like some gruesome textile. A left-handed swing.

But Helen Watson had died earlier that night, hadn't she? There'd been no blood on her. *Neither* girl had been a credible suspect. They were both high out of their minds and too small to have done that kind of damage, and Alex wasn't left-handed.

But Helen Watson was.

Hellie.

Alex was looking at him in the dark. She had the cautious look of someone who knew she'd said too much. Darlington knew he should pretend a lack of concern. *Act natural.* Yes, act natural. Standing in a basement crackling with storm magic, beside a portal to who knows where, next to a girl who can see ghosts. No, not just see ghosts.

Maybe let them in.

Act natural. Instead, he stood stock still, staring into Alex's black eyes, his mind rifling through what he knew about possessions by Grays. There had been other people Lethe had followed, people who could supposedly see ghosts. Many had lost their minds or become "no longer tenable" as candidates. There were stories of people going mad and destroying their hospital rooms or attacking their caretakers with unheard-of strength—the kind of strength it might take to wield a bat against five grown men. After the outbursts, the subjects were always left in a catatonic state that made them impossible to question. But Alex wasn't ordinary, was she?

Darlington looked at her. Undine with her slick black hair, the center part like a naked spine, her devouring eyes.

"You killed them," he said. "All of them. Leonard Beacon. Mitchell Betts. Helen Watson. *Hellie.*"

The silence stretched. The dark sheen of her eyes seemed to harden. Hadn't he wanted magic, a doorway to another world, a fairy girl? But faeries were never kind. *Tell me to fuck off,* he thought. *Open that vulgar mouth and tell me I'm wrong. Tell me to go to hell.*

But all she said was, "Not Hellie."

Darlington could hear the rush of wind through the portal, the ordinary groans of the building settling above them, and somewhere, distantly, the sound of a siren.

He'd known. The first day he met her, he'd known there was something wrong with her, but he never could have guessed the depth of it. *Murderer.*

But who had she killed, really? No one who would be missed. Maybe she'd done what she had to. Either way, the Lethe board had no idea who they were dealing with, *what* they'd brought into the fold.

"What are you going to do?" Alex asked. Those hard black eyes, stones in the river. No remorse, no excuses. Her only drive was survival.

"I don't know," said Darlington, but they both knew that was a lie. He would have to tell Dean Sandow. There was no way around it.

Ask her why. No, ask her how. Her motive should matter more to him, but Darlington knew it was the *how* that would obsess him, and probably the board as well. But they could never let her continue at Lethe. If something happened, if Alex hurt someone again, they would be liable.

"We'll see," he said, and turned toward the deep shadow in the corner. He didn't want to keep looking at her, to see the fear in her face, the knowledge of all she was about to lose.

Was she ever really going to make it anyway? A cold part said she'd never really had what it took to be Lethe. To be Yale. This girl of the West, of easy sunshine, plywood, and Formica.

"Someone was here before us," he said, because it was easier to talk about the work in front of them rather than the fact that she was a killer. Leonard Beacon had been beaten unrecognizable. Mitchell Betts's organs had been nearly liquefied, pummeled into pulp. Two men in the back rooms had holes in their chests that indicated they'd been staked in the heart. The bat had been left in fragments so small it had been impossible to lift fingerprints. But Alex had been clean. No blood on her. The crime techs had even checked the drains.

Darlington gestured to the dark blot in the corner. "Someone opened a portal."

"Okay," she said. Cautious, unsure. The camaraderie and ease they'd earned over the last months gone like passing weather.

"I'll ward it," he said. "We'll go back to Il Bastone and talk this out." Did he mean that, he wondered? Or did he mean, *I'll learn what I can before I turn you in and you go quiet.* Tonight, she'd still be looking to barter—a trade of information for his silence. She was his Dante. That should matter. *She's a killer. And a liar.* "This isn't something I can keep from Sandow."

"Okay," she said again.

Darlington drew two magnets from his pocket and traced a clean sign of warding over the portal. Doorways like this were strictly Scroll and Key magic, but it was a ridiculous risk for the Locksmiths to try to open a portal away from their tomb. Nevertheless, it was their own magic he would use to close it.

"Alsamt," he began. *"Mukhal—"* The breath was sucked from his mouth before he could finish the words.

Something had hold of him, and Darlington knew he'd made a terrible mistake. This was not a portal. Not at all.

He realized in that last moment how few things he had to tether him to the world. What could keep him here? Who knew him well enough to keep hold of his heart? All of the books and the music and the art and the history, the silent stones of Black Elm, the streets of this town. *This town.* None of it would remember him.

He tried to speak. A warning? The last gasp of a know-it-all? *Here lies the boy with all the answers.* Except there would be no grave.

Danny was looking at Alex's old young face, at her dark well eyes, at the lips that remained parted, that did not move to speak. She did not step forward. She cast no words of protection.

He ended as he had always suspected he would, alone in the dark.

19

Last Summer

Alex couldn't trace where the trouble began at Ground Zero that night. It all went too far back. Len had been trying to move up, to get Eitan to let him take on more weight. Weed paid the bills, but the private school kids at Buckley and Oakwood wanted Adderall, Molly, oxy, ketamine, and Eitan just didn't trust Len with more than dime bags of green, no matter how much he kissed up.

Len loved to bitch about Eitan, called him an oily Jewish prick, and Alex would squirm, thinking of her grandmother lighting the prayer candles on Shabbat. But Eitan Shafir had everything Len wanted: money, cars, a seemingly endless line of aspiring models on his arm. He lived in a mega mansion in Encino with an infinity pool that overlooked the 405 freeway surrounded by a crazy amount of muscle. The problem was that Len didn't have anything Eitan wanted—until Ariel came to town.

"Ariel," Hellie had said. "That's an angel's name."

Ariel was Eitan's cousin or brother or something. Alex was never sure. He had wide-set eyes with heavy lids, a handsome face framed by perfectly groomed stubble. He made Alex nervous from moment one. He was too still, like a creature hunting, and she could sense the violence in him waiting. She saw it in the way even Eitan deferred to him, the way the parties at the house in Encino grew more frantic, desperate to impress him, to keep him entertained, as if boring Ariel might be a very dangerous thing.

Alex had the sense that Ariel, or some version of him, had always been there, that the messy clockwork of men like Eitan and Len could not operate without someone like Ariel looming above it all, leaning back in his seat, his slow blink like a countdown.

Ariel got a kick out of Len. Len made him laugh, though somehow Ariel never seemed to smile when he was laughing. He loved to wave Len over to his table. He'd slap him on the back and get him to freestyle.

"This is our in," Len said the day Ariel invited himself to Ground Zero.

Alex couldn't understand how Len didn't see that Ariel was laughing at him, that he was amused by their poverty, excited by their want. The survivor in her understood that there were men who liked to see other people grovel, liked to push to see what humiliations the needs of others would allow. There were rumors floating around Eitan's place, passed from one girl to the next: *Don't end up alone with Ariel. He doesn't just like it rough; he likes it ugly.*

Alex had tried to make Len see the danger. "Don't mess around with this guy," she'd told him. "He's not like us."

"But he likes me."

"He just likes playing with his food."

"He's getting Eitan to level me up," Len said, standing at the chipped yellow counter at Ground Zero. "Why do you have to shit on anything good that happens to me?"

"It's garbage-can fentanyl, for fuck's sake. He's giving it to you because no one wants it." Eitan didn't mess with fentanyl unless he knew exactly where it had come from. He liked to stay off law-enforcement radar, and killing your clients tended to draw attention. Someone had paid off a debt to him in what was supposed to be heroin cut with fentanyl, but it had passed through too many hands to be considered clean.

"Don't screw this up for me, Alex," Len said. "Make this shithole look nice."

"Let me get my magic wand."

He'd slapped her then, but not hard. Just an "I mean business" slap.

"Hey," Hellie had protested. Alex was never sure what Hellie intended when she said, "Hey," but she was grateful for it anyway.

"Relax," Len said. "Ariel wants to party with real people, not those plastic assholes Eitan keeps around. We're going to go get Damon's speakers. Get everything cleaned up." He'd looked at Hellie, then at Alex. "Try to look nice. No attitude tonight."

"Let's go," Alex had said as soon as Len left the apartment, Betcha in the passenger seat, already lighting up. Betcha's real name was Mitchell, but Alex hadn't known that until he got picked up on a possession charge and they had to scrape together bail. He'd run with Len since long before Alex and was always just there, tall, stocky, and soft-bellied, his chin perpetually flecked with acne.

Alex and Hellie started walking, heading toward the concrete bed of the L.A. River, then up to the bus stop on Sherman Way, with no destination in mind. They'd done it before, even sworn they were leaving for good, gotten as far as the Santa Monica Pier, Barstow, once all the way to Vegas, where they'd spent the first day wandering hotel lobbies and the second day stealing quarters from old ladies playing the slots until they had enough for bus fare home. Speeding down the 15 in the air-conditioning on the way back to L.A., they'd fallen asleep leaning on each other's shoulders. Alex had dreamed of the garden at the Bellagio, the water wheels and piped-in perfume, the flowers arranged like a jigsaw puzzle. Sometimes it took Alex and Hellie hours, sometimes days, but they always came back. There was too much world. There were too many choices, and those only seemed to lead to more choices. That was the business of living, and neither of them had ever acquired the skill.

"Len says we're going to lose Ground Zero if Ariel doesn't come through," Hellie said as they boarded the RTD. No grand plans today. No Vegas, just a trip to the West Side.

"It's talk," said Alex.

"He's going to be pissed we didn't clean up."

Alex looked out the murky window and said, "You notice Eitan sent his girlfriend away?"

"What?"

"When Ariel came to town. He sent Inger away. He hasn't had any of the usual girls around. Only Valley trash."

"It's not that big a deal, Alex."

They both knew what Ariel was coming to Ground Zero for. He wanted to slum it for a while and Alex and Hellie were supposed to be part of the fun.

"It never feels like a big deal until it is," Alex said. There had been other favors. The first time was a film guy, or at least someone Len said was a film guy, who was going to get them lots of Hollywood business, but Alex learned later he was just a production assistant, straight out of film school. She'd ended up sitting on his lap all night, hoping that might be all there was to it, until he'd taken her back to the little bathroom and put their filthy bath mat down on the tiles—a weirdly chivalrous gesture—so that she could blow him in greater comfort while he sat on the toilet. *I'm fifteen,* she'd thought as she'd rinsed out her mouth and cleaned up her eye makeup. *What does fifteen look like?* Was another Alex going to slumber parties and kissing boys at school dances? Could she climb through the mirror above the sink and slide into that girl's skin?

But she was fine. Really okay. Until the next morning, when Len kept slamming cabinet doors and smoking in this way he had where it seemed like he wanted to eat the cigarette with every drag, until at last Alex had snapped and said, "What is your problem?"

"My problem? My girlfriend is a whore."

Alex had heard that word so many times from Len it barely registered anymore. Bitch, slut, occasionally cunt when he was feeling particularly angry or when he was affecting British gangster. But he'd never called her that. That was a word for other girls.

"You said—"

"I didn't say shit."

"You told me to make him happy."

"And that means *suck his dick* in Whore?"

Alex's head had done a dizzy spin. How did he know? Had the film guy walked right out of that bathroom and just announced it? And even if he had, why was Len angry? She knew what "make him happy" meant. Alex had felt nothing but rage and it was better than any drug, burning doubt from her mind.

"What the fuck did you think I was going to do?" she demanded, surprised at how loud she sounded, how sure. "Impressions? Make him some balloon animals?"

She'd picked up their blender, the one Len used for protein shakes, and smashed it against the refrigerator, and for a moment she'd seen fear in Len's eyes and she had wanted very badly to keep making him feel afraid. Len had called her crazy, slammed out of the apartment. He had run from *her*. But once he was gone, the adrenaline had poured out of Alex in a rush that left her feeling limp and lonely. She didn't feel angry or righteous, just ashamed and so scared that somehow she'd ruined everything, ruined herself, that Len would never want her again. And then where would she go? All she'd wanted was for him to come back.

In the end she apologized and begged him to forgive her and they got high and turned the air-conditioning up and fucked right next to it, the air coming in cooling gusts that masked their panting. But when Len had said she was a good little slut, she hadn't felt sexy or wild; she'd felt so small. She was afraid she might cry and she was afraid he might like that too. She'd turned her face to the vent and felt the icy breath of the AC unit blow the fine hairs back from her face. She squeezed her eyes shut, and as Len had jackrabbited away behind her, she'd imagined herself on a glacier, naked and alone, the world clean and empty and full of forgiveness.

But Ariel wasn't a film student looking for some strange. He had a reputation. There were stories that he was only in the States because he was dodging the Israeli police after roughing up two underage girls in Tel Aviv, that he ran a dog-fighting ring, that he liked to dislocate girls' shoulders as a kind of foreplay, like a boy pulling the wings off a fly.

Len would be furious when he returned home to find the apartment still a mess. He'd be even madder when they didn't come back to Ground Zero for the party. But they could survive Len's anger better than Ariel's attention.

Alex understood that Len had expected some kind of jealousy when he'd brought Hellie home with them that day from Venice Beach. He hadn't predicted Hellie's warm laugh, her easy way of looping her arm around Alex, the way she'd pluck a paperback from Alex's shelf of thrillers and old sci-fi and say, "Read to me." Hellie had made this life bearable. Alex wasn't going down the path that led to Ariel and she wasn't going to let Hellie go either, because somehow she knew they would not come back from him intact. They didn't have a great life. It wasn't the kind of life anyone imagined or asked for, but they managed.

They took the bus over the hill, down the 101 to the 405 to Westwood, and walked all the way to UCLA, up the slope to campus and through the sculpture garden. They sat on the steps beneath the pretty arches of Royce Hall and watched the students playing Frisbee and lying in the sun reading. *Leisure.* These golden people pursued leisure because they had so many things they had to do. Occupations. Goals. Alex had nothing she needed to do. Ever. It made her feel like she was falling.

When it got bad, she liked talking about the Two Year Gameplan. She and Hellie would start community college in the fall or they'd take online classes. They'd both get jobs at the mall and put their money toward a used car so they wouldn't have to take the bus everywhere.

Usually Hellie liked to play along, but not that day. She'd been sullen, cranky, poking holes in everything. "No one is going to give us enough shifts at the mall to afford a car *and* rent."

"Then we'll be secretaries or something."

Hellie had cast a long look over Alex's arms. "Too many tattoos." Not on Hellie. Lying there on the steps of Royce in her jean shorts, her golden legs crossed, she looked like she belonged. "I like that you think this is really happening. It's cute."

"It could happen."

"We can't lose the apartment, Alex. I was homeless for a while after my mom kicked me out. I'm not doing that again."

"You won't have to. Len's just talking. Even if he's not, we'll figure it out."

"If you stay in the sun much longer, you're gonna look all *Mexicana.*" Hellie rose and dusted off her shorts. "Let's smoke and go see a movie."

"We won't have enough money for the bus back."

Hellie winked. "We'll figure it out."

They'd found a movie theater, the old Fox, where Alex sometimes saw the staff putting up red ropes for premieres. Alex had nestled against Hellie's shoulder, smelling the sweet coconut scent of her still sun-warm skin, feeling the silk of her blond hair brushing occasionally against her forehead.

Eventually she'd dozed off, and when the theater lights came up, Hellie was gone. Alex had gone out into the lobby, then the bathroom, then texted Hellie, and it was only after the second text that she finally got a reply: *It's ok. I figured it out.*

Hellie had gone back for the party. She'd gone back to Len and Ariel. She'd made sure Alex wouldn't be there in time to stop her.

Alex had no money left, no way to get to home. She tried hitching, but no one wanted to pick up a girl with tears streaming down her face, dressed in a dirty T-shirt and the nubs of black jean shorts. She'd walked up and down Westwood Boulevard, unsure of what to do, until at last she'd sold the last of her pot to a redhead with dreads and a skinny dog.

When she got back to the apartment, her feet were bloody where blisters had formed and burst inside her Converse low-tops.

The party was in full swing at Ground Zero, the music filtering outside in thuds and chirps.

She crept inside but didn't see Hellie or Ariel in the living room. She waited in line for the bathroom, hoping no one would report her presence to Len or that he'd be too wasted to care, washed her feet in the tub, then went to the back bedroom and lay down on the mattress. She texted Hellie again.

Are you here? I'm in the back.

Hellie please.

Please.

She'd fallen asleep but woke to the sound of Hellie lying down beside her. In the dim shine of the security light from the alley, she looked yellow all over. Her eyes were huge and glassy.

"Are you okay?" Alex had asked. "Was it bad?"

"No," Hellie said, but Alex didn't know which question Hellie was answering. "No, no, no, no, no." Hellie wrapped her arms around Alex and drew her close. Her hair was damp. She had showered. She smelled like Dial soap, devoid of the usual sweet coconut Hellie smell. "No no no no no no," she kept saying. She was giggling, her body shaking in the way it did when she was trying to keep from laughing too loudly, but her hands clutched Alex's back, the fingers digging in as if she were being pulled out to sea.

Hours later, Alex had woken again. She felt as if she'd never have a real night's sleep or a real morning, just these short naps broken by half waking. It was three a.m., and the party had died down or moved elsewhere. The apartment was quiet. Hellie was on her side, looking at her. Her eyes still looked wild. She'd vomited on her shirt at some point in the night.

Alex wrinkled her nose at the stink. "Good morning, Smelly Hellie," she said. Hellie smiled, and there was such sweetness in her face, such sadness. "Let's get the fuck out of here," Alex said. "For good. We're done with this place."

Hellie nodded.

"Take that shirt off. You smell like hot lunch," Alex said, and reached for the hem. Her hand passed straight through it, straight through the place where the firm skin of Hellie's abdomen should have been.

Hellie blinked once, those eyes so sad, so sad.

She just lay there, still looking at Alex, studying her, Alex realized, for the last time.

Hellie was gone. But she wasn't. Her body was lying on the mattress, on her back, a foot away, her tight T-shirt splattered with vomit, still and cold. Her skin was blue. How long had her ghost lain there waiting for Alex to wake? There were two Hellies in the room. There were no Hellies in the room.

"Hellie. *Hellie.* Helen." Alex was crying, leaning over her body, feeling for a pulse. Something broke inside her. "Come back," she sobbed, reaching for Hellie's ghost, her arms passing through her again and again. With each swipe she glimpsed a bright shard of Hellie's life. Her parents' sunny house in Carpinteria. Her callused feet on a surfboard. Ariel with his fingers jammed into her mouth. "You didn't have to do it. You didn't have to."

But Hellie said nothing, just wept silently. The tears looked like silver against her cheeks. Alex started screaming.

Len slammed through the door, his shirt untucked, his hair a messy tangle, already swearing that it was three in the morning and couldn't he get some rest in his own house, when he saw Hellie's body.

Then he was saying the same thing over and over again. "Fuck fuck fuck." Just like Hellie's *no no no.* Rat-a-tat-tat. A moment later he had his palm pressed against Alex's mouth. "Shut up. Shut the fuck up. God, you stupid bitch, be quiet."

But Alex couldn't be quiet. She sobbed in loud torrents, her chest heaving as he squeezed her tighter and tighter. She couldn't breathe. Snot was running from her nose, and his hand was clamped tight against her lips. She scrabbled against him as he squeezed. She was going to black out.

"Jesus fuck." He shoved her away, wiped his hands on his pants. "Just shut up and let me think."

"Oh shit." Betcha was in the doorway, his big belly hanging over his basketball shorts, his T-shirt gapping. "Is she?"

"We've got to clean her up," said Len, "get her out of here."

For a moment, Alex was nodding, thinking he meant to make her look nice. Hellie shouldn't have to go to the hospital with vomit on her shirt. She shouldn't be found that way.

"It's still early. No one's out there," said Len. "We can get her in the car, drop her . . . I don't know. That nasty-ass club on Hayvenhurst."

"Crashers?"

"Yeah, we'll put her in the alley. She looks used up enough, and there's got to be plenty of shit still in her system."

"Yeah," said Betcha. "Okay."

Alex watched them, her ears ringing. Hellie was watching them too, from her place beside her own body on the mattress, listening to them talk about throwing her out like trash.

"I'm calling the cops," Alex said. "Ariel must have given her—"

Len hit her, openhanded but hard. "Don't be fucking stupid. You want to go to jail? You want Eitan and Ariel coming after us?" He hit her again.

"Shit, man, calm down," said Betcha. "Don't be like that." But he wasn't going to step in. He wasn't going to actually do anything to stop Len.

Hellie's ghost tipped her head back, looked at the ceiling, started drifting toward the wall.

"Come on," said Len to Betcha. "Grab her ankles."

"You can't do this to her," Alex said. It was what she should have said the previous night. Every night. *You can't do this to her.*

Hellie's ghost was already starting to fade through the wall.

Len and Betcha had her body slung between them like a hammock. Len had his arms under Hellie's armpits. Her head lolled to the side. "God, she smells like shit."

Betcha gripped her ankles. One of her pearly pink jelly shoes dangled from her foot. She hadn't taken them off before she came to bed. She probably hadn't noticed. Alex watched it slide off her toe and thunk to the ground.

"Shit, put that back on her."

Betcha fumbled awkwardly with it, setting down her feet, then trying to jam the shoe back on like some kind of a footman in *Cinderella*.

"Oh for fuck's sake, just bring it with you. We'll throw it in with her."

It was only when Alex followed them into the living room that she saw Ariel was still there, asleep on the couch in his undershorts. "I'm tryina sleep, for shit's sake," he said, blinking drowsily at them. "Oh shit, is she . . . ?"

And then he giggled.

They paused in front of the door. Len tried to reach for the knob, knocked over his stupid gangster bat that he kept there for "protection." But he couldn't balance Hellie's body and get the knob to turn.

"Come on," he snapped. "Open the door, Alex. Let us out."

Let me in.

Hellie's ghost hung halfway through the window and the sky. She was fading to gray. Would she trail them all the way down to that grimy alley? "Don't go," Alex begged her.

But Len thought she was talking to him. "Open the door, you useless bitch."

Alex reached for the knob. *Let me in.* The metal was cold in her hand. She started to open the door, then shut it. She flipped the lock and turned to face Len and Betcha and Ariel.

"What now?" Len said impatiently.

Alex held her hand out to Hellie. *Stay with me.* She didn't know what she was asking. She didn't know what she was offering. But Hellie understood.

She felt Hellie rush toward her, felt herself splitting, being torn open to make room for another heart, another pair of lungs, for Hellie's will, for Hellie's strength.

"What now, Len?" Alex asked. She picked up the bat.

Alex didn't remember much of what happened next. The sense of Hellie inside her like a deep, held breath. How light and natural the bat felt in her hand.

There was no hesitation. She swung from her left, just as Hellie had when she'd played for the Midway Mustangs. Alex was so strong it made her clumsy. She hit Len first, a hard crack to the skull. He stepped sideways and she stumbled, knocked off-balance by the force of her own swing. She hit him again and his head gave way with a thick *crunch,* like a piñata breaking open, chips of skull and brain flying, blood spattering everywhere. Betcha still had Hellie's ankles in his hands when Alex turned the bat on him— she was that fast. She struck him behind the knees first and he screamed as he collapsed, then she brought the bat down like a sledgehammer on his neck and shoulders.

Ariel rose and at first she thought he might reach for a gun, but he was backing away, eyes terrified, and as she passed the sliding glass door, she understood why. She was glowing. She chased him to the door—no, not chased. She flew at him, as if her feet were barely touching the ground. Hellie's rage was like a drug inside her body, setting her blood on fire. She knocked Ariel to the floor and hit him again and again, until the bat broke against his spine. Then she took the two jagged pieces in her hands and went to find the rest of the vampires, a coven of boys, asleep in their beds, wasted and drooling.

When it was done, when there were no more people left to kill and she felt her own exhaustion creeping into Hellie's limitless energy, Hellie was the one who guided her, made her put the pink plastic shoes on her own feet and walk the two miles down to where Roscoe crossed the Los Angeles River. She saw no one along the way; Hellie steered her down each empty street, telling her where to turn, when to wait, when it was safe, until they reached the bridge and climbed down in the dawning gray of early morning. They waded in together, the water cold and foul. The city had broken the river when it had flooded one too many times, had sealed it up in concrete to make sure it could never do damage again. Alex let it wash her clean, the shattered remnants of the bat flowing from her hands like seeds. She followed the river's course most of the way back to Ground Zero.

She and Hellie placed Hellie's body back where it had been, and then they lay down together in the cold of that room. She didn't care what happened now, if the police came, if she froze to death on this floor.

"Stay," she told Hellie, hearing the thunder of their hearts beating together, feeling the weight of Hellie curled into her muscles and bones. "Stay with me."

But when she woke, a paramedic was shining a light into her eyes and Hellie was gone.

20

Winter

What had Alex been thinking the night that Darlington vanished? That she just had to get him back to the Hutch. They would talk. She would explain . . . What exactly? That they'd deserved it? That killing Len and the others had given not only Hellie but her some kind of peace? That the world punished girls like them, like Tara, for all their bad choices, every mistake. That she had liked doling out the punishment herself. That whatever conscience she'd always assumed she possessed just hadn't shown up for work that day. And she certainly wasn't sorry.

But she could say she was. She could pretend she didn't remember the feel of the bat in her hand, that she wouldn't do it again. Because that's what Darlington feared—not that she was bad, but that she was dangerous. He feared chaos. So Alex could tell him that Hellie had possessed her. She would turn it into a mystery that they could solve together. He would like that. She would be something for him to fix, a project like his broken town, his crumbling house. She could still be one of the good guys.

But Alex never had to tell those lies. The thing in the basement made sure of that. Darlington was not abroad. He was not in Spain. And she didn't really believe he'd vanished into some pocket realm to be retrieved like a child who'd wandered away from the group. Dawes and Dean Sandow hadn't been there that night. They hadn't felt the finality of that darkness.

"It's not a portal," he'd said in the basement of Rosenfeld Hall. "It's a muh—"

One minute he was there and the next he was enveloped in blackness.

She'd seen the terror in his eyes, the plea. *Do something. Help me.*

She meant to. At least, she thought she meant to. She'd replayed that moment a thousand times, wondering why she'd frozen—if it had been fear or lack of training or distraction. Or if it had been a choice. If the thing in the corner had given her a solution to the problem Darlington presented.

This isn't something I can keep from Sandow. Darlington's words like fingers reaching into her mouth, pinching her tongue, keeping her from crying out.

At night, she thought of Darlington's perfect face, of the feel of his body bracketing hers in the sleep-warmed sheets of his narrow bed.

I let you die. To save myself, I let you die.

That is the danger in keeping company with survivors.

The mechanic leaned over her, smiling. "Nowhere to run, bitch."

His grip felt so heavy on her neck, like his thumbs might push right through her skin and sink into her windpipe.

Alex hadn't wanted to think of that night at Ground Zero. She hadn't wanted to look back. She hadn't even been sure what had happened, if it had been Hellie or her that had made it possible.

Let me in.

Stay with me.

Maybe she'd been afraid that if she opened the door again something terrible might step inside. But that was exactly what she needed now. Something terrible.

Alex's right hand closed over the discarded golf club—a putter. She extended her left hand toward North, remembered the sense of herself splitting, willed herself to do it again. *Open the door,*

Alex. She had time to register the look of surprise on his face, and then the dark cold of him rushed toward her.

Hellie had come to her willingly, but North fought. She sensed his confusion, his desperate terror to remain free, and then a tide of her own need swallowed his concerns.

North felt different than Hellie. She had been the powerful curve of a wave. North's strength was dark and limber, springy as a fencer's foil. It filled her limbs, made her feel like molten metal ran through her veins.

She twirled the putter once in her hand, tested its weight. *Who said I'm running?* She swung.

The mechanic managed to get his hand up, protecting his head, but Alex heard the bones of his hand give way with a satisfying crunch. He yowled and stumbled backward into the couch.

Alex went for his knee next. The big ones were easier to handle on the ground. He collapsed with a thud.

"Who are you?" she demanded. "Who sent you?"

"Fuck off," he snarled.

Alex brought the putter down and struck the hard slats of the floor. He was gone—as if he'd melted straight through the floorboards. She stared at the empty place where he had been, the recoil of the strike reverberating through her arms.

Something smacked her from behind. Alex fell forward as pain exploded through her skull.

She hit the floor and rolled, scrabbling backward. The mechanic was half in and half out of the wall, his body split by the mantel.

Alex sprang to her feet, but in the next second he was beside her. His fist shot out, cracking across her jaw. Only North's strength kept her from crumpling. She swung the putter, but the mechanic was already gone. A fist cracked into her from the other side.

This time she went down.

The mechanic kicked her hard in the side, his boot connecting with her broken ribs. She screamed. He kicked again.

"Get your hands on your head!"

Detective Turner. He was standing at the door, his weapon drawn.

The mechanic looked at Turner. He threw his middle fingers up and vanished, melting into the mantel.

Alex slumped against the wall and felt North flood out of her, saw him leave her in a blurry tide, reassuming his form, his face frightened and resentful. Was she supposed to feel sorry for him?

"I get it," Alex muttered. "But I didn't have a choice." He touched his hand to the wound at his chest as if she'd been the one to shoot him.

"Just find Tara," she snapped. "You have the retainer."

"The what?" said Turner. He was patting the mantel and the bricked-up hearth beneath it as if expecting to find a secret passage.

"Portal magic," Alex grunted out.

North looked back once over his shoulder and vanished through the wall of the apartment. Pain came at her in a sudden swell, a time-lapse photograph of a blooming flower, as if North's presence had kept the worst of it at bay and now that she was empty the damage could rush in. Alex tried to push herself up. Turner had holstered his weapon.

Turner slammed his fist on the counter. "That isn't possible."

"It is," said Alex.

"You don't understand," said Turner. He looked at her the way North had, as if Alex had done him a wrong. "That was Lance Gressang. That was my murder suspect. I left him less than an hour ago. Sitting in a jail cell."

Is there something unnatural in the very fabric of New Haven? In the stone used to raise its buildings? In the rivers from which its great elms drink? During the War of 1812, the British blockaded New Haven Harbor, and poor Trinity Church—not yet the Gothic palace now gracing the green—had no way of accessing the necessary lumber for its construction. But Commander Hardy of the Royal British Navy heard of the purpose for which the great roof beams were intended. He permitted them to pass and they were floated down the Connecticut River. "If there is any place on earth that needs religion," he said, "it is this New Haven. Let the rafts go through!"

—*from* Lethe: A Legacy

Why do you think they built so many churches here? Somehow the men and women of this city knew: Their streets were home to other gods.

—Lethe Days Diary of Elliot Sandow
(Branford College '69)

21

Winter

Turner had his phone out and Alex knew what came next. Part of her wanted to let it happen. She wanted the steady beep of hospital machines, the smell of antiseptic, an IV full of the strongest dope they had to knock her into sleep and away from this pain. Was she dying? She didn't think so. Now that she'd done it once, she figured she'd know. But it *felt* like she was dying.

"Don't." She forced the word out in a rasp. Her throat still hurt like it was being squeezed by Lance Gressang's enormous hands. "No hospital."

"Did you see that in a movie?"

"How are you going to explain this to a doctor?"

"I'll say I found you this way," said Turner.

"Okay, how am *I* going to explain this? And the messed-up crime scene. And how I got in here."

"How *did* you get in here?"

"I don't need a hospital. Take me to Dawes."

"Dawes?"

Alex was annoyed that Turner had somehow forgotten Dawes's name. "Oculus."

"Fuck this," said Turner. "All of you with your code names and your secrets and your bullshit." She could see the way he was leaping from rage to fear and back again. His mind was trying to erase everything he'd seen. It was one thing to be told magic existed, quite another to have it literally give you the finger.

Alex wondered how much Lethe had shared with Centurion. Did they hand him the same *Life of Lethe* booklet? A long file full of horror stories? A commemorative mug that said *Monsters Are Real*? Alex had spent her life surrounded by the uncanny and it had still been hard to let in the reality of Lethe. What would it be like for someone who had grown up in what he believed was an or-dinary city—*his* city—who had been an instrument of order on its streets, to suddenly know that the most basic rules did not apply?

"She need a doctor?" A woman stood in the hall, her cell phone in her hand. "I heard a commotion."

Turner flashed his badge. "Help is on the way, ma'am. Thank you."

That badge was a kind of magic too. But the woman turned to Alex. "You okay, honey?"

"I'm good," Alex managed, feeling a pang of warmth for this stranger in a bathrobe, even as she cradled her phone to her chest and shuffled away.

Alex tried to raise her head, the pain spiking through her like a whip crack. "You need to take me somewhere warded. Someplace they can't get to me, understand?"

"They."

"Yes, *they*. Ghosts and ghouls and inmates who can walk through walls. It's all real, Turner, not just a bunch of college kids dressing up in robes. And I need your help."

Those were the words that woke him. "There's a uniform out front, and I can't carry you past him without answering a whole heap of questions—and you sure can't walk out on your own."

"I can." But, God, she didn't want to. "Reach into my right pocket. There's a little bottle in there with a dropper."

He shook his head but dug into Alex's pocket. "What is this?"

"Basso belladonna. Just put two drops in my eyes."

"Drugs?" asked Turner.

"Medication."

Of course that placated him. Turner the Eagle Scout.

As soon as the first drop hit her eyes, she knew she'd made a bad miscalculation. She felt instantly energized, ready to move, act, but the basso belladonna did nothing to ease the pain, only made her more aware of it. She could *feel* the places where her broken bones were pressing that they shouldn't, where the blood vessels had burst, the capillaries ruptured and swelling.

The drug was telling her brain that everything was okay, that anything was possible, that if she willed it, she could heal herself right now. But the pain was shrieking panic, banging on her awareness, a fist against glass. She could feel a splinter starting, her sanity like a windshield that wasn't meant to break. She'd been called crazy countless times, had sometimes believed it, but this was the first time she'd *felt* insane.

Her heart was thundering. *I'm going to die here.*

You're fine. Through how many late nights and long afternoons had she said that to someone who'd smoked too much, swallowed too much, snorted too much? *Breathe through it. You're fine. You're fine.*

"Meet me on Tilton," she told Turner, pushing to her feet. He was beautiful. The basso belladonna had lit his brown skin like a late-summer sunset. Light bounced off the short stubble of his shaved head. *Medication, my ass.* The pain screamed as her broken ribs shifted.

"This is a terrible idea," he said.

"The only kind I have. Go on."

Turner blew out an exasperated breath and went.

Alex's hyped-up mind had already plotted a route down the back hall and out onto the rickety landing. The air was cool and moist against her fevered skin. She could see every grain of the weathered gray wood, feel sweat blooming on her cheeks and turning cold in the winter air. It was going to snow again.

Down the little row of steps. *Just hop them,* said the drug lighting up her system.

"Please shut up," gasped Alex.

Everything seemed to be coated in a smooth, silvery sheen, painted in high gloss. She forced herself to walk instead of run, her bones scraping against each other like a violin bow. The blacktop of the alley behind Tara's apartment glittered, the stink of garbage and piss like a thick, visible haze that she had to push through as if she were underwater. She passed between two row houses and onto Tilton. A moment later, a blue Dodge Charger rounded the corner and slowed. Turner hopped out and opened the back door, letting Alex slide into the back seat.

"Where are we going?" he asked.

"Il Bastone. The house on Orange."

It was almost worse to lie down and stop moving. All she could think about as she sank into the new-car smell of Turner's leather seats was the pain rolling through her. She stared at the bits of sky and rooftop passing by the window, trying to follow their path to Il Bastone in her head. How much longer? Dawes would be there. Dawes was always there, but could she help? *It's my job.*

"Oculus isn't answering her phone," said Turner. Was Dawes in section? Somewhere in the stacks? "What was I seeing back there?" he asked.

"Told you. Portal magic." She said it with confidence, though she couldn't really be sure. She'd thought portal magic was used for traveling big distances or entering secure buildings. Not getting the jump on someone in a beatdown. "Portals are Scroll and Key magic. I thought Tara and Lance might be dealing to them because of Colin Khatri. And Tara's tattoo."

"Which one?"

"*Rather die than doubt.* From *Idylls of the King.*" She had the strange sense that she'd taken Darlington's place. Did that mean he'd taken hers? God, she hated being this high. "Lance said something when he was kicking the crap out of me. He wanted to know who hurt Tara. He didn't do it."

"Do I need to remind you that he's a criminal?"

Alex tried to shake her head, then winced. "He wasn't bullshitting me." In the panic and fear of the attack, she'd thought she was being hunted again, like with the *gluma*. But now she wasn't so sure. "He was interrogating me. He thought I'd broken in."

"You did break in."

"He wasn't there for me. He came back to the apartment for something else."

"Yeah, let's talk about that. I explicitly told you not to go anywhere near—"

"Do you want answers or do you want to keep being an asshole? Lance Gressang didn't kill Tara. You have the wrong guy."

Turner said nothing and Alex laughed softly. The effect was not worth the effort. "I get it. Either you're crazy and seeing shit or I'm crazy, and wouldn't it be nicer if I was the crazy one. I have bad news for you, Turner. Neither of us is nuts. Someone wanted you to believe Lance is guilty."

"But you don't think he is." There was a long silence. Alex heard the *tick tock tick tock* of the turn signal in time with her heartbeat. At last, Turner said, "I checked into the whereabouts of the society members you mentioned."

So he'd followed up. He was too good a detective to turn down a lead. Even if it came from Lethe. "And?"

"We already knew it was impossible to confirm Tripp Helmuth's whereabouts, because no one had eyes on him the whole night. Kate Masters claims she was at Manuscript until just after three in the morning."

Alex grunted as the Charger hit a bump. It hurt to talk, but it also helped keep her distracted. "Her whole delegation should have been there," she managed. "It was a Thursday night. A meeting night."

"My impression is they were partying late. It's a big building. She easily could have come and gone with no one the wiser."

And Manuscript was only a few blocks from the crime scene. Could Kate have snuck out, glamoured as Lance, to meet Tara? Had it been some kind of game? A high gone wrong? Had Kate intended to hurt Tara? Or was all of this just in Alex's head?

"What do you know about the kid from Scroll and Key, Colin Khatri?" Turner asked.

"I like him," Alex was surprised to hear herself say. "He's nice and he dresses sharp like you but more European."

"That's great intel."

Alex searched her memory. The basso belladonna made it easy to remember the elaborate interior of the Scroll and Key tomb, the patterns of the tiles on the floor. The night of the botched attempt to open a portal to Budapest, Colin had given her an excited little wave when he'd seen her, as if they were rushing the same sorority. "Darlington said Colin was one of the best and brightest, doing graduate-level chem work as an undergrad. Headed someplace prestigious next year. Stanford, I think."

"He never showed at Scroll and Key last Thursday. He was at a party at a professor's house. Bell-something. A French name."

She wanted to laugh. "Not a party. A salon." Colin had been at Belbalm's salon. Alex was supposed to attend the next one . . . tomorrow? No, tonight. Her magical summer working in the professor's quiet office and watering her plants had never seemed more far away. But had Colin actually *been* at the salon? Maybe he'd slipped away. Alex hoped that wasn't the case. Belbalm's world of peppery perfume and gentle conversation felt like a refuge, the reward she probably didn't deserve but would happily accept. She wanted to keep it separate from all of this mess.

Alex felt her awareness drifting, that first bright burst of the basso belladonna letting go. She heard a beep that sounded too loud, then Turner talking over the radio, explaining the damage at

Lance and Tara's apartment. Someone looking for drugs. He had pursued on foot but lost the perp. He gave a vague description of a suspect who might have been male or female in a parka that might have been black or dark blue.

Alex was surprised to hear him lying, but she knew he wasn't covering for her. He didn't know how to explain Lance or what he'd seen.

At last, Turner said, "We're coming up on the green."

Alex forced herself to sit up so she could direct him. The world felt red, as if even the air touching her body was out to get her.

"Alley," she said, as the dark brick and stained glass of Il Bastone came into view. There were lights on in the parlor window. *Be home, Dawes.* "Park in back."

Alex shut her eyes and released a sigh when the engine stopped. She heard Turner's door slam and then he was helping her climb out of the car.

"Keys," he said.

"No keys."

She had a worried moment when Turner fumbled with the doorknob, wondering if the house would let him in. But either her presence was enough or it recognized Centurion. The door swung open.

Il Bastone made a worried rattle as she entered, the chandeliers tinkling. To anyone else it probably would have felt like a truck rolling by, but Alex could feel the house's concern and it put a lump in her throat. Maybe it just disapproved of so much blood and trauma crossing its threshold, but Alex wanted to believe that the house did not like the suffering of one of its own.

Dawes was lying on the parlor carpet in her lumpy sweatshirt, headphones on.

"Hey," said Turner, and repeated, "Hey!" when she didn't answer.

Dawes jumped. It was like watching a big beige rabbit come to life. She startled and cringed backward at the sight of Turner and Alex in the parlor.

"Is she a racist or just twitchy?" asked Turner.

"I'm not a racist!" said Dawes.

"We're all racists, Dawes," said Alex. "How did you even make it through undergrad?"

Dawes's mouth went slack as Turner dragged Alex into the light. "Oh my God. *Oh my God.* What happened?"

"Long story," said Alex. "Can you fix me?"

"We should go to the hospital," said Dawes. "I've never—"

"No," said Alex. "I'm not leaving the wards."

"What got you?"

"A very big dude."

"Then—"

"Who can walk through walls."

"Oh." She pressed her lips together and then said, "Detective Turner, I . . . could you—"

"What do you need?"

"Goat's milk. I think Elm City Market stocks it."

"How much?"

"As much as they have. The crucible will do the rest. Alex, can you get up the stairs?"

Alex glanced at the staircase. She wasn't sure she could.

Turner hesitated. "I can—"

"No," said Alex. "Dawes and I will manage."

"Fine," he said, already heading toward the back door. "You're lucky this dump of a town is gentrifying. Like to see me walk into the Family Dollar looking for goat's milk."

"You should have let him carry you," Dawes grunted as they made their slow way up the stairs.

Alex's body was fighting every step. "Right now he feels guilty for not listening to me. I can't let him make up for it just yet."

"Why?"

"Because the worse he feels, the more he'll do for us. Trust me.

Turner doesn't like to be in the wrong." Another step. Another. Why didn't this place have an elevator? A magical one full of morphine. "Tell me about Scroll and Key. I thought their magic was waning. The night Darlington and I observed, they couldn't even open a portal to Eastern Europe."

"They've had a few bad years, trouble getting the best taps. There's been some speculation in Lethe that portal magic is so disruptive it's been eroding the power nexus their tomb is built on."

But maybe the Locksmiths had been pretending, running a little con, trying to look weaker than they actually were. Why? So that they could perform rituals in secret without Lethe interference? Or was there something shady about the rituals themselves? But how would that connect Colin Khatri to Tara? All Tripp had said was that Tara had mentioned Colin once in passing. There had to be more to it. That tattoo couldn't just be coincidence.

Dawes led Alex to the armory and propped her up against Hiram's Crucible. It felt like it was vibrating gently, the metal cool against Alex's skin. She had never used the Golden Bowl, just watched Darlington mix his elixir in it. He had treated it with reverence and resentment. Like any junkie with a drug.

"The hospital would be safer," Dawes said, rummaging through the drawers in the vast cabinet, opening and closing one after another.

"Come on, Dawes," Alex said. "You gave me that spider-egg stuff before."

"That's different. It was a specific magical cure for a specific magical ailment."

"You didn't hesitate to drown me. How hard can it be to fix me up?"

"I did hesitate. And none of the societies specialize in healing magic."

"Why?" Alex said. Maybe if she kept talking, her body couldn't give up. "Seems like there'd be money in it."

Dawes's disapproving frown—that "learning should be for the

sake of learning" look—reminded her painfully of Darlington. Actually, everything she did in this moment was painful.

"Healing magic is messy," said Dawes. "It's the most commonly practiced by laypeople, and that means power gets distributed more broadly instead of being drawn to nexuses. There are also strong prohibitions against tampering with immortality. And it isn't like I know exactly what's wrong with you. I can't x-ray you and just cast a spell to mend a broken rib. You could have internal bleeding or I don't know what."

"You'll think of something."

"We're going to try reversion," said Dawes. "I can take you back . . . will an hour do it? Two hours? I hope we have enough milk."

"Are you . . . are you talking about time travel?"

Dawes paused with a hand on a drawer. "Are you serious?"

"Nope," said Alex hurriedly.

"I'm just helping your body revert to an earlier version of itself. It's an undoing. Much easier than trying to make new flesh or bone. It's actually a kind of portal magic, so you can thank Scroll and Key for it."

"I'll send them a note. How far back can you go?"

"Not far. Not without stronger magic and more people to work it."

An undoing. *Take me back. Make me into someone who has never been done harm. Go as far as you can. Make me brand-new. No bruises. No scars.* She thought of the moths in their boxes. She missed her tattoos, her old clothes. She missed sitting in the sun with Hellie. She missed the gentle, dilapidated curves of her mother's couch. Alex didn't really know what she missed, only that she was homesick for something, maybe for someone, she'd never been.

She ran her hand along the edge of the crucible. *Could this thing burn me new? Make it so I'd never have to see another ghost or Gray or whatever they decided to call it?* And would she even wish for that now?

Alex remembered Belbalm asking what she wanted. Safety. A chance at a normal life. That was what had come to mind in that moment—the quiet of Belbalm's office, the herbs blooming in the window boxes, a matched set of teacups instead of the chipped mugs of jobs lost and promotional giveaways. She wanted sunlight through the window. She wanted peace.

Liar.

Peace was like any high. It couldn't last. It was an illusion, something that could be interrupted in a moment and lost forever. Only two things kept you safe: money and power.

Alex didn't have money. But she did have power. She'd been afraid of it, afraid of staring directly at that blood-soaked night. Afraid she'd feel regret or shame, of saying goodbye to Hellie all over again. But when she'd finally looked? Let herself remember? Well, maybe there was something broken and shriveled in her, because she felt only a deep calm in knowing what she was capable of.

The Grays had plagued her life, changed it horribly, but after all of those years of torment, they'd finally given something back to her. She was owed. And she'd liked using that power, even the alien feeling of North inside her. She had enjoyed the surprise on Lance's face, on Len's face, on Betcha's. *You thought you saw me. See me now.*

"You have to take your clothes off," said Dawes.

Alex unbuttoned her jeans, trying to hook her fingers into the waist. Her movements were slow, hampered by pain. "I need your help."

Reluctantly, Dawes stepped away from the shelves and helped shove the jeans over Alex's hips. But once they were around her ankles, Dawes realized she needed to take off Alex's boots, so Alex stood there in her underwear while Dawes untied her boots and yanked them off.

She stood, eyes jumping from Alex's bruised face to the tattooed snakes at her hips, which had once matched those at her clavicles. She'd gotten them after Hellie told her there was a rattler inside her. She liked the idea. Len had wanted to try tattooing her in their kitchen. He'd gotten his own gun and inks online, insisted it was all sterile. But Alex hadn't trusted him or their filthy apartment and she hadn't wanted him to leave a mark on her, not that way.

"Can you lift your arms over your head," Dawes said, cheeks red.

"Uh-uh," Alex grunted. Even forming words was getting difficult.

"I'll get shears."

A moment later, she heard the snip of scissors, felt her shirt pulled away from her skin, the fabric sticking to the drying blood.

"It's okay," said Dawes. "You'll feel better as soon as you're in the crucible."

Alex realized she was crying. She'd been choked, drowned, beaten, choked again, and nearly killed, but now she was crying—over a shirt. She'd bought it new at Target before she'd come to school. It was soft and fit well. She hadn't owned many new things.

Alex's head felt heavy. If she could just close her eyes for a minute. For a day.

She heard Dawes say, "I'm sorry. I can't get you in. Turner will have to help."

Was he back from the market? She hadn't heard him return. She must have blacked out.

Something soft moved over Alex's skin and she realized Dawes had wrapped her in a sheet—pale blue, from Dante's room. *My room.* Bless Dawes.

"Is she in some kind of shroud?" Turner's voice.

Alex forced herself to open her eyes, saw Turner and Dawes emptying cartons of milk into the crucible. Turner's head moved back and forth like a searchlight, a slow scan, taking in the strangeness of the upper floors. Alex felt proud of Il Bastone, the armory with its cabinet of curiosities, the bizarre golden bathtub at its center.

She meant to be brave, to grit her teeth through the pain, but she screamed when Turner lifted her. A moment later, she was sinking beneath the cool surface, the sheet unwrapping, blood staining the goat's milk in veins of pink. It looked like a strawberry sundae cup, the kind with the wooden spoon.

"Don't touch the milk!" Dawes was shouting.

"I'm trying to keep her from drowning!" Turner barked back. He had his hands cradled around her head.

"I'm all right," said Alex. "Let me go."

"You're both nuts," said Turner, but she felt his grip ease.

Alex let herself sink beneath the surface. The cool of the milk seemed to seep straight through her skin, coating the pain. She held her breath as long as she could. She wanted to stay below, feel the milk cocoon around her. But eventually she let her toes find the bottom of the crucible and pushed back to the surface.

When she emerged, Dawes and Turner were both shouting at her. She must have stayed beneath the surface a little too long.

"I'm not drowning," she said. "I'm fine."

And she was. There was still pain but it had receded, her thoughts felt sharper—and the milk was changing too, becoming clearer and more watery.

Turner looked like he might be sick, and Alex thought she understood why. Magic created a kind of vertigo. Maybe the sight of a girl on the brink of death descending into a bathtub and then emerging whole and healthy seconds later was just one spin too many on this ride.

"I need to get to the station," he said. "I—"

He turned and strode out the door.

"I don't think he likes us, Dawes."

"It's okay," Dawes said, picking up the heap of Alex's bloodied clothes. "We had too many friends already."

Dawes left to make Alex something to eat, claiming she'd be famished once the reversion was complete. "Do not drown while

I'm gone," she said, and left the door to the armory open behind her.

Alex lay back in the crucible, feeling her body change, the pain leaching out of her, and something—the milk or whatever it had become in Dawes's enchantment—filling her up. She heard music coming from the tinny sound system, the sound so staticky it was hard to pick out a tune.

She dunked her head beneath the surface again. It was quiet here, and when she opened her eyes it was like looking through mist, watching the last traces of milk and magic fade. A pale shape loomed before her, came into focus. A face.

Alex sucked in a breath, choking down water. She burst through the surface, coughing and sputtering, arms crossed over her breasts. The Bridegroom's reflection stared up at her from the water.

"You can't be here," she said. "The wards—"

"I told you," his reflection said, "wherever water pools or gathers, we can speak now. Water is the element of translation. It is the mediary."

"So you're going to be showering with me?"

North's cold face didn't change. She could see the dark shore behind him in the reflection. It looked different than it had the first time, and she remembered what Dawes had said about the different borderlands. She must not be looking into Egypt this time—or whatever version of Egypt she had traveled to when she'd crossed the Nile. But Alex could see the same dark shapes on the shore, human and inhuman. She was glad they couldn't reach her here.

"What did you do to me at Tara's apartment?" North said. He sounded haughtier than ever, his accent more clipped.

"I don't know what to tell you," said Alex, because it felt truer than most things. "There wasn't really time to ask for permission."

"But what did you *do*? How did you do it?"

Stay with me.

"I don't really know." She didn't understand any of it. Where the ability had come from. Why she could see things no one else could. Was it buried somewhere in her bloodline? In the genes of the father she'd never met? Was it in her grandmother's bones? The Grays had never dared approach in Estrea Stern's house, the candles lit at the windows. If she'd lived longer, would she have found a way to protect Alex?

"I gave you my strength," said North.

No, thought Alex. *I took it.* But she doubted North would appreciate the distinction.

"I know what you did to those men," said North. "I saw when you let me inside."

Alex shivered. All the warmth and well-being that had poured into her as she'd soaked in the milk bath was no match for the thought of a Gray rattling around in her head. What else had the Bridegroom seen? *It doesn't matter.* Unlike Darlington, North couldn't share her secrets with the world. No matter how many layers of the Veil he pierced, he was still trapped in death.

"You have enemies on this side of the Veil, Galaxy Stern," he continued. "Leonard Beacon. Mitchell Betts. Ariel Harel. A whole host of men you sent to the darker shore."

Daniel Arlington.

Except he'd said Darlington wasn't on the other side. A murmur rose from the shapes behind the Bridegroom, the same sound she'd heard when she waded into the Nile. *Jean Du Monde. Jonathan Mont.* It might not even be a name. The syllables sounded strange and wrong, as if spoken by mouths not made to form human language.

And what about Hellie? Was she happy where she was? Was she safe from Len? Or would they find each other behind the Veil and make their own misery there?

"Yeah, well, I have enemies on this side too. Instead of looking up my old buddies, how about you find Tara?"

"Why don't you seek out Darlington's notebooks?"

"I've been busy. And it's not like you're going anywhere."

"How glib you are. How sure of yourself. There was a time when I had the same confidence. Time took it. Time takes everything, Miss Stern. But I didn't have to go looking for your friends. After what you did to me at Tara Hutchins's residence, they came looking for me. They could smell your power on me like stale smoke. You've deepened the bond between us."

Perfect. Exactly what she needed. "Just find Tara."

"I have hope that repellent object will draw her to me. But her death was brutal. She may be recovering somewhere. The other side can be a dismaying place for the new dead."

Alex hadn't thought of that. She had just assumed people crossed over into some kind of understanding. Painlessness. Tranquility. She looked again at the surface of the water, that wobbling reflection of the Bridegroom, at those monstrous shapes somewhere behind him, and shivered.

How had Hellie passed into the next world? Her death had been . . . well, in some ways, compared to Tara, compared to Len and Betcha and Ariel, she had passed in relative peace.

It was still death. It was still death too soon.

"Find her," said Alex. "Find Tara so I can figure out who hurt her and Turner can put him away before he hurts me."

North frowned. "I don't know that the detective is a good partner in this endeavor."

Alex leaned back against the curve of the crucible. She wanted to get out of the water but she wasn't sure if she was supposed to. "Not used to seeing a black man with a badge?"

"I haven't been holed up in my tomb for the last hundred years, Miss Stern. I know the world has changed."

His tomb. "Where are you buried?"

"My bones are in Evergreen." His lip curled. "It's quite the tourist attraction."

"And Daisy?"

"Her family had her interred in their mausoleum on Grove Street."

"That's why you're always lurking around there."

"I'm not lurking. I go to pay my respects."

"You go because you're hoping she'll see you doing your penance and forgive you."

When North was mad, his face changed. It looked less human. "I did not hurt Daisy."

"Temper temper," crooned Alex. But she didn't want to provoke him further. She needed him and she could make a gesture toward peace. "I'm sorry about what I did at the apartment."

"No, you're not."

So much for peace. "No, I'm not."

North turned his head away. His profile looked like it had been cut for a coin. "It wasn't an entirely unenjoyable experience."

Now, that surprised her. "No?"

"It was . . . I had forgotten what it felt like to be in a body."

Alex considered. She shouldn't deepen the bond. But if he could look inside her head when he entered her, maybe his thoughts would be open to her too. She'd gotten little sense of him in the panic of the fight. "You can come back in if you like."

He hesitated. Why? Because there was intimacy in the act? Or because he had something to hide?

Dawes bustled through the door, a tray heaped with dishes in her hands. She set it down on the map cabinet. "I kept it simple. Mashed potatoes. Macaroni and cheese. Tomato soup. Green salad."

As soon as the smell hit, Alex's stomach began to rumble and saliva filled her mouth. "Bless you, Dawes. Can I get out of this thing?"

Dawes glanced at the tub. "It looks clear."

"If you're going to eat, I'll stay," said North. His voice was steady, but he looked eager in the mirror of the water.

Dawes handed Alex a towel and helped her climb awkwardly from the tub.

"Can I be alone for a minute?"

Dawes's eyes narrowed. "What are you going to do?"

"Nothing. Just eat. But if you . . . If you hear anything, don't worry about knocking. Just come on in."

"I'll be downstairs," Dawes said warily. She closed the door behind her.

Alex leaned over the crucible. North was waiting in the reflection.

"Want in?" she asked.

"Submerge your hand," he muttered, as if asking her to disrobe. But, of course, she'd already disrobed.

She dunked her hand beneath the surface.

"I'm not a murderer," said North, reaching for her.

She smiled and let her fingers clasp his. "Of course not," she said. "Neither am I."

She was looking through a window. She felt excited, a sense of pride and comfort she'd never known. The world was hers. This factory, more modern than Brewster's or Hooker's. The city before her. The woman beside her.

Daisy. She was exquisite, her face precise and lovely, her hair in curls that brushed the collar of her high-necked dress, her soft white hands buried in a fox-fur muff. She was the most beautiful woman in New Haven, maybe Connecticut, and she was his. Hers. *Mine.*

Daisy turned to him, her dark eyes mischievous. Her intelligence sometimes unnerved him. It was not quite feminine, and yet he knew it was what elevated her over all of the belles of the Elm City. Perhaps she was not really the most beautiful. Her nose was too sharp, her lips too thin—but oh the words that spilled from them, laughing and quick and occasionally naughty. And there was absolutely nothing to fault in her figure or her clever smile. She was simply more alive than anyone he'd ever met.

These calculations were made in a moment. He could not stop making them, because always they tallied to a sense of triumph and contentment.

"What is it you're thinking, Bertie?" she asked in her playful voice, sidling closer. Only she used that name with him. Her maid had come with them, as was proper, but Gladys had hung back in the hallway and now he saw her through the window drifting toward the green, the strings of her bonnet trailing from her hand as she plucked a sprig of dogwood from the trees. He hadn't had much cause to speak to Gladys, but he would make more of an effort. Servants heard everything, and it would pay to have the ear of the woman closest to the woman who would be his wife.

He turned away from the window to Daisy glowing like a piece of milky glass against the polished wood of his new office. His desk, along with the new safe, had been built especially for the space. He'd already spent several late nights here working in comfort. "I was thinking of you, of course."

She tapped him on the arm, drawing closer still. Her body had a sway to it that might have been unseemly in another woman, but not in Daisy.

"You needn't flirt with me anymore." She held up her hand, fluttered her fingers, the emerald glinting on them. "I've already said yes."

He snatched her hand from the air and pulled her near. Something in her eyes kindled, but with what? Desire? Fear? She was sometimes impossible to read. In the mirror above the mantel, he saw the two of them, and the image thrilled him.

"Let's go to Boston after the wedding. We can drive up to Maine for our honeymoon. I don't want a long sea voyage."

She only lifted a brow and smiled. "Bertie, Paris was part of the bargain."

"But why? We have time to see the whole world."

"You have time. I will be a mother to your children and a hostess to your business partners. But for a moment . . ." She stood on tiptoe, her lips a bare breath from his, the heat of her body palpable as her fingers pressed against his arm. "I might simply be a girl seeing Paris for the first time, and we might simply be lovers."

The word hit him like a hammer swing.

"Paris it is," he said on a laugh, and kissed her. It was not their first kiss, but like every kiss with Daisy it felt new.

A creak sounded on the stairs, then a rolling sound, like someone stumbling.

Daisy pulled away. "Gladys has the very worst timing."

But over Daisy's shoulder, Bertie could see Gladys still drifting dreamily along the green, her white cap bright against the dogwoods.

He turned and saw—nothing, no one, an empty doorway. Daisy sucked in a startled breath.

The edge of his vision blurred, a dark blot spreading like flame catching at the corner of a page, eating along its edge. He cried out as he felt something like pain, something like fire, pierce his skull. A voice said, *They cut me open. They wanted to see my soul.*

"Daisy?" he gasped. The word came out garbled. He was lying on his back in an operating theater. Men stood above him—boys, really.

Something's wrong, one said.

Just finish! shouted another.

He looked down. His stomach had been cut open. He could see, oh God, he could see himself, his gut, the meat of his organs, displayed like winding snakes of offal in a butcher's case. One of the boys was pawing at him. *They cut me open.*

He screamed, doubled over. He clutched his stomach. He was whole.

He was in a room he didn't recognize, some kind of office, polished wood everywhere. It smelled new. The sunlight was so bright it hurt his eyes. But he wasn't safe from those boys. They'd followed him here. They wanted to kill him. They'd taken him from his good spot at the train yard. They'd offered him money. He knew they wanted to have their fun, but he hadn't known, he didn't know. They'd cut him open. They were trying to take his soul.

He couldn't let them drag him back to that cold room. There was protection here. If he could only find it. He reached for the desk, pulling open drawers. They seemed too far away, as if his arms were shorter than he remembered.

"Bertie?"

That wasn't his name. They were trying to confuse him. He looked down and saw a black shape in his hand. It looked like a shadow, but it felt heavy in his palm. He knew the name for it, tried to form the word for it in his mind.

There was a gun in his hand and a woman was screaming. She was pleading. But she wasn't a woman; she was something terrible. He could see night gathered around her. The boys had sent her to bring him back so they could cut him open again.

Lightning flashed but the sky was still blue. *Daisy.* He was supposed to protect her. She was crawling across the floor. She was weeping. She was trying to get away.

There, a monster, staring back at him from above the mantel, his white face filled with horror and rage. They'd come for him and he had to stop them. There was only one way to do it. He had to ruin their fun. He turned the shadow in his hand, pressed it to his gut.

Another flash of lightning. When had the storm come on?

He looked down and saw that his chest had come apart. He'd done the work. Now they couldn't cut him open. They couldn't take his soul. He was on the floor. He saw sunlight crisscrossing the slats, a beetle crawling over the dusty floorboards. Daisy—he knew her—lay still beside him, the roses fading from her cheeks, her wicked, lively eyes gone cold.

22

Winter

Alex staggered backward, nearly knocking the tray from the table where Dawes had placed it. She clutched her chest, expecting to find an open wound there. Her mouth was full of food and she realized that she'd been standing in front of the tray, shoveling macaroni into her mouth, as she relived North's death. She could still sense him inside her, oblivious, lost to the sensations of eating for the first time in more than a hundred years. With all of her will, she shoved him from her, resealing the breach that had allowed him inside.

She spat out the macaroni, gasped for air, lurched to the edge of the crucible. The only face looking back at her from the surface of the water was her own. She slapped her hand against it, watching the ripples spread.

"You killed her," she whispered. "I saw you kill her. I felt it."

But even as she said it, she knew she hadn't been North in that moment. There had been someone else inside him.

Alex stumbled down the hall to the Dante bedroom and pulled on a pair of Lethe House sweats. It felt like days had passed but it had only been hours. There was a lingering soreness where her ribs had been broken, the only sign of the beating she'd endured. And yet she was so tired. Each day had started to feel like a year, and she wasn't sure if it was the physical trauma or the heavy exposure to the uncanny that was wearing her down.

Afternoon light streamed through the stained-glass windows, leaving bright patterns of blue and yellow on the polished slats of the floor. Maybe she would sleep here tonight, even if it did mean she had to go to class in sweats. She was literally running out of clothes. These attempts on her life were playing havoc with her wardrobe.

The bathroom off the big bedroom had two standing pedestal sinks and a deep claw-footed tub that she'd never used. Had Darlington? She had trouble imagining him sinking into a bubble bath to relax.

She cupped her hand beneath the sink to drink, then spat into the basin. Alex flinched back—the water was pink and speckled with something. She stoppered the drain before it could vanish.

She was looking at North's blood. She felt sure of it. Blood he had himself swallowed nearly a hundred years ago when he died.

And parsley.

Little bits of it.

She remembered Michael Reyes lying unconscious on an operating table, the Bonesmen gathered around him. *Dove's heart for clarity, geranium root, a dish of bitter herbs.* The diet of the *victima* before a prognostication.

There had been someone inside North that day at the factory— someone who had been used by Bones for a prognostication, long before there was a Lethe House around to keep watch. *They cut me open. They wanted to see my soul.* They'd let him die. She felt sure of it. Some nameless vagrant who would never be missed. *NMDH. No more dead hobos.* She'd seen the inscription in *Lethe: A Legacy.* A little joke among the old boys of the Ninth House. Alex hadn't quite believed it somehow, even after she'd seen Michael Reyes cut open on a table. She should check on him, make sure he was okay.

Alex let the sink drain. She rinsed her mouth again, wrapped her wet hair in a fresh towel, and sat down at the little antique desk by the window.

Bones had been founded in 1832. They hadn't built their tomb until twenty-five years later, but that didn't mean they weren't trying their hand at rituals before that. No one had been keeping an eye on the societies back then, and she remembered what Darlington had said about stray magic breaking loose from the rituals. What if something had gone wrong with that early prognostication? What if a Gray had disrupted the rite, sent the *victima's* spirit flying wild? What if it had found its way into North? He hadn't even seemed to recognize that he was holding a gun—*a shadow in my hand.*

The terrified *victima* inside North, North inside Alex. They were like a nesting doll of the uncanny. Had the spirit somehow chosen North's body to escape to, or had he and Daisy simply been in the wrong place at the wrong time, two innocent people mowed down by power they couldn't begin to understand? Was that what Darlington had been investigating? That stray magic had caused the North-Whitlock murder?

Alex climbed the stairs to the third floor. She'd spent little time here, but she found the Virgil bedroom on her second try. It was directly above the Dante room but far more grand. Alex supposed that if she survived three years of Lethe and Yale, it would one day be hers.

She went to the desk and opened the drawers. She found a note with a few lines of poetry inside, some stationery stamped with the Lethe hound, and not much else.

There was a statistics textbook on the desk. Had Darlington left it there the night they'd gone to the basement of Rosenfeld Hall?

Alex padded back down the stairs to the bookshelf that guarded the library. She pulled down the Albemarle Book. The smell of horses rose from its pages, the sound of hooves on cobblestones, a snatch of Hebrew—the memory of the research she'd done on golems. Darlington had used the library regularly and the book's rows were full of his requests, but most seemed focused on feeding his obsession with New Haven—manufacturing history, land deeds, city planning. There were entries from Dawes too, all about tarot and ancient mystery cults, and even a few from Dean Sandow. But then there it was, early in the fall semester, two names in Darlington's jagged scrawl: Bertram Boyce North and Daisy Whitlock. The Bridegroom was right. Darlington had been looking into his case. But where were his notes? Had they been in his satchel that night at Rosenfeld and been swallowed up with the rest of him?

"Where are you, Darlington?" she whispered. *And can you forgive me?*

"Alex."

She jumped. Dawes was standing at the top of the stairs, her headphones clamped around her neck, a dishrag in her hands. "Turner's back. He has something to show us."

Alex retrieved her socks from the armory and joined Turner and Dawes in the parlor. They sat shoulder to shoulder at a clunky-looking laptop, matching frowns on their faces. Turner had changed into jeans and a button-down shirt but still managed to look sharp, especially next to Dawes.

He waved Alex over, a stack of folders piled beside him.

On the screen, Alex saw black-and-white footage of what looked like a prison hallway, a row of inmates moving along a corridor of cells.

"Look at the time stamp," said Turner. "That's right about the time you were headed into my crime scene."

Turner hit play and the inmates shuffled forward. A huge shape lumbered into view.

"That's him," said Alex. It was unmistakably Lance Gressang. "Where does he go?"

"He turns a corner and then he's just gone." He struck a few keys and the scene changed to a different angle on another hallway, but Alex didn't see Gressang anywhere. "Here's number one on the long, long list of things I don't understand: Why did he go back?" Turner hit the keys again and Alex saw a wide view of what looked like a hospital ward.

"Gressang went back to jail?"

"That's right. He's in the infirmary with a busted hand."

Alex remembered the crunch of bones when she'd hit him with the putter. But why the hell would Gressang have returned to jail to await trial?

"Are these for me?" Alex asked, gesturing at the folders.

Turner nodded. "That's everything we have on Lance Gressang and Tara Hutchins right now. Look your fill, but they're going back with me tonight."

Alex took the stack to the velvet sofa and settled in. "Why such generosity?"

"I'm stubborn, not stupid. I know what I saw." Turner leaned back in his chair. "So let's hear it, Alex Stern. You don't think Gressang did the murder. Who's responsible?"

Alex flipped open the top folder. "I don't know, but I do know Tara has connections to at least four societies, and you don't get stabbed over the occasional twenty bag, so this isn't about a little weed."

"How do you tally four societies?"

"I'll get the whiteboard," said Dawes.

"Is it a magical whiteboard?" asked Turner sourly.

Dawes cast him a baleful look. "All whiteboards are magical."

She returned with a handful of markers and a whiteboard that she propped up on the mantel.

Turner rubbed a hand over his face. "Okay, give me your list of suspects."

Alex felt suddenly self-conscious, like she was being asked to work a complicated math problem in front of the class, but she took a blue marker from Dawes and went to the board.

"Four of the Ancient Eight may have connections to Tara: Skull and Bones, Scroll and Key, Manuscript, and Book and Snake."

"The Ancient Eight?" asked Turner.

"The Houses of the Veil. The societies with tombs. You should have read your *Life of Lethe*."

Turner waved her on. "Start with Skull and Bones. Tara was selling weed to Tripp Helmuth, but I don't see how that's a motive for murder."

"She was also sleeping with Tripp."

"You think it was more than casual?"

"I doubt it," Alex admitted.

"But if Tara thought so?" asked Dawes tentatively.

"I'm guessing Tara knew the score." You had to. All the time. "Still, Tripp's family is real old money. She might have tried to get something out of him."

"That sounds like a soap opera motive," said Turner.

He wasn't going to be an easy sell. "But what if they were dealing in harder stuff? Not just pot? I think a senior named Blake Keely was getting a drug called Merity from them."

"That's impossible," said Dawes. "It only grows—"

"I know, on some mountaintop. But Blake bought from Lance and Tara. Tripp said he saw Tara with Kate Masters, and Kate is in Manuscript—the only society with access to Merity."

"You think Kate sold Merity to Tara and Lance?" asked Dawes.

"No," said Alex, turning the idea over in her head. "I think Kate paid Tara to find a way to grow it. Lance and Tara lived within spitting distance of the forestry school and the Marsh greenhouses. Kate wanted to cut out the middleman. Get Manuscript its own supply."

"But then . . . how did Blake get his hands on it?"

"Maybe they started growing their own stash of Merity and sold it to Blake. Money is money."

"But that would be . . ."

"Unethical?" asked Alex. "Irresponsible? Like handing a socio-pathic toddler a magical machete?"

"What exactly does this drug do?" Turner sounded reluctant, as if he wasn't sure he wanted to know.

"It makes you . . ." Alex hesitated. *Obedient* wasn't the right word. *Eager* didn't cover it either.

"An acolyte," said Dawes. "Your only desire is to serve."

Turner shook his head. "And let me guess, it isn't a regulated substance because no one's ever heard of it to regulate it." He had the same nauseated expression he'd worn when he saw Alex healed by the crucible. "All you children playing with fire, looking surprised when the house burns down." He scrubbed a hand over his face. "Back to the board. Tara is connected to Bones by Tripp, Manuscript by Kate Masters and this drug. Is Colin Khatri her only connection to Scroll and Key?"

"No," said Alex. "She had words from a poem called *Idylls of the King* tattooed on her arm, and that text is all over the Locksmiths' tomb." She passed the file full of photos to Dawes. "Right forearm."

Dawes glanced at the autopsy photos displaying Tara's tattoos, then shuffled hurriedly past.

"That doesn't feel like a casual connection," said Alex.

"What's this?" Dawes asked, tapping a photo of Tara's bedroom.

"Just a bunch of jewelry-making tools," said Turner. "She had a little business on the side."

Of course she had. That was what girls did when their lives fell apart. They tried to find a window to climb out of. Community college. Homemade soaps. A little jewelry-making business on the side.

Dawes was gnawing at her lower lip hard enough that Alex thought she might draw blood. Alex leaned over and peered at the picture, at the cheap knockoff gemstones and dishes of curved hooks for earrings, the pliers. But one of the dishes looked different than the others. It was shallower, the metal beaten and raw, the leavings of something like ash or a ring of lime around its base.

"Dawes," said Alex. "What does that look like to you?"

Dawes pushed the file away as if she could banish it. "It's a crucible."

"What would Tara have used it for? To process the Merity?"

Dawes shook her head. "No. Merity is used in its raw form."

"Hey," said Turner. "How about we pretend for a minute I don't know what a crucible is."

Dawes tucked a strand of her auburn hair behind her ear and without looking at him said, "They're vessels created for magical and alchemical use. They're usually made of pure gold and highly reactive."

"That big gold bathtub Dawes just put me in is a crucible," said Alex.

"You're telling me the thing in Tara's apartment is real gold? It's the size of an ashtray. No way Gressang and his girl could afford something like that."

"Unless it was a gift," said Alex. "And unless whatever they were making in it was worth more than the metal itself."

Dawes pulled her sweatshirt sleeves over her hands. "There are stories about holy men who would use psilocybin—mushrooms—to literally open doorways to other worlds. But the drugs had to be purified . . . in a crucible."

"Doorways," said Alex, remembering the night she and Darlington had observed the botched ritual at Scroll and Key. "You mean portals. You said there are rumors of the magic at Scroll and Key failing. Could Lance and Tara's secret sauce have helped with that?"

Dawes expelled a long breath. "Yes. In theory, a drug like that could help facilitate opening the portals."

Alex picked up the photo of the tiny crucible. "Do you have this stuff in, uh . . . custody or whatever?"

"In evidence," said Turner. "Yes, we do. If there's enough residue left in that thing we can have it tested, see if it matches the hallucinogen we found in Tara's system."

Dawes had taken her headphones from around her neck. She sat with them cradled in her lap like a sleeping animal.

"What is it?" Alex asked her.

"You said Lance was walking through walls, maybe using portal magic to attack you. If someone from Scroll and Key allowed outsiders access to their tomb, if they brought Lance and Tara into their rituals . . . The Houses of the Veil consider that unforgivable. *Nefandum*."

Alex and Turner exchanged a glance.

"What's the penalty for sharing that kind of information with outsiders?" Alex asked.

Dawes clutched her headphones. "The society would be stripped of its tomb and disbanded."

"You know what that sounds like?" said Turner.

"Yeah," replied Alex. "Motive."

Had Colin Khatri inducted Lance and Tara into the secrets of the society? Had it been some kind of payment, one he didn't want to continue to make? Was that what had gotten Tara killed? It was hard for Alex to imagine clean, cheerful Colin committing violent murder. But he was a boy with a bright future, and that meant he had plenty to lose.

"I'm going to Professor Belbalm's salon tonight," said Alex. She would have preferred to fall asleep right here in front of the fire, but she didn't intend to piss off the one person who seemed to be looking out for her future. "Colin works for Belbalm. I can try to find out how late he stayed at her house the night Tara died."

"Alex," Dawes said quietly, looking up at last. "If Darlington found out about the drugs, about what Colin and the other Locksmiths were doing with Lance and Tara, maybe . . ." She trailed off, but Alex knew what she was suggesting: Maybe Scroll and Key had been responsible for the portal that had disappeared Darlington that night in the Rosenfeld basement.

"Where *is* Darlington?" asked Turner. "And if you say Spain, I'm going to pack up my files and go home. My bed is looking real good right now."

Dawes squirmed in her chair.

"Something happened to him," said Alex. "We're not sure what. There's a ritual to try to reach him, but it can only be attempted at the new moon."

"Why the new moon?"

"The timing matters," said Dawes. "For a ritual to work, it helps if it's built around an auspicious date or an auspicious place. The new moon represents the moment before something hidden is revealed."

"Sandow wanted you to keep it quiet?" asked Turner. Alex nodded, feeling guilty. She hadn't exactly wanted to trumpet the news either. "What about Darlington's family?"

"Darlington is our responsibility," said Dawes sharply, protective to the last. "We'll get him back."

Maybe.

Turner leaned forward. "So what you're saying is that Scroll and Key may be involved in a murder *and* a kidnapping?"

Alex shrugged. "Sure. Let's call it that. But we can't rule out Manuscript. Maybe Kate Masters found out Tara sold the Merity to Blake Keely and that he was using it on girls, or maybe something went wrong with their deal. If Lance didn't kill Tara, someone was glamoured to look like him. Manuscript has plenty of tricks and gimmicks that would let Kate spend a few hours wearing his face. And none of this explains the *gluma* that was sent after me." Alex reached into her pocket and felt the reassuring tick of the watch.

Turner looked like he might do murder himself. "The what now?"

"The thing that chased me down Elm. Don't fucking look at me like that. It happened."

"Fine, it happened," said Turner.

"*Glumae* are servants of the dead," said Dawes. "They're errand boys."

Alex scowled. "That was a highly homicidal errand boy."

"You give them a simple task, they accomplish it. Book and Snake uses them as messengers to and from the other side of the Veil. They're too violent and unpredictable to really be good for much else."

Except for making a girl look crazy and maybe shutting her up permanently.

"So Book and Snake is on the board," said Turner. "Motive unknown. You realize none of this is evidence, right? We can draw no credible connections to these societies beyond what Tripp told you. I don't even have enough to get a warrant to look inside those forestry greenhouses."

"I'm guessing Centurion can pull all kinds of strings with his superiors." A shadow crossed Turner's face. "Except you don't want to pull strings."

"That isn't the way things should work. And I can't just go to my captain. He doesn't know about Lethe. I'd have to go all the way up the chain to the chief." And Turner wasn't going to make that move unless he was sure that all of their theories added up to more than some lunatic scrawl on a whiteboard. Alex couldn't blame him. "I'll pull the LUDs for the liquor store near Tara's apartment. It's possible they were using the store's phone to do business. Kate Masters wasn't in Tara's cell or Lance's. Neither was Colin Khatri or Blake Keely."

"If Tara and Lance were using the greenhouses, then they were working with someone at the forestry school," said Dawes. "Warrant or not, we should try to find out who."

"I'm a student," said Alex. "I can walk right in."

"I thought you wanted me to start pulling strings," Turner said.

She had, but now she was thinking better of it. "We can handle this on our own. If you go up the food chain, someone might tell Sandow."

Turner raised a brow. "That a problem?"

"I want to know where he was the night of the murder."

Dawes's spine straightened. "Alex—"

"He pushed to make me stop looking, Dawes. Lethe is here to keep the societies in line. Why did he yank so hard on the reins?"

We are the shepherds. Lethe had been built on that mission. Or had it? Had Lethe ever really been intended to protect anyone? Or were they just supposed to maintain the status quo, to make it look like the Houses of the Veil were being monitored, that some standard was being kept to without ever really checking the societies' power? *This is a funding year.* Had Sandow somehow known that if they looked too closely, they'd find connections to the society rosters? Bones, Book and Snake, Scroll and Key, Manuscript—four of the eight societies responsible for funding Lethe. That added up to half the money needed to keep the Ninth House alive—more since Berzelius never paid in. Was Lethe that precious to Sandow?

"What kind of salary does Dean Sandow get from Lethe?" Alex asked.

Dawes blinked. "I don't actually know. But he has tenure. He makes plenty from the university."

"Gambling?" suggested Turner. "Drugs? Debt?"

Dawes's spine seemed to straighten even more, as if she were an antenna being adjusted to receive information. "Divorce," she said slowly, reluctantly. "His wife left him two years ago. They've been in court ever since. Still—"

"It's probably nothing," said Alex, though she wasn't at all sure that was true. "But it couldn't hurt to know where he was that night."

Dawes's teeth dug into her lip again. "Dean Sandow would never do anything to hurt Lethe."

Turner rose and began to collect his folders. "For the right price, he just might. Why do you think I said yes to being Centurion?"

"It's an honor," protested Dawes.

"It's a *job,* on top of the very intense job I already have. But the money meant I could pay down my mother's mortgage." He slid the folders into a messenger bag. "I'll see what I can find out about Sandow without tipping him off."

"I should do it," Dawes said quietly. "I can talk to his housekeeper. If you start asking questions, Yelena will go to Sandow right away."

"Do you feel up to that?" Turner said skeptically.

"She can handle it," said Alex. "We just need a look at his schedule."

"I like money as a motive," said Turner. "Nice and clean. None of this hocus-pocus bullshit." He shrugged into his coat and headed for the back door. Alex and Dawes followed.

Turner paused with the door open. Behind him, Alex could see the sky turning the deep blue of dusk, the streetlamps coming on. "My mother couldn't just take the check," he said, a rueful smile on his lips. "She knows cops don't get bonuses. She wanted to know where the money came from."

"Did you tell her?" asked Alex.

"About all this? Hell no. I said I hit a lucky streak at Foxwoods. But she still knew I'd gotten myself into something I shouldn't have."

"Mothers are like that," said Dawes.

Were they? Alex thought of the photo her mom had texted her the week before. She'd had one of her friends snap a picture of her in the apartment. Mira had been wearing a Yale sweatshirt, the mantel behind her crowded with crystals.

"Do you know what my mother said?" Turner asked. "She told me there's no doorway the devil doesn't know. He's always waiting to stick his foot in. I never really believed her until tonight."

Turner pulled up his collar and disappeared into the cold.

23

Winter

Alex trudged upstairs to retrieve her boots from the armory. The crucible had healed her wounds, but she was short on sleep and her body knew it. Still if she'd had a choice, she thought she might take another brawl, even with a bruiser like Lance, rather than face the salon tonight, classes tomorrow, and the day after—and the day after that. When she was fighting for her life, it was strictly pass/fail. All she had to do was survive and she could call it a win. Even sitting in the parlor with Dawes and Turner, she'd felt like she was keeping up, not just playing along. She didn't want to go back to feeling like a fraud.

But you are still pretending, she reminded herself. Dawes and Turner didn't really know her. They never would have guessed at what Darlington had learned about her past. And if the new-moon rite worked? If Darlington returned two days from now and told them all the truth, would anyone speak for her then?

Alex found a stack of clothes on her bed in the Dante room.

"I brought them from my apartment," Dawes said, hovering in the doorway, hands curled into her sleeves. "They're not stylish, but they're better than sweats. I know you like black, so . . ."

"They're perfect." They weren't. The jeans were too long and the shirt had been washed so many times it was closer to gray than black, but Dawes hadn't needed to share her closet. Alex wanted to soak up every kindness while she still could.

As she set out for Belbalm's house, Alex felt jumpy. She'd wound her watch tight in case the *gluma* was stalking her, stuffed a jar of graveyard dirt into her satchel, placed two magnets in her pocket, and studied the signs of warding needed to close a portal temporarily. They felt like small protections. The list of suspects in Tara's murder had become a list of possible threats, and they were all packing too much magical firepower.

Belbalm lived on St. Ronan, a twenty-minute walk north from Il Bastone, not far from the divinity school. Her house was one of the smaller ones on the street, two stories high, and built of red brick covered in gray vines like an old woman's hair. Alex entered through a garden gate beneath a white lattice arch, and the same sense of calm she'd felt in Belbalm's office descended over her. The garden smelled of mint and marjoram.

Alex paused on the path. It was some kind of crushed gravel the color of slate. Through the tall windows, she could see a circle of people gathered in a variety of chairs, a few crowded onto a piano bench, some on the floor. She glimpsed glasses of red wine, plates poised on knees. A boy with a beard and a wild mane of curls was reading from something. She felt like she was looking into another Yale, a Yale beyond Lethe and the societies, one that might open and keep opening if she could just learn its rituals and codes. At Darlington's house she had felt like a trespasser. Here she had been invited. She might not belong but she was welcome.

She knocked softly at the door and, when there was no answer, pushed gently. It was unlocked, as if there were never unwanted visitors. There were coats hung in heaps and in piles along a row of hooks. The floor was littered with boots.

Belbalm saw her hovering in the door and gestured Alex toward the kitchen.

Then Alex understood. She was staff.

Of course she was staff.

Thank God she was staff and wouldn't have to try to pretend to be anything else.

Over Belbalm's shoulder, Alex spotted Dean Sandow talking to two students on a settee. She slipped into the kitchen, hoping he hadn't seen her, and then wondered why she should worry about it. Did she really think he had hurt Tara? That he was capable of something that gruesome? In the parlor back at Il Bastone, it had seemed possible, but here, in this place of warmth and easy conversation, Alex couldn't quite get her head around it.

The kitchen was vast, the cupboards white, the countertops black, the floor a clean checkerboard.

"Alex!" crowed Colin when she appeared. Murder suspects on all sides. "I didn't know you were coming! We need extra hands. What are you wearing? Black is fine, but next time a white button-down."

Alex didn't own a white button-down. "Okay," she said.

"Just come over here and set these on a baking sheet."

Alex fell into the rhythm of following orders. Isabel Andrews, Belbalm's other assistant, was there too, arranging fruit and pastries and mysterious stacks of meats on different platters. The food they were serving seemed utterly foreign to her. When Colin said to hand him the cheese, it took her a long moment to realize it was right in front of her: not platters of cubed cheddar but giant hunks of what looked like quartz and iolite, a tiny pot of honey, a spray of almonds. All of it art.

"After the readings and the talk they'll do dessert," Colin explained. "She always does meringues and mini tartes aux pommes."

"Was Dean Sandow here last week?" Alex asked. If he had been, then Alex could cross him off their list, and if Colin didn't know, then maybe *he* hadn't really been at the salon all night.

But before he could answer, Professor Belbalm sailed through the swinging doors.

"Of course he was," she said. "That man loves to drink my bourbon." She popped a tiny wild strawberry into her mouth and wiped her fingers on a towel. "He said the most inane thing about Camus. But it's hard not to be inane about Camus. I'm not sure why I expected better—he has a *Rumi quote* framed beside his desk. It pains me. Darling Colin, please make sure we always have white and red at hand?" She held up an empty bottle and Colin's face went ashen. "It's all right, love. Grab a bottle and come join us. Alex and the others can keep things under control here, yes? Did you bring something to read?"

"I . . . yes." Colin drifted from the kitchen as if his ankles had just sprouted wings.

"Meringues," commanded Isabel.

"Meringues," repeated Alex, walking over to the mixer and handing the bowl to Isabel. She snapped a picture of the kitchen for her mom and texted, *At work.* This was the way she wanted Mira to think of her. Happy. Normal. Safe. Everything Alex had never been. She texted Mercy and Lauren too. *At Belbalm's salon. Fingers crossed for leftovers.*

"I cannot believe Colin gets to read tonight," Isabel complained, piping the meringue onto a baking sheet. "I've been with her a semester longer than he has, and I aced her Women and Industrialism seminar."

"Next time," murmured Alex, brushing melted butter over the tiny apple tarts. "Was it this crowded last week?"

"Yes, and Colin bitched the entire night. We were here cleaning up until after two."

Then Colin's alibi was good. Alex felt a rush of relief. She liked Colin, liked sour Isabel, liked this kitchen, this house, this comfortable space. She liked this piece of world that had nothing to do with murder or magic. She didn't want to see it disrupted by brutality. But that didn't mean she could cross all of Scroll and Key off her list. Even if Colin hadn't killed Tara, he'd known her. And someone had taught Lance portal magic.

"Did Sandow stick around for the whole salon last week?"

"Unfortunately," said Isabel. "He always drinks way too much. Apparently he's been going through some kind of awful divorce. Professor Belbalm tucked him away in her study with a blanket. He left a ring of urine around the powder room toilet that Colin had to clean up." She shuddered. "On second thought, Colin totally deserves to read. You have so much to look forward to, Alex."

Isabel had no reason to lie, so Dean Sandow's bad aim had just earned him an alibi. Dawes would be glad. And Alex supposed she was too. It was one thing to be a murderer, quite another to work for one.

It was a long, late night in the kitchen, but Alex couldn't resent it. It felt like working toward something.

Around one in the morning, they finished serving, tidied up the kitchen, packed bottles into the recycling bins, accepted air kisses from Belbalm, and then floated into the night with platters of leftovers in hand. After the violence and strangeness of the last few days, it felt like a gift. It was a beautiful taste of what life might become, of how little the societies mattered to most people at Yale, of work that asked nothing of you but time and a bit of attention in a house full of harmless people high on nothing more than their own pretensions.

Alex saw a Gray in Rollerblades ahead of her, weaving her way between the lampposts, drawing closer. Her skull and torso looked like they'd been crushed, a deep dimple left by the wheels of some careless driver's car.

Pasa punto, pasa mundo, Alex whispered, almost kindly, and watched the girl vanish. A moment passes, a world passes. *Easy.*

Alex didn't have classes the next morning. She got up early to eat breakfast and to try to do a little reading before trekking up to Marsh, but as she was finishing her pile of eggs and hot sauce, she caught sight of the Bridegroom. His expression turned disapproving when she followed up with a hot fudge sundae, but ice cream was available at all meals in every dining hall, and that was not an opportunity to be squandered.

After breakfast, she ducked into the bathroom off the JE common room and filled the sink. She wasn't eager to talk to him; she wasn't ready to discuss what she'd witnessed in his memories. But she also wanted to know if he'd had any luck finding Tara.

After a moment, North's face appeared in the reflection.

"Well?" she said.

"I haven't found her yet."

Alex flicked the surface of the water with her finger and watched his reflection fracture. "Seems like you're not much good at this."

When the water stilled, North's expression was grim. "And what have you discovered?"

"You were right. Darlington was interested in your case. But his notes weren't in his desk at Il Bastone. I can look at Black Elm tomorrow night." When the new moon would rise. Maybe then Darlington would be able to answer the Bridegroom's questions himself.

"And?"

"And what?"

"What did you see when you were in my head, Miss Stern? You were distressed when you cast me out."

Alex contemplated how much she wanted to tell him. "What do you remember from the moment you died, North?"

His face seemed to go still, and she realized she'd spoken his name out loud. *Damn it.*

"Is that what you saw?" he asked slowly. "My death?"

"Just answer me."

"Nothing," he admitted. "One moment I was standing in my new office, talking to Daisy, and then . . . I was no one. The mortal world was lost to me."

"You were on the other side." Alex could see how that could mess with your head. "Did you ever try to find Gladys O'Dona-ghue behind the Veil?"

"Who?"

"Daisy's maid."

North frowned. "The police interviewed her. She found our . . . bodies, but she wasn't even there to witness the crime."

"And she was just a maid?" said Alex. Guys like this never noticed the help. But North was right. Alex had spotted Gladys outside enjoying the spring weather herself. If Gladys had seen or heard something strange at the scene, she had every reason to share that information with the police. And Alex suspected there had been no one to see—just magic, invisible and wild, the frightened spirit of a man who had been brutalized by the Bonesmen and somehow found his way into North. "I'll let you know what I find at Black Elm. Quit following me around and go hunt down Tara."

"What did you see in my head, Miss Stern?"

"Sorry! You're breaking up!" Alex released the plug in the drain.

She headed out of the common room and texted Turner that she was on her way to the Marsh greenhouses. On her way, she placed a phone call to the hospital to ask after Michael Reyes. She should have checked in on the *victima* from Skull and Bones's latest prognostication sooner, but she'd been more than a little distracted. It took her a while to get the right person on the line, but eventually Jean Gatdula came on to tell her that Reyes was recovering well and would be sent home in the next two days. Alex knew "home" was Columbus House, a shelter far away from campus. She hoped Bones at least left him with a pocketful of cash for his trouble.

The Marsh Botanical Garden sat at the top of Science Hill, the old mansion topped by what looked like a bell tower, the grounds of the former estate rolling down the slope toward the apartment Tara had shared with Lance. There was no real security and Alex blended in easily with the students coming and going from the facility. Four massive forestry school greenhouses stood near the back entrance, surrounded by a cluster of smaller glass structures. Alex had worried she wouldn't be able to identify where Tara had tended her dangerous garden, but as she made a circuit around the grounds, she detected the stink of the uncanny beneath the smells of manure and turned soil. Though the little greenhouse looked ordinary enough, Alex suspected it had the remnants of a glamour on it—probably courtesy of Kate Masters and Manuscript. How else would Tara have cultivated her crops without inviting suspicion?

But when Alex pulled open the door, she found nothing but empty planters and overturned pots on the tables. Someone had cleaned the place out. Kate? Colin? Someone else? Had Lance opened a portal from his jail cell and come here to destroy potential evidence?

A single, slender tendril of some unknown plant lay in a pile of dirt beside a toppled plastic container. Alex touched her finger to it. The little vine unfurled, a lone white bud appearing from its leaves. Its petals parted in a burst of glittering seeds like a firework, with a soft but audible *puh,* and it withered to nothing.

Outside, Alex found a lean woman in jeans and a barn jacket digging through a bucket of some kind of mulch with gloved hands.

"Hey," she said, "can you tell me who uses that greenhouse?"

"Sveta Myers. She's a grad student."

Alex didn't remember her name from Tara's case file.

"You know where I can find her?"

The woman shook her head. "She left a couple days ago. Took the rest of the semester off."

Sveta Myers had gotten spooked. Maybe she'd done the work of destroying the greenhouse herself. "You ever see her with a couple? Skinny little blond girl and a big guy, looked like he lived at the gym?"

"I saw the girl here a lot. She was Sveta's cousin or niece or something?" Alex highly doubted that. "I might have seen the guy once or twice. Why?"

"Thanks for your help," said Alex, and headed for the gates.

She tried to shake off her feeling of disappointment as she made her way back down the hill. She'd hoped to find more of Tara in the gardens, not just piles of dirt heaped like a fresh grave.

Turner had said he'd meet Alex outside Ingalls Rink, and she spotted his Dodge idling by the curb. It was blessedly warm inside.

"Anything?" he asked.

She shook her head. "Someone cleaned the whole place out, and the student they were working with skipped town too. Some-one named Sveta Myers."

"Doesn't ring a bell, but I'll see if I can track her down."

"I'll check the alumni rosters to see if she's connected to any of the societies," said Alex. "I want to talk to Lance Gressang."

"You're back on that?"

Alex had almost forgotten she'd feigned interest in talking to Gressang before. "Someone has to question him about the new information we have."

"If the case goes to trial—"

"It will be too late. Someone sent a monster after me. They killed Tara, stole all her plants. Maybe they got to Sveta Myers too. They're cleaning house."

"Even if I could get an interview with Gressang, I'm not bring-ing you with me."

"Why not? We need Gressang to believe we understand more about all of this than he does. It will take him about thirty seconds to realize you don't know your ass from a hot rock."

"What a colorful turn of phrase."

"I saw you in that apartment, Turner. You almost wet yourself when Lance disappeared through that wall."

"You have a real way about you, y'know that, Stern?"

"Is it my charm or my looks that you can't get enough of?"

Turner twisted in his seat to give her a long stare. "You don't always have to come out swinging. What are you so angry at?"

Alex felt an irritating jolt of embarrassment. "Everything," she muttered, gazing at the fogged-up windshield. "Anyway, you know I'm right."

"Maybe so, but Lance is represented by counsel. Neither of us can talk to him without his lawyer."

"Would you like to?"

"Of course I'd like to. I'd also like a rare steak and a moment of peace without you yapping in my ear."

"Can't oblige. But I think I can get you an interview with Gressang."

"Let's say that's true. Nothing we learn will be admissible in a court of law, Stern. Lance Gressang could tell us he killed Tara twelve times over and we wouldn't be able to pin it on him."

"But we'll still get answers."

Turner rested his gloved hands on the steering wheel. "I'm pretty sure when my mother was talking about the devil, she had you in mind."

"I'm a delight."

"If I said yes, what would we need?"

Turner already had a nice enough suit. "You own a briefcase?"

"I can borrow one."

"Great. Then all we need is this." She pulled the mirror she'd used to gain access to Tara's apartment from her pocket.

"You want me to walk into a secure jail with a compact and a nice attaché case?"

"It's worse than that, Turner." Alex flipped the mirror in her hand. "I want you to believe in magic."

24

Winter

The plan was trickier than Alex had anticipated. The mirror would fool the guards they encountered but not the cameras in the jail.

Dawes came to the rescue with an actual tempest in a teapot. Alex hadn't thought Darlington was being literal when they'd walked through the bizarre basement of Rosenfeld Hall, but apparently back in their heyday, St. Elmo's had managed all kinds of interesting magic.

"It's not just the vessel," Dawes explained to Alex and Turner the next day, standing at the counter in the kitchen at Il Bastone, a golden teapot and jeweled strainer before her. "It's the tea itself." She carefully measured out dried leaves from a tin stamped with the St. Elmo's crest, a sinister little design referred to as "the goat and boat."

"Darlington said they're campaigning for a new tomb," Alex said.

Dawes nodded. "Losing Rosenfeld Hall broke them. They've been petitioning for years, claiming all sorts of new applications for their magic. But without a nexus to build over, there's no point to a new tomb." She poured the water over the leaves and set the timer on her phone. The lights flickered. "Make the brew too strong and you could short the grid for the entire Eastern Seaboard."

"Why are the tombs so important?" Turner asked. "This is just a house and you're standing there . . . working *magic*." He ran his tongue over his teeth as if he didn't like the taste of the word.

"Lethe House magic is spell- and object-based, borrowed enchantments, very stable. We don't rely on rites. It's why we can keep the wards up. The other societies are trafficking with far more powerful forces—telling the future, communicating with the dead, altering matter."

"Big magic," said Alex.

Turner leaned back against the counter. "So they have machine guns and you're working with a bow and arrow?"

Dawes looked up, startled. She rubbed her nose. "Well, more like a crossbow, but yes."

The timer sounded. Dawes swiftly removed the strainer and poured the tea into a thermos. She handed it to Alex. "You should have about two hours of real disruption. After that . . ." She shrugged.

"But you're not going to knock the power out, right?" Turner asked. "I don't want to be at a jail when all the lights go down."

"Aw, look how far you've come!" Alex said. "Now you're worried about magic being *too* powerful."

Dawes tugged at her sweatshirt sleeves, the surety she'd displayed while caught up in brewing the tea evaporating. "Not if I got it right."

Alex took the thermos and stowed it in her satchel, then yanked her hair into a tight bun. She'd told Mercy she had a job interview as an excuse to borrow her fancy black pantsuit.

"I hope you get the job," Mercy had said, and hugged Alex so tight it felt like her bones were bending.

"I hope I get it too," Alex had replied. She'd been happy to play dress-up, happy to have this adventure to fill the hours, regardless of the danger. The new-moon rite had felt distant, impossibly far off, but tonight it would happen. She was having trouble thinking about anything else.

She checked her phone. "No signal."

Turner did the same. "Me neither."

Alex turned on the little television that sat above the breakfast nook. Nothing but static. "A perfect brew, Dawes."

Dawes looked pleased. "Good luck."

"I'm about to commit career suicide," said Turner. "Let's hope we've got more on our side than luck."

The drive to the jail was short. No one there knew Alex, so she didn't have to worry about being recognized. She made a perfectly reasonable assistant in her borrowed corporate drag. Turner was another matter. He'd had to pop by the courthouse that morning to bump into Lance Gressang's attorney and secure his visage in the compact.

They passed through security without incident.

"Stop looking at the cameras," Alex whispered as she and Turner were escorted down a dingy hallway lit by buzzing fluorescents.

"They look like they're working."

"The power is on, but they're just recording static," Alex said with more confidence than she felt. The thermos was tucked into her bag, its weight resting reassuringly against her hip.

Once they were inside the meeting room, they'd be safe at least. There was no video or audio recording allowed in a conference between an attorney and his client.

Lance was seated at the table when they entered. "What do you want?" he said when he caught sight of Turner, who had pocketed the compact after flashing it at the scowling guard.

"You've got one hour," the guard said. "Don't push it."

Gressang shoved back from the table, looking from Turner to Alex. "What the fuck is this? Are you two working together?"

"One hour," the guard repeated, and locked the door behind him.

"I know my rights," Gressang said, standing. He looked even

bigger than he had at the apartment, and his bandaged hand didn't do much to put Alex at ease. She had made it her business not to get trapped in small spaces with men like Lance Gressang. You didn't want to be the only thing in sight when their moods went sour.

"Sit down," said Turner. "We need to have a conversation."

"You can't talk to me without my lawyer."

"You walked through a wall yesterday," said Turner. "That in the penal code?"

Lance looked almost sheepish at the accusation. *He knows he's not supposed to be using portal magic,* Alex thought. And he most definitely wasn't supposed to be seen doing it by a cop. Lance had no way of knowing that Turner was associated with the Houses of the Veil.

"Sit down, Gressang," Turner repeated. "You might be glad you did."

Alex wondered if Lance would just pop a mushroom in his mouth and vanish through the floor. But slowly, sullenly, he dropped back into his seat.

Turner and Alex took chairs opposite him at the table.

Lance's jaw set and he jutted his chin toward Alex. "Why were you at my place?"

My place. Not our place. She said nothing.

"I'm trying to find out who killed Tara," said Turner.

Lance threw up his hands. "If you know I'm innocent, why don't you get me out of this shithole?"

"'Innocent' is a big word for what you are," Turner said in that same pleasant, condescending tone he'd used on Alex just a few days ago. "Maybe you're innocent of this particular bit of brutality, and if that's the case it will be my great pleasure to make sure the murder charge against you is vacated. But right now what I want to convey to you is that no one knows we're here. The guards all think you're chatting with your lawyer, and what you need to absorb is that we can do whatever we want."

"Am I supposed to be afraid?"

"Yes," said Turner. "You are. But not of us."

"Hey, he can be afraid of us," said Alex.

"He can, but he has bigger problems to worry about. If you didn't kill Tara, then someone did. And that someone is just waiting to lay hands on you too. Right now you're a useful scapegoat. But for how long? Tara knew things she wasn't supposed to, and maybe you do too."

"I don't know shit."

"I'm not the one you need to convince. You've seen what these people can do. Do you think that they care about wiping away a little shitstain like you? Do you think they will hesitate to eradicate you or your friends or that entire neighborhood if it will help them sleep a little better at night?"

"People like you and me don't matter," said Alex. "Not when we stop being useful."

Lance placed his injured hand gingerly on the table and leaned forward. "Who the *fuck* are you?"

Alex held his gaze. "I'm the only person who thinks you didn't kill Tara. So help me figure out who did before Turner loses patience, shuffles me out that door, and leaves you to rot."

Lance's eyes darted back and forth between Alex and Turner. At last he said, "I didn't hurt her. I loved her."

Like those things couldn't go hand in hand. "When did you start working with Sveta Myers?"

Lance shifted in his seat. He obviously didn't like that they knew that name. "I don't remember. Two years back? Tara went up there for a plant sale, got to chatting with her. They got on real good, talking about community gardening and shit. We sold to her for a while, then we started growing with her, giving her a cut."

"Tell us about the Merity," Alex said.

"The what?"

"You weren't just growing cush. What did you grow for Blake Keely?"

"That model guy? He was always sniffing around Tara, flashing cash like he's a celebrity. I can't stand that asshole."

Alex didn't know how she felt about finding common ground with Lance Gressang.

"What were you growing for him?" Turner pushed.

"It wasn't for him. Not at first. We were selling green to his frat for a while—none of this shit is admissible, all right? It's all off the record?" Turner waved him on. "Nothing special. Dime bags, twenty bags. The usual shit. Then this year, this girl Katie shows up—"

Alex sat forward. "Kate Masters?"

"Yeah. Blond, real cute, but kinda butch?"

"Tell me more about your taste in women."

"Really?"

"No, you ass. What did *Katie* want?"

"She wanted to know where we were growing and if Tara could make some space at the greenhouses for something new. Some medicinal shit, had all these specific rules about moisture or I don't know what. Tara got real into working on it with Sveta. Took a minute but eventually it started growing pretty well. I tried some of it once. Didn't even give me a buzz."

Jesus. Lance Gressang had gotten his hands on Merity and he hadn't even known it. When Alex thought of the damage he might have done if he'd realized the control it could give him over others . . . But someone else had gotten there first.

"You thought it was worthless," said Alex. "A shit buzz. So you sold it to Blake."

"Yeah," Gressang said, grinning.

"And what did you think when he came back for more?"

Gressang shrugged. "Happy to take his money."

"Did Kate Masters know you sold Merity to Blake?"

"Nah, she was real uptight. Told us it was poisonous and whatever, not to mess with it. I knew she'd be pissed if she found out. But Blake kept hitting us up for more, and then he brings this other guy around who wants to know if we can get mushrooms."

"Who?" Turner asked Lance. But Alex already knew what Lance was going to say.

Lance wriggled in his seat. He looked uneasy, almost scared.

"It was Colin Khatri, wasn't it?" said Alex. "From Scroll and Key."

"Yeah. He . . ." Lance leaned back. The bravado had gone from him. He looked at the wall as if expecting to find some kind of answer there. The clock was ticking, but Alex and Turner stayed quiet. "I didn't know what we were starting."

"Tell me," said Turner. "Tell me how it began."

"Tara was at the greenhouses all the time," Lance said haltingly. "Coming home late, staying up to try mixing shit, putting the mushrooms together with I don't know what. She had this little yellow dish Colin gave her. Called it her witch's cauldron. Colin couldn't get enough of the tabs she made. He kept coming back for more."

"Tabs?" asked Turner. "I thought you were dealing with mushrooms."

"Tara distilled that shit down. It wasn't acid. I don't know what it was." Lance rubbed his good hand up his other arm, and Alex could see his skin had puckered with goosebumps. "We wanted to know what Colin was using it for, but he was real cagey about it. So Tara's like, guess I won't be cooking for you guys anymore." Lance held his hands out like he was pleading with Alex. "I told her. I *told* her to just leave it alone, just keep taking Colin's cash."

"But it wasn't enough," Alex said. *Rather die than doubt.* Tara had sensed something big at play and she'd wanted to be part of it. "So what happened?"

"Colin caved." Alex couldn't tell if he sounded more smug or regretful. "One weekend, he and his buddies come get us at the apartment. We all take the tabs Tara made and then they blindfold us and take us into this building, this room. It was real pretty, with these screens with, like, Jewish stars on them, and the roof was open so you could see the skies." Alex had been in that room the night of the failed Locksmith ritual, when they'd tried to get to Budapest. Had they staged the whole thing knowing it wouldn't work without Tara's tabs? "We stand in a circle at this round table and they start chanting in, like, I don't know, Arabic maybe and the table just . . . opens up."

"Like a passage?" asked Turner.

Lance was shaking his head. "No, no. You don't understand: There was no bottom. It was night down there—some other night—and night up top, our night. It was all stars." There was real awe in his voice. "We walked through and we were standing on a mountaintop. You could see for miles. It was so clear you could see the bend in the horizon. It was incredible. I was sick as shit the next day, though. And, God, we smelled. It didn't wash off for days." Lance sighed and said, "I guess it just went on from there. Colin and that whole crew wanted Tara to keep cooking up her stuff for them. We wanted to keep tripping. Tara wanted to see the world. I only wanted to fuck around. We went to the Amazon, Morocco, those hot pools in Iceland. We went to New Orleans for New Year's. It was like the best video game ever." Lance released a little laugh. "Colin couldn't figure out how Tara was mixing the shit. He acted like he thought it was funny, but I could tell it pissed him off."

Alex tried to reconcile this Colin—greedy, jealous, tripping with drug dealers—with the ambitious, perfectly groomed boy she'd seen at Belbalm's house. Where had he thought this would end?

"How did Blake and Colin know each other?" Alex asked. She couldn't imagine them hanging out.

Lance shrugged. "Lacrosse or some shit?"

Lacrosse. Colin seemed so distinctly un-jocklike it was hard to picture. Had he seen one of Blake's nasty little videos and recognized Merity the way Alex had? The Locksmiths' magic had started to fail. The nexus beneath their tomb wasn't working anymore and they were desperate for ways to open portals. And Colin—bright, friendly, polished Colin—hadn't reported what Blake had been doing with the Merity. He hadn't stopped him from hurting girls. Instead, he'd seized an opportunity for himself and his society.

"What about Tripp Helmuth?" said Turner. It felt strange to ask about rosy-cheeked, good-vibes-only Tripp, but Alex was glad he wasn't ruling anyone out.

"Who?"

"Rich kid," said Alex, "sailing team, always seems to have a tan?"

"That could be a lot of guys around Yale."

Alex didn't think he was playing dumb, but she couldn't be sure.

"The other day you opened a portal in the jail," said Turner.

"I had a tab on me when you guys picked me up." Lance grinned. "Plenty of places to stash something that small."

"Why not just escape?" asked Turner. "Go to Cuba or something?"

"What the fuck would I do in Cuba?" Lance asked. "Besides, you can't portal big distances from anywhere but the table."

He meant the tomb. Scroll and Key still needed the nexus. Tara's tabs weren't enough on their own.

"Wait," said Alex. "You wasted your only tab going back to your apartment?"

"I thought I could get some cash, maybe make a run for it or get something to trade in here, but your asshole cops had tore the whole place apart."

"Why didn't you just portal to the tomb—the table—and then go wherever you wanted?"

Lance blinked. "Shit." He slumped back in his chair. *"Shit."* He trained his gaze on Alex. He looked impossibly mournful. "You're going to help me, right? You're going to protect me?"

Turner stood. "Keep your head down, Gressang. As long as you look like you're taking the fall, you should be safe in here."

Alex expected Lance to protest, try to bargain, maybe even

threaten them. Instead, he just sat there, his big body frozen like a stone idol beneath the fluorescent lights. He didn't say a word when Turner knocked on the door and the guard came to fetch them, didn't look up when they left. He'd been to the jungles of the Amazon, explored the markets of Marrakesh. He'd seen into the mysteries of the world, but the mysteries of the world had taken no notice of him, and after all of it, he'd still ended up here. The doors had closed. The portals too. Lance Gressang wasn't going anywhere.

Turner and Alex rode back to campus in silence, the Dodge's heater cranked up against the bitter cold. She texted Dawes to let her know they were in the clear and that she'd be at Black Elm by eight at the latest, then slipped off the pumps she'd borrowed from Mercy. They were a half size too small and her feet were killing her.

It wasn't until they were exiting the highway that Turner said, "Well?"

"I think we may have more motives than we started with."

"I'm not taking Gressang off the table. Not until we can put someone else at the scene. But Colin Khatri and Kate Masters are looking a lot more interesting." He tapped his gloved hands on the wheel. "It's not only Colin and Kate, though, is it? It's all of them. All the little children in their robes and hoods pretending they're wizards."

"They're not pretending." But Alex knew exactly what he meant. Colin was the most direct connection between Scroll and Key and Tara, but all of the Locksmiths had shared their rituals with outsiders and hidden the truth from Lethe. If Tara had become a danger to the society, any one of them could have decided to shut her up. It also didn't seem likely Kate Masters had opted to go rogue from Manuscript. Alex remembered what Mike Awolowo had said about the rarity of the drug. Maybe they'd all thought they could cut out their Khingan Mountain supplier and start growing their own. He'd seemed genuinely surprised that the Merity had gotten out, but that could have been an act.

"Who do you like for this?" Turner asked.

Alex tried not to show her surprise. Turner might just be using her as a sounding board, but it felt good to be asked. She wished she had a better answer.

Alex flexed her aching feet. "Any member of Manuscript could have used a glamour to make Tara think she was meeting Lance. Plus if Keys relied on Tara for the secret sauce, why would they want her dead? Their magic has been a mess the last few years. They needed her."

"Unless she was pushing too hard," said Turner. "We have no idea what her relationship with Colin was really like. We don't even know exactly what was in those tabs of hers. We aren't talking about magic mushrooms anymore."

That was true. Maybe Colin the chem whiz hadn't liked being shown up by a town girl. And Alex doubted anyone in Scroll and Key liked being blackmailed into sharing their rites. It was also possible someone had cracked Tara's recipe and decided they didn't want her around anymore.

"Colin Khatri had an alibi that night," Alex said. "He was at Belbalm's salon."

"You're telling me he couldn't just open up a convenient little portal, pop through, kill Tara, be back before anyone noticed?"

Alex wanted to smack herself. "Smart, Turner."

"It's almost like I'm good at my job."

Alex knew she should have thought of it herself. Maybe she would have if she wasn't too busy hoping Colin wasn't involved in the worst of this, that her perfect, promising summer with Belbalm could remain untouched by the ugliness of Tara's murder.

Turner steered the car up Chapel and pulled in at the Vanderbilt gates. She saw North hovering by the steps to her entryway. How long had he been waiting? And had he found Tara on the other side? With a shiver, she realized he'd been killed—or killed pretty Daisy and himself—only blocks from where she was sitting.

"What would you say if I told you there's a ghost outside my dorm?" asked Alex. "Right there in the courtyard?"

"Honestly?" asked Turner. "After everything I've seen the last few days?"

"Yeah."

"I'd still think you were screwing with me."

"What if I told you he's working our case?"

Turner's real laugh was completely unlike his false chuckle, a deep, full belly laugh. "I've had weirder CIs."

Alex shoved her feet into the too-tight pumps and pushed open the car door. The night air was so cold it hurt to breathe, and the sky was black above her. New moon rising. She was due at Black Elm in a matter of hours. When Dean Sandow had first started talking about the ritual, Alex assumed they would try to contact Darlington from Il Bastone, maybe even using the crucible. But Sandow really did intend to call him home.

"I'll shake Kate Masters's tree tomorrow," said Turner. "Colin Khatri too. See what falls out."

"Thanks for the ride-along." Alex shut the car door and watched Turner's headlights recede down Chapel. She wondered if she'd ever get to speak to the detective again.

Everything might change tonight. Alex had longed for Darlington's return, and she'd feared it—and she couldn't quite pull apart those feelings. She knew that when he told Dean Sandow what she'd done, what she really was, it would mean the end for her and Lethe. She knew that. But she also knew that Darlington was Tara's best chance at justice. He spoke the language of this world, understood its protocols. He would make the connections that the rest of them were missing.

She could admit she missed his pompous, know-it-all ass. But it was more than that. He would protect her.

The thought was embarrassing. Alex the survivor, Alex the rattler, should be harder than that. But she was tired of fighting. Darlington wouldn't stand for any of what she and Dawes had been put through. He might not believe she belonged in Lethe, but she knew he believed she was worthy of Lethe's protection. He had promised to place himself between her—between all of them—and the terrible dark. That meant something.

North kept his distance, hovering in the golden light of the streetlamp, murderer or victim, but partner either way. For now.

She nodded to him and left it at that. Tonight she had other debts to pay.

25

Winter

How'd it go?" Mercy asked, as soon as Alex entered the common room. She sat cross-legged on the couch, surrounded by books. It took Alex a moment to remember she was supposed to have been on a job interview.

"I'm not sure," she said, heading back to their bedroom to change. "Maybe good? It was interesting. These pants are too tight."

"Your ass is too big."

"My ass is just right," Alex called back. She pulled on black jeans, one of the last of her good long-sleeved shirts, and a black sweater. She considered making up an excuse about a study group, then opted for brushing her hair and applying some dark plum lipstick.

"Where are *you* going?" Mercy asked when she caught sight of Alex's look.

"I'm meeting someone for coffee."

"Hold up," said Lauren, poking her head out of her bedroom. "Is Alex Stern going on a date?"

"First Alex Stern had a job interview," said Mercy. "And now she's going on a date."

"Who *are* you, Alex Stern?"

Hell if I know. "If y'all are done, who stole my hoops?"

"What college is he in?" asked Lauren.

"He's town."

"Ooh," said Lauren. She placed Alex's fake silver hoops in her hand. "Alex loves a working man. That lipstick is way too much."

"I like it," said Mercy.

"It looks like she's going to try to eat his heart."

Alex stuck the hoops in her ears and blotted her lips with a tissue. "Just right."

"Feb Club is almost over," said Mercy. Every night in February, some group or organization hosted an event, a protest against the deep gloom of winter. "We should hit the last party on Friday."

"Should we?" Alex asked, wondering if Mercy was really ready for that.

"Yeah," said Mercy. "I'm not saying we should stay long or anything, but . . . I want to go. Maybe I'll borrow your lipstick."

Alex grinned and took out her phone to request a ride. "Then we're definitely going." *If I'm still a Yale student tomorrow.* "Don't wait up, Ma."

"You beautiful slut," said Lauren.

"Be careful," said Mercy.

"Tell *him* to be careful," said Alex, and locked the door behind her.

She had the driver drop her off at the stone columns of Black Elm and walked up the long driveway on foot. The garage was open, and Alex could see Darlington's burgundy Mercedes parked inside.

Lights shone from the first and second stories of the house, and Alex saw Dawes through the kitchen window, stirring something on the stove. As soon as she entered, she recognized the lemony smell. Avgolemono. Darlington's favorite.

"You're early," said Dawes over her shoulder. "You look nice."

"Thanks," Alex said, feeling suddenly shy. Had the earrings and the lipstick been her version of lemon soup?

Alex stripped off her coat and hung it on a hook by the door. She wasn't sure what to expect from the night, but she wanted a chance to search Darlington's office and bedroom before the others arrived. She was glad Dawes had turned all the lights on. The last time she'd been here, the loneliness of the place had overwhelmed her.

Alex checked the office first, a room of wood paneling and packed bookshelves located just off of the pretty sunroom where she'd written her report for Sandow on Tara's death. The desk was fairly well organized, but its file cabinets just seemed to be full of documents pertaining to Black Elm. In the top drawer, Alex found an old-fashioned datebook and a crushed pack of Chesterfields. She couldn't imagine Darlington taking a drag on a bargain smoke.

Her search through his monk's chamber on the third floor was equally fruitless. Cosmo followed her inside and stared at her judgmentally as she pulled open drawers and thumbed through stacks of books.

"Yes, I'm violating his privacy, Cosmo," she said. "But it's for a good cause."

Apparently that was enough for the cat, who twined through Alex's legs, pressing his head against her combat boots and purring loudly. She gave him a scratch between the ears as she flipped through the books piled closest to Darlington's bed—all of them devoted to New England industry. She paused on what looked like an old carriage catalog, the paper yellowing and torn at the edges, sealed in a plastic baggie to protect it from the elements. North's family had been carriage makers.

Alex removed it carefully from the bag. On closer inspection it seemed to be a kind of newsy trade magazine for the various carriage makers in New Haven and the businesses that supported them. There were hand-drawn pictures of wheels and locking mechanisms and lanterns and, on the third page, an announcement in large bold type of the construction of North & Sons' brand-new factory, which would be fronted by a showroom for prospective buyers. In the margin, in Darlington's distinctive scrawl, was a note that read: *the first?*

"That's it? Come on, Darlington. The first *what?*"

Alex heard the sound of tires on gravel and looked down to the driveway to see headlights from two cars—a slightly beat-up Audi and, close behind it, a shiny blue Land Rover.

The Audi pulled into the garage beside Darlington's Mercedes, and a moment later Alex saw Dean Sandow and a woman who had to be Michelle Alameddine emerge. Alex wasn't sure what she'd expected, but the girl looked perfectly ordinary. Thick curls in a tangle around her shoulders, an angular face with elegantly manicured brows. She wore a well-cut black coat and knee-high black boots. She looked very New York to Alex, though Alex had never been to New York.

Alex slipped the carriage catalog back in its bag and hurried downstairs. Sandow and Michelle were already hanging up their coats in the mudroom, trailed by an older woman and a gawky-looking boy with a Mohawk and a huge backpack slung over his shoulders. It took Alex a long minute to recognize them out of their white robes, but then the memory locked into place: Josh Zelinski, the president of the Aurelian delegation, and the alumna who had led the ritual last fall with that novelist that had almost gone so wrong. *Amelia.*

Darlington had convinced Aurelian the fault had been theirs and not Alex's. And on that same night, much to Dawes's confusion, Alex and Darlington had gotten very drunk on expensive red wine and smashed a cupboardful of innocent crystal to bits— along with a tacky set of china chafing dishes that had probably deserved to die. She remembered standing in a room full of broken glass and crockery shards, feeling better than she had in years. Darlington had surveyed the damage, topped off his glass, and blearily said, *There's a metaphor in this, Stern. I'll figure it out when I'm sober.*

Now introductions were made and Sandow opened a bottle of wine. Dawes set out a plate of cheese and sliced vegetables. It felt like the prelude to a bad dinner party.

"So," Michelle said, popping a slice of cucumber into her mouth. "Danny got himself disappeared?"

"He could be dead," Dawes said quietly.

"I doubt it," Michelle replied. "Or he'd be haunting the hell out of her." She hooked her thumb at Alex. "You were with him, right?"

Alex nodded, feeling her stomach clench.

"And you're the magic girl who can see Grays. Has he been hanging around?"

"No," said Alex. And North hadn't seen him on the other side. Darlington was alive somewhere and he was coming home tonight.

"Such an extraordinary gift," Amelia said. She had thick honey-brown hair that fell just below her chin and wore a navy twinset over starched jeans. "Lethe is lucky to have you."

"Yes," said Sandow kindly. "We are."

Josh Zelinski shook his head. "Crazy. They're just all floating around? Are there any Grays here right now?"

Alex took a long sip of her wine. "Yup. One has his hand on your ass."

Zelinski whirled. Sandow looked pained.

But Michelle laughed. "Darlington must have been pissing himself when he found out what you can do."

Sandow cleared his throat. "Thank you for coming," he said. "All of you. This is a difficult situation and I know you're all busy."

It's not a fucking board meeting, Alex wanted to shout. *He disappeared.*

Michelle refilled her wineglass. "I can't say I was surprised to get the call."

"No?"

"I feel like I spent most of Darlington's freshman year making sure he didn't kill himself or set something on fire. Wherever he is, he's probably thrilled things finally got exciting around here."

Sandow chuckled. "I'll wager."

Alex felt a stab of irritation. She didn't like Sandow and Michelle sharing a smile over Darlington. He deserved better.

"He's a sensation seeker?" asked Amelia, sounding a little thrilled herself.

"Not exactly," said Michelle. "He's just always ready to jump in. He fancied himself a knight, a boy standing at the door to the underworld with a sword in his hand."

Alex had scoffed whenever Darlington described himself or Lethe that way. But it didn't feel silly now, not when she thought of Tara, of drugs like Merity, boys like Blake. The Houses of the Veil had too much power, and the rules they had put in place were really about controlling access to that power, not limiting the damage it could do.

"Isn't that kind of what we are?" Alex said before she could stop herself. "*We are the shepherds* and all that?"

Michelle laughed again. "Don't tell me he got to you too?" She looped her arm through Sandow's as they strolled out of the kitchen, followed by Zelinski and Amelia. "I wish I'd been able to come earlier and see this place in the daylight. He did so much work to it."

Dawes's hand brushed against Alex's, startling her. It was a little thing, but Alex let her knuckles do the same. Darlington had been *right* about the need for Lethe, about why they were here. They weren't just mall cops keeping a bunch of unruly kids in line. They were supposed to be detectives, soldiers. Michelle and Sandow didn't get it.

Do I? Alex wondered. How had she gone from barely getting by to holy warrior? And what was going to happen when they pulled Darlington back to their world from wherever he'd been cooling his heels?

Maybe her work on the Tara Hutchins case would be a mark

in her favor, but she very much doubted he was just going to say, *Way to take the initiative; all is forgiven.* She would tell him she was sorry, that she hadn't known what Hellie intended that morning at Ground Zero. She would tell him whatever she had to and hold on to this life with both hands.

"Where do we think he is?" Michelle was asking as they took the stairs up to the second floor.

"We don't know. I thought we'd use a hound-dog casting." Sandow sounded almost pleased with himself. Alex sometimes forgot that the dean had actually *been* in Lethe, and had been pretty good at it too.

"Very nice! What are we using for his scent?"

"The deed to Black Elm."

"Was it bound by Aurelian?"

"Not that I know of," said Amelia. "But we can activate the language to summon the signatories."

"From anywhere?" asked Michelle.

"From anywhere," Zelinski said smugly.

They went through a long description of the mechanics of the contract and how the summoning should work so long as the commitment to the contract was made in good faith and the parties had some emotional connection to the agreement.

Alex and Dawes exchanged a glance. That much at least they could be sure of: Darlington loved Black Elm.

The second-floor ballroom had been lit with lanterns at the four compass points. Darlington's exercise mats and gear had been set off to the side.

"This is a good space," said Zelinski, unzipping his backpack. He and Amelia drew out four objects wrapped in cotton batting.

"We don't need someone to open a portal?" Alex whispered to Dawes, watching Josh unwrap the cotton to reveal a large silver bell.

"If Sandow is right and Darlington is just stuck between worlds or in some kind of pocket space, then the activation of the deed should create enough pull to bring him through to us."

"And if it isn't?"

"Then we'll have to get Scroll and Key involved at the next new moon."

But what if the Locksmiths had been the ones to create the portal in the basement that night? What if they wanted Darlington to stay gone?

"Alex," called Sandow, "please come help me make the marks."

Alex felt strange warding the circle, as if she'd somehow fallen backward through time and become Sandow's Dante.

"We'll leave the northern gate open," he said. "True north to guide him home. I'll need you to be on the lookout for Grays on your own. I would take Hiram's elixir but. . . . I'm at an age when the risk is just too high." He sounded embarrassed.

"I can handle it," said Alex. "Is there blood involved?" She at least wanted to be ready if a flood of Grays came on.

"No," said Sandow. "No blood. And Darlington planted the Black Elm borders with protective species. But you know strong desire can draw Grays, and strong desire is what we need to bring him back."

Alex nodded and took her position at the northern compass point. Sandow took the southern point; Dawes and Michelle Alameddine faced each other at east and west. With only the candlelight to give shape to the space, the ballroom felt even more vast. It was a big, cold room, built to impress people long since gone.

Amelia and Josh stood at the center of the circle with a sheaf of papers—the deed to Black Elm—but they would have nothing to do unless Sandow's casting worked.

"Are we ready?" he asked. When no one answered, Sandow forged ahead, murmuring first in English, then in Spanish, then in a whispery language that Alex recognized as Dutch. Was that Portuguese next? Mandarin followed. She realized he was speaking the languages that Darlington knew.

She wasn't sure if it was her imagination or if she really did hear the patter of paws, panting. A *hound-dog* casting. She thought of the hounds of Lethe, the surprisingly beautiful jackals Darlington had set on her that first day at Il Bastone. *I forgive you,* she thought. *Just come home.*

She heard a sudden howl and then the very distant sound of barking.

The candles flared, their flames gone vibrant green.

"We've found him!" cried Sandow in a trembling voice. He sounded almost frightened. "Activate the deed!"

Amelia touched a candle to the papers lying at the center of the circle. Green light kindled and rose around the piles. She tossed something into the flame and it ignited in bright sparks like a firework.

Iron, Alex realized. She'd seen an experiment just like that in a science class once.

Words seemed to hover in the green flame over the document as the iron filings sparked.

WITNESSETH
THAT THE
SAID GRANTOR
FOR GOOD AND VALUABLE
CONSIDERATION
FOR GOOD
FOR GOOD

The words curled in on themselves, rising in the fire and vanishing like smoke.

The candle flames shot even higher, then sputtered. The fire covering the deed banked abruptly. They were left in darkness.

And then Black Elm came alive. All at once, the sconces on the walls flared to brightness, music blared from the speakers in the corner, and the halls echoed with the sound of a late-night newscast as somewhere in the house a television came on.

"Who the hell left all the lights on?" said an old man standing outside the circle. He was frighteningly thin, his hair a wisp on his head, his bathrobe hanging open to reveal an emaciated chest and shriveled genitals. A cigarette hung from his mouth.

He wasn't sharp and clear the way Grays usually were to Alex; he looked . . . well, gray. As if she were viewing him through layers of milky chiffon. *The Veil.*

She knew she was looking at Daniel Tabor Arlington III. A moment later he was gone.

"It's working!" shouted Josh.

"Use the bells," cried Amelia. "Call him home!"

Alex lifted the silver bell at her feet and saw the others do the same. They rang the bells, the sweet sound rolling over the circle, over the din of the music and the chaos of the house.

The windows blew open. Alex heard a squeal of tires and a loud crash from somewhere below. Around her, she saw people dancing; a young man with a heavy mustache who distinctly resembled Darlington floated past, dressed in a suit that looked like it belonged in a museum.

"Stop!" shouted Sandow. "Something's wrong! Stop the ringing!"

Alex seized the clapper of her bell, trying to silence it, and saw the others do the same. But the bells did not stop ringing. She could feel her bell still vibrating in her hand as if struck, hear the peals growing louder.

Alex's cheeks felt flushed. The room had been icy moments before, but now she was sweating in her clothes. The stink of sulfur filled the air. She heard a groan that seemed to rumble through the floor—a deep bass rattle. She remembered the crocodiles calling to each other from the banks of the river in the borderlands. Whatever was out there, whatever had entered the room, was bigger. Much, much bigger. It sounded hungry.

The bells were screaming. They sounded like an angry crowd, a mob about to do violence. Alex could feel the vibrations making her palms buzz.

Boom. The building shook.

Boom. Amelia lost her footing, clutched at Zelinski to keep her balance, the bell tumbling from her hands, still ringing and ringing.

Boom. The same sound Alex had heard that night at the prognostication, the sound of something trying to break through the circle, to break through to their world. That night the Grays in the operating theater had pierced the Veil, splintered the railing. She'd thought they were trying to destroy the protection of the circle, but what if they were trying to get inside it? What if they were afraid of whatever was coming? That low rumbling groan shook the room again. It sounded like the jaws of something ancient creaking open.

Alex gagged, then retched, the scent of sulfur so heavy she could taste it, rotten in her mouth.

Murder. A voice, hard and loud, above the bells—Darlington's voice, but deeper, snarling. Angry. *Murder,* he said.

Well, shit. So much for him keeping his mouth shut.

And then she saw it, looming over the circle, as if there were no ceiling, no third story, no house at all, a monster—there was no other word for it—horned and heavy-toothed, so big its hulking body blotted out the night sky. A boar. A ram. The rearing, segmented body of a scorpion. Her mind leapt from terror to terror, unable to make sense of it.

Alex realized she was screaming. Everyone was screaming. The walls seemed lit by fire.

Alex could feel the heat on her cheeks, searing the hair on her arms.

Sandow strode forward to the center of the circle. He tossed down his bell and roared, *"Lapidea est lingua vestra!"* He threw his arms open as if conducting an orchestra, his face made golden in the flames. He looked young. He looked like a stranger. *"Silentium domus vacuae audito! Nemo gratus accipietur!"*

The windows of the ballroom blew inward, glass shattering. Alex fell to her knees, covering her head with her hands.

She waited, heart pounding in her chest. Only then did she realize the bells had stopped ringing.

The silence was soft against her ears. When Alex opened her eyes, she saw that the candles had bloomed to light again, bathing everything in a gentle glow. As if nothing had happened, as if it had all been a grand illusion—except for the pebbles of broken glass littering the floor.

Amelia and Josh were both on their knees, sobbing. Dawes was huddled on the floor with her hands clasped over her mouth. Michelle Alameddine paced back and forth, muttering, "Holy shit. Holy shit. Holy *shit*."

Wind gusted through the shattered windows, the smell of the night air cold and sweet after the thick tang of sulfur. Sandow stood staring up at where the beast had been. His dress shirt was soaked through with sweat.

Alex forced herself to stand and make her way to Dawes, boots crunching over glass.

"Dawes?" she said, crouching down and laying a hand on her shoulder. "Pammie?"

Dawes was crying, the tears making slow, silent tracks down her cheeks. "He's gone," she said. "He's really gone."

"But I heard him," Alex said. Or something that sounded very much like him.

"You don't understand," Dawes said. "That thing—"

"It was a hellbeast," said Michelle. "It was talking with his voice. That means it consumed him. Someone let it into our world. Left it like a cave for him to walk into."

"Who?" said Dawes, wiping the tears from her face. "How?"

Sandow put his arm around her. "I don't know. But we're going to find out."

"But if he's dead, then he should be on the other side," said Alex. "He isn't. He—"

"He's gone, Alex," Michelle said. Her voice was harsh. "He's not on the other side. He's not behind the Veil. He was devoured, soul and all."

It's not a portal. That was what Darlington had said that night in the Rosenfeld basement. And now she knew what he had meant to say, what he had tried to say, before that thing had taken him. *It's not a portal. It's a mouth.*

Darlington had not disappeared. He had been eaten.

"No one survives that," said Sandow. His voice was hoarse. He took off his glasses and Alex saw him wipe at his eyes. "No soul can endure it. We summoned a poltergeist, an echo. That's all."

"He's gone," Dawes said again.

This time Alex didn't deny it.

They collected Aurelian's bells and Dean Sandow said he would make calls to have the windows of the ballroom boarded up the next morning. It was starting to snow, but it was too late in the evening to do anything about it now. And who was there left to care? Black Elm's keeper, its defender, would never return.

They made their slow way out of the house. When they entered the kitchen, Dawes began to cry harder. It all looked so impossibly stupid and hopeful: the half-full glasses of wine, the tidily arranged vegetables, the pot of soup waiting on the stove.

Outside, they found Darlington's Mercedes smashed into Amelia's Land Rover. That was the crash Alex had heard, Darlington's car possessed by whatever echo they'd drawn into this world.

Sandow sighed. "I'll call a tow truck and wait with you, Amelia. Michelle—"

"I can take a car to the station."

"I'm sorry, I—"

"It's fine," she said. She seemed distracted, confused, as if she couldn't quite make the numbers tally, as if she'd only now realized that in all her years at Lethe she'd been walking side by side with death.

"Alex, can you see Dawes home?" Sandow asked.

Dawes wiped her sleeve across her tearstained face. "I don't want to go home."

"To Il Bastone, then. I'll join you as soon as I can. We'll . . ." He trailed off. "I don't know exactly what we'll do."

"Sure," said Alex. She used her phone to request a ride, then put her arm around Dawes and herded her down the driveway after Michelle.

They stood in silence by the stone columns, Black Elm behind them, the snow gathering around them.

Michelle's car came first. She didn't offer to share it, but she turned to Alex as she got in.

"I work in gifts and acquisitions in the Butler Library at Columbia," she said. "If you need me."

Before Alex could reply, she ducked inside. The car vanished slowly down the street, cautious in the snow, its red taillights dwindling to sparks.

Alex kept her arm around Dawes, afraid that she might pull away. Until this moment, until this night, anything had been possible and Alex had really believed that somehow, inevitably, maybe not on this new moon but on the next, Darlington would return. Now the spell of hope was broken and no amount of magic could make it whole.

The golden boy of Lethe was gone.

26

Winter

Y ou'll stay, won't you?" Dawes asked as they entered the foyer at Il Bastone. The house sighed around them as if sensing their sadness. Did it know? Had it known from the start that Darlington would never come back?

"Of course." She was grateful Dawes wanted her there. She didn't want to be alone or to try to put on a cheerful face for her roommates. She couldn't pretend right now. And yet she couldn't stop reaching for some scrap of hope. "Maybe we got it wrong. Maybe Sandow screwed up."

Dawes switched on the lights. "He's had almost three months to plan. It was a good ritual."

"Well, maybe he got it wrong on purpose. Maybe he doesn't want Darlington back." She knew she was grasping at smoke, but it was all she had. "If he's involved in covering up Tara's murder, you think he really wants a crusader like Darlington around instead of me?"

"But you *are* a crusader, Alex."

"A more competent crusader. What did Sandow say to stop the ritual?"

"*Your tongues are made stone*—he used that to silence the bells."

"And the rest?"

Dawes shucked off her scarf and hung her parka on the hook.

She kept her back to Alex when she said, *"Hear the silence of an empty home. No one will be made welcome."*

The thought of Darlington being forever banned from Black Elm was horrible. Alex rubbed her tired eyes. "The night of the Skull and Bones prognostication, I heard someone—some*thing*—pounding on the door to get in right at the moment Tara was murdered. It sounded just like tonight. Maybe it was Darlington. Maybe he saw what was happening to Tara and he tried to warn me. If he—"

Dawes was already shaking her head, her loose bun unwinding at her neck. "You heard what they said. It . . . that thing ate him." Her shoulders shook and Alex realized she was crying again, clutching her hanging coat as if without its support she might topple. "He's gone." The words like a refrain, a song they'd be singing until the grief had passed.

Alex touched a hand to Dawes's arm. "Dawes—"

But Dawes stood up straight, sniffled deeply, wiped the tears from her eyes. "Sandow was wrong, though. Technically. Someone could survive being consumed by a hellbeast. Just no one human."

"What could, then?"

"A demon."

Far above our pay grade.

Dawes took a long, shuddering breath and pushed her hair back from her face, re-fastening her bun. "Do you think Sandow will want coffee when he gets here?" she asked as she retrieved her headphones from the parlor carpet. "I want to work for a while."

"How's it going?"

"The dissertation?" Dawes blinked slowly, looked down at the headphones in her hand as if wondering how they'd gotten there. "I have no idea."

"I'll order pizza," said Alex. "And I'm taking first shower. We both reek."

"I'll open a bottle of wine."

Alex was halfway up the stairs when she heard the knock at the door. For a second, she thought it might be Dean Sandow. But why would he knock? In the six months she'd been a part of Lethe, *no one* had knocked at Orange.

"Dawes—" she began.

"Let me in." A male voice, loud and angry through the door.

Alex's feet had carried her all the way to the base of the stairs before she realized it. *Compulsion.*

"Dawes, don't!" she cried. But Dawes was already unlocking the door.

The lock clicked and the door slammed inward. Dawes was thrown back against the banister, headphones flying from her hand. Alex heard a loud *crack* as her head connected with the wood.

Alex didn't stop to think. She snatched up Dawes's headphones and shoved them down over her ears, using her hands to keep them tight to her head as she ran up the stairs. She glanced back once and saw Blake Keely—beautiful Blake Keely, the shoulders of his wool coat dusted with snow as if he'd emerged from the pages of a catalog—step over Dawes's body, his eyes locked on Alex.

Dawes will be okay, she told herself. *She has to be okay. You can't help her if you lose control.*

Blake was using Starpower or something like it. Alex had felt the pull of it in his voice through the door. It was the only reason Dawes had flipped the lock.

She bolted toward the armory, punching Turner's number into her phone, and slammed her hand against the old stereo panel on the wall by the library, hoping that for once it would oblige. Maybe the house was fighting alongside her, because music boomed through the hallways, louder and clearer than she'd ever heard it before. When Darlington had been around, it would have been Purcell or Prokofiev. Instead, it was the last thing Dawes had listened to—if Alex hadn't been so frightened, she would have laughed as Morrissey's warble and the jangle of guitars filled the air.

The words were muted by the headphones, the sound of her own breathing loud in her ears. She hurtled into the armory, throwing open drawers. Dawes was down and bleeding. Turner was far away. And Alex didn't want to think about what Blake might do to her, what he might make her do. Would it be revenge for what she'd done? Had he figured out who she was and somehow followed her here? Or was it Tara who had brought him to her door? Alex had been so focused on the societies, she hadn't noticed another suspect right in front of her—a pretty boy with a rotten core who didn't like the word "no."

She needed a weapon, but nothing in the armory was made to fight a living, human body hyped up on super charisma.

Alex glanced over her shoulder. Blake was right behind her. He was saying something, but thankfully she couldn't hear him over the music. She reached into the drawers, grabbing anything heavy she could find to throw. She wasn't even sure what priceless thing she was hurling at him. An astrolabe. A glittering paperweight with a sea frozen inside it.

Blake batted them aside and seized the back of her neck. He was strong from lacrosse and vanity. He tore the headphones from her ears. Alex screamed as loud as she could and raked her nails across his face. Blake shrieked and she fled down the hall. She'd fought monsters before. She'd won. But not on her own. She needed to get outside, away from the wards, where she could draw on North's strength or find another Gray to help her.

The house seemed to be humming, buzzing its anxiety. *A stranger is here. A killer is here.* The lights crackled and flared, the static from the stereo rising.

"Calm down," Alex told the house as she pounded down the hallway, back to the stairs. "You're too old for this shit."

But the house continued to whir and rattle.

Blake tackled her from behind. She hit the floor hard. "Be still," he crooned in her ear.

Alex felt her limbs lock up. She didn't just stop moving—she was glad to do it, thrilled, really. She would be perfectly still, still as a statue.

"Dawes!" she screamed.

"Be quiet," said Blake.

Alex clamped her lips shut. She was happy to have the chance to do this for him. He deserved it. He deserved everything.

Blake rolled her over and stood, towering over her. He seemed impossibly tall, his golden, tousled head framed by the coffered ceiling.

"You ruined my life," he said. He lifted his foot and rested his boot on her chest. "You ruined me." Some part of her mind screamed, *Run. Push him off. Do something.* But it was a distant voice, lost to the contented hum of submission. She was so happy, so very happy to oblige.

Blake pressed down with his boot and Alex felt her ribs bend. He was big, two hundred pounds of muscle, and all of it felt like it was resting just beneath her heart. The house rattled hysterically, as if it could feel her bones crying out. Alex heard a table topple somewhere, dishes crashing from their shelves. Il Bastone giving voice to her fear.

"What gave you the right?" he said. "Answer me."

He'd granted her permission.

"Mercy and every girl before her," Alex spat, even as her mind begged for another command, another way to please him. "They gave me the right."

Blake lifted his boot and brought it down hard. Alex screamed as pain exploded through her.

At the same moment the lights went out. The stereo went with it, the music fading, leaving them in darkness, in silence, as if Il Bastone had simply died around her.

In the quiet, she heard Blake crying. His left hand was clenched in a fist, as if readying to strike her. But the light from the streetlamps filtering in through the windows caught on something silver in his other hand. A blade.

"Can you be quiet?" he asked. "Tell me you can be quiet."

"I can be quiet," said Alex.

Blake giggled, that high-pitched giggle she remembered from the video. "That's what Tara said too."

"What did she say?" Alex whispered. "What did she do to make you mad?"

Blake leaned down. His face was still beautiful, cut in sharp, almost angelic lines. "She thought she was better than all my other girls. But everyone gets the same from Blake."

Had he been stupid enough to use the Merity on Tara? Had she realized what he was using it for? Had she threatened him? Did any of it matter now? Alex was going to die. In the end, she'd been no smarter than Tara, no more able to protect herself.

"Alex?" Dean Sandow's voice from somewhere down below.

"Don't come up here!" she screamed. "Call the cops! He has—"

"Shut the fuck up!" Blake drew back his foot and kicked her hard in the side. Alex went silent.

It was too late anyway. Sandow was at the top of the stairs, his expression bewildered. From her place on the floor, Alex saw him register her on her back, Blake above her, the knife in his hand.

Sandow lunged forward, but he was too slow.

"Stop!" snapped Blake.

The dean went rigid, nearly toppling.

Blake turned to Alex, a smile spreading across his lips. "He a friend of yours? Should I make him throw himself down the stairs?"

Alex was silent. He'd told her to be silent and she just wanted to make him happy, but her mind was mule-kicking around her skull. They were all going to die tonight.

"Come here," Blake said. Sandow strode forward eagerly, a spring in his step. Blake bobbed his head at Alex. "I want you to do me a favor."

"Whatever I can do to help," said Sandow, as if inviting a promising new student to office hours.

Blake held out the knife. "Stab her. Stab her in the heart."

"A pleasure." Sandow took the knife and straddled Alex.

A cold wind gusted through the house from the open door. Alex felt it on her flushed face. She couldn't speak, couldn't fight, couldn't run. Behind Sandow the top of the open door and the brick path were visible. Alex remembered the first day Darlington had brought her here. She remembered Darlington's whistle. She remembered the jackals, spirit hounds, bound to serve the delegates of Lethe.

We are the shepherds.

Alex's hand lay against the floorboards. She could feel the cool, polished wood beneath her palm. *Please,* she begged the house silently. *I am a daughter of Lethe, and the wolf is at the door.*

Sandow raised the knife high above his head. Alex parted her lips—she wasn't speaking, no, she wasn't talking—and desperately, hopelessly, she whistled. *Send me my hounds.*

The jackals burst through the front door in a snapping, snarling pack. They raced up the stairs, claws clattering and paws sliding. *Too late.*

"Do it," said Blake.

Sandow brought the knife down. Something slammed into him, driving him off Alex. The hallway was suddenly full of jackals, trampling over her in a snarling mass. One of them crashed into Blake. The weight of their bodies drove the breath from Alex's lungs, and she cried out as their paws smacked over her broken bones.

They were wild with excitement and bloodlust, yelping and snapping. Alex had no idea how to control them. She'd never had reason to ask. They were a mess of gleaming canines and black gums, muzzles frothing. She tried to push up, push away. She felt jaws clamp closed on her side and screamed as long teeth sank into her flesh.

Sandow shouted a string of words she didn't understand and Alex felt the jaws open, hot blood gushing from her. Her vision was turning black.

The jackals retreated, slinking back toward the stairs, bodies bumping against each other. They crouched by the banister, whining softly, jaws snapping at the air.

Sandow lay bleeding on the hall runner beside her; his pant leg was torn. She could see that the jackal's jaws had snapped clean through his femur, the white jut of bone gleaming like a pale tuber. Blood was gouting from his leg. He was gasping, fumbling in his pocket, trying to find his phone, but his movements were slow, sluggish.

"Dean Sandow?" she panted.

His head lolled on his shoulders. She saw the phone slip from his fingers and fall to the carpet.

Blake was crawling toward her. He was bleeding too. She saw where the jackals had sunk their teeth into the meat of his biceps, his thigh.

He pulled himself up the length of her body, resting against her like a lover. His hand was still clenched in a fist. He struck her once, twice. The other hand slid into her hair.

"Eat shit," he whispered against her cheek. He sat up, gripped her hair in his hand, and slammed her skull against the floor. Stars exploded behind her eyes. He lifted her head again, yanking on her hair, tilting her chin back. "Eat shit and die."

Alex heard a wet, heavy thud and wondered if her skull had split open. Then Blake fell forward onto her. She shoved at him, scrabbling against his chest, his weight impossible, and finally rolled him off her. She touched her hand to the back of her head. No blood. No wound.

She couldn't say the same for Blake. One side of his perfect face was a bloody red crater. His head had been smashed in. Dawes stood over him, weeping. In her hands she clutched the marble bust of Hiram Bingham III, patron saint of Lethe, his stern profile covered with blood and bits of bone.

Dawes let the bust slip from her fingers. It hit the carpet and rolled to its side. She turned away from Alex, fell to her knees, and vomited.

Blake Keely stared at the ceiling, eyes unseeing. The snow had melted on his jacket, and the wool glittered like something far finer. He looked like a fallen prince.

The jackals padded down the stairs, vanishing through the open door. Alex wondered where they went, what they spent their hours hunting.

Somewhere in the distance she heard what might have been a siren or some lost thing howling in the dark.

27

Winter

When Alex woke, she thought she was back in the hospital in Van Nuys. The white walls. The beeping machines. Hellie was dead. Everyone was dead. And she was going to jail.

The illusion was fleeting. The pain burning in the wound at her side brought her back to the present. The horror of what had happened at Il Bastone returned in a rapid blur: red lights flashing, Turner and the cops flooding up the stairs. The uniforms had sent a jolt of panic through her, but then . . . *What's your name, kiddo? Talk to me. Can you tell me what happened? You're all right now. You're all right.* How gently they spoke to her. How gently they handled her. She heard Turner talking: *She's a student, a freshman.* Magic words. Yale falling over her, shroud and shield. *Take courage; no one is immortal.* Such power in a few words, an incantation.

Alex pushed her blankets back and yanked at her hospital gown. Every movement hurt. Her side had been stitched up and was covered in bandages. Her mouth was dry and cottony.

A nurse bustled in with a big smile on her face as she rubbed hand sanitizer between her palms. "You're up!" she said brightly.

Alex read the name on the tag attached to her scrubs and felt a chill creep over her. *Jean.* Was this Jean Gatdula? The woman Skull and Bones had paid to take care of Michael Reyes, to care for all of their *victimae* for the prognostications? It couldn't be coincidence.

"How are you, sweetheart?" the nurse asked. "How's your pain?"

"I'm good," Alex lied. She didn't want them doping her up. "Just a little groggy. Is Pamela Dawes here? Is she okay?"

"Down the hall. She's being treated for shock. I know you've both been through it, but you have to rest now."

"That sounds good," Alex said, letting her eyelids flutter closed. "Could I have some juice?"

"You bet," said Jean. "Back before you know it."

As soon as the nurse was gone, Alex made herself sit up and slide out of bed. The pain forced her to breathe shallowly, and the sound of her own panting made her feel like an animal caught in a trap. She needed to see Dawes.

She was hooked to her IV so she took it with her, wheeling it along beside her, grateful for the support. Dawes's room was at the end of the hall. She was propped up in her hospital bed on top of the covers, dressed in NHPD sweats. They were far too big for her and dark navy, but otherwise they would have fit perfectly into her grad student uniform.

Dawes turned her head on the pillow. She said nothing when she saw Alex, just wriggled over to the edge of the bed to make room.

Carefully, Alex hoisted herself into the bed and laid down beside her. There was barely space for the two of them, but she didn't care. Dawes was okay. She was okay. They had somehow survived this.

"The dean?" she asked.

"He's stable. They put him in a cast and pumped him full of blood."

"How long have we been here?"

"I'm not sure. They sedated me. I think at least a day."

For a long time, they lay in silence, the sounds of the hospital filtering down the hall to them, voices at the nurses' station, the click and whir of machines.

Alex was drifting into sleep when Dawes said, "They're going to cover it all up, aren't they?"

"Yeah." Jean Gatdula was a sure sign of that. Lethe and the other societies would use every bit of their influence to make sure that the true details of the night never came to light. "You saved my life. Again."

"I killed someone."

"You killed a predator."

"His parents are going to know he was murdered."

"Even alligators have parents, Dawes. That doesn't stop them from biting."

"Is it over now?" Dawes asked. "I want . . . normal."

If you ever find it, let me know.

"I think so," Alex said. Dawes deserved some kind of comfort, and it was all she could offer. At least now this whole gnarled mess would unravel. Blake would be the thread that pulled it all apart. The drugs. The lies. There would be some kind of reckoning among the Houses of the Veil.

Alex must have fallen asleep, because she woke with a start when Turner wheeled Dean Sandow into the room. She sat up too quickly and hissed in a breath at the pain, then nudged Dawes, who drowsily came awake.

Sandow looked exhausted, his skin sagging and almost powdery. His leg was extended before him in a cast. Alex remembered that white spike of bone jutting from his thigh and wondered if she should apologize for calling the jackals. But if she hadn't, she would be dead, and Dean Sandow would be a murderer—and more than likely dead too. How had they even explained these wounds to the police? To the doctors who had sewn them up? Maybe they hadn't had to explain. Maybe power like Lethe, power like the societies, like the dean of Yale University, made explanations unnecessary.

Detective Abel Turner looked fresh as ever, dressed in a charcoal suit and a mauve tie. He perched at the end of the big recliner tucked into the corner for overnight guests.

Alex realized this was the first time they'd all been in a room together—Oculus, Dante, Centurion, and the dean. Only Virgil was missing. Maybe if they'd started the year this way, things would have gone differently.

"I suppose I should begin with an apology," said Sandow. His voice sounded ragged. "It's been a hard year. A hard couple of years. I wanted to keep that poor girl's death away from Lethe. If I had known about the Merity, the experiments with Scroll and Key . . . but I didn't want to ask, did I?"

Dawes shifted in the narrow bed. "What's going to happen?"

"The murder charge against Lance Gressang will be vacated," said Turner. "But he'll still face charges on dealing and possession. He and Tara were dealing psychotropics to Scroll and Key, possibly to Manuscript, and we had a look at Blake Keely's phone. Someone got in there to delete a bunch of big files recently." Alex kept her face blank. "But the voicemails were enlightening. Tara found out what Merity could do and what Blake was using it for. She was threatening to tell the police. I don't know if Blake was more afraid of blackmail or exposure, but there was no love lost between them."

"So he killed her?"

"We've been interviewing a lot of Blake Keely's friends and associates," Turner went on. "He was not someone who liked women. He may have been escalating in some way or using drugs himself. His behavior lately has been truly bizarre."

Bizarre. Like eating the contents of a clogged toilet. But the rest made a kind of sense. Blake had barely seen the girls he used as human. If Tara had challenged his control, maybe the leap to murder hadn't been a big one. When Alex had relived Tara's death, it had been Lance's face she saw looming above her, and she'd assumed it was a glamour disguising the real murderer. But what if Blake had somehow dosed Tara with Merity and simply commanded her to see Lance's face? Was the drug that powerful?

Something else was bothering her. "Blake told me he didn't kill Tara."

"He was clearly out of his right mind when he attacked you—" said Sandow.

"No," said Alex. "When . . ." When she'd been seeking revenge for what he'd done to Mercy. "A few days ago. He was under compulsion."

Turner's eyes narrowed. "You were questioning him?"

"I had an opportunity and I took it."

"Is this the time to critique Alex's methods?" Dawes asked quietly.

Alex bumped Dawes's shoulder with her own. "Excellent point. Neither of you would have looked past Lance if I hadn't been a tack in your ass."

Turner laughed. "Still coming out swinging, Stern."

Sandow gave a pained sigh. "Indeed."

"But she's not wrong," said Dawes.

"No," said Sandow, chastened. "She's not wrong. But Blake may have believed in his own innocence. He may not have remembered committing the crime if he was under the influence when it happened. Or he may have been trying to please whoever was compelling him. Compulsion is complicated."

"What about the *gluma* that came after me?" Alex asked.

"I don't know," said Sandow. "But I suspect whoever sent that . . . monster for Darlington sent the *gluma* after you as well. They didn't want Lethe investigating."

"Who?" demanded Alex. "Colin? Kate? How did they get their hands on a *gluma*?" Had they deliberately used a monster that would cast suspicion on Book and Snake?

You asked me to tell you what you were getting into. Now you know. That was what Darlington had said after he'd unleashed the jackals on her. But had *he* known? Had he understood that his own intelligence, his love of Lethe and its mission, would paint a target on his back?

"We'll find out," Sandow said. "I promise you that, Alex. I won't rest until it's done. Colin Khatri has been questioned. It's clear he and Tara were experimenting heavily together. With portal magic, money spells, very dangerous stuff. It's not apparent who was the instigator, but Tara wanted to go deeper and she wouldn't let Colin put on the brakes, not if he and the society wanted more of the . . . assistance she was providing."

Because Tara had gotten a taste of something more. She'd glimpsed true power and she knew it was her one chance to take it.

"She was essentially extorting him," said Sandow. "All of it a disgrace—and all of it happening right beneath my nose." He slumped in his wheelchair. He looked old and gray. "You were in danger and I didn't protect you. You were keeping the spirit of Lethe alive, and I was so focused on Darlington's disappearance, on trying to make it seem as if all was well, on maintaining an illusion for the alumni. It was . . . It *is* shameful. Your tenacity is a credit to Lethe, and both Turner and I will say so in our reports to the board."

"And what does she get for her trouble?" asked Dawes, arms crossed. "You were so eager to wash your hands of Tara's murder, Alex almost died twice."

"Three times," noted Alex.

"Three times. She should get something for it."

Alex's brows rose. Since when was Dawes part hustler?

But Sandow just nodded. This was the world of quid pro quo. *See, Darlington?* Alex thought. *Even I know a little Latin.*

Turner rose. "Whatever bullshit you all come up with, I don't want to hear it. You can dress this up in talk, but Blake Keely, Colin Khatri, Kate Masters—they're rich kids getting wasted and wrapping a sports car they have no business driving around a tree." He gave Alex's shoulder a gentle squeeze on his way out. "I'm glad no one ran you over. Try not to get your ass kicked for a week or two."

"Try not to buy any new suits."

"I make no promises."

Alex watched him saunter away. She wanted to say something to call him back, to make him stay. Good-guy Turner with his shiny badge. Sandow was looking at his clasped hands as if he were concentrating on a particularly difficult magic trick. Maybe he'd unfold his palms and release a dove.

"I know this semester has been a struggle," he said at last. "It's possible I could help you with that."

Alex forgot Turner and the pain smoldering in her side. "How?"

He cleared his throat. "I could, possibly, make sure you pass your classes. I don't think it would be wise to go too far, but—"

"A 3.5 GPA should do it," said Dawes.

Alex knew she should say no, that she wanted to earn her way. It was what Darlington would do, what Dawes would do, probably what Mercy and Lauren would do. But Tara would say yes. Opportunity was opportunity. Alex could be honest next year. Still . . . Sandow had agreed too fast. What exactly were the terms of this bargain?

"What's going to happen to Scroll and Key?" Alex asked. "To Manuscript? To all of these assholes?"

"There will be disciplinary action. Heavy fines."

"*Fines?* They tried to kill me. They as good as killed Darlington."

"The trust of each House of the Veil has been contacted, and a meeting will be held in Manhattan."

A meeting. With a seating chart. Maybe some minted slush punch. Alex felt a wild anger building inside her. "Tell me someone is going to pay for what they did."

"We'll see," said Sandow.

"*We'll see?*"

Sandow raised his head. His eyes were fierce, lit by the same fire she'd seen when he'd faced down a hellbeast on new-moon night. "You think I don't know what they're getting away with? You think I don't care? Merity being passed around like candy. Portal magic revealed to outsiders and used by one of them to attack a delegate of Lethe. Manuscript and Scroll and Key should *both* be stripped of their tombs."

"But Lethe won't act?" asked Dawes.

"And destroy two more of the Ancient Eight?" His voice was bitter. "We are kept alive by their funding, and this isn't Aurelian or St. Elmo we're talking about. These are two of the strongest Houses. Their alumni are incredibly powerful and they're already lobbying for clemency."

"I don't get it," said Alex. She should just let it all go, take her boosted GPA and be glad she was alive. But she couldn't. "You had to know something like this would happen eventually. Turner's right. You soup up the car. You hand them the keys. Why leave magic, all this power, to a bunch of kids?"

Sandow sagged further in his chair, the fire leaving him. "Youth is a wasting resource, Alex. The alumni need the societies; an entire network of contacts and cohorts depends on the magic they can access. This is why the alumni return here, why the trusts maintain the tombs."

"So no one pays," said Alex. Except Tara. Except Darlington. Except her and Dawes. Maybe they were knights—valuable enough, but easy to sacrifice in the long game.

Dawes turned cold eyes on the dean. "You should go."

Sandow looked defeated as he wheeled himself into the hall.

"You were right," Dawes said when they were alone. "They're all going to get away with it."

A brisk knock sounded at the open door.

"Ms. Dawes, your sister is here to pick you up," said Jean. She pointed at Alex. "And you should be resting in your own bed, little miss. I'm coming back with a wheelchair."

"You're leaving?" Alex hadn't meant to sound so accusatory. Dawes had saved her life. She could go wherever she wanted. "I didn't know you had a sister."

"She lives in Westport," Dawes said. "I just need . . ." She shook her head. "This was supposed to be a research job. It's too much."

"It really is," said Alex. If her mom's place had been a few train stops away instead of a few thousand miles, she wouldn't have minded curling up on the couch there for a week or twelve.

Alex climbed out of the bed. "Be safe, Dawes. Watch lots of bad TV and just be normal for a while."

"Stay," Dawes protested. "I want you to meet her."

Alex made herself smile. "Come see me before you go. I need to get some of that sweet, sweet Percocet before I collapse, and I don't want to wait for good nurse Jean to wheel me away."

She moved as fast as she could out the door, before Dawes could say more.

Alex returned to her room only long enough to retrieve her phone and yank out her IV. Her clothes and boots were nowhere to be found, taken to be entered into evidence. She'd probably never see them again.

She knew what she was doing was irrational, but she didn't want to be here anymore. She didn't want to pretend to talk reasonably about something that made no sense.

Sandow could make all of the apologies he wanted. Alex didn't feel safe. And she had to wonder if she'd ever feel safe again. *We are the shepherds.* But who would protect *them* from the wolves? Blake Keely was dead and gone, his pretty skull smashed to bits. But what was going to happen to Kate Masters and Manuscript, who had unleashed Merity for the sake of saving a few dollars? What about Colin—eager, brilliant, scrubbed-face Colin—and the rest of Scroll and Key, who had sold their secrets to criminals and possibly sent a monster to devour Darlington? And what about the *gluma*? She'd nearly been murdered by a golem in glasses, and no one seemed to care. Dawes had been attacked. Dean Sandow had nearly bled out on the hall rug. Were they all really that expendable?

Nothing was going to be dismantled. Nothing would change. There were too many powerful people who needed the magic that lived in New Haven and that was tended by the Houses of the Veil. Now the investigation belonged to Sandow and to faceless groups of wealthy alumni who would dole out punishment or forgiveness as they saw fit.

Alex snagged a doctor's lab coat off the back of a chair and headed for the elevators in her hospital socks. She thought someone might stop her, but she strolled by the nurses' station without incident. The pain was bad enough that she wanted to bend double and cling to the wall, but she wasn't going to risk drawing attention.

The elevator doors opened on a woman with auburn hair in a cream-colored sweater and snug jeans. She looked like Dawes but Dawes winnowed down and polished to a high shine. Alex let her pass and stepped inside the elevator. As soon as the doors closed, she slumped against the wall, trying to catch her breath. She didn't really have a plan. She just couldn't be here. She couldn't make small talk with Dawes's sister. She couldn't act like what had happened was somehow fair or right or okay.

She shuffled out into the cold, limped a half block away from the hospital, and requested a ride on her phone. It was late and the streets were empty—except for the Bridegroom. North hovered in the glow of the hospital lights. He looked worried as he moved toward her, but Alex couldn't bring herself to care. He hadn't found Tara. He hadn't done a damn thing to help her.

It's over, she thought. *Even if you don't want it to be, buddy.*

"*Unwept, unhonored, and unsung,*" she growled. North recoiled and vanished, his expression wounded.

"How are you tonight?" the driver asked as she slid into the back seat.

Half dead and disillusioned. How 'bout you? She wanted to be behind the wards, but she couldn't bear the idea of returning to Il Bastone. "Can you take me to York and Elm?" she said. "There's an alley. I'll show you."

The streets were quiet in the dark, the city faceless.

I'm done, Alex thought, as she dragged herself out of the car and up the staircase to the Hutch, the smell of clove and comfort surrounding her.

Dawes could run off to Westport. Sandow could go home to his housekeeper and his incontinent Labrador. Turner . . . well, she didn't know who Turner went home to. His mother. A girl-friend. The job. Alex was going to do what any wounded animal would. She was going where the monsters couldn't reach her. She was going to ground.

Others may falter and take the false step. What penalty but pride?
Ours is the calling of the final trumpet on the horseman's last
    ride.
Ours is the answer given without pause and none too soon.
Death waits on black wings and we stand hoplite, hussar,
    dragoon.

—"To the Men of Lethe," *Cabot Collins*
(Jonathan Edwards College, '55)

Cabsy wasn't actually any good as far as poets go. Seems to have missed the last forty years of verse and just wants to write Longfellow. It's ungenerous to carp, what with him losing his hands and all, but I'm not sure even that justifies two hours cooped up at Il Bastone, listening to him read from his latest masterpiece while poor Lon Richardson is stuck turning the pages.

—Lethe Days Diary of Carl Roehmer
(Branford College '54)

28

Early Spring

Alex woke to the sound of glass breaking. It took her a moment to remember where she was, to take in the hexagon pattern of the Hutch's bathroom floor, the dripping faucet. She grabbed the lip of the sink and pulled herself up, pausing to wait out the head rush before she padded through the dressing room to the common room. For a long moment she stared at the broken window—one leaded pane smashed, the cool spring air whistling through, the glass slivers scattered on the plaid wool of the window seat beside her discarded falafel and *Suggested Requirements for Lethe Candidates,* the pamphlet still open to the page where Alex had stopped reading. *Mors irrumat omnia.*

Cautiously, she peered down at the alley. The Bridegroom was there, just as he had been every day for the last two weeks. Three weeks? She couldn't be sure. But Mercy was there too, in a belted jacket patterned with cabbage roses, her black hair pulled into a ponytail, a guilty expression on her face.

Alex thought about just not doing anything. She didn't know how Mercy had found her, but she didn't have to stay found. Eventually her roommate would get tired of waiting for Alex to show and she'd leave. Or throw another rock through the window.

Mercy waved and another figure stepped into view, dressed in a purple crochet coat and glittery mulberry-colored scarf.

Alex leaned her head against the window frame. "Shit."

She pulled on a Lethe House sweatshirt to cover her filthy tank top and limped barefoot down the stairs. Then she took a deep breath and pushed the door open.

"Baby!" her mom cried, lunging toward her.

Alex squinted against the spring sunshine and tried not to actually recoil. "Hi, Mom. Don't hug—"

Too late. Her mother was squeezing her and Alex hissed in pain.

"What's wrong?" Mira asked, pulling back.

"Just dealing with an injury," Alex said.

Mira bracketed Alex's face with her hands, pushing the hair back, tears filling her eyes. "Oh, baby. Oh, my little star. I was afraid this might happen."

"I'm not using, Mom. I swear. I just got really, really sick."

Mira's face was disbelieving. Otherwise, she looked good, better than she had in a long time. Her blond hair had fresh highlights; her skin was glowing. She looked like she'd put on weight. *It's because of me,* Alex realized with a pang. *All those years that she looked tired and too old for her age, she was worrying about me.* But then her daughter had become a painter and gone to Yale. Magic.

Alex saw Mercy hovering near the alley wall. *Snitch.*

"Come on," Alex said. "Come in."

She was breaking Lethe House rules by allowing outsiders into the Hutch, but if Colin Khatri could show Lance Gressang how to portal to Iceland, she could have her mother and her roommate in for tea.

She glanced at the Bridegroom. "Not you."

He started moving toward her and she hurriedly closed the door.

"Not who?" said her mother.

"Nobody. Nothing."

Climbing the stairs left Alex winded and dizzy, but she still had enough sense to be embarrassed when she opened the door to the Hutch and let them inside. She'd been too out of it to realize just how bad her mess had gotten. Her discarded blankets were crumpled in a heap on the couch, and there were dirty dishes and containers of spoiled food everywhere. Now that she'd had a breath of fresh air, she could also tell the common room stank like a cross between a swamp and a sick ward.

"Sorry," said Alex. "It's been . . . I haven't been up to house-keeping."

Mercy set to opening the windows, and Mira began picking up trash.

"Don't do that," said Alex, skin prickling with shame.

"I don't know what else to do," said Mira. "Sit down and let me help. You look like you're going to fall over. Where's the kitchen?"

"On the left," Alex said, directing her to the cramped galley kitchen, which was just as messy as the common room if not worse.

"Whose place is this?" asked Mercy, removing her coat.

"Darlington's," Alex said. It was true in a way. She lowered her voice. "How did you know I was here?"

Mercy shifted uneasily. "I, uh . . . may have followed you here once or twice."

"What?"

"You're very mysterious, okay? And I was worried about you. You look like hell, by the way."

"Well, I feel like hell."

"Where have you been? We've been worried sick. We didn't know if you'd gone missing or what."

"So you called my mom?"

Mercy threw up her hands. "Don't expect me to be sorry. If I disappeared, I hope you'd come looking." Alex scowled, but Mercy just jabbed her shoulder with her finger. "You rescue me. I rescue you. That's how this works."

"Is there recycling?" Mira called from the kitchen.

Alex sighed. "Under the sink."

Maybe good things were the same as bad things. Sometimes you just had to let them happen.

Mercy and Mira were a surprisingly efficient team. They got the garbage packed away, made Alex shower, and got her an appointment at the university health center to get on a course of antibiotics, though she didn't go so far as to show them her wound. She said she'd just been dealing with some kind of flu or virus. They made her shower and change into clean sweats, then Mira went to the little gourmet market and got soup and Gatorade. She went back out again when Alex told them she'd had to throw away her boots.

"Tar," she said. "They were ruined." *Tar, blood spatter. Same difference.*

Mira returned an hour later with a pair of boots, a pair of jeans, two Yale T-shirts, and a set of shower sandals that Alex didn't need but thanked her for anyway.

"I got you a dress too."

"I don't wear dresses."

"But you might."

They settled in front of the fireplace with cups of tea and instant cocoa. Unfortunately, Alex had eaten all of Dawes's fancy gourmet marshmallows. It wasn't quite cold enough for a fire, but the room felt snug and safe in the late-afternoon light.

"How long are you here for?" Alex asked. It came out with an ungrateful edge she hadn't intended.

"First flight out in the morning," said Mira.

"You can't stay longer?" Alex wasn't sure how much she wanted her to. But when her mother beamed, so happy to be asked, Alex was glad she'd made the gesture.

"I wish I could. Work on Monday."

Alex realized it must be the weekend. She'd only checked her email once since she'd holed up in the Hutch and hadn't read any of Sandow's messages. She'd let her phone go dead. For the first time she wondered if the societies had continued meeting without Lethe to oversee them. Maybe activity had been suspended after the attack at Il Bastone. She didn't much care. She *did* wonder if her mom could afford a last-minute cross-country flight. Alex wished she'd extorted some money from Lethe along with that grade bump.

Mercy had brought notes from the three weeks of classes she'd missed and was already talking about a plan of attack before finals. Alex nodded along, but what was the point? The fix was in. Sandow had said he'd make sure Alex would pass, and even if he didn't, Alex knew she didn't have the will to catch up. But she could pretend. For Mercy's sake and for her mother's.

They ate a light dinner and then made the slow walk back to Old Campus. Alex showed her mom the Vanderbilt courtyard and their shared suite, her map of California and the poster of Leighton's *Flaming June,* which Darlington had once rolled his eyes at. She let Mira coo over the sketchbook she'd tried to make herself pick up once in a while for the sake of appearances but admitted she hadn't been drawing or painting much.

When her mom lit up a bundle of sage and started smudging the common room, Alex tried not to melt into the floor in embarrassment. Still, she was surprised at how good it felt to be back in the dorms, to see Lauren's bike leaning up against the mantel, the toaster oven topped by boxes of Pop-Tarts. It felt like home.

When it was time for Mira to head back to her hotel, Alex walked outside with her, trying to hide how much it took out of her just to descend the few steps to the street.

"I didn't ask what happened and I'm not going to," said Mira, gathering her glittery scarf around her neck.

"Thank you."

"It's not for you. It's because I'm a coward. If you tell me you're clean, I want to believe you."

Alex wasn't sure what to say to that. "I think I may have a job lined up for the summer. But it means I won't be coming home."

Mira looked down at her shoes, handmade leather booties she'd been getting from the same guy at the same craft fair for the last ten years. She nodded, then brushed tears from her eyes.

Alex felt her own tears rising. How many times had she made her mother cry? "I'm sorry, Mama."

Mira drew a tissue from her pocket. "It's okay. I'm proud of you. And I don't want you to come home. After all of those horrible things with those horrible people. This is where you belong. This is where you were meant to bloom. Don't roll your eyes, Galaxy. Not every flower belongs in every garden."

Alex couldn't quite untangle the wave of love and anger that rushed through her. Her mother believed in faeries and angels and crystal visions, but what would she make of real magic? Could she grasp the ugly truth of it all? That magic wasn't something gilded and benign, just another commodity that only some people could afford? But the car was pulling up and it was time to say goodbye, not time to start arguments over old wounds.

"I'm glad you came, Mom."

"I am too. I hope . . . If you aren't able to manage your grades—"

"I've got this," Alex said, and it felt good to know that thanks to Sandow she wasn't lying. "Promise."

Mira hugged her and Alex breathed in patchouli and tuberose, the memory of being small. "I should have done better," her mother said on a sob. "I should have set clearer boundaries. I should have let you have fast food."

Alex couldn't help but laugh, then winced at the pain. No amount of strict bedtimes and trans fats could have kept her safe.

Her mother slid into the back seat of the car, but before Alex closed the door, she said, "Mom . . . my dad . . ." Over the years, Mira had made an effort to answer Alex's questions about her father. Where was he from? *Sometimes he told me Mexico, sometimes*

Peru, sometimes Stockholm or Cincinnati. It was a joke with us. It doesn't sound funny. *Maybe it wasn't.* What did he do? *We didn't talk about money. He liked to surf.* Did you love him? *I did.* Did he love you? *For a while.* Why did he leave? *People leave, Galaxy. I hope he finds his bliss.*

Had her mother meant it? Alex didn't know. When she'd gotten old enough to realize how much the questions hurt her mother and to realize the answers were never going to change, she stopped asking. She decided not to care. If her father couldn't be bothered with her, she wasn't going to bother with him.

But now she found herself saying, "Was there anything unusual about him?"

Mira laughed. "How about everything?"

"I mean . . ." Alex struggled for a way to describe what she wanted to know without sounding crazy. "Did he like the same stuff you did? Tarot and crystals and all that? Did you ever get the sense he could see things that weren't there?"

Mira looked down Chapel Street. Her gaze turned distant. "Have you ever heard of the arsenic eaters?"

Alex blinked, confused. "No?"

"They would ingest a little bit of arsenic every day. It made their skin clear and their eyes bright and they felt wonderful. And all the while they were just drinking poison." When Mira turned her eyes back to Alex, they were sharper and steadier than Alex ever remembered them being, free of the usual determined cheer. "That's what being with your father was like." Then she smiled and the old Mira was back. "Text me after you see the doctor."

"I will, Mom."

Alex closed the door and watched the car drive away. The Bridegroom had stood a respectful distance away, watching the whole exchange, but now he drew closer. Was he ever going to let up? She really didn't want to go to Il Bastone, but she was going to need the Lethe library to figure out how to break their connection.

"No one is immortal," she snapped at him, and saw him reluctantly shrink back, vanishing through the bricks.

"Your mom okay?" Mercy asked as Alex entered the common room. She'd put on her hyacinth robe and curled up on the couch.

"I think so. She's just worried about me getting through the rest of the year."

"And you're not?"

"Sure," Alex said. "Of course."

Mercy snorted. "No, you're not. I can tell. So continues the mystery of Alex Stern. It's okay. Mystery is good. I played softball for two years in high school."

"You did?"

"See? I have secrets too. Did you hear about Blake?"

She hadn't. She hadn't heard about anything during the weeks she'd hid at the Hutch. That had been the point. But according to Mercy, Blake Keely had attacked a woman in her home and her husband had fought him off with a golf club. Forensics had matched the knife he'd been carrying with the weapon in the Tara Hutchins murder investigation. There was no mention of Dawes, or the mansion on Orange, or Hiram Bingham III's fatal marble noggin. No discussion of Merity. Not a single word about the societies. Case closed.

"I could have ended up dead," said Mercy. "I guess I should be grateful."

Grateful. The word hung in the air, its wrongness like the sour clang of a bell.

Mercy tilted her head back, letting it flop on the arm of the couch, staring up at the ceiling. "My great-grandmother lived to be one hundred and three years old. She was doing her own taxes and swimming at the Y every morning until she keeled over dead in the middle of a yoga class."

"She sounds great."

"She was a total asshole. My brother and I hated going to her house. She served the nastiest-smelling tea and she never stopped complaining. But you always felt a little tougher at the end of a visit. Like you'd endured her."

Alex figured she'd be lucky if she made it to the end of the semester. But it was a nice sentiment. "I wish my grandmother had made it to a hundred and three."

"What was she like?"

Alex sat down in Lauren's ugly recliner. "Superstitious. Religious. I'm not sure which one. But she had a steel spine. My mom told me when she brought my father home, he took one look at my grandmother, turned right around, and never came back." Alex had asked her grandmother about it once, after her first heart attack. *Too pretty,* she'd said, waving her hand dismissively. *Mal tormento que soplo.* He was a bad wind that blew through.

"I think you have to be like that," Mercy said. "If you're going to survive to get old."

Alex looked out the window. The Bridegroom had returned. His face was taut, determined. As if he could wait forever. And he probably could.

What do you want? Belbalm had asked her. Safety, comfort, to feel unafraid. *I want to live to grow old,* Alex thought as she pulled the curtains closed. *I want to sit on my porch and drink foul-smelling tea and yell at passersby. I want to survive this world that keeps trying to destroy me.*

29

Early Spring

The next morning when Alex set out for class, determined to at least try to make a good show of it, North was still there. He seemed agitated, cutting in and out of her path, hovering in her field of vision so that she couldn't see the board in Spanish.

I know you're not around, Alex texted Dawes when she got out of section. *But did you ever find anything about severing connections to Grays? I've got a Bridegroom situation.*

Temper fraying, she cut into the bathroom in the entryway to Commons and waved North inside.

"Just tell me one thing," she said to him. "Did you find Tara behind the Veil?"

He shook his head.

"Then I'm going to need you to fuck off for a good long while. The deal is off. The case is solved and I don't want to hang with your girl-murdering ass." Alex didn't really believe North had been responsible; she just wanted him to leave her alone.

The Bridegroom jabbed a finger at the sink.

"If you think I'm going to run a bath in there so we can have a chat, you're wrong. Take a break."

She thought about ditching lecture and just going back to the quiet of her warded dorm room. But she'd gone to the trouble of putting on clothes. She might as well make the most of it. At least it was Shakespeare and not Modern British Novels.

She crossed Elm to High Street and Linsly-Chittenden Hall, and took a seat on the aisle, tucking herself into a desk. Whenever the Bridegroom swooped into her view, she shifted her focus. She hadn't done the reading, but everyone knew *The Taming of the Shrew,* and she liked this bit they were covering about the sisters and music.

Alex was looking at a slide of Sonnet 130 when she felt her head split open with a sudden bolt of pain. A deep wash of cold gusted through her. She saw flashes of a street lit by gas lamps, a smokestack belching dark clouds into the gray sky. She tasted tobacco in her mouth. *North.* North was inside her and she hadn't invited him in. She had time to feel a flash of rage and then the world went black.

In the next second she was looking down at her paper. The professor was still talking but Alex couldn't quite understand what she was saying. She could see the trail of the pen where her notes had left off. Three dates had been scrawled across the page in wobbly handwriting.

1854 1869 1883

There was blood spattered across the page.

Alex reached up and nearly smacked herself in the face. It was as if she'd forgotten how long her arm was. Hastily, she wiped her sleeve across her face. Her nose was bleeding.

The girl to her right was staring at her. "You okay?"

"I'm great," Alex said. She pinched her nostrils with her fingers, trying to get the bleeding to stop, as she hastily shut her notebook. North hovered just in front of her, his face stubborn. "You son of a bitch."

The girl beside her cringed, but Alex couldn't be bothered with putting on a good front. North had possessed her. He'd been inside her. He might as well have shoved his hand up her ass and used her as a puppet.

"You fucking *bastard,*" she snarled beneath her breath.

She shoved her notebook into her satchel, seized her coat, and hurried down the aisle, out of the lecture hall, and through the back door of L-C. She headed straight for Il Bastone, texting Dawes furiously: *SOS*.

Alex was limping by the time she reached the green, the pain in her side making it hard to breathe. She wished she'd brought some Percocet with her. North was still following a few feet behind. "*Now* you're keeping a respectful distance, you disembodied fuck?" she barked over her shoulder.

He looked grim, but he sure as hell didn't look sorry.

"I don't know what bad shit you can do to a ghost," she promised him. "But I'm going to figure it out."

All of her bluster was cover for the fear rattling around in her heart. If he'd gotten in once, could he get in again? What could he make her do? Hurt herself? Hurt someone else? She'd used North in pretty much the same way when Lance had attacked her, but her life had been in danger. She hadn't been bullying him into going on a fact-finding mission.

What if other Grays found out and came barging through? It had to be the result of the bond she'd formed with him. She'd invited him in twice. She knew his name. She'd called him by it. Maybe once that door was open, it couldn't be locked again.

"Alex?"

Alex whirled, then caught her side, the pain from her wound splintering through her. Tripp Helmuth stood on the sidewalk in a navy sailing-team windbreaker and a backward cap.

"What do you want, Tripp?"

He held up his hands defensively. "Nothing! I just . . . Are you okay?"

"No, I'm really not. But I will be."

"I just wanted to thank you for, y'know, keeping that stuff with Tara quiet."

Alex had done no such thing, but if Tripp wanted to think she had, that was fine. "You bet, buddy."

"That's crazy about Blake Keely, though."

"Is it?" said Alex.

Tripp lifted his cap, ran a hand through his hair, settled it back on his head. "Maybe not. I never liked him. Some guys are just made mean, y'know?"

Alex looked at Tripp in surprise. Maybe he wasn't quite as useless as he seemed. "I do know."

She cast a warning glance at North, who was pacing back and forth, passing through Tripp again and again.

Tripp shivered. "Shit, I think I'm coming down with a flu."

"Get some rest," said Alex. "There's something bad going around."

Something that looks like a dead Victorian.

Alex hurried down Elm to Orange, eager to be behind the wards. She pulled herself up the three porch steps to Il Bastone, a sense of ease flowing through her as soon as she opened the door and crossed the threshold. North was hovering in the middle of the street. She slammed the door and, through the window, saw a gust of air knock him backward—as if the whole house had given a great *harumph*. Alex rested her forehead against the closed door. "Thanks," she murmured.

But what would stop him the next time he tried to push his way into her? Would she have to return to the borderlands to sever the connection? She'd do it. She'd throw herself on Salome Nils's mercy to be let back into Wolf's Head. She'd let Dawes drown her a thousand times.

Alex turned, keeping her back against the door. It felt like safe harbor. Afternoon light filtered through the remaining stained-glass window in the foyer. The other had been boarded up, the pebbles and shards of shattered glass lying dull in the deep shadow. There was blood on the old wallpaper where Dawes had hit her head. No one had made an attempt to clean it.

Alex peered through the archway to the parlor, half-expecting to see Dawes there. But there was no sign of her or her binders or her index cards either. The house felt empty, battered and wounded. It put a hollow ache in Alex's heart. She'd never had to return to Ground Zero. And she'd never loved Ground Zero. She'd been happy to turn her back on it and never look into the face of the horrors she'd done there.

But maybe she did love Il Bastone, this old house with its warm wood and its quiet and its welcome.

She pushed away from the door and got a dustpan and broom from the pantry. It took her a long while to sweep up the broken glass. She poured it all into a plastic bag, sealed it with a strip of tape. She just wasn't sure if she should throw it out. Maybe they could put the broken pieces in the crucible with some goat's milk, make it whole.

It was only when she went to wash her hands in the little powder room that she realized there was dried blood all over her face. No wonder Tripp had asked if she was okay. She rinsed it off, watching the water swirl in the basin before it vanished.

There was bread and cheese that hadn't spoiled yet in the refrigerator. She made herself eat lunch, though she wasn't hungry. Then she went upstairs to the library.

Dawes hadn't replied to her text. She probably wasn't even looking at her phone. She'd gone to ground too. Alex couldn't blame her, but that meant she would have to find a way to block her connection to the Bridegroom on her own.

Alex yanked the Albemarle Book from the shelf but hesitated. She'd recognized the first date North had forced her to scrawl in her notebook instantly: 1854, the year of his murder. The others had been meaningless to her. She owed North nothing. But Darlington had thought the Bridegroom murder was worth investigating. He would want to know what those dates meant. Maybe Alex wanted to know too. It felt like giving in, but North didn't have to find out he'd snagged her curiosity.

Alex unslung her satchel and took out her Shakespeare notebook, opening it to the blood-spattered page: *1854 1869 1883*. If she did some kind of search for all those years, the library would go mad. She had to find a way to narrow the parameters.

Or maybe she just needed to find Darlington's notes.

Alex remembered the words he'd written in the carriage catalog: *the first?* If he'd actually done any research on North's case, she hadn't found it in the Virgil bedroom or at Black Elm. But what if his notes were here, in the library? Alex opened the Albemarle Book and looked at Darlington's last entry—the schematic for Rosenfeld. But right above it was a request for something called the *Daily New Havener.* She copied the request exactly and returned the book to the shelf.

When the bookcase stopped shaking, she pried it open and entered the library. The shelves were filled with stack after stack of what looked less like newspapers than flyers packed with tiny type. There were thousands of them.

Alex stepped outside and opened the Albemarle Book again. Darlington had been working in the library the night he'd disappeared. She wrote out a request for the Rosenfeld schematics.

This time when she pulled the door open, the shelves were empty except for a single book lying flat on its side. It was large and slender, bound in oxblood leather, and completely free of dust. Alex set it on the table at the center of the room and let it fall open. There, between elevations of the third and fourth subterranean levels of Rosenfeld Hall, was a sheet of yellow legal paper, folded neatly and covered in Darlington's tiny, jagged scrawl—the last thing he'd written before someone sent him to hell.

She was afraid to unfold the page. It might be nothing. Notes on a term paper. A list of repairs needed at Black Elm. But she didn't believe that. That night in December, Darlington had been working on something he cared about, something he'd been picking at for months. He'd been distracted as he worked, maybe thinking of the night ahead, maybe worried about his apprentice, who never did the damn reading. He hadn't wanted to bring his notes with him, so he'd stashed them someplace safe. Right here, in this book of blueprints. He'd thought he would be back soon enough.

"I should have been a better Dante," she whispered.

But maybe she could do better now.

Gently, she unfolded the page. The first line read: *1958-Colina Tillman-Wrexham. Heart attack? Stroke?*

A series of dates followed—coupled with what seemed to be women's names. The last three dates on the list matched those North had forced her to write in her notebook.

1902-Sophie Mishkan-Rhinelander-Brain fever?

1898-Effie White-Stone-Dropsy (Edema?)

1883-Zuzanna Mazurski-Phelps-Apoplexy

1869-Paoletta DeLauro-Kingsley-Stabbing

1854-Daisy Fanning Whitlock-Russell-Gunshot

The first? Darlington had believed that Daisy was the first, but the first what? Daisy had been shot, Paoletta had been stabbed, but the others had died of natural causes.

Or someone had gotten smarter about killing girls.

I'm seeing things, thought Alex. *I'm making connections that aren't there.* According to every single TV show she'd ever watched, serial killers always had a modus operandi, a way they liked to kill. Besides, even if a murderer had been operating in New Haven, if these dates were right, this particular psychopath had been preying on girls from 1854 to 1958—over one hundred years.

But she couldn't say it was impossible, not when she'd seen what magic could do.

And there was something about the way the dates clustered that felt familiar. The pattern matched the way the societies had been founded. There'd been a flurry of activity in the 1800s—and then a new tomb hadn't been built for a very long time, not until Manuscript in the sixties. An unpleasant shiver crawled over Alex's skin. She knew Skull and Bones had been founded in 1832 and that date didn't line up with any of the deaths, but it was the only year she could remember.

Alex took the notes and padded down the hall to the Dante room. She grabbed a copy of *The Life of Lethe* from the desk drawer. Scroll' and Key had been founded in 1842, Book and Snake in 1865, St. Elmo in 1889, Manuscript in 1952. Only the founding date of Wolf's Head matched up with 1883, but that could be coincidence.

She ran her finger down the list of names.

1854-Daisy Fanning Whitlock-Russell-Gunshot

She hadn't seen Daisy's name hyphenated anywhere else. She'd always just been Daisy Fanning Whitlock.

Because it wasn't a hyphen. None of them were hyphens. Rhinelander. Stone. Phelps. Kingsley. Russell. Wrexham. They were the names of the trusts, the foundations and associations that funded the societies—that paid for the construction of their tombs.

Alex ran back to the library and slammed the shelf shut; she yanked the Albemarle Book free again but made herself slow down. She needed to think about how to phrase this. Russell was the trust that funded Skull and Bones. Carefully, she wrote out: *Deed for land acquired by Russell Trust on High Street, New Haven, Connecticut.*

A ledger was waiting for her on the middle shelf. It was marked with the Lethe spirit hound, and there, one after another, were deeds of acquisition for land all over New Haven, the locations that would one day house each of the eight Houses of the Veil, each one built over a nexus of power created by some unknown force.

But Darlington had known. *The first.* 1854: The year the Russell Trust had acquired the land where Skull and Bones would build their tomb. Darlington had pieced together what had created those focal points of magic that fed the societies' rituals, that made all of it possible. Dead girls. One after another. He'd used the old editions of the *New Havener* to match the places they'd died to the locations of the societies' tombs.

What had been special about these deaths? Even if all these girls had been murdered, there had been plenty of homicides in New Haven over the years that hadn't resulted in magical nexuses. And Daisy hadn't even died on High Street, where Skull and Bones erected their tomb, so why had the nexus formed there? Alex knew she was missing something, failing to connect the dots Darlington would have.

North had given her the dates; he had seen the connections too.

Alex sprinted back to the bathroom and filled the basin of the sink.

"North," she said, feeling like a fool. *"North."*

Nothing. Ghosts. Never there when you needed them.

But there were plenty of ways to get a Gray's attention. Alex hesitated, then took the letter opener from the desk. She slashed it across the top of her forearm and let the blood drip into the water, watching it plume.

"Knock knock, North."

His face appeared in the reflection so suddenly she jumped.

"Daisy's death created a nexus," she said. "How did you find out?"

"I couldn't find Tara. It should have been easy with that object in hand, but there was no sign of her on this side of the Veil. Just like Daisy. There's no sign of Gladys O'Donaghue either. Something happened that day. Something bigger than my death or Daisy's. I think it happened again when Tara died."

Daisy had been an aristocrat, one of the city's elite. Her death had started it all. But the other girls? Who had they been? Names like DeLauro, Mazurski, Mishkan. Had they been immigrant girls working in the factories? Housemaids? Daughters of freed slaves? Girls who would have no headlines or marble headstones to mark their passing?

And was Tara meant to be one of them too? A sacrifice? But why had her murder been so gruesome? So public? And why now? If these really were killings, it had been over fifty years since the last girl died.

Someone needed a nexus. One of the Houses of the Veil was in need of a new home. St. Elmo's had been petitioning to build a new tomb for years—and what good was a tomb without a nexus beneath it? Alex remembered the empty plot of land where Tara's body had been found. Plenty of room to build.

"North," she said. "Go back and look for the others." She read their names to him, one after another: *Colina Tillman, Sophie Mishkan, Effie White, Zuzanna Mazurski, Paoletta DeLauro.* "Try to find them."

Alex plucked a towel from the rack and pressed it against her bleeding arm. She sat down at the desk, looked out the window onto Orange Street, trying to think. If Darlington had uncovered the cause of the nexuses, the first person he would have told was Sandow. He'd probably been proud, excited to have made a new discovery, one that would shed new light on the way that magic worked in his city. But Sandow had never mentioned it to her or Dawes, this final project Darlington had been pursuing.

Did it matter? Sandow couldn't be involved. He'd been violently attacked only a few feet from where she was sitting. He'd almost died.

But not because of Blake Keely. Blake had hurt Dawes, had nearly killed Alex, but he hadn't hurt the dean. It had been the snarling half-mad hounds of Lethe that had come to Alex's defense. She remembered Blake's clenched fist. He'd struck her with that hand but then he'd kept it closed.

She walked back to the hallway at the top of the stairs. Ignoring the dark stains on the rug, the lingering scent of vomit, she got down on her knees and began to search—the slats of the floor, under the runner. It wasn't until she peered beneath an empty wicker planter that she saw a glint of gold. She wrapped her hand in the sleeve of her shirt and carefully pulled it into the light. A coin of compulsion. Someone had been controlling Blake. Someone had given him very specific orders.

This is a funding year.

Darlington had brought his theory of the girls and the tombs to Sandow. But Sandow had already known. Sandow, who was strapped for cash after his divorce and hadn't published in years.

Sandow, who wanted so desperately to keep Darlington's disappearance quiet. Sandow, who had delayed the ritual to find him until after that first new moon and who had used that ritual to bar Darlington from ever returning to Black Elm. Because maybe Sandow had been the one to set a trap for Darlington in the Rosenfeld basement in the first place. Even then, he'd been planning for Tara Hutchins to die—and he'd known only Darlington would comprehend what her murder really meant. So he got rid of him.

Sandow had never intended to bring Darlington back. After all, Alex was the perfect patsy. *Of course* everything had gone wrong the year they'd brought in an unknown as a Lethe delegate. It was to be expected. They'd be more cautious in the future. Next year, brilliant, competent, steady Michelle Alameddine would come back to see to educating their wayward Dante. And Alex would be in Sandow's debt, forever grateful thanks to that grade bump.

Maybe I'm wrong, she thought. And even if she was right, that didn't mean she had to speak up. She could stay quiet, keep her passing grades, get through her calm, beautiful summer. Colin Khatri would graduate in May, so she wouldn't have to make nice with him. She could survive, *bloom,* in Professor Belbalm's care.

Alex turned the coin of compulsion over in her hand.

In the days after the massacre at the apartment in Van Nuys, Eitan had run all over Los Angeles, trying to find out who'd killed his cousin. There were rumors it was the Russians—except the Russians liked guns, not bats—or the Albanians, or that someone back in Israel had made sure Ariel would never return from California.

Eitan had come to see Alex in the hospital, despite the police officer posted at her door. Men like Eitan were like Grays. They found a way in.

He'd sat by her bed in the chair Dean Elliot Sandow had occupied only a day before. His eyes were red and the stubble on his chin was growing out. But his suit was as slick as ever, the gold chain at his neck like some throwback to the seventies, as if it had been handed down by another generation of pimps and panderers, the passing of the torch.

"You almost die the other night," he'd said. Alex had always liked his accent. She'd thought it was French at first.

She hadn't known how to reply, so she licked her lips and gestured to the pitcher of ice chips. Eitan had grunted and nodded.

"Open your mouth," he'd said, and spooned two ice chips onto her tongue.

"Your lips are very chapped. Very dry. Ask for Vaseline."

"Okay," she'd croaked.

"What happen that night?"

"I don't know. I got to the party late."

"Why? Where were you?"

So this was an interrogation. That was fine. Alex was ready to confess.

"I did it." Eitan's head shot up. "I killed them all."

Eitan slumped back in his chair and ran a hand over his face. "Fucking junkies."

"I'm not a junkie." She didn't know if that was true. She'd never gotten into the hard stuff. She'd been too afraid of what might happen if she lost too much control, but she'd kept herself in a carefully modulated haze for years now.

"*You* kill them? Tiny little girl. You were pass out, full of fentanyl." Eitan cut her a sidelong glance. "You owe me for the drugs."

The fentanyl. It had come into her blood from Hellie somehow, left enough in her system to make it look like she'd almost overdosed too. A last gift. A perfect alibi.

Alex laughed. "I'm going to Yale."

"Fucking junkies," Eitan repeated in disgust. He rose and dusted off his perfectly tailored trousers.

"What are you going to do?" Alex asked.

He glanced around the room. "You have no flowers. No balloons or anything. That's sad."

"I guess it is," said Alex. She wasn't even sure if her mother knew she was in the hospital. Mira had probably been waiting for that call a long time.

"I don't know what I will do," said Eitan. "I think your asshole boyfriend got into debt with the wrong person. He rip someone off or piss someone off and Ariel was in the wrong place at the wrong time." He rubbed his face again. "But it doesn't matter. Once you are chump, is like a tattoo. Everyone can see it. So someone will die for this." Alex wondered if it would be her. "You owe me for fentanyl. Six thousand dollars."

After Eitan had left, she asked the nurse to move the hospital phone closer. She took out the card Elliot Sandow had left with her and called his office.

"I'll take your offer," she told him, when his secretary put her through. "But I'm going to need some money."

"That shouldn't be a problem," he'd replied.

Later, Alex wished she'd asked for more.

Alex flipped the coin of compulsion once more. She pulled herself to her feet, ignoring the throb of pain that shot through her. She walked back to the desk where she'd spread Darlington's scribblings beside her bloody Shakespeare notebook.

Once you are chump, is like a tattoo. Everyone can see it.

She took out her phone and called the dean's house. His housekeeper picked up, as Alex had known she would. "Hi, Yelena. It's Alex Stern. I have something to drop off for the dean."

"He is not home," Yelena said in her heavy Ukrainian accent. "But you can bring package by."

"Do you know where he went? Is he feeling better?"

"Yes. Went to president's house for big party. Is welcome back."

Alex had never been to the university president's house, but she knew the building. Darlington had pointed it out—a pretty stack of red brick and white trim on Hillhouse.

"That's great," said Alex. "I'll be by in a bit."

Alex texted Turner: *We got it wrong. Meet me at the president's house.*

She folded the list of names and placed it in her pocket. She was done being Sandow's chump. "All right, Darlington," she whispered, "let's go play knight."

30

Early Spring

Alex stopped back at her dorm room to shower and change. She combed her hair carefully, checked her bandages, put on the dress her mother had bought for her. She didn't want to look out of place. And if something bad went down, she wanted as much credibility as possible. She poured herself a cup of tea and waited for North to appear in the cup.

"Any luck?" she asked, when his pale face emerged in the reflection.

"None of them are here," he said. "Something happened to those girls. The same thing that happened to Daisy. Something worse than death."

"Meet me outside the wards. And be ready. I'm going to need your strength."

"You'll have it."

Alex didn't doubt it. Stray magic had killed North and his fiancée, Alex felt sure of it. But something else had gone on in the aftermath, something Alex couldn't explain. All she knew was that it had kept Daisy from passing behind the Veil, where she might have found peace.

She took a car to the president's house. There was a valet out front, and through the windows, she could see people crowding the rooms. Good. There would be witnesses.

Even so, she texted Dawes. *I know you've gone MIA, but if*

anything happens to me, it was Sandow. I left a record in the library. Just ask the Albemarle Book.

No reply from Turner yet. Now that he thought his case was solved was he done with her? She was glad of North's presence beside her as she walked up the path.

Alex had expected someone checking names at the door, but she entered without incident. The rooms were warm and smelled of damp wool and baked apples. She slipped off her coat and hung it on top of two others on a peg. She could hear a piano being played beneath the murmur of conversation. She snatched a couple of stuffed mushroom caps from a passing server. Hell if she was going to die on an empty stomach.

"Alex?" the server asked, and she realized it was Colin.

He looked a little tired maybe, but not distressed or angry.

"I didn't know you worked for the president too," Alex said cautiously.

"I'm on loan from Belbalm. I have to drive her home later if you want a ride. You working today?"

Alex shook her head. "No, just dropping something off. For Dean Sandow."

"I think I saw him by the piano. Come back to the kitchen when you're done. Someone sent Belbalm a bottle of champagne and she brought it by for us."

"Nice," Alex said, feigning enthusiasm.

She found the powder room and darted inside. She needed a moment to compose herself, to make sense of Colin's easy demeanor. He should be mad. He should hate her for uncovering his connections to Tara, for revealing that Scroll and Key had shared their secrets with outsiders, that they had been using illegal drugs. Even if Sandow had kept her name out of the disciplinary proceedings, she was still a representative of Lethe.

But hadn't Alex known there would be no real repercussions? A slap on the wrist. A fine. The blood price was for someone else to pay. And yet she'd thought there would be *some* kind of reckoning.

Alex leaned her hands on the sink, staring into the mirror. She looked exhausted, dark shadows carving trenches beneath her eyes. She'd worn an old black cardigan over the cream wool sheath her mother had bought for her. Now she stripped it off. Her skin looked sallow and her arms had the lean, ropy look of someone who would never be full. She could see pink from her wound seeping through the wool of her dress; her new bandage must have come loose at the edges. She'd meant to look reputable, like a good girl, a girl who tried, someone to be trusted. Instead, she looked like the monster at the door.

Alex could hear the sounds of glasses clinking and civilized conversation in the living room. She had tried so hard to be a part of it all. But if this was the real world, the normal world, did she really want in? Nothing ever changed. The bad guys never suffered. Colin and Sandow and Kate and all of the men and women who had come before them, who had filled those tombs and worked their magic—they weren't any different than the Lens and Eitans and Ariels of the world. They took what they wanted. The world might forgive them or ignore them or embrace them, but it never punished them. So what was the point? What was the point of her passing GPA and her bargain cashmere sweaters when the game was rigged from moment one?

Alex remembered Darlington placing the address moths on her skin in the dim light of the armory. She remembered watching her tattoos fade, believing for the first time that anything might be possible, that she might find a way to belong to this place.

Be careful in the throes, he'd said. Saliva could reverse the magic.

Alex made her hands into fists. She ran her tongue along the knuckles of her left hand, did the same to the right. For a moment nothing happened. Alex listened to the faucet drip.

Then ink bloomed dark over the skin of her arms. Snakes and peonies, cobwebs and clusters of stars, two clumsy koi circling each other on her left biceps, a skeleton on one forearm, the arcane symbols of the Wheel on the other. She still had no idea what those symbols meant. She'd pulled that card from Hellie's tarot deck moments before they'd walked into a tattoo shop on the boardwalk. Alex watched in the mirror as her history spilled over her skin, the scars she had chosen for herself.

We are the shepherds. The time for that was done. Better to be a rattler. Better to be a jackal.

Alex stepped out of the powder room and let herself be absorbed into the crowd, the clouds of perfume, the suits and St. John knitwear. She saw the nervous glances cast her way. She did not look right. She did not look wholesome. She did not belong.

She glimpsed Sandow's salt-and-pepper hair in a cluster of guests by the piano. He was balanced on a pair of crutches. She was surprised he hadn't healed himself, but she also couldn't imagine him dragging a dozen cartons of goat's milk up the stairs at Il Bastone without help.

"Alex!" he said in some confusion. "What an unexpected pleasure."

Alex smiled warmly. "I was able to find the file you requested and I thought you'd want to know as soon as possible."

"File?"

"On the land deeds. Dating back to 1854."

Sandow startled, then laughed unconvincingly. "Of course. I'd forget my head if it wasn't screwed on tight. Excuse us for just a moment," he said, and led them through the crowd. Alex stayed behind him. She knew he was already calculating what she knew and how to question her, maybe how to silence her. She took her phone out and hit record. She would have liked the protection of the crowd, but she knew the microphone would never be able to pick up his voice in all of the party noise.

"Stay close," she whispered to North, who hovered at her side.

Sandow opened a door to an office—a lovely, perfectly square room with a stone-manteled fireplace and French doors that looked out on a back garden caught between the leavings of snow and the green beginnings of the spring thaw. "After you."

"You go ahead," Alex said.

The dean shrugged and entered. He set his crutches aside and leaned against the desk.

Alex left the door open so they would be at least partially visible to the partygoers. She didn't expect Sandow to pick up a fancy paperweight and club her with it, but he'd already killed one girl.

"You murdered Tara Hutchins."

Sandow opened his mouth, but Alex stopped him with a hand. "Don't start lying yet. We've got a lot of territory to cover and you'll want to pace yourself. You killed her—or you had her killed—on a triangle of unused land, one I'm guessing the Rhinelander Trust is going to move to acquire."

The dean took a pipe from his pocket, then brought out a pouch of tobacco and gently began filling the bowl. He set the pipe down beside him without lighting it.

At last, he folded his arms and met her gaze. "So what?"

Alex wasn't sure what she'd expected, but that wasn't it. "I—"

"*So what,* Miss Stern?"

"Did they pay you?" she asked.

He glanced over her shoulder, making sure no one was lingering in the hallway.

"St. Elmo's? Yes. Last year. My divorce left me with nothing. My savings were gutted. I owed outrageous alimony. But a few dedicated St. Elmo's alumni wiped all of that trouble away with a single check. All I had to do was provide them with a nexus to build over."

"How did they know you could create one?"

"They didn't. I approached them. I'd guessed at the pattern during my days at Lethe. I knew it would repeat. We were so long overdue. I didn't think I'd actually have to *do* anything. We simply had to wait."

"Were the societies involved in the murders of those other girls? Colina and Daisy and the rest?"

Again he glanced behind her. "Directly? I've wondered that myself over the years. But if any of the societies had solved the riddle of creating a nexus, why would they have stopped at one? Why not use that knowledge? Barter it?" He picked up his pipe. "No, I don't think they were involved. This town is a peculiar one. The Veil is thinner here, the flow of magic easier. It eddies in the nexuses, but there is magic in every stone, every bit of soil, every leaf of every old elm. And it is hungry."

"The town . . ." Alex remembered the strange feeling she'd had at the crime scene, the way it had mirrored the map of the New Haven colony. Dawes had said that rituals worked best if they were built around an auspicious date. Or an auspicious place. "That's why you chose that intersection to kill Tara."

"I know how to build a ritual, Alex. When I want to." Hadn't Darlington told her that Sandow was a brilliant Lethe delegate? That some of the rites he'd fashioned were still in use?

"You killed her for money."

"For a great deal of money."

"You took the payoff from the board of St. Elmo's. You told them you could control the location of the coming nexus."

"That I would prepare a site. I thought all I had to do was wait for the cycle to run its course. But it didn't happen. No one died. No new nexus formed." He shook his head in frustration. "They were so impatient. They . . . they said they would demand their money back, that they would go to the Lethe board. They had to be appeased. I created a ritual I knew would work. But I needed an offering."

"And then you found Tara."

"I knew her," Sandow said, his voice almost fond. "When Claire was sick, Tara got her marijuana."

"Your wife?"

"I nursed her through two bouts of breast cancer and then she left me. She . . . Tara was in my house. She heard things she probably shouldn't have. I was not focused on discretion. What did it matter?"

What did it matter what some town girl knew? "And Tara was nice, wasn't she?"

Sandow looked away guiltily. Maybe he'd fucked her; maybe he'd just been happy to have someone to talk to. That was what you did. You made nice with clients. Sandow had needed a sympathetic shoulder and Tara had provided it.

"But then Darlington found the pattern, the trail of girls."

"The same way I did. I suppose it was inevitable. He was too bright, too inquisitive for his own good. And he always wanted to know what made New Haven different. He was trying to make a map of the unseen. He brought it up to me just in passing, an academic exercise, a wild theory, a possible subject for his graduate work. But by then—"

"You'd already planned on killing Tara."

"She'd taken what she'd heard at my house and built a nice little business on it, dealing to the societies. She was in too deep with Keys and Manuscript. The drugs. The rituals. It was all going to come crashing down. She was nineteen, a drug user, a criminal. She was—"

"An easy mark." *Just like me.* "But Darlington would have figured it out. He knew about the girls that had come before. He was smart enough to connect them to Tara. So you sent the hellbeast to consume him that night."

"Both of you, Alex. But it seems Darlington was enough to sate the beast's appetite. Or maybe he saved you in some final, foolish act of heroism."

Or maybe the monster hadn't wanted to consume Alex. Maybe it had known she might burn going down.

Sandow sighed. "Darlington liked to talk about how New Haven was always on the brink of success, always about to tip over into good luck and good fortune. He didn't understand that the city walks a tightrope. On one side, success. On the other, ruin. The magic of this place and the blood shed to retain it is all that stands between the city and the end."

This town has been fucked from the start.

"Did you do it yourself?" Alex asked. "Or did you not have the balls?"

"I was once a knight of Lethe, you know. I had the will." He actually sounded proud.

Isabel had said that Sandow was sleeping off too much bourbon in Belbalm's study the night Tara died, but he could have slipped out somehow or even used the same portal magic she'd suspected Colin of using. He still would have had to manage a glamour—but of course that was no problem for Sandow. Alex thought of the compact she'd used to get into Tara's apartment and then the jail. When she'd taken it from the drawer, there had been a smudge on it. But Dawes never would have put it away dirty. Someone had used it before Alex.

"You put on Lance's face. You got Tara high so she wouldn't hurt and then you murdered her. Did you send the *gluma* after me?"

"I did. It was risky, maybe foolish. I have no talent for necromancy. But I didn't know what you might have discovered at the morgue."

She remembered Sandow sitting across from her at the Hutch, his teacup perched on his knee, telling her that her power had brought on the *gluma* attack, that *she* was to blame for it, for Tara's murder. "You told me it was my fault."

"Well, you weren't meant to survive. I had to say something." He sounded so reasonable. "Darlington knew you would be trouble. But I had no idea how much."

"You still don't know," said Alex. "And Darlington would loathe everything about you."

"Darlington was a gentleman. But this isn't a time for gentlemen." He picked up his pipe. "Do you know the terrible thing?"

"That you murdered a girl in cold blood so some rich kids can build a fancy clubhouse? Seems pretty terrible."

But he didn't seem to hear her. "It didn't work," he said, shaking his head, his steepled brows creasing his forehead. "The ritual was sound. I built it perfectly. But no nexus appeared."

"So Tara died and you're still screwed?"

"I would have been if not for you. I'm advocating for Manuscript to be stripped of their tomb. St. Elmo's will have a new home by the next school year. They'll get what they want. I'll get my money. So the question is, Alex, what do *you* want?"

Alex stared at him. He was actually trying to negotiate with her. "What do I want? *Stop killing people.* You don't get to murder a girl and disappear Darlington. You don't get to use me and Dawes and Lethe because you want to live in a nice neighborhood and drive a nice car. We aren't supposed to be walking that tightrope. We are the goddamn shepherds."

Sandow laughed. "We are beggars at the table. They throw us scraps, but the real magic, the magic that makes futures and saves lives, belongs to them. Unless we take a bit of it for ourselves."

He lifted his pipe, but instead of lighting it, he tapped the contents of the bowl into his mouth. It glittered against his lips—Astrumsalinas. Starpower. *Compulsion.* He'd given it to Blake to use on Alex that night at Il Bastone. The night Sandow had sent Blake Keely to kill her.

Not this time.

Alex reached out to North and, with a sudden rush, felt him flood into her, filling her with strength. She launched herself toward Sandow.

"Stay right there!" said the dean. Alex's steps faltered, wanting only to obey. But the drug had no power over the dead.

No, said North, the voice clean and true inside her head.

"No," said Alex. She shoved the dean down into a chair. His crutches clattered to the floor. "Turner is coming. You're going to tell him what you did. There isn't going to be another tomb for St.

Elmo's. This isn't all going away with fines and suspensions. You're all going to pay. Fuck the societies, fuck Lethe, and fuck you."

"Alexandra?" She and Sandow turned. Professor Belbalm hovered in the doorway, a glass of champagne in her hand. "What's going on here? Elliot . . . are you all right?"

"She attacked me!" he cried. "She's unwell, unstable. Marguerite, call campus security. Get Colin to help me subdue Alex."

"Of course," said Belbalm, the compulsion taking hold.

"Professor, wait—" Alex began. She knew it was futile. Under the influence of Starpower, there would be no reasoning with her. "I have a recording. I have proof—"

"Alexandra, I don't know what's gotten into you," Belbalm said with a sad shake of her head. Then she smiled and winked. "Actually, I know exactly what's gotten into you. Bertram Boyce North."

"Marguerite!" snapped Sandow. "I told you to—"

"Oh, Elliot, stop." Professor Belbalm shut the door behind her and turned the lock.

31

Early Spring

Alex stared. It wasn't possible. How was Belbalm resisting the Starpower? And could she somehow *see* North?

Belbalm set her champagne on a bookshelf. "Please, won't you sit, Alex?" she asked with the gracious air of a hostess.

"Marguerite," said Sandow sternly.

"We're overdue for a talk, yes? You're a desperate man, not a stupid one, I think. And the president is already pleasantly sozzled and settled in front of the fire. No one will interrupt us."

Warily, Sandow sat back in the desk chair.

But Alex wasn't ready to oblige. "You can see North?"

"I can see the shape of him," said Belbalm. "Tucked inside you like a secret. Didn't you notice my office was protected?"

Alex remembered the sense of peace she'd had there, the plants growing in the window boxes—mint and marjoram. They'd bloomed in the borders around Belbalm's house too, though it had been the dead of winter. But she couldn't quite grasp what Belbalm was suggesting. "You're like me?"

Belbalm smiled and gave a single nod. "We are Wheelwalkers. All worlds are open to us. If we are bold enough to enter."

Alex felt suddenly dizzy. She sank into a chair, the creak of the leather strangely reassuring.

Belbalm picked up her champagne and relaxed into the seat

opposite her, elegant and poised as ever, as if they were a mother and daughter who had come to meet with the dean.

"You can let him out if you like," she said, and it took Alex a second to realize Belbalm meant North.

Alex hesitated, then gave North a gentle nudge and he poured out of her, taking shape beside the desk, wary eyes darting between Alex and Belbalm.

"He's not quite sure what to do, is he?" Belbalm asked. She cocked her head to the side and a lively smile played over her lips. "Hello, Bertie."

North flinched backward.

Alex remembered that sunlit afternoon in the office at North & Sons, sawdust still in the corners, a deep feeling of contentment. *What is it you're thinking, Bertie?*

"Daisy?" Alex whispered.

Dean Sandow leaned forward, peering at Belbalm. "Daisy Fanning Whitlock?"

But that couldn't be.

"I prefer the French, *Marguerite*. So much less provincial than *Daisy*, yes?"

North shook his head, his expression turning angry.

"No," said Alex. "I saw Daisy. Not just her photo. I saw *her*. You look nothing like her."

"Because this is not the body I was born into. This is not the body my smug, adoring Bertie destroyed." She turned to North, who was glaring at her now, his face disbelieving. "Don't worry, Bertie. I know it wasn't your fault. It was mine in a way." Belbalm's accent seemed to have vanished, her voice taking on North's broad vowels. "I have so many memories, but that day at the factory is the clearest." She closed her eyes. "I can still feel the sun pouring through the windows, smell the wood polish. You wanted to honeymoon in Maine. *Maine,* of all places . . . A soul shoved into me, frantic, blood soaked, bristling with magic. I had spent my life in communion with the dead, hiding my gift, borrowing their strength and their knowledge. But I had never had a spirit over-take me in that way." She gave a helpless shrug. "I panicked. I pushed him into you. I didn't even know I could do such a thing."

Frantic, blood soaked, bristling with magic.

Alex had suspected that something had gone wrong with a prognostication back in 1854, that the Bonesmen had accidentally killed the vagrant they'd used as *victima*. She'd wondered why that spirit had been drawn to that particular room, why it had sought refuge in North, if it had just been some awful coincidence. But, no, that magic, that wayward soul cut free of its body and caught between life and death, had been drawn to a young girl's power. It had been drawn to Daisy.

"It was a foolish mistake," Belbalm said on a sigh. "And I paid for it. You couldn't contain that soul and its anger. It took your gun. It used your hand to shoot me. I had lived so little and, just like that, my life was over."

North began to pace, still shaking his head.

Belbalm sank back in her seat and released a snort. "My God, Bertie, can you possibly be this obtuse? How many times have you passed me on the streets without a second glance? How many years have I had to watch you moping around New Haven in all your Byronic glory? I was robbed of my body, so I had to steal a new one." Her voice was calm, measured, but Alex could hear the anger beneath it. "I wonder, Bertie, how many times you looked at Gladys without really seeing her."

Guys like this never noticed the help. Alex remembered gazing through the windows of North's office, seeing Gladys strolling through the dogwoods in her white bonnet. No—that wasn't right. She'd had the bonnet in her hand. It was her hair that had been white, smooth and sleek as a seal's head. Just like Belbalm's.

"Poor Gladys," Belbalm said, resting her chin in her hand. "I'll warrant you'd have noticed if she'd been prettier." North was peering at Belbalm now, his expression caught between belief and stubborn refusal. "I wasn't ready to die. I left my ruined body and I claimed hers. She was the first."

The first.

Gladys O'Donaghue had discovered Daisy's and North's bodies and run screaming up Chapel to High Street, where the authorities found her. High Street, where Daisy's desperate spirit chased her. High Street, where the first nexus was created and the first of the tombs would be built.

"You possessed Gladys?" said Alex, trying to make sense of what Belbalm was saying. North had shoved himself into Alex's head but only for a short time. She knew there were stories of possessions, real hauntings, but nothing like . . . whatever this was.

"I fear that is too kind a word for what I did to Gladys," Belbalm said gently. "She was Irish, you know. Very stubborn. I had to barge into her, just as that miserable soul had tried to push into me. It was a struggle. Do you know that the Irish had a taboo against the word 'bear'? No one knows why exactly, but it was most likely because they feared even saying the word would summon the creature. So they called it 'the shaggy one' or 'the honey eater.' I always loved that phrase. *The honey eater.* I ate her soul to make room for mine." She clicked her tongue against her teeth, surprised. "It was so sweet."

"That isn't possible," Sandow said. "A Gray can't simply seize someone's body. Not in any permanent way. The flesh would wither and die."

"Clever boy," said Belbalm. "But I was no ordinary girl and I am no ordinary Gray. My new body had to be sustained and I had the means to do it." She shot Alex a small, mischievous smile. "You already know you can let the dead inside. Have you never wondered what you might do to the living?"

The words had weight, sinking into Alex's understanding. Daisy hadn't just killed Gladys. That had been almost incidental. She had consumed Gladys's soul. It was *that* violence that had created a nexus. So what had created the other nexuses? *My new body had to be sustained.*

Gladys had been the first. But not the last.

Alex stood, backing away toward the mantel. "You killed them all. All of those girls. One by one. You ate their souls."

Belbalm gave a single nod. It was almost a bow. "And left their bodies. Husks for the undertaker. It's no different than what you do when you draw a Gray inside you for strength, but you cannot imagine the vitality of a living soul. It could sustain me for years. Sometimes longer."

"Why?" Alex asked desperately. It made no sense. "Why these girls? Why this place? You could have gone anywhere, done anything."

"Wrong." Belbalm's laugh was bitter. "I have had many professions. Changed my name and my identity, building false lives to disguise my true nature. But I never made it to France. Not in my old body, not in this one. No matter how many souls I consume, I cannot leave without starting to decay."

"It's the town," said Sandow. "You need New Haven. This is where the magic lives."

Belbalm smacked her palm against the arm of her chair. "This dump of a town."

"You had no right," said Alex.

"Of course not." Belbalm looked almost confused. "Did the boys of Skull and Bones have the right to cut that poor man open?" She bobbed her chin at Sandow. "Did *he* have the right to murder Tara?"

Sandow flinched in surprise.

"You knew?" asked Alex. "Did you eat her soul too?"

"I am not a dog to come running when the dinner bell rings. Why would I trifle with a soul like that when I had a feast set before me?"

"Oh," said Sandow, pressing his fingertips together. "I see. Alex, she means you."

Belbalm's glance was cold. "Don't look so pleased, Elliot. I'm not here to tidy up your mistakes, and I don't intend to waste any time worrying about you blabbing my secrets. You're going to die in that chair."

"I think not, Marguerite." Sandow stood, his face suffused with the same determination that had possessed him the night of the new-moon rite, when he'd looked into the fires of hell. *"The curfew tolls the knell of parting day, the lowing herd wind slowly o'er the lea—"*

North cringed backward. He cast a desperate look at Alex, scrabbling futilely at the walls as he began to fade through the bookshelf, fighting his banishment even as fear of the death words seized him.

"North!" Alex cried, holding out her hand to him, trying to pull him back into her. But it was too late. He disappeared through the wall.

"The plowman homeward plods his weary way," declared Sandow, his voice ringing loud through the room. *"And leaves the world to darkness and to me—"*

Belbalm rose slowly from her chair and shook out the sleeves of her elegant black tunic. "Poetry, Elliot?"

Death words. But Belbalm didn't fear death. Why would she? She'd already met it, bested it.

Sandow focused his hard eyes on Belbalm. *"Perhaps in this neglected spot is laid some heart once pregnant with celestial fire—"*

Belbalm drew a deep breath and thrust out her hand to Sandow—the same gesture Alex had used to welcome Hellie, to draw North into her.

"Stop!" Alex shouted, lunging across the room. She grabbed Belbalm's arm, but her skin was hard as marble; she didn't budge.

Sandow's eyes bulged and the high whistle of a teapot beginning to boil emerged from his parted lips. He gasped and fell back into the chair, with enough force to send it rolling across the floor. His hands gripped the armrests. The sound faded, but the dean remained sitting upright, staring at nothing, like a bad actor miming shock.

Belbalm pursed her lips in distaste and daintily wiped the corner of her mouth. "Soul like a mealy apple."

"You killed him," Alex said, unable to look away from the dean's body.

"Did he really deserve better? Men die, Alexandra. It's rarely a tragedy."

"He won't pass behind the Veil, will he?" Alex said, beginning to understand. "You eat their souls and they never move on." That was why North hadn't been able to find Gladys or any of the other girls on the other side. And what had become of Tara's soul, sacrificed to Sandow's ritual? Where had she gone in the end?

"I've upset you. I see that. But you know what it is to carve out a place in the world, to have to fight for your life at every turn. You can't imagine how much worse it was in my time. Women were sent to madhouses because they read too many books or because their husbands tired of them. There were so few paths open to us. And mine was stolen from me. So I forged a new one."

Alex jabbed a finger at Belbalm. "You don't get to turn this into some kind of feminist manifesto. You forged your new path from the lives of other girls. Immigrant girls. Brown girls. Poor girls." *Girls like me.* "Just so you could buy yourself another few years."

"It is so much more than that, Alexandra. It is a divine act. With each life I took, I soon saw a new temple raised to my glory—built by boys who never stopped to wonder at the power they claimed, only took it as their due. They toy with magic while I fashion immortality. And you will be part of it."

"Lucky me." Alex didn't have to ask what she meant. Belbalm had rejected Sandow's offering because she hadn't wanted to spoil her appetite. "I'm the prize."

"I've learned patience in this long life, Alexandra. I didn't know what Sophie was when I met her, but when I consumed her soul?

It was wild and gamey, bitter as yew, lightning in the blood. It sustained me for over fifty years. Then, just as I was beginning to weaken and age, Colina appeared. This time, I recognized the smell of her power. I scented her in a church parking lot and followed her for blocks."

Their deaths had been the foundations of the tombs for St. Elmo's and Manuscript.

What was the word Belbalm had used? "They were Wheelwalkers."

"It was as if they were drawn here to feed me. Just like you."

That was why the killings had paused in 1902. Girls had died in rapid succession through the late 1800s as Daisy fed on ordinary girls to stay alive. But then she'd found her first Wheelwalker, Sophie Mishkan, a girl with a power just like hers. That soul had kept her sated until 1958, when Belbalm had murdered Colina Tillman, another gifted girl. And now it was Alex's turn.

This town. Did New Haven draw Wheelwalkers here? Daisy. Sophie. Colina. Had Alex always been on a collision course with this place and this monster? Magic feeding magic?

"When did you know what I was?" Alex asked.

"From the moment we met. I wanted to let you ripen for a while. Wash the stink of the common from you. But . . ." Belbalm gave a profound shrug. She threw out her hand.

Alex felt a sudden sharp pain in her chest, as if a hook had lodged beneath her sternum, notched into her heart. Around her, she saw blue flames ignite, a ring of fire surrounding her and Belbalm. A wheel. She felt herself falling.

Hellie had been sunlight. North had been cold and coal smoke. Belbalm was teeth.

Alex was swaying next to the grill on the tiny balcony at Ground Zero, the smell of charcoal thick in the air, smog smeared across the hills in the distance. She could feel the bass track thumping through her bare feet. She held up her thumb, blotting out the rising moon, then making it reappear.

A woman leaned over her crib, reaching for her again and again, her hands passing through Alex's body. She wept, silver tears that fell on Alex's chubby arms and vanished through her skin.

Hellie had hold of Alex's hand. She was pulling her along the Venice boardwalk. She slid the Nine of Wands from a tarot deck. Alex already had a card in her hands. *No way I'm getting that inked on me*, said Hellie. *Let me draw again.*

Len took one of the leather bracelets from his arm and fastened it around Alex's wrist. *Don't tell Mosh,* he whispered. His breath smelled like sour bread, but Alex had never been so happy, never felt so good.

Her grandmother stood in front of the stove. Alex smelled cumin, meat roasting in the oven, tasted honey and walnuts on her tongue. *We're eating vegetarian now,* Mira said. *At your own house,* said her grandmother. *When she comes here I feed her strength.*

In the garden, a man lingered, pruning the hedges that never changed, squinting at the sun even on cloudy days. He tried to talk to Alex, but she couldn't hear a word.

One by one, Alex felt the memories plucked away like threads, caught on the spikes of Belbalm's teeth, unraveling her bit by bit. Belbalm—Daisy—wanted them all, the good and the bad, the sad and the sweet, all equally delicious.

There was nowhere to run. Alex tried to remember the smell of her mother's perfume, the color of the couch in the common room, anything that would help her hold on to herself as Daisy swallowed her down.

She needed Hellie. She needed Darlington. She needed . . . what was her name? She couldn't recall, a girl with red hair, headphones around her neck. *Pammie?*

Alex was curled up on a bed. She was surrounded by monarchs that became moths. A boy was behind her, nestled against her. He said, *I will serve you 'til the end of days.*

Belbalm's teeth sank deeper. Alex couldn't remember her body, her arms. She'd be gone soon. Was there some relief along with the fear? Each sadness and loss and mistake would be wiped away. She'd be nothing at all.

Belbalm was going to crack her open. She was going to drink Alex dry.

A wave rose over the stone plaza of Beinecke; a beautiful dark-haired boy was shouting. *Let all become mid-ocean!*

She could drift into the Pacific, past Catalina, watch the ferries come and go.

The wave crashed over the plaza, carrying away a tide of Grays.

Alex remembered cowering on the floor of that beautiful library, tears streaming down her cheeks, singing her grandmother's old songs, speaking her grandmother's words. She'd been hiding from the Grays, hiding behind . . . Darlington, his name was Darlington . . . Darlington in his dark coat. She'd been hiding the way she had her whole life. She'd sealed herself away from the world of the living, for the sake of being free of the dead.

Let all become mid-ocean.

Alexandra. Belbalm's voice. A warning. As if she knew the thought as soon as it entered Alex's head.

She didn't want to hide anymore. She'd thought of herself as a survivor, but she'd been no better than a beaten dog, snapping and snarling in any attempt to stay alive. She was more than that now.

Alex stopped fighting. She stopped trying to close herself off from Belbalm. She remembered her body, remembered her hands. What she intended was dangerous. She was glad.

Let all become mid-ocean. *Let me become the flood.*

She threw her arms wide and let herself open.

Instantly she felt them, as if they had been waiting, ships on an endless sea, forever searching the dark horizon, waiting for some light, some beacon to guide them on. Throughout New Haven she felt them. Down Hillhouse. Up Prospect. She felt North climbing his way back from the old factory site where the death words had thrown him, felt that kid forever looking to score tickets outside the vanished Coliseum, felt the Gray running wind sprints outside Payne Whitney, felt a thousand other Grays she'd never let herself look at—old men who had died in their beds; a woman pushing a crumpled pram with mangled hands; a boy with a gunshot wound to his face, reaching blindly for the comb in his pocket. A desiccated hiker limped down the slope of East Rock, dragging her broken leg behind her, and out in Westville, in the ruined maze of Black Elm, Daniel Tabor Arlington III drew his bathrobe tight and sped toward her, a cigarette still hanging from his mouth.

Come to me, she begged. *Help me.* She let them feel her terror, her fear burning bright like a watchtower, her longing to live another day, another hour, lighting the way.

There was no end to them, flowing over the streets, past the garden, through the walls, crowding into the office, crowding into Alex. They came on in a cresting wave.

Alex felt Belbalm recoil and suddenly she could see the room, see Belbalm before her, arm outstretched, eyes blazing. The Wheel still encircled them, bright blue flame. They stood at its center, surrounded by its spokes.

"What is this?" Belbalm hissed.

"Call to the missing!" Alex cried. "Call to the lost! I know their names." And names had power. She spoke them one after another, a poem of lost girls: "Sophie Mishkan! Colina Tillman! Zuzanna Mazurski! Paoletta DeLauro! Effie White! Gladys O'Donaghue!"

The dead whispered their names, repeated them, drawing closer, a tide of bodies. Alex could see them packed into the garden, halfway in and out of the walls. She could *hear* them moaning *Sophie, Colina, Zuzanna, Paoletta,* a rising wail.

The Grays were speaking, calling out to the scraps of those souls, a murmur of voices that rose in a broken chorus, louder and louder.

"Alexandra," snarled Belbalm, and Alex could see sweat on her brow. "I will not relinquish them."

It wasn't up to her anymore.

"My name is Galaxy, you fucking glutton."

At the sound of Alex's name, the Grays released a unified sigh that gusted through the room. It ruffled Alex's hem, blew Belbalm's hair back from her face. Her eyes went wide and white.

A girl seemed to emerge from inside her, peeling away from Belbalm like a pale onion skin. She had thick dark curls and wore the apron of a factory worker over a gray blouse and skirt. A blonde in a plumed hat appeared, skin like a faded apricot, her plaid dress high-necked, her waist cinched to an impossible size; then a black girl, shimmering in a soft pink cardigan and circle skirt, her hair pressed into shining waves. One after another they pulled themselves from Belbalm, joining the crowd of Grays.

Gladys was the last and she did not want to come. Alex could feel it. Despite all of the years she'd spent cowering within Daisy's consciousness, she was afraid to leave her body.

"She doesn't get to keep you," Alex pleaded. "Don't be afraid."

A girl emerged, barely visible, a scrap of a Gray. She was a far younger version of Belbalm, slender and sharp-featured, her white hair bound in a braid. Gladys turned to stare at herself, at Belbalm in her black tunic and rings. She held up her hands as if to ward her off, still frightened, shrinking back into the crowd as the other girls gathered her to them.

Belbalm opened her mouth as if to scream, but the only sound that emerged was that high teakettle whistle Alex had heard the dean make.

North was beside Alex now; maybe he'd been there all along.

"She isn't a monster," he said, begging. "She's just a girl."

"She knew better," said Alex. There was no room for mercy in her. "She just thought her life was more important than all of ours."

"I didn't know she was capable of such things," he said over the clamor of the crowd. "I never knew she had such a heart."

"You never knew her at all."

Careful Daisy, who had kept her secrets close, who had seen

ghosts, who had longed to see the world. Wild Daisy, cut down before she could even start to live. Cruel Daisy, who had refused her fate and had stolen life after life to keep herself fed.

Alex spoke the final name. "Daisy Fanning Whitlock!"

She thrust out her hand and felt Daisy's spirit inch toward her, slowly, grudgingly, fighting to hold on to her body like a plant determined to curl its roots in the ground and remain.

Alex took strength from the Grays surrounding her, passing through her. She let her mind form teeth, let them sink into Daisy's consciousness. She pulled.

Daisy's soul hurtled toward her. Alex cast it free before it could enter her and seize hold.

For the briefest moment, she glimpsed a dark-haired, pixie-faced girl in wide skirts and ruffled sleeves. Her chest had been blown open by a gunshot; her mouth was stretched in a scream. The Grays surged forward.

North threw himself in front of Daisy. "Please," he said. "Leave her be!"

But Gladys stepped forward, thin as air. "No."

"No," chorused the lost girls. Sophie and Zuzanna, Paoletta and Effie and Colina.

The Grays surged past North. They fell upon Daisy in a whirling horde.

"*Mors irrumat omnia,*" Alex whispered. Death fucks us all.

The Wheel spun and Alex felt her stomach lurch. She thrust her hands out, trying to find something, anything, to hold on to. She smacked into something solid, fell to her knees. The room went suddenly still.

Alex was on the carpeted floor of the president's office. She looked up, her head still spinning. The Grays were gone—all but the Bridegroom. She could hear her heart pounding in her chest and, through the door, the sounds of the party. The dean lay dead in the desk chair. When she closed her eyes, an afterimage of the Wheel burned blue against her lids.

Belbalm's body had collapsed in on itself, her skin dissolving to a powdery husk, her bones crumbling as the weight of a hundred years fell upon them. She was little more than a pile of ash.

The Bridegroom stood staring at the heap of dust that had once been a girl. He knelt and reached out, but his hand passed right through it.

Alex used the edge of the desk to pull herself to her feet. She stumbled to the French doors that led onto the garden. Her legs felt wobbly. She was pretty sure the wound in her side had reopened. She unlocked the door and cold air blew through. It felt clean on her flushed cheeks and scattered Belbalm's ashes.

Helplessly, North watched them gust up from the carpet.

"Sorry," Alex muttered. "But you have shit taste in women."

She looked at the dean's body and tried to make her mind work, but she felt wrung out, empty. She couldn't quite keep hold of her thoughts. In the garden, daffodils were just pushing up through the soil of the flower beds.

Turner, she thought. Where was he? Had he gotten her message?

She took out her phone. There was a message from the detective. *Working a case. Stay put. Will call when I'm done. DON'T DO ANYTHING STUPID.*

"It's like he doesn't even know me."

A burst of laughter floated through the door. She needed to think. If the records from the other deaths ascribed to Daisy were correct, then Sandow's death would most likely look like a heart attack or stroke. But Alex wasn't taking any chances. She could sneak out through the garden, but people had seen her going into the office with him. She hadn't exactly been discreet.

She would have to slip back into the party, try to mingle. If anyone asked, she'd claim she last saw the dean talking to Professor Belbalm.

"North," she said. He glanced up from where he'd been kneeling. "I need your help."

It was possible he wouldn't be willing, that he would blame her for Daisy's final death. Alex wondered if the Grays would leave any part of her to pass beyond the Veil. North's presence here, his grief, didn't make it seem likely.

Slowly, North rose. His eyes were dark and mournful as ever, but there was a new caution in them as he looked at Alex. *Is he afraid of me?* She didn't mind the idea. Maybe he'd think twice about jumping into her skull again. Still, she felt for North. She knew loss, and he'd lost Daisy twice—first the girl he loved, and then the dream of who she'd been.

"I need you to make sure there's nobody in the hall," Alex said. "No one can see me leave this room."

North drifted through the door, and for a long moment Alex wondered if he'd just leave her here with a dead body and a carpet covered in powdered evil.

Then he passed back through the wall and nodded the all-clear.

Alex made herself walk. She felt strange, wide open and exposed, a house with all its doors thrown open.

She smoothed her hair, tugged down the hem of her dress. She would have to act normal, pretend nothing had happened. But Alex knew that wouldn't be a problem. She'd been doing it her whole life.

We say "the Veil," but we know there are many Veils, each a barrier between our world and the beyond. Some Grays remain sequestered behind all of them, never to return to the living; others may be glimpsed in our world by those willing to risk Hiram's Bullet, and others may pierce still further into our world to be seen and heard by ordinary folk. We know too that there are many borderlands where the dead may commune with the living, and we have long suspected that there are many afterlives. A natural conclusion is that there are also many hells. But if there are such places, they remain opaque to us, unknown and undiscovered. For there is no explorer so intrepid or daring that he would dare to walk the road to hell—no matter how it may be paved.

—*from* The Life of Lethe: Procedures and
Protocols of the Ninth House

Cuando ganeden esta acerrado, guehinam esta siempre abierto.
While the Garden of Eden may be closed, Hell is always open.

—*Ladino saying*

32

Spring

Alex met Dawes at the Hutch and they walked up Elm to Payne Whitney, to the intersection that Sandow had chosen for his murder rite, the place where Tara Hutchins had died. *Auspicious.* Spring flowers had begun to emerge on the edges of the empty plot of land, pale purple crocus, tiny white bells of lily of the valley on their hesitant bent necks.

It was hard for Alex to be away from the wards. All her life she'd seen Grays—the Quiet Ones, she'd called them. They weren't keeping quiet anymore. She could *hear* them now. The dead woman clad in a nightgown singing softly to herself outside the music school. Two young men in coats and breeches, perched on the Old Campus fence, exchanging gossip, the left sides of their bodies charred black from some long-ago fire. Even now she had to actively ignore the drowned rower running wind sprints outside the gym. She could hear his heavy breathing. How was that possible? Why would a ghost need to breathe? Was it just the memory of needing air? An old habit? Or a performance of being human?

She gave her head a little shake. She would find a way to silence them somehow or lose her mind trying.

"Someone talking?" Dawes asked, keeping her voice low.

Alex nodded and rubbed her temples. She didn't know how she was going to fix this particular problem, but she did know she had to make certain the Grays didn't realize she could still hear them, not when so many were desperate for connection with the living world.

She hadn't seen North since the afternoon of the party at the president's house. Perhaps he was somewhere grieving what Daisy had become. Maybe he'd created a support group on the other side of the Veil for the souls she'd kept captive for so many years. Alex didn't know.

They paced the perimeter of the land the dean had intended for St. Elmo's. Alex hoped flowers would grow over the place where Tara had died. She had sent the recording of Sandow's confession to the Lethe board. It was horrible, they agreed. Grotesque. But mostly it was dangerous. Even if Sandow's ritual had failed, they didn't want anyone getting the idea there might be a way to create a nexus through ritual homicide—and they didn't want Lethe connected to Tara's death. Excluding a few members of the board, everyone still believed Blake Keely was responsible for the murder, and Lethe intended to keep it that way.

This time, Alex wasn't going to push. She had too many new secrets that needed keeping. Sandow's death had been chalked up to a sudden, massive heart attack during his welcome-home party. He'd had a bad fall only a few weeks before. He was under tremendous financial stress. His passing had been cause for sadness, but it had drawn little attention—especially since Marguerite Belbalm had disappeared after being seen with him at the same party. She'd last been observed entering the president's office to speak to Dean Sandow. No one knew where she was or if she'd come to harm, and the New Haven PD had opened an investigation.

Lethe had no idea what Belbalm had been or how she was connected to Sandow's death. Alex had made sure to cut off the recording before the professor entered the office. The Lethe board had never heard the term "Wheelwalker" and they were never going to, because unless Alex was very much mistaken, she had the ability to create a nexus anytime she wanted—all she had to do was develop a taste for souls. She'd seen the way Lethe and the societies worked. That wasn't knowledge any of them needed.

Dawes glanced at the time on her phone, and in silent agreement they left Payne Whitney behind and turned right down Grove Street. Ahead, Alex saw the massive mausoleum of Book and Snake, a gloomy block of white marble surrounded by black wrought iron. Now that Alex knew they hadn't sent the *gluma* after her, that they hadn't had any involvement in what happened to Tara, she had to wonder if they could help her find Tara's soul. Though she didn't like the idea of stepping beneath that portico or of what the Lettermen might demand in trade, Lethe owed Tara Hutchins some kind of rest. But that would have to wait. She had another task to accomplish before she could help Tara. One she might not survive.

Alex and Dawes passed under the massive neo-Egyptian gates of the cemetery, beneath the inscription that had pleased Darlington SO: THE DEAD SHALL BE RAISED.

Maybe not just the dead if Alex put her mind to it.

They passed the graves of poets and scholars, presidents of Yale. A small crowd was gathered at a new headstone. Dean Sandow was still keeping the best company.

Alex knew there might be Lethe alumni in the crowd today, but the only one she recognized was Michelle Alameddine. She wore the same stylish coat, her dark hair pulled back in a neat twist. Turner was there too, but he gave her the barest nod. He wasn't happy with her.

"You left me a *body* to find?" he'd growled at her when she'd agreed to meet him at Il Bastone.

"Sorry," Alex had said. "You're really hard to shop for."

"What happened at that party?"

Alex had leaned against the porch column. It felt like the house was leaning on her too. "Sandow killed Tara."

"What happened to *him*?"

"Heart attack."

"Like hell. Did you kill him?"

"I didn't have to."

Turner had looked at her for a long moment, and Alex had been glad that for once she was telling the truth.

They hadn't spoken since, and Alex suspected that Turner wanted to be done with her and all of Lethe. She couldn't blame him, but it felt like a loss. She'd liked having one of the good guys in her corner.

The service was long but dry, a recitation of the dean's accomplishments, a statement from the president, a few words from a slender woman in a navy dress that Alex realized was Sandow's ex-wife. There were no Grays at the cemetery today. They didn't like funerals, and there wasn't enough emotion at this graveside to overcome their revulsion. Alex didn't mind the quiet.

As the dean's coffin was lowered into the earth, Alex met Michelle Alameddine's eyes and gave a brief bob of her head—an invitation. She and Dawes drifted away from the graveside, and Alex hoped Michelle would follow.

They took a winding path to the left, past the tomb of Kingman Brewster, planted with a witch hazel tree that bloomed yellow every year in June—almost always on his birthday—and that lost its leaves in November at the time of his death. Somewhere in this cemetery, Daisy's first body was buried.

When they reached a quiet corner between two stone sphinxes, Dawes said, "Are you sure about this?" She'd worn mom slacks and pearl earrings to the funeral, but her red bun had slid gently to one side.

"No," admitted Alex. "But we need all the help we can get."

Dawes wasn't going to argue. She'd been full of apologies once Lethe had reached her at her sister's house in Westport and she'd heard the real story of what happened at the president's party from Alex. Besides, she wanted this quest, this mission, as much as Alex did. Maybe more.

Alex saw Michelle headed their way through the grass. She

waited for her to join them, then dove right in. "Darlington isn't dead."

Michelle sighed. "That's what this is about? Alex, I understand—"

"He's a demon."

"Excuse me?"

"He didn't die when he was eaten by the hellbeast. He was transformed."

"That isn't possible."

"Listen," said Alex. "I've spent some time in the borderlands recently—"

"Why am I not surprised?"

"Every time I heard . . . well, I don't know what they were— Grays? Monsters? Some kind of creature that wasn't quite human on the darker shore. They were saying something I couldn't quite make out. I thought it was a name at first, Jonathan Desmond or Jean Du Monde. But that wasn't it at all."

"And?" Michelle's expression was rigidly impassive, as if she was fighting to appear open-minded.

"*Gentleman demon.* That's what they were saying. They were talking about Darlington. And I think they were scared."

Darlington was a gentleman. But this isn't a time for gentlemen. Alex had barely registered the dean's words at the time. But when she'd played back the recording of their conversation, they'd stuck in her head. Darlington: the gentleman of Lethe. People had always described him that way. Alex had thought of him like that herself, as if he'd somehow stepped into the wrong time.

But it had still taken her a while to put it together, to realize that the creatures on that dark shore had always muttered those strange sounds when Alex mentioned Darlington or even thought about him. They hadn't been angry, they'd been frightened, the same way the Grays had been frightened the night of the prognostication. It *had* been Darlington who had spoken "murder" at the new-moon rite, not just some echo—but it was Sandow he'd been accusing, not Alex. The man who had murdered Tara. The man who had tried to murder him. At least, Alex hoped that was the case. Daniel Tabor Arlington, always the gentleman, a boy of infinite manners. But what had he become?

"What you're suggesting isn't possible," said Michelle.

"I know it sounds that way," said Dawes. "But humans can become—"

"I know the process. But demons are created one way: the union of sulfur and sin."

"What kind of sin are we talking about?" said Alex. "Masturbation? Bad grammar?"

"You're in a graveyard," chided Dawes.

"Trust me, Dawes. The dead don't care."

"There's only one sin that can make a man into a demon," Michelle said. "Murder."

Dawes looked stricken. "He would never, could never—"

"You killed someone," Alex reminded her. *And so have I.* "'Never' is a big word."

"Darlington?" Michelle said incredulously. "The teacher's pet? The knight in shining armor?"

"There's a reason knights carry swords, and I didn't tag you in so we could argue. You don't want to help, that's fine. I know what I know: A hellbeast was sent to kill Darlington. But he survived and that thing shat him out in hell. We're going to go get him."

"We are?" said Michelle.

"We are," said Dawes.

A cold wind blew through the cemetery trees and Alex had to restrain a shiver. It felt like winter trying to hold on. It felt like a warning. But Darlington was on the other side of something terrible, waiting for rescue. Sandow had stolen the golden boy of Lethe from this world, and someone had to steal him back.

"So," she said as the wind picked up, shaking the new leaves on their branches, moaning over the gravestones like a mourner lost to grief. "Who's ready to go to hell?"

The Houses of the Veil

"The Ancient Eight"

MAJOR HOUSES

Skull & Bones — 1832

Rich or poor, all are equal in death.

Teachings: Extispicy and splanchomancy. Divination using human and animal entrails.

Notable Alumni: William Howard Taft, George H. W. Bush, George W. Bush, John Kerry.

Scroll & Key — 1842

Have power on this dark land to lighten it, and power on this dead world to make it live.

Teachings: *Duru dweomer,* portal magic. Astral and etheric projection.

Notable Alumni: Dean Acheson, Gary Trudeau, Cole Porter, Stone Phillips.

Book & Snake — 1863

Everything changes, nothing perishes.

Teachings: *Nekyia* or *nekromanteía,* necromancy and bone conjuring.

Notable Alumni: Bob Woodward, Porter Goss, Kathleen Cleaver, Charles Rivkin.

Wolf's Head — 1883

The strength of the pack is the wolf. The strength of the wolf is the pack.

Teachings: Therianthropy.

Notable Alumni: Stephen Vincent Benét, Benjamin Spock, Charles Ives, Sam Wagstaff.

Manuscript — 1952

Dream delivers us to dream, and there is no end to illusion.

Teachings: Mirror magic and glamours.

Famous Alumni: Jodie Foster, Anderson Cooper, David Gergen, Zoe Kazan.

LESSER HOUSES

Aurelian — 1910

Teachings: Logomancy—word binding and divination through language.

Notable Alumni: Admiral Richard Lyon, Samantha Power, John B. Goodenough.

St. Elmo's — 1889

Teachings: *Tempestate Artium,* elemental magic, storm calling.

Notable Alumni: Calvin Hill, John Ashcroft, Allison Williams.

Berzelius — 1848

Teachings: None. Founded in the tradition of its namesake, Jöns Jacob Berzelius, the Swedish chemist who created a new system of chemical notation that left the secrecy of alchemists in the past.

Notable Alumni: None.

Acknowledgments

In New York: Many thanks to everyone at Flatiron Books, particularly Noah Eaker, who took a gamble on this book early, Amy Einhorn, Lauren Bittrich, Patricia Cave, Marlena Bittner, Nancy Trypuc, Katherine Turro, Cristina Gilbert, Keith Hayes, Donna Noetzel, Lena Shekhter, Lauren Hougen, Kathy Lord, and Jennifer Gonzalez and her team. Thank you to New Leaf Literary—Pouya Shahbazian, Veronica Grijalva, Mia Roman, Hilary Pecheone, Meredith Barnes, Abigail Donoghue, Jordan Hill, Jo Volpe, Kelsey Lewis, Cassandra Baim, and Joanna Volpe, who championed me and this idea from the start.

In New Haven and at Yale: Professor Julia Adams of Hopper College, Angela McCray, Jenny Chavira if the Association of Yale Alumni, Judith Ann Schief in Manuscripts and Archives, Mark Branch of the *Yale Alumni Magazine*, David Heiser of the Yale Peabody Museum of Natural History, Michael Morand at the Beinecke, and Claire Zella. Thank you to Rabbi Shmully Hecht for granting me access to the Anderson Mansion and to Barbara Lamb, who shared her extensive knowledge of Connecticut and squired me through many cemeteries. I have taken the occasional liberty with New Haven history and geography. Most notably, Wolf's Head built their first hall on Prospect Street in 1884. The new hall on High Street was built more than forty years later.

In California: David Peterson for the Latin assists, Rachael Martin, Robyn Bacon, Ziggy the Human Cannonball, Morgan Fahey, Michelle Chihara, Sarah Mesle, Josh Kamensky, Gretchen McNeil, Julia Collard, Nadine Semerau, Marie Lu, Anne Grasser, Sabaa Tahir, Robin LaFevers, Victoria Aveyard, and Jimmy Freeman. Thank you also to my mom, who first sang to me in Ladino, to Christine, Sam, Emily, Ryan, Eric who has somehow kept me laughing, and the manatee.

In the Hall: Steven Testa, Laini Lipsher, and my own wolf pack of '97.

Everywhere else: Max Daniel at UCLA and Simone Salmon for their help with Sephardic ballads, Kelly Link, Daniel José Older, Holly Black, Robin Wasserman, Sarah Rees Brennan, Rainbow Rowell, Zoraida Córdova, Cassandra Clare, Ally Carter, Carrie Ryan, Marie Rutkoski, Alex Bracken, Susan Dennard, Gamynne Guillote, and Michael Castro.

Many books helped build the world of *Ninth House: Yale in New Haven: Architecture and Urbanism* by Vincent Scully; Patrick Pinnell's *Yale University: An Architectural Tour;* Loomis Havemeyer's *Go to Your Room: A story of undergraduate Societies and Fraternities at Yale;* Brooks Mather Kelley's *Yale: A History;* Joseph A. Soares's *The Power of Privilege: Yale and America's Elite Colleges;* David Alan Richards's *Skulls and Keys: The Hidden History of Yale's Secret Societies;* Craig Steven Wilder's *Ebony and Ivy: Race, Slavery, and the Troubled History of America's Universities; Carriages and Clocks, Corsets and Locks: The Rise and Fall of an Industrial City* by Preston Maynard and Marjorie B. Noyes; *New Haven: A Guide to Architecture and Urban Design* by Elizabeth Mills Brown; *Model City Blues: Urban Space and Organized Resistance in New Haven* by Mandi Isaacs Jackson; and *The Plan for New Haven* by Frederick Law Olmsted and Cass Gilbert. I found the ballad "La Moza y El Huerco" in the article "Sephardic Songs of Mourning and Dirges" by Paloma Díaz-Mas. Thanks also to the Pan-Hispanic Ballad Project.

About the Author

Taili Song Roth

Leigh Bardugo is a #1 *New York Times* bestselling author of fantasy short stories and novels, including *Shadow and Bone* and *Six of Crows*. She was born in Jerusalem, grew up in California, and graduated from Yale University. These days she lives and writes in Los Angeles.

leighbardugo.com

About the Type

This book was set in Garamond, a typeface created by and named for Claude Garamond, a sixteenth-century Parisian engraver and typefounder. A perennial masterpiece of old style serif, Garamond is distinguished by its graceful irregularity among individual letters and contrast between light and heavy strokes, which give the sense of a calligrapher's handwriting. This version of Garamond, Adobe Garamond Pro, was designed by Robert Slimbach, who captured the gracefulness of the original Garamond typefaces while creating a typeface family that is well-suited for contemporary digital printing.

Ninth House
by Leigh Bardugo

PLEASE NOTE: In order to provide reading groups with the most informed and thought-provoking questions possible, it is necessary to reveal important aspects of the plot of this novel—as well as the ending. If you have not finished reading *Ninth House,* we respectfully suggest that you may want to wait before reviewing this guide.

1. Alex's life before Yale is lived on the fringes of society. At Yale, she finds herself in a somewhat similar situation: an outsider in a world of privilege. How does Alex's sense of identity change over the course of the book? What kinds of attempts to assimilate into the culture does Alex make, and do they help or hinder her work for Lethe, and later, her attempts to solve Tara's murder?

2. While Alex is in the hospital, Dean Sandow offers her a chance to remake her life by joining Lethe and attending Yale. If you were Alex, would you have said yes? What if you knew the challenges ahead? Have you ever been offered a second chance, and how did it impact your own journey? If you haven't, is there a second chance you would like to be offered?

3. In contemplating Tara and Hellie's death—and contemplating the possibility of her own death—Alex laments that "There are always excuses for why girls die." How is violence against women in the novel made better or worse by magic? How does magic work differently for each of the main characters in the novel? How is this impacted by a character's background and education?

4. Themes of class, race, and ethnicity are woven throughout *Ninth House.* How does having Alex as a narrator influence our view of the story and the world of Yale and New Haven? How would it be different if the story were narrated by Darlington, Dawes, or Turner?

5. Despite Darlington being absent for much of the novel, he's still a big presence in Alex's life and in the house of Lethe. Why do you think Alex has such a connection with Darlington despite how different they are in both background and personality? To what extent do you think their relationship transcends that of mentor and mentee and why?

6. There are many kinds of fantastical magic and houses in this novel. If you had to choose one house to be in, which would it be—and if your friends or family had to pick for you, do you think they would choose differently, and why?

7. Throughout the novel we see magic in Yale and New Haven used for both good and bad. If you were in charge of Lethe, would you run it differently? If you had the power to ban the use of magic by the Houses of the Veil, would you or wouldn't you, and why?

8. At one point in the novel it's said that New Haven is a place where magic took root. The idea of magic being drawn to certain places is a new way of looking at a map—is there a place you've visited that you felt magic might be lurking? What was that place, and why?

9. There are many ghosts in this novel. Some of them become allies, like the Bridegroom; others are more insidious and even evil. Most people have ghosts of a different variety, namely ghosts from our pasts—a difficult ex, our younger selves, or friends from a time long gone. How do you think those kinds of ghosts are similar to the ghosts in *Ninth House*? How are they different, and what allows them to exert influence over us?